Lizzie Lane was born and brought up in one of the toughest areas of Bristol, the eldest of three siblings who were all born before her parents got round to marrying. Her mother, who had endured both the Depression and war years, was a natural-born story teller, and it's from her telling of actual experiences of the tumultuous first half of the twentieth century that Lizzie gets her inspiration.

Lizzie put both city and rat race behind her in 2012 and moved on to a boat, preferring to lead the simple life where she can write and watch the sun go down without interruption.

LIZZIE LANE

War Baby

EBURY
PRESS

3 5 7 9 10 8 6 4

Ebury Press, an imprint of Ebury Publishing
20 Vauxhall Bridge Road
London SW1V 2SA

Penguin
Random House
UK

Ebury Press is part of the Penguin Random House
group of companies whose addresses can be found at
global.penguinrandomhouse.com
Copyright © Lizzie Lane, 2015

Lizzie Lane has asserted her right to be identified as
the author of this work in accordance with the Copyright,
Designs and Patents Act 1988

First published in 2015 by Ebury Press
This edition published 2016

www.eburypublishing.co.uk

A CIP catalogue record for this book is
available from the British Library

ISBN 9781785036101

Typeset in Times LT Std by Palimpsest Book Production Limited,
Falkirk, Stirlingshire

Penguin Random House is committed to a sustainable future for our business,
our readers and our planet. This book is made from Forest Stewardship
Council® certified paper.

Printed and bound in Great Britain by Clays Ltd, Elcograf S.p.A.

CHAPTER ONE

April 1941, London

On the evening before the bombers came it had been an ordinary street in the East End of London, where little girls played hopscotch and boys rolled marbles in the gutter. But by the early hours of the next morning twisted gas pipes hissed and great clouds of smoke and steam arose from blackened buildings.

Thousands of gallons of water had been poured on to the burning buildings, but the heat was still intense enough to scorch the faces of the firefighters if they got too close.

Dawn was just beginning to lighten the sky to the east, but for the firemen, air-raid wardens and the civilians from all walks of life lending a hand the job was not yet over. Fires blazed where Victorian terraced houses once stood, and some of those who had lived in them still had to be accounted for. A few had made it to the air-raid shelter or the Underground where the rattle of trains was preferable to the sound of explosions. Others had refused to leave their homes because of their fear of looters or simply because they were sound asleep and hadn't heard the siren. The volunteers who were to sift through the bombed-out buildings were under no illusion of what to expect.

Harry Norton, a stevedore on a Thames barge by day, was standing by, waiting for the go ahead from the firemen to begin looking for survivors.

'Looks like hell!' he shouted to his friend Clancy Cowell, a man of few words but who had more muscles than a fairground strongman.

They had to shout to hear each other above the hissing of steam, gas and water jetting from the ends of fire hoses.

'It is hell,' Clancy shouted back to him.

Harry blinked. Clancy was right. The incendiary raid had started an inferno, some of which might not burn out for days. He sighed. If there were any survivors buried under this little lot, it would be nothing short of a miracle, but both he and the other voluntary firefighters tried to remain hopeful.

'For this lot here, take these houses from here to here. Just give us a minute.'

He went back to the line of men heaving on hoses, stinking of sweat and smoke. Deep down inside all of them was the feeling of sickness that comes with the prospect that, for all their good intent, the army of volunteers would be digging nothing but corpses from the ruins.

The hissing stopped when the gas was turned off at the mains. Steam still rose from the smouldering buildings, but the sound of surging water also ceased as the hoses were turned off.

Once the noise lessened, the order to move in and begin the search was given.

Harry pulled on a pair of asbestos gloves. The fire in this particular street had been put out, but the bricks and other debris would still be hot. Even the ground beneath their feet was scorching. Like most of the men there, he was wearing his steel-capped work boots. The thick soles would protect him from the heat and, at one time, he thought the toe caps would too, but there had been times when it had felt as though the devil was toasting his toes. Not that discomfort would deter him from doing his job. If there were people to be rescued, then it was all hands to the pump, sorting through the smoking debris, and stopping every so often to listen for the slightest sound of somebody still alive.

Clancy worked beside him, methodically pulling at huge pieces of brickwork, ceiling joists and concrete. He tackled the real heavy items that usually took two men to lift.

Harry just missed being hit by a window frame. Up until then it had been held in place along the sill and up one side. It fell in slow motion, its movement almost indiscernible. Somebody shouted. Harry reacted instantly, leaping over a pile of broken bricks and a smashed-up fireplace.

The glass panes, having survived bomb damage, smashed into jagged pieces either side of a heavy roof truss, which now lay flat among bricks and bits of wood.

There was a strange silence following the sound of breaking glass and broken timbers, not a real silence, just a contrast with the noise that had gone before.

In that silent moment he heard something. At first it sounded like the mewing of a cat. They'd found plenty of trapped animals following an air raid. Plenty of dead ones too.

'If there are any pets, they'll be roasted,' somebody close by muttered.

He tilted his head to one side.

'Hear that, Clancy?'

Clancy did the same as Harry, tilting his head to one side in an effort to hear better.

A door left swinging at an angle on one hinge creaked and fell.

Harry looked around him and shook his head. 'Blimey. This place is still falling down.'

3

It was also still steaming and although the firemen had done sterling work, Harry kept his eyes peeled for any flare up of the fire ignited by the incendiary bomb. He rubbed at his chest. It felt tight. He knew he'd inhaled his fair share of black smoke and brick dust. All the same he could do with a bit of light relief.

'I badly need a smoke, funny that, what with all this . . .'

His face was black with sweat and soot, his eyes streaming and sore on account of the steam and the smoke.

There was that noise again. He cupped his ear the same way he'd seen his old father do when he couldn't catch what was being said. 'Hear anything, Clancy?'

He looked at his friend, a hulking figure among the ruins. Clancy raised his hand and pointed to a spot beneath what was left of the stairs.

Harry listened. There it was again. A mewing sound? That wasn't a mewing sound! It was crying. A baby! It sounded like a baby!

'I hear something!' he shouted out to the men behind him.

Clancy heard it too, but being a big man with chunky limbs he was clumsy and his movements slow. Harry got to the sound first.

Bits of brick, tile and plaster began to slide under his feet as he dug desperately and carefully, his bare hands less likely to do damage than any shovel or crowbar.

George Poster, the civil defence volunteer in charge of the job, climbed carefully over the rubble that lay between a bathtub and a broken lavatory pan, aware that disturbing anything too much might cause the whole lot to slide or fall into a hidden cellar. A lot of the houses round here had cellars. Rather than go to the air-raid shelter and chance their houses being looted, some people went down there. It was because of those cellars that some survived, trapped in air pockets beneath the destruction.

4

The intensity of the men listening was suddenly interrupted by the loud clanging of a bell, which preceded the arrival of an ambulance. There were one or two injured people to take to hospital. Quite a few dead ones too.

George stood up and flung a stone at the culprit. 'Stop that bloody racket! Can't you see we're trying to listen 'ere?'

The bell stopped, the driver hurriedly getting out of her ambulance, sliding on the slick of mud and water, her tin hat toppled to one side. She whispered sorry, but nobody was really interested. All eyes returned to what was happening among the ruins.

Harry got down on his hands and knees so he could hear better, turning his head so his ear was close to the glass shards and other bits and pieces that had once been part of a house, that had once been a family home.

'Here,' he shouted. 'Beneath this. I'm sure of it!'

It was a slow process, but gradually the piled muck was shifted, slid sideways and behind them on to other piles, the rescuers forming a human chain.

'There's a door,' shouted Harry. 'It's coming from beneath this door.'

The door was pinned flat beneath a roof truss, one of the many A-frames whose ends had scorched in the walls before falling to earth when the walls supporting them had fallen down. Six men, including Clancy and Harry, three one side and three the other, heaved up the massive piece of wood.

'Just enough so we can move it off the door,' ordered George.

Sweat streaked their dirty faces as every muscle in their body strained and shook.

'We need it held up in the middle,' shouted Harry. 'If we could jam something underneath it, I reckon two of us could pull that door out.'

Eyes sore from smoke and lack of sleep searched the seared bombsite. There was not one piece of material suitable for jacking up the piece of wood, nothing that wouldn't disintegrate into cinders when it took the weight.

'Let me try.'

Clancy crouched down as low as he could, feet apart, knees bent. Hands the size of shovels clasped the massive piece of wood and slowly, very slowly, he began to rise.

A gasp of amazement went up before the rest of the men sprang into action.

'Give him a hand, boys,' George ordered.

Lifted by Clancy's broad shoulders, the crossbeam of the truss began to rise. Other men put their shoulders beneath it too, straining for all they were worth.

Choosing just the right moment, Harry let go and with the help of a young lad of barely sixteen, they managed to slide the door out from beneath the beam. The roof truss was shifted to one side, though only enough to give them access to the space beneath the door.

Harry was closest to the hole and it was him who called for a flashlight. As his fingers were cramped with tiredness, he held the flashlight with both hands. Although the gap was filled with dust and it was difficult to see at first, its beam eventually picked out the body of a woman pinned face downwards. Even before checking for a pulse they knew she was dead.

'I heard a baby,' Harry said. 'I know I heard a baby.'

The same thought came to each of them: there had been a baby. They'd heard a baby, but they couldn't hear it now.

'Right,' said George, the voice of authority. 'Let's move her, but carefully, right? If there is anyone else down there, we don't want to disturb anything loose and bury them, now do we?'

Clancy and Harry moved the woman's body gently. Then the baby cried. It was alive.

'She threw her body over the baby,' Harry exclaimed. Not for the first time, he was awestruck at a mother's bravery and self-sacrifice, throwing her body over her child so her little one might live.

'She protected the little tyke,' Clancy said.

The baby was handed over to the proper authorities. Harry made enquiries regarding the woman, and was told that her name was Gilda Jacobsen and she had two older children who had been staying with their father's parents at the time of the raid. This fact gave him enormous relief. 'At least the poor mite will have his grandparents to care for him.'

Unfortunately, Harry was wrong.

CHAPTER TWO

April 1941, Bristol

'Sorry love. You can't go through 'ere. The buggers dropped a big 'un, if you'll excuse my French.'

The man's face was soaked with sweat and there were bags under his red-rimmed eyes. Mary Sweet guessed he hadn't slept a wink all night.

'Is it very bad?

He nodded. 'Nearly as bad as the November raid, though different types of bomb. One of 'em didn't go off. I 'eard one of the sappers call it Satan.' Mary understood, as everyone did, that he was referring to a detachment of Royal Engineers; sappers was the name by which bomb disposal experts were more generally know.

Resigned that speaking on BBC's *Kitchen Front* wouldn't happen today, Mary sighed, pushed the gear stick forward and prepared to do a U-turn. The car, a basic black Austin bestowed upon the Sweet sisters by the Ministry of Food, made grating noises as though reluctant to be turned back. Mary felt pretty much the same. Although she'd been nervous first off, she quite enjoyed making these radio broadcasts, airing useful tips on how best to stretch the family budget but concentrating on baking. Baking was the most difficult subject of all in wartime cooking, purely because most of the ingredients for making pastry or a cake were on ration.

The windscreen wipers slapped backwards and forwards, not that it was raining. They just seemed to come on when she least expected it.

Usually the car was driven by Corporal John Smith, Mary's twin sister, Ruby, sitting in the back seat as a passenger. Today the privilege had been hers purely because while Ruby was fine demonstrating delicious ration-based recipes in front of people, giving out that same information over the airwaves terrified her.

The gearbox continued to make crunching noises, metal grating against metal. It really was a stubborn car.

Perhaps it wants to be a tank, she thought, and was putting up a show of defiance, relegated as it was to driving someone who talked to housewives about how best to make pies with ingredients they never would have dreamed of using before the war.

After shunting backwards and forwards a few times, she was finally facing the right direction. Homeward bound, she thought resignedly.

Although she was far enough out from the city centre not to be immersed in smoke, she could see it billowing skywards in the distance. She could also smell it, the very air dried and tarnished with its sooty heat and blown in her direction by a prevailing westerly wind.

She should have known better, of course. She knew there had been yet another raid on the city. Half the village had turned out last night after hearing the drone of bombers flying overhead. Even the pub regulars had poured out from the Apple Tree pub and the Three Horseshoes, their beer mugs tightly clutched in their fists.

First off the searchlights had picked out the black moving

marks that were German bombers, vague X-shapes crossing the sky. Then the bombs began to fall, an awesome glow painting the sky a frighteningly beautiful orange-red over Bristol, the city of churches, their spires sharply black against the red glow.

'Well, that ain't no shepherd's delight,' somebody said.

Red sky at night, shepherd's delight. The meaning being that the following day would be fine.

In happier times it might have been said in jest to lighten the moment and lift the spirits of the gathered crowd, but it didn't happen. Those watching the terrible display had fallen to silence, perhaps thinking of how much damage had been done or, more likely, how many people had died.

'Bleedin' Germans,' somebody said. 'They got a lot to answer for.'

Against her better judgement Mary had still set out for the BBC studios in Bristol. Andrew Sinclair, her contact at the Ministry of Food, had promised to be there too, but had telephoned yesterday to say he couldn't come. London was also under siege, bombs everywhere.

'Another raid tonight, I'm sure. My mother is very frightened,' he'd added. 'I have to stay close to her.'

She'd told him she could find her way there by herself. She'd done so before. She'd appreciated the Ministry providing them with a telephone, but wondered sometimes if it was something of a curse: Andrew Sinclair was the only person who phoned regularly.

Not having him come was something of a relief. Although Andrew knew she was getting married in June, he couldn't hide the fact that he was attracted to her.

She'd told him she'd be fine. 'The corporal left the car here last night. He knew I could drive and besides he was due some extended leave.'

She'd got up early this morning, skipping breakfast because she was feeling nervous. It wasn't the first time she'd done this, but the butterflies came every time.

Ruby had been surprised that she was still going. 'We all saw the bombs last night. Bristol's had another bashing.'

Mary scanned her notes. 'Yes, but they haven't said much about it on the wireless, only that a city in the south-west had been attacked by enemy bombers. They didn't say it was bad.'

'That don't mean it ain't bad,' remarked her father. 'And that's a straight road into the city centre. It might be dangerous.'

Mary was undaunted. 'I'll skip the main road and skirt around the edge.'

'You'll have to be careful. You don't have to go.'

What he meant was that he didn't want her to go.

'I'll be fine, Dad.'

'Your brother thought he'd be fine too.'

She'd looked at him tellingly, her hands slowing in the process of straightening her hat, her best one in a shade of blue that matched her eyes.

'It's my duty, Dad,' she said softly. 'I have to do my duty. I owe it to Charlie.'

At mention of his son, missing presumed dead, he'd turned away, heading in the direction of the bread oven and the freshly baked loaves he'd left there turning golden brown.

So much for getting up early; now here she was on her way home again. She caught herself in a yawn, her eyes flickering half shut. It was on blinking herself fully awake that she saw the WVS van, a monstrous affair with a drop side that opened up to serve as a counter. She guessed it had been there all night, a marshalling point for the emergency teams helping to put out fires, organise rescue centres and dig for the poor souls buried under tons of rubble. She prayed that casualties were light.

The women running the tea wagon were stalwart souls sporting stiffly curled iron-grey hair that peeked out under humble headscarves that had been tied into turbans. Each had a no-nonsense attitude, even though they must have been up all night. At present it seemed they were all enjoying a cuppa themselves, the lines beneath their eyes evidence of how long they'd been on their feet.

Mary pulled the car over, stopped the engine and got out.

'Any chance of a cuppa?' she asked as cheerfully as she could. Her stomach rumbled. 'Wouldn't mind a currant bun too or a tea cake if you happen to have one going.'

'You're welcome, love. We've no butter, mind you. The air-raid warden had the last of that.'

'I can manage without.'

The woman in charge wore a felt hat sporting the WVS badge. She peered at her with narrowed eyes that made Mary think she might be a bit short-sighted.

'You been there, love?' She nodded in the direction of the city centre some four or five miles away. Her accent betrayed her humble origins, certainly not like the upper-crust Women's Voluntary Service type Mary had come across before.

'I got turned back. I was trying to get to Whiteladies Road.'

She didn't want to mention the BBC studios; it might sound too superior and she badly needed that cup of tea.

'What you doin' going there?' asked another of the women.

'I work for the Ministry of Food. I was ordered to go there. You know how it is, ours is not to reason why . . .'

She left the rest of the words from the poem hanging in the air . . . *Ours is but to do or die.*

She gulped the hot tea and quickly ate the currant bun they'd found for her. It was a little dry, especially without butter, but she was hungry and very grateful. Eating and drinking helped her blank out the unsaid words. Charlie, her brother, was dead at twenty-two. How many more, she wondered?

The women asked her about her work and Mary told them about her and her sister's job: showing women how to use their rations to make economical – and delicious – food.

The woman with the tightest iron-grey curls Mary had ever seen placed her cup into its saucer and sighed. 'It's pastry and cakes that's the problem. There are never enough eggs and never enough fat.'

'I can give you an eggless recipe,' Mary said to her. She went on to tell her to use self-raising flour *and* baking powder. 'It makes a good sponge recipe without eggs. You're using more raising ingredient instead. Add margarine, milk, golden syrup and sugar – if you have enough. Sift the flour and baking powder. Mix the other ingredients together. Plus whatever jam you have for the filling.'

In turn they bombarded her with their own labour-saving cooking tips and favourite recipes.

Mary took out her notebook and wrote down everything studiously. Some recipes she would use and some were already familiar. However, it didn't do to upset people's feelings. This would have been the whole point of her wireless broadcast today: to have her listeners feel they were contributing in whatever small way they could, including sending in their recipes and home front tips.

'So how come you got involved with all this then? You don't look old enough.' The woman in charge was straightforward and to the point, which was probably why she'd got the job in the first place.

Mary smiled politely, though it still grated when her youth was pointed out. The same point had been made so many times.

'My family run a bakery. I've been baking and cooking all

my life. I've had to, really. My mother died when I was very young. The work's divided between me and my twin sister. We won a baking competition and the Ministry offered us a job. I did have a brother serving on a merchant ship, bringing in food supplies, but . . .' She took a quick sip of tea to quell the short sob that threatened to escape. 'His ship was torpedoed.'

There was much mutual nodding of heads. They understood and sympathised.

'We all got men away fighting. Even the old blokes 'ereabouts aren't out of danger what with all this bombing. Even an ARP warden can get killed.'

Somebody else asked if she had a sweetheart.

Mary found herself blushing over the rim of her teacup. 'Yes. We're getting married next month.'

The women erupted with cries of congratulations.

'Bin courtin' long?'

She shook her head. It was the one question she hated facing. 'No. Not very long at all, but . . .' She shrugged suggestively.

'Grab the chance, dear. A fighting man I take it?'

'Royal Air Force. He's Canadian. Even though we haven't known each other long, he kept asking.'

Suddenly out it all came. They were complete strangers, yet in their company, a cup of hot tea in one hand and a bun in the other, opening up to them seemed the natural thing to do.

'My sister is making me a wedding dress and a bridesmaid's dress for my cousin Frances. It could also lift my father's spirits; he's been so down since my brother was lost at sea.'

'Never you mind, dear. It'll all turn out right in the end. You wait and see. When you seeing him again?'

Mary shrugged. 'I'm not sure. He's a bomber pilot. They're

pretty busy at present.' She didn't add that sometimes she couldn't help having second thoughts about their imminent wedding. It had all happened so quickly but she couldn't back out now. Everything was arranged around the leave he'd managed to get.

'Good for him,' exclaimed one of the women. 'Give them as much as they're giving us.'

'There's no sense in waiting. Who knows what tomorrow may bring,' said the woman in charge. She introduced herself as Doris. The two women with her were named Ivy and Edith.

'Grab a bit of happiness while you can, love, that's what I say,' declared Edith, a woman with a triple chin, the lowest of which totally obliterated her neckline.

'Have you heard whether there has been much damage in the city?' asked Mary, keen to change the subject.

There followed a jerking of heads and the expelling of sad sighs. 'Enough. After the docks again, as if there weren't enough damage back in November when they destroyed all around Castle Street and Wine Street. It was sad to see the Old Dutch House go and St Peter's Hospice and the church. We've known them all our lives.'

'Gone for ever,' said Ivy mournfully then sighed. 'That's where I met my ole man, Harold, up Castle Street.'

Edith pursed her lips after leaving a lipstick imprint on the side of her cup. 'We all met our sweethearts around Castle Street, well, either there or up Park Street. No money for doing much else. You just paraded up and down and when you saw somebody you fancied, that was how you met your intended.'

There rose another collective sigh before Doris suggested they all had another cuppa.

'I have to go,' Mary said, declining a second cup. 'I've got other things scheduled. Must keep going, mustn't we.'

She hadn't wanted to say that everyone at home in the village had seen the sky on fire. She hadn't wanted them to feel perhaps that she was better off than them living outside the areas that had been bombed. Everyone had it bad, each in their own way.

Fingers firmly gripping the steering wheel, she headed away from the city and back to Oldland Common. Ahead of her she saw a row of tramcars, all at a standstill, people pouring out of them looking pretty disgruntled.

Why had the trams stopped?

She opened the window a little, just enough for some air to come in and disperse the condensation on the windscreen. Through the small gap she heard troubled voices calling Adolf Hitler and his bombers all manner of names.

'Fancy blowing up the tramlines! How we gonna get to work?'

Mary settled back behind the wheel. Suddenly she felt very tired. How many more privations would people have to endure? She was lucky to have use of the car. Even at this time of day there were not many on the roads as few could afford cars or get hold of petrol. She was lucky in being in receipt of a generous petrol allowance, plus that allocated to the bakery business. The old bakery van was used only sparingly; adding what was left over from that with that for the car, there was some left over for private use.

Travelling, whether on trains, buses or trams, was disrupted each time there was a raid. London was fast becoming isolated, or at least the journey to the capital was being lengthened thanks to the more frequent raids. People were being urged not to travel unless necessary. Movement of armed personnel was first priority.

Her thoughts naturally turned to Michael Dangerfield, her fiancé. He would be travelling from Scampton in Lincolnshire for their wedding at St Anne's Church. She ought to be worried about him getting to the church on time, but oddly enough she didn't feel like that at all. In fact she was half hoping he couldn't get there, that he would call it off.

Her sister Ruby sometimes accused her of thinking too deeply. That's what she was doing now, trying to recall every detail of Mike's face and failing. Why was that? Was it perhaps that he didn't mean as much to her as he should?

She sucked in her bottom lip, tasting the sweet slickness of her bright red lipstick. She'd also dabbed a little on her cheeks, just enough to give her some colour.

She leaned forward so she could see better through the misted-up windscreen. Concentrating on the road helped put her misgivings from her mind. She found herself wishing the shops were lit up like they used to be, that there were no white lines along the edge of the pavement, that so many people didn't have to walk or cycle to work thanks to the destruction of the tramlines.

A crowd suddenly gathered in the middle of the road, all looking upwards and pointing. For one brief moment she thought it was another air raid, but then saw they were all laughing. Adults and children alike were skipping and jumping up and down with joy.

The tail of a barrage balloon, a big fat balloon designed to keep dive bombers at bay, slid over the side of a house, its fat bulk seemingly trapped on the roof.

She stopped and watched as people in navy-blue uniforms and tin hats sporting the letters ARP ran up and down the road in front of the shops, shouting and trying to reach for the damaged ropes that should have been tethered to the ground.

'Michael!'

Michael?

Steel curlers poked out from beneath a woollen turban and a cigarette hung from the lips of the woman shouting for her boy.

Michael! He was nothing like her Michael of course; just a tousle-haired lad with a dirty face and hair that looked as though it had never been introduced to a comb or a hairbrush.

Mike, her Mike, was a dream. She'd seen the way other girls looked at him. But it was she who was going to marry him. Everything was arranged. Rations had been scrupulously saved. The cake was made, the lack of traditional dried fruit more than made up for with fruits they'd dried themselves, plus over-generous amounts of brandy donated by Mike's aunt Bettina Hicks from her late husband's collection.

The wedding dress had been more of a problem, fabric being in such short supply. Mrs Hicks had found two yards of lace. 'You could trim up something a little plain. I'm sure it would work. And perhaps just a little teaser of a hat with a small veil at the front . . . what do you think? Oh, and I do have some lovely blue material that might do for the bridesmaids' dresses. I presume you'll be wearing your mother's dress?'

Mary had assured her that the lace was beautiful and of course it would change something quite plain into something quite wonderful. As regards her mother's wedding dress . . .

She bit her lip anew as she recalled her father's response when she'd asked to wear her mother's wedding dress, though it would have to be altered of course.

'He said he didn't think it would be appropriate,' she had told Mrs Hicks.

Actually his response had been quite sharp. 'It's Sarah's dress!'

Mary had bitten back the obvious response that her mother was dead and had no need of it. That if she'd still been alive

18

she would have wanted her daughter to wear it. Stan Sweet had changed since they'd lost Charlie. It was hard accepting that he wouldn't be coming back.

'The softness has gone from him,' Bettina Hicks had confided.

'Will it come back?' Mary had asked.

Bettina had shaken her head sorrowfully. 'Who can say? I do hope this wedding brings him out of himself. We can but hope.'

Mary hoped she was right.

CHAPTER THREE

Row after row of golden-crusted bread occupied the bakery shelves and the air was warmed by its yeasty presence.

Ruby Sweet breathed in the delicious aroma.

'There's nothing like the smell of freshly baked bread,' she said out loud, her hands on her slim hips. She liked bread and, though you wouldn't know it from her slender frame, ate a lot of it.

She turned as her father came from out back and through the shop. Having finished baking for the day, he was wearing his outdoor coat and his hat.

'No sign of Mary?'

'No.' Ruby shook her head, eyeing him from behind a curtain of dark gold hair.

He sighed. 'She shouldn't have gone. I hear the tramlines got blown up. Anything could have happened.'

'We would know if it had. Dad, there's something I want to—'

'I told her not to go. We all saw the sky last night.'

'Dad, about the wedding—'

'What about it?'

Ruby thought he should show more enthusiasm, but that was the way he was at present. Still in mourning. God knows when he'd finally snap out of it.

'Mary would love to wear white.'

'So?'

Ruby took a deep breath and jumped in with what she had to say. 'Mum's dress wouldn't need that much alteration . . .'

'No! It's Sarah's dress. Nobody else's. Not yours. Not Mary's!'

'Dad, Mum's been gone for over twenty years, and I think she would have—'

'You don't know.' He waved his finger in front of her face. 'That's just it. You do not know! Now let that be an end to it.'

There was so much more she wanted to say, but it was useless arguing with him when he was in this kind of mood.

Clamping her lips tightly together, she went to the wooden drawer that served as a cash register and bent her head over the order book. Thanks to her 'peek-a-boo' hairstyle, adopted to hide the mole on her face, a lock of hair fell forward, preventing him from seeing her expression: anger mixed with concern.

She was angry that he was so intractable when it came to Mary wearing their mother's dress; she was concerned because her father had changed since he'd lost his only son. 'Going for a walk?' she asked in an absent-minded fashion. Inside she continued to bristle.

He pulled the brim of his hat down over his face. 'Won't be long,' he said gruffly.

A draught of chill air came in as he dragged the door open. The drop in temperature persisted even after the door had closed behind him.

While supposedly counting the loose change in the till, Ruby contemplated where her father might be going. Before Charlie's death it would have been one of two places: either Stratham House to visit Bettina Hicks, who was also aunt to Michael, Mary's fiancé, or to his wife's grave.

Sarah Sweet had died in the flu epidemic immediately following the end of the Great War. Her passing had left their father with a small boy and twin baby girls to raise on his own. He'd done handsomely, and rose to the occasion again when his brother died and his sister-in-law shot off, leaving him to bring up Frances, their daughter, his niece.

Since Charlie's death, his last resting place known only unto God, Stan Sweet had stopped visiting Bettina Hicks for a cup of tea or a tot of something stronger. Bettina's view, which she had confided to Mary, was that he felt guilty at still being alive and his only son dead. 'As though having happy moments were a sin,' she'd said, a look of profound sadness in her eyes.

Slamming the cash drawer shut, Ruby came out from behind the counter. She watched as her father made his way towards West Street, the top of his hat bobbing along before he disappeared around the corner. Her guess was that he was heading for St Anne's churchyard and her mother's grave.

'She can't be that good company,' Ruby muttered to herself.

Before she could get too melancholy, she marched through the door behind the counter and brought through the other items they had for sale that day: cheese straws, rock cakes and scones. She'd used the last of the dried fruit they'd preserved last year to make the scones and rock cakes. The cheese for the straws had been grated from the end rind of a piece of Cheddar cheese given them by one of the local farmers' wives.

The tray containing all this wasn't so much heavy as bulky. As she carried it through to the shop, the headscarf she'd wound loosely around her hair, like an Alice band, slipped off and her hair fell forward, obscuring her vision.

Muttering under her breath, Ruby placed the tray on the counter and picked up the scarf. It was blue and matched her eyes.

Rather than leave the shop and use the mirror over the fireplace, she used her reflection in the shop door to put her scarf straight again. Her hair fell in her usual peek-a-boo hairstyle. It seemed a shame to alter it, but it made sense to tie it back whilst serving in the shop.

As she began to rewind the scarf around her head she caught sight of the mole that blighted one side of her face. Once the scarf was retied, she pulled a section of hair from beneath it, looping it over the mole that she preferred to keep hidden.

Although her reflection in the shop door was faint, she could still see that mole. A thought occurred to her. Perhaps it's the reason why Mary is engaged to a handsome flier and I don't even have a sweetheart. If I were to get married, I'd present Dad with a grandchild right away, she thought to herself. That would perk him up.

But she wasn't getting married. She'd vowed not to fall for anyone ever again after Gareth Stead, the landlord of the Apple Tree pub, had made a fool of her. He'd been sentenced to prison shortly after he was caught dealing on the black market. Mrs Darwin-Kemp, who lived in the biggest house in the village with her retired colonel husband, had been the presiding magistrate at his trial and he'd gone down for two years.

'Day-dreaming again, Ruby?' She shook her head. 'Talking to oneself is the first sign of madness.' She shrugged. 'Oh well. In this crazy world, who's going to notice?'

She placed the tray of cheese straws and cakes on the counter just as the jangling of the brass bell above the shop door announced a customer.

Miriam Powell came in, her pale countenance made paler on account of her black knitted hat and a worn black coat with a threadbare collar speckled with dandruff. It reeked of mothballs.

Ruby plastered on a smile to hide the pity she felt for Miriam, unfortunate enough to live and work with a mother who spouted religion from her thin lips. She'd always been scruffy, but never more so than she was now.

'Hello, Miriam. What can I get for you?'

'My usual, please. And mother said can she have some cheese straws to sell in the shop. The children like them if they've used up their sweet ration.'

'She lets them come into the shop?' Ruby couldn't avoid sounding surprised. Miriam's mother was a right old dragon and not particularly fond of children. It had always amazed Ruby that she'd actually had a child of her own, though Miriam had been a one-off.

Miriam held her head slightly to one side as she shook it, her eyes downcast.

'Oh no. Mother doesn't let them come into the shop. She lets their parents buy for them. That is her rule. Mother sticks to her rules.'

'You know what they say, Miriam. Rules are meant to be broken.'

The moment the words were out, Ruby knew from Miriam's face that rules in the Powell household were never broken. Miriam wouldn't dare.

'It's a lovely day,' said Ruby brightly as she took the money and put it in the wooden drawer behind the counter. She jerked her chin at Miriam's coat as she passed her the change. 'Aren't you a bit hot in that coat?'

She shook her head. 'No! No! In fact I find it a little chilly.'

'Perhaps you're sickening for something. I'd get to bed if I were you.'

'I can't. I've got things to do. Mother needs me.'

The glass in the shop door rattled as Miriam left. Ruby came out from behind the counter and watched her dashing off home, the full skirt of her black coat flapping around her legs.

Ruby sighed and rubbed her arms. Poor Miriam. Trapped in that shop with a domineering mother, her social life comprising only of church, still in her mother's company. At one time Miriam had been sweet on Charlie, not that he'd been interested.

It was mid-morning when Mary returned tugging off her gloves as though they were irritating her hands.

Ruby understood the situation in one swift look. 'You didn't make it.'

Mary shook her head. 'The city's in ruins. I smell of smoke.'

Ruby sniffed. 'You're right. You smell like a kipper.'

'I need a bath.'

'That can be arranged as long as you stick to the few inches allowed by the powers that be.' Their father had measured and painted a line around the bath.

'Have you had a busy morning?'

Ruby shook her head a little too vigorously. The long tress half covering one side of her face flew out of place. She swiftly pulled it back again.

'Not especially. Miriam Powell came in early as she always does. She never used to look so downtrodden and scruffy.'

Mary shook her head. 'I know it's uncharitable, but I sometimes think she'd have a better life if her mother wasn't around.'

Ruby's laughter was as bright as a bell. 'If you mean dead, say dead. She's always in church so the churchyard should feel like home to her.'

'Ruby!' said Mary in mock disapproval. 'You are wicked.'

'No, I'm not,' said Ruby, amusement written all over her face. 'I'm just stating the facts.'

'No wonder Ada Perkins hardly visits.'

Ada Perkins, Miriam's grandmother, lived alone in the Forest of Dean. At one point she'd taken Frances in as a refugee.

'Cuppa?' Ruby lifted the glossy brown teapot.

'Lovely. I'll tell Dad I'm home and see if he wants one.'

She went behind the counter and made to go through to the back where the bread oven was situated, but seeing the look on Ruby's face she stopped.

'Again? All morning?'

Ruby waved a hand dismissively. 'Again! All morning! He's going to make himself ill if he goes on like this. It wouldn't be so bad if he still visited Bettina, but he only goes there to look after her garden. The rest of the time, it's our mother's grave.'

They might have discussed things in more detail, but suddenly half a dozen customers flooded into the shop before they closed for lunch. One loaf after another disappeared from the shelves, and even then the shop failed to empty entirely. Everyone was talking about the previous night's air raid and how many were killed and whether a bomb was ever likely to fall on them, though it wasn't thought likely.

'We're too far out.'

'But if they've got one left, they'll drop it on us. They don't like taking 'em home.'

From air raids the conversation turned to recipes and the fact that everyone was baking potatoes in the ash of the fire grate, the best fuel-saving method they knew of.

After home cooking came talk about how best to grow good vegetables and keep chickens including the best way to kill them once their egg-laying lives were over.

'I favour knocking 'em over the 'ead with a block of wood before cutting their throats. Otherwise they're still running round . . .'

'My husband does the killing. Slits their throat without a second thought . . .'

'Mine prefers opening their beaks and getting the knife down their throats . . .'

Ruby suddenly disappeared out back, then just as quickly reappeared with a piece of paper in her hand.

'Diversionary tactics,' she whispered to Mary. 'Before I'm sick!'

Mary glanced at her, then the piece of paper on which was written the recipe she had been going to air on the radio that morning. Smiling, she faced the customers.

'Ladies,' she declared loudly. She waved the piece of paper in the air. 'This is our cake recipe for this week. Butterfly cakes with chocolate. The kids will love them. I'll stick it on the door so everyone can see.'

She managed to stick it to the glass with a few scraps of sticky tape left on the door from out of date official notices. Receiving new government directives was becoming a weekly event.

The women thronged around, each one peering with interest at the latest recipe. Nutritious meals were all well and good, but cakes were a delightful luxury.

'They'd be nice after a bit of stew.'

Once stew was mentioned, the conversation veered in that direction. All the women in the shop agreed it was a good plan to keep a stockpot going all week, but everyone had their own secret ingredient.

'Put the meat in first and never put the vegetables in until the end or it goes sour.'

'Only if you keep it a week. My stockpot only lasts two days – and my boys insist on 'avin' plenty of meat in their stews. They're growing boys.' Mrs Martin slapped her big hand down on the counter in an act of finality.

Everyone agreed that red-blooded men needed to eat plenty of meat.

Mrs Gates, a heavily pregnant lady, added her opinion. 'I like my stew with dumplings, but instead of using suet I save the fat from the Sunday roast. Oh, I do like a few dumplings.'

'Looks like you got yer own dumpling,' one of the other women said to her.

Much laughter followed. Mrs Gates had five children already. Her husband had been called up. Rumour had it he'd made sure she wouldn't stray by getting her pregnant before leaving.

'He needn't think he's done for me,' Mrs Gates declared loudly. 'Does he think I'm daft? Him away down the pub with his mates and all them loose women floating around. He does like his sauce, do my Bob, and what's sauce for the goose is sauce for the gander.'

The women laughed. So did Ruby. Mary turned pink. Such talk embarrassed her.

'Are you going to do this every week?' Mrs Gates asked jerking her chin at the recipe stuck to the door.

'I don't see why not.'

Ruby looked at her sister. 'What do you think, Mary? Something sweet from the Sweet sisters?'

Everyone laughed and remarked what a good line that was.

Mary scrutinised the recipe prominently displayed on the door.

'Yes,' she said thoughtfully. 'I think putting a new recipe up there every week is a good idea.'

Mary glanced at the clock. It had been like a women's church club that morning, talking about growing food, cooking food – and even how best to kill it, but now it was getting close to midday and the last customer had left. The shelves were almost empty. The surplus she'd give to some deserving family, though not before she'd taken a loaf for themselves and some for using in recipes. Breadcrumbs were becoming an acceptable alternative to pastry.

The bell above the door jangled as Mary brought down the blind. 'Sweet things from the Sweet sisters,' she said to her sister. 'When did you first think up that line? It's really catchy.'

Ruby grinned. 'Just thought it up on the spot!' Her grin turned to a grimace. 'Anything rather than hear more about how best to kill a chicken!'

'We'll do the same next week. Shall we take it in turns?'

'If you like, but in the meantime can I suggest you have your bath? I quite like smoked kippers, but I can hear the neighbourhood cats mewing around the back door.'

Mary laughed before turning pensive. 'I suppose Dad will be back for lunch, though he usually isn't gone this long.'

Ruby shrugged. 'It must be something I said . . .'

Mary paused. 'What did you say to him, Ruby?'

Ruby shook her head defiantly and peered beyond her sister to the shop door at the same time as reaching for a duster. 'Nothing much. My, but look at that glass. Finger marks all over the place.'

'Ruby! What did you say to him?'

The finger marks weren't that stubborn to remove, but Ruby pretended they required her undivided attention. But her sister's look meant she had to give a response.

'I said that you'd prefer to be married in white. I asked him whether he'd allow you to wear our mother's dress.'

'Oh, Ruby!'

Ruby spun round. 'Well you do, don't you?'

Now it was Mary who averted her eyes. There were so many things she wasn't sure about.

'I don't know. I haven't really thought about it. I wish I'd had more time to think about it . . . the wedding I mean. Everything.'

Ruby frowned. She'd been surprised when Mary announced she had accepted Michael Dangerfield's proposal. Mary had always been cautious, the twin who thought things through very carefully before committing herself. Agreeing to marry a man she had known for only a short time had seemed out of character, but that was her business. Could she be having second thoughts?

'Still,' Mary said, looking suddenly brighter. 'The blue dress will look lovely I'm sure.'

Ruby was certain she had not misread the look that had flashed over her sister's face. 'You could always postpone the wedding until Dad gives in and lets you have Mum's dress to wear.'

Mary clenched her hands together. 'I can't. Everyone is counting on me.'

Her sister could hardly believe her ears. What she'd said was outrageous. 'Mary, you shouldn't be getting married because everyone is counting on you. It's a lifelong commitment between you and Mike.' She paused as a thought came to her. 'You do love him, don't you?'

'Yes. Of course I do.'

'Do you want to talk about it?'

'Some other time. I'm going to have a bath.'

Left alone in the shop Ruby contemplated those words. *Everyone is counting on me.* She shook her head. They were the wrong words. Mary should have said I love Mike and we're going to get married as planned, regardless of whether I'm wearing white or blue. The fact that she hadn't was worrying.

CHAPTER FOUR

The bakery was shut, lunch was overdue and still Stan Sweet hadn't come home.

Mary was drying her hair in front of the fire when Ruby declared her intention to go and fetch him. She was stirring a thick stew made from pork bones and plenty of vegetables. Once the meat had fallen off the bones she'd taken them out and added rolled oats to the stew to thicken it.

'I'll tell him he's missing a lovely stew and it will be ruined if he doesn't get back here soon.'

'I'll make sure to keep an eye on it.' Mary did not raise her eyes but concentrated on making her hair nice and dry.

Snatching her coat and scarf, Ruby flounced out, annoyed with her sister for a host of things: for being the way she was, for not demanding their mother's wedding dress, for not confiding in her as Ruby had expected her to.

The fresh breeze blew in Ruby's face as she walked briskly along West Street before turning into Court Road down over the hill and over the hump-backed bridge.

As she made her way up the incline towards the church, she turned up the furry collar of her coat until she could feel the soft fabric tickling her ears. The collar had been plain but a little frayed. Mrs Hicks had given her an old fox fur which she'd cut up and made into a fur collar sewing it neatly on to the old one.

Ruby commented on how new it looked. Bettina even had the original box.

'It seems a shame to cut it up,' she'd said to Bettina. 'There's nothing wrong with it.'

Mrs Hicks had sighed but been resolute. 'My late husband bought it for me. I could never admit to him that I hated the glassy eyes of that fox looking at me. It made me feel guilty. The poor creature was far happier running around a field. Cut it up, dear. Do as you like with it.'

So Ruby had cut off enough to cover the frayed collar of her coat and made a hat out of the tail. Like Mrs Hicks, she didn't like the glass eyes and the snapping mouth that served as a clasp to pin both ends together. She'd been about to throw the head away but Frances, home for Charlie's funeral at the time, had intervened, stating she would take it with her if she should ever go back to the Forest of Dean where she'd been evacuated. The reason wasn't clear, but Frances was adamant. Shuddering with distaste, Ruby gave her the whole of the head with its glassy eyes and spring-loaded jaw.

Ruby stopped at the church gate, her eyes scouring the lichen-covered gravestones, the sad-eyed angels, the army of crosses and stone books engraved with the names of those lying there.

A few dead leaves blew through the long grass from the edge of the churchyard and across her mother's grave. There was no sign of her father.

She eyed her mother's headstone as though that might give her inspiration. A bouquet of spring flowers, yellow and purple, overflowed from the marble urn in the centre of the grave. The smell was fresh and sweet, and despite the overcast sky and lack of spring weather, there was something hopeful and happy about it.

She reached out and touched the headstone. The speckled

marble felt oddly warm, which surprised her. She'd expected it to feel cold. Perhaps it was due to that unexpected warmth that she suddenly found herself wanting to speak to her mother. She'd never done so before. Only her father did that.

She heaved her shoulders in a huge sigh and knelt down, her knee resting on the marble sill that surrounded her mother's plot.

One voice inside told her she was about to talk to a stone – nothing more. Another voice said otherwise and urged her on.

'It's Ruby, Mum. I hope you can hear me. It's about Dad. He's depressed, Mum. It's ever since we lost our Charlie. You'd think our Mary getting married would buck him up, but it hasn't. He's happy for her, yes, but there's a big gap in his life. Charlie's gone. His only son. Sometimes I think he'll never get over it and that worries me. I've heard it said that grief can shorten your life. I don't want him to die, but nothing we do seems to help. I just wish something would happen to take him out of himself, but that would take a miracle. I wish there was some way you could help. I wish there was something I could do, but try as I might, things stay the same. If there is a God and a heaven, perhaps you might put in a good word.'

She got up on to her feet shaking her head and almost laughing, thinking how foolish this was. As though talking to her mother's headstone would solve anything. That's all you've been doing, she thought to herself. The dead hear nothing and can do nothing.

Turning her back on the grave she retraced her steps along the path and out of the church, down the incline and slowly back up the hill.

Stratham House was on the way and Ruby decided to call in on Bettina in case her father was in there. He hadn't had much to do with Bettina since Charlie's death, but there was always the chance that he might have relented and dropped in.

Daffodils danced in big clay pots to either side of the front door. Cowslips and crocuses dotted the small areas of lawn that were left closest to the house. The rest of the garden had been dug up and planted with vegetables. Ruby reminded herself that her father had planted most of those. He still tended the garden, but kept himself to himself, declining offers of refreshment from the woman who he'd once counted as a friend.

At the sound of the gate creaking open, the tall figure of Bettina Hicks came out from the garden shed, a stone-built affair attached to one end of the house. She was wearing gumboots and the rough webbed gloves she used for gardening. Despite her age, Bettina was a fine figure of a woman. Her back was ramrod straight, her eyes clear and her cotton-fine hair was fashioned into a cottage-loaf style, the sort favoured by the Gibson girls before the Great War.

She hesitated for only a moment before recognising which twin was visiting. Ruby's peek-a-boo hairstyle gave her away.

'Ruby! How nice to see you. Would you like a cup of tea?'

Ruby tucked a tress of unruly hair back behind her right ear. 'I was looking for Dad to tell him his lunch is ready. Obviously he's not here.'

'No. I've not seen him all day. Not seen a soul in fact.'

A sad smile accompanied her words. Bettina was on her own most of the time now. Gilda Jacobsen, a friend of a friend, she'd once had staying with her, had gone back to London shortly after Charlie's death taking her two children with her. She'd gone without saying a proper goodbye. Ruby found it hard to forgive her for that. She'd so wanted to talk with her, make her a friend and even part of the family. Gilda, already widowed by the war, had been having a relationship with their brother. Like everyone else she'd been devastated at his death, especially considering that he'd survived one sinking only to die in another shortly afterwards.

Bettina had also taken Gilda leaving hard. What with her nephew Mike Dangerfield away serving with Bomber Command and Stan Sweet no longer taking tea with her, she was alone much of the time.

Ruby wished she could do something about it, but her father wouldn't take kindly to her giving him a good shake and telling him to buck up. Anyway, he had the right to be sad. But life goes on, she told herself. Life has to go on.

'You look as though you're busy,' Ruby said to her after rousing herself from her thoughts. 'I don't want to intrude.'

Bettina smiled. 'You're not intruding. I'm glad of the company. Come on into the kitchen.'

Although Stratham House was grandly titled, there were only two reception rooms, a kitchen, bathroom and two bedrooms. Mrs Hicks had forsaken a third bedroom to have it converted into an upstairs bathroom, quite a luxury in the area.

'An old woman's indulgence. I'm too old to be paying visits down the garden or hanging a tin bath from the back wall,' she'd explained early on when Ruby's father had been a regular visitor.

Bettina talked about the garden as she took the kettle from the hob, warmed the willow-patterned teapot and then put two spoonfuls of leaf tea from the caddy into it.

'Would you like a biscuit? They're very good.' She laughed. 'Of course you know they're very good. Mary made them. I must admit you girls bake the best biscuits ever, far better than I could make myself or even buy in a shop. Not that there's that much choice in a shop nowadays *and* you have to queue, even for biscuits!'

The tea was poured into bone china cups decorated with roses. The biscuits – four of them – were set out on a separate plate.

Bettina went on talking about the garden for a while then switched to talking about the wedding.

'I'm so looking forward to it. I thought about buying a new hat, but then thought Mary might have need of my ration quota for a going away outfit.' She paused. 'I take it your father hasn't relented and let her have your mother's wedding dress to alter?'

Ruby shook her head. 'No. He's not the easiest man in the world to get on with at present.'

'Ah yes,' sighed Bettina. 'Only to be expected of course, but hard to live with. Charlie's loss was so unexpected.' She looked down into her lap, for the moment lost in thought. When she raised her head and Ruby saw the sadness in her eyes, she felt her heart would break.

'I miss Gilda and the children. I never thought I would, but I do. She used to write at first and then a month or two ago it stopped. I don't know why.'

'And your son? He writes frequently?'

'Oh yes. He does, but . . .' Again her gaze dropped to her lap. 'He's so busy doing war work over in Canada, and anyway, writing is all very well. But you can't beat contact with another human being. Face to face, so to speak. And somebody of one's own age.'

'After Charlie died everything changed,' remarked Ruby.

Bettina jerked her chin. Her expression was one of sad regret.

'I'm grateful that he takes care of my garden, but he declines my offer of a cup of tea. In fact, he doesn't even come in the house, because his boots are too muddy and he can't take them off because his socks are in need of darning.'

'That is not true,' Ruby protested. 'Mary and I make sure of that.'

Bettina forced a little laugh. 'I know that. It's just his excuse. Still,' she said visibly brightening. 'At least we've got the wedding to look forward to and seeing as I'm not buying a hat, I think I'll alter and trim my favourite one. It's a cloche style but I'm sure that with a little ingenuity I can make it into a pillbox and even add a little veil and a silk rose – or a real one if I can find one.'

'A Charles Stuart, perhaps,' said Ruby. 'It's already in flower and there are lots of buds just waiting to burst open. Mary is planning to use some for her bouquet.'

Aware that the rose bush, Charles Stuart growing in the Sweets' garden, had been bought to commemorate both Christmas 1939 and Charlie's surviving the sinking of his first ship, Bettina nodded silently.

'We'll see if there's enough for Mary's bouquet first. I can make do with something else, and isn't that what we're supposed to do? Make do and mend?'

'I'm wearing yellow. Actually it's the material you gave to Mary. There's only enough of the blue for Mary's dress and for Frances as a bridesmaid.'

'You don't want to be a bridesmaid?'

'I would if there was enough of the blue material, but there isn't. All we had in the rag bag was Mary's old dress that got ripped by the dog!'

Bettina laughed. 'Blasted dog. Still, it's thanks to him that Mary and Mike are getting married.'

They talked about the time Mike Dangerfield had been staying with his aunt and had brought a friend's dog with him. The dog's teeth had connected with Mary's dress and torn it. They both smiled at the memory.

'So how about you, Ruby? Do you have a sweetheart? Oh, I'm sorry. I don't mean to pry . . .'

Ruby put down her teacup which was now empty. 'You're not prying. There's nobody serious. I'm enjoying myself while I can. I work hard. I think I deserve a little fun. I'm not a nun!' Normally she wouldn't have revealed so much to somebody who was basically only a neighbour, but Bettina was such a kindly, motherly person. Ruby felt comfortable telling her.

'Nobody said you were or that you should be a nun.' Bettina looked at her with kindly eyes.

'Good!'

'More tea?'

'Why not?'

It had always surprised her how easy it was to talk to Bettina. Her father must have found it easy too; shame that things had fallen so desperately apart.

'I've made a point of not going out on a date with anyone from the village. Most of the men I meet are through work. Some of them have been soldiers – officers mainly – home on leave. A few days and they're gone. They ask me to write to them, but . . . well . . . I haven't encouraged it.'

Bettina saw her slight smile. 'I can't say I blame you for enjoying life as it is.'

'As I've already said, I enjoy my work. I didn't think I would enjoy standing up in front of a group of women and talking about baking, but I love doing it. It's safe to say that I don't have a care in the world, except . . .' She looked down at her teacup, turning it around on its saucer. 'Except for Dad of course.' She sighed. 'I just wish he was his old self again.'

'So do I,' Bettina said quietly.

'Oh well. I'd better be off. Lunch will be getting cold and I still haven't found him. I wonder where he's got to.'

Actually, she suspected he was in the pub. He'd always liked the odd pint, but never during lunchtime, not until Charlie had died. The thought of it was worrying. Too much to drink and he became somebody else, somebody with a temper and the fists to match.

They'd only ever seen it once, on the occasion of his brother Sefton dying and Sefton's wife, Frances's mother, taking off and leaving her child behind.

There'd been a man involved. Stan Sweet had found out about him, following him to a pub in East Bristol where he'd faced him down and given him a licking he was likely to remember for some time. Not that it made much difference to Mildred. She'd still shot off. The last they'd heard she was in London.

On Ruby's return home, she found Mary putting away the dishes. Stan Sweet was sound asleep in one of the old armchairs placed either side of the fireplace.

His mouth was open, his eyes closed and his arms were flopped over the chair arms. His snores were loud and clear. His breath smelled of beer.

'He came in ten minutes ago,' she said when Ruby glanced accusingly at their father.

'No need to tell me where he's been. I can smell it.'

Mary shrugged. 'He's our father. We can't tell him what to do.'

Ruby gritted her teeth. She wanted to say that he could do with somebody telling him that life goes on, but held back. She thought about what she'd said over her mother's grave. It was too much to hope for, but it was something. Hope, as somebody said, springs eternal.

'I take it Mrs Hicks wouldn't let you go until you'd had

at least two cups of tea,' said Mary, an amused smile on her face.

'You're right,' whispered Ruby. She crooked her finger so that Mary would come closer, nodding to where her father was really sending the snores home!

'Best not to disturb him. He's not sleeping well.'

Mary agreed with her.

'I told Bettina about the time Frances came to live with us. Do you remember what he was like then?'

'Very angry with her mother. I don't remember Mildred very well except that she wore a lot of make-up and never left the house unless she was looking her best. Dad called her a hussy.'

'That's right. But he didn't dwell on Mildred leaving. He brightened up for the sake of Frances I think. At least, that's how I recall that time.'

Mary nodded and kept her voice low. 'He felt responsible for her so he brightened up. That's how Dad is.'

'That's what he needs now,' whispered Ruby. 'A responsibility to face up to and live for.'

Mary agreed with her. 'He's only got us and we're grown up and don't need anyone to be responsible for us. Neither does Frances. She's growing up too.'

Ruby fiddled with the collar of her dress. 'Poor Dad. What he needs is grandchildren. Imagine how happy that would make him.'

'Ruby!' Mary managed to keep her voice down, but had no control over the heat spreading over her face. 'Give me a chance. I have to get married first.'

Ruby grinned. 'Not necessarily, my dear sister. In fact, you don't need to get married at all. Do I have to point out to you that babies do not come from under the gooseberry bush?'

Mary's blush deepened. 'Of course I know where babies

40

come from! Don't be so silly! Honestly, Ruby, at times I can hardly recognise you as my sister.'

'At times I think I need to speak to you about the facts of life!'

To Mary it felt as though her face was on fire. 'I'm off upstairs. I need to finish dusting the bedroom.'

After she'd gone, Ruby stood thoughtfully. Heading upstairs to dust the bedroom was only an excuse. She told herself her sister just had a case of wedding nerves. Everything would be fine – including having babies.

CHAPTER FIVE

Spring had come to the forest. Days of watery sunshine inter-mingled with breezy days, and days when it rained, though lightly.

Frances stood in a forest glade, enjoying the chirping of birds in the trees and watching their coming and going with twigs and bits of sheep's wool tugged from barbed wire fences.

When evacuation had first been suggested to her, she hadn't wanted to leave home and stay with Ada Perkins – mother to Gertrude Powell and grandmother to Miriam – across the River Severn in the Forest of Dean. She'd wanted to stay with her uncle and cousins in the only safe home she'd ever known. As it turned out, she settled in well with both Ada and the local kids and hadn't grumbled too much when it had been decided, in light of the recent bombing raids, that she should come back for a while. For the rest of her life she would remember this carefree time, days of learning how to tickle trout, how to snare rabbits and how to forage for lunch when it was too late to go home.

Frances was now thirteen. In another year she'd be leaving school, probably to help out in the family bakery in Oldland Common, unless she obtained a job in a factory producing war materials. There was one at the bottom of Cherry Garden

Hill that used to produce lawn mower parts before the war. Apparently it was now producing nuts and bolts. There was a chance she might get a job there, although her age might count against her.

In the meantime she was enjoying her few days back in the forest. Soon she would be returning home to be a bridesmaid at her cousin Mary's wedding.

'Mary's marrying a pilot,' Frances proudly told her school-friends while on a foray to pick wild mushrooms and garlic and to see if the odd rabbit or two had got caught in one of Ralphie's traps.

Deacon, with his cheeky face and tumbling hair, was the friend she most wanted to impress. She was over the moon when his face lit up with awestruck delight.

'Get on! Bombers or fighters?'

'Bombers,' said Frances, his response causing her to glow with delight.

'What sort of bombers? Hampdens? Wellingtons? Halifaxes? Lancasters?'

All Frances knew was that he flew in bombers. She hadn't a clue about what *type* of bomber. 'I'm not sure: He didn't say. I think it's a secret.'

Deacon narrowed his eyes so he could better read her expression. 'You don't know, do you?'

'Yes I do,' Frances replied hotly. 'But I can't tell you. Remember what that poster in school says: "Careless talk costs lives".'

Deacon winced. She could see by his expression that he wanted to know more, but was an out-and-out patriot so wouldn't dare press her further.

'Are you going to be a bridesmaid?' asked Merlyn, the only girl Frances had really latched on to.

Uncertain whether being a bridesmaid would impress them,

she considered denying it. She'd spent most of her childhood in the company of boys, preferring to climb trees and make dens rather than play with a doll and pram.

It was only remembering Deacon's reaction to Susan, a blond-haired girl at school who lisped a little, but was full of confidence and favoured wearing dresses with bows and an Alice band in her hair, and how Deacon became dumbstruck when Susan was in the room, that Frances finally admitted, 'I suppose so.'

Merlyn persisted. 'What colour?'

'Na, na, na-na, na. Frances is going to wear a dress and bows in her hair,' mocked Ralph – or Ralphie as they usually called him. He was a scruffy boy from a large family. On account of there being rarely enough food to eat at home, he had become a skilled hunter of anything edible. This included salmon, trout, rabbits and pheasants.

Deacon clipped the back of his head with the flat of his hand. 'She's a girl, Ralph. Girls wear pretty dresses. Haven't you noticed?'

Ralphie, scornful of anything sissy, wiped his nose on his shirtsleeve in an act of contempt. He'd never actually quite taken it on board that Frances was a girl. From the moment she'd arrived in the forest, she'd joined in every scrape they'd ever got up to and could climb a tree quicker than anyone else.

'What colour?' Merlyn repeated. Merlyn had also spent most of her childhood ranging the forest with the boys. Of late she'd taken to wearing a ribbon in her hair. And now she was asking about the colour of the bridesmaid's dress Frances would wear. Like Frances, Merlyn was growing up.

Confused by conflicting emotions, Frances shrugged. 'I'm not sure. Blue, I think.' Blue was the first colour to come into her head, mainly because she'd glanced around her and Deacon was wearing a navy-blue pullover. 'Not navy blue,' she added as an afterthought. 'I think sky blue.'

'I like pink best,' said Merlyn. The answer was not surprising. The ribbon in her hair was pink.

Frances didn't know quite how to respond except to say that it most definitely wouldn't be pink. 'I don't care what colour you like, Merlyn. I like blue best and my dress will be blue.'

There were plenty of mushrooms growing, especially around a part of the forest frequented by deer.

'Deer's poo! You can't beat it for growing mushrooms,' Deacon had declared.

Frances gathered up enough mushrooms to fry in butter, perhaps with a few scraps of bacon added.

Deacon was close by doing the same. The line of mushrooms she was following joined up with those he was picking. She could have gone in the other direction, there were plenty growing there too, but Deacon was like a magnet. She was drawn to him, but couldn't as yet understand why.

They ended up standing next to each other, out of earshot of the rest of them.

'You can have one of these.'

He handed her one of the rabbits he and Ralphie had trapped earlier that day.

'I thought you only caught two today,' she asked, thinking perhaps that she'd got it wrong, though she didn't want it to be wrong. She wanted to be favoured by him. She wanted him to like her more than he liked Susan, the girl with the lisp and the pretty dresses.

Deacon, undisputed leader of the local lads and heartthrob of every adolescent girl in school, turned a touching shade of pink.

'It's a present, seeing as you're off to this wedding by and by. And I'm leaving school before you. Got a job an' all.'

Frances let the rabbit dangle from her fingers and blushed just as brightly as Deacon. 'I will be back you know.'

He shrugged. 'You might. You might not. Anyway, I'm starting my job at the quarry. I might not be around when you're over here visiting.'

'I'll find you.'

'Come elvering tonight?'

'Yes. I think so.'

Ada Perkins looked at Frances searchingly when she asked about going elvering with young Deacon Fielding. She had recognised the besotted look in her young charge's eyes. She'd seen the same in her daughter Gertrude's eyes when she'd been in love. Seen the disappointment too when the man she loved had left her and she'd been forced to marry someone who had demanded her complete obedience. To Ada's eternal sorrow, her daughter had buckled under his domineering ways. She had become as hard and as sanctimonious as he was. There had been no forgiveness in his religion. Gertrude tried her best, but her best had never been good enough. She'd been stripped of compassion, stripped also of the affection she should have given her daughter.

Ada sighed. But that was Gertrude. Her daughter. This was Frances Sweet, Stan Sweet's niece. She only hoped a dark evening in the forest didn't lead to the same scenario. Even if Frances was a lot younger, the forest lived and breathed the ways of nature and wasn't easily resisted.

'Seeing as you're back home on the other side of the Severn shortly, you can.'

'I'll get my coat!'

Ada grabbed her arm as she swept by. 'You'll eat your supper. Then you can get ready. I'll get my net.'

'You're coming too?'

46

'Of course I am! I go elvering every year, don't I?'

As dusk fell, men, women and children trooped along the slippery paths at the side of the river, some of them lugging home-made elver scoops over their shoulders.

Netting that might once have been hung up at a window were spread tautly over a frame, the resultant shape vaguely resembling a small bathtub. There was a handle at one end, this slung over the shoulder, the scoop hanging over behind.

Elver fishermen not carrying a net or a parcel of sandwiches, carried torches with which to attract the young eels; others had storm lanterns and a few, notably those that worked in the forest coal mines, used the Davey lamps on their pit helmets.

Ada kept her home-made scoop sitting on top of the shed roof. Once she had shaken the leaves out of it, she and Frances joined the others, seeking out and claiming what they considered the best pitch possible.

'Just here,' she said, pointing at a favourite spot where a natural jetty of fallen stones speared out into the dark water.

Ada was one of those lucky enough to own a storm lantern, the little flame flickering into life once they were settled beside the river. Ada attached it to a long pole so the light fell directly on to the water.

Ada told Frances what to do. 'Scoop it in. Shine yer light down into it and the little critters will come swimming in.'

Frances fixed her eyes on the spot of light, which looked as bright as the moon. Even though this was her second spring in the forest, it was the first time she'd been elvering. She felt very confident of success, Ada leaving her to it while she sat back on the wet grass, her boots in the mud, her smoking pipe clenched in the corner of her mouth.

Intent on what she was doing, she didn't notice Deacon

and his father Joe walking along the path behind them, but Ada did. 'Off early, Joe?'

'I am that. Just been brought a message that our Roger is shipping out so got a bit of leave. Waiting fer us at home, along with Will Pegg and his daughter.'

Mention of Will Pegg's daughter was uttered with apprehension.

'I won't ask what that's about,' Ada muttered, shifting her pipe from one side of her mouth to the other.

'You don't need to,' grumbled Joe.

Deacon's eyes met those of Frances before he followed soundlessly behind his father, the elver scoop bouncing over his back.

Will Pegg's daughter was named Della. Frances hadn't had anything much to do with her. She merely knew her as one of the older girls, though she had noticed she had a winning smile and an ample bosom. She'd overheard Deacon and the other boys remarking about those breasts using their hands to describe the size of them. Once when Roger Peters had been home on leave, they'd almost tripped over him and Della in the forest. Della's dress had been up around her waist and Roger had been lying on top of her.

They'd hidden in the undergrowth, watching in silent fascination until the pair had finished and stood up, rearranging their clothes.

They didn't speak much, mostly just kissed and fondled each other. The only thing Frances remembered Della saying was that she hoped Roger hadn't got her in the family way.

'I suppose Della Pegg's in the family way,' Frances said to Ada.

Ada opened one eye; she had been dozing. A whorl of smoke rose from her pipe. 'Aye. I suppose she is.'

'Roger Peters's for it,' she heard somebody say.

'Before he goes off to war by the sound of it,' shouted somebody else.

Another voice rang through the forest, high as the sound of metal ringing against metal. 'Won't be the first.'

'Won't be the last either,' muttered Ada.

It wasn't a bad haul of elvers, and although Frances was delighted, she still couldn't bring herself to eat them. They'd cooked some up in the forest once, she and the other kids. Ralphie had brought them along, a mass of wriggling in a tin can. He'd told her he'd got them from the river and that they were quite fresh. One look had been enough to turn her stomach.

She half turned, hands still holding the net, as she informed Ada that she wouldn't be eating the elvers.

In the glow of the storm lantern that Ada had hung from a low hanging branch, Frances saw her eyes narrow. 'No need to. We can sell them to people who do like eating them.'

Just a few days later Frances was standing at the door of the little house in the forest that she'd stayed in ever since she was evacuated. There were logs piled up outside the smoke house where Ada smoked salmon poached fresh from the river. There was also a leg of ham, courtesy of a wild boar that everyone said didn't exist in the forest. They did. It was just that you had to know where to look.

Ada noticed her reluctance. 'My door's always open.' The pipe in the corner of her mouth jiggled as she spoke.

Frances nodded. A thought came to her. 'Will you be coming over to visit Mrs Powell and Miriam?'

Sadness clouded the old lady's eyes but was swiftly hidden. 'I visit there when I think there's a need – like there was with you. You needed me to be there.'

It seemed a strange answer, but then, Frances thought to

herself, Ada Perkins was a strange woman, but likeable, very likeable.

Frances grimaced. 'I've never liked wearing dresses, but I suppose I have to get used to it.'

There was a wise look on Ada's face as she regarded her charge – not without some affection. 'You don't have to, but you will. You're still a child,' she said, patting Frances's shoulder. 'That's what you are this week. But next?'

Frances frowned. Ada sometimes talked in riddles. 'Don't be silly, Ada. I'll still be thirteen.'

'And then you'll be fourteen, and one year is going to make all the difference in your life – whether you like to wear fancy dresses or not!'

'Why doesn't Miriam ever wear pretty dresses?'

Ada's eyes darkened, as though her thoughts were going somewhere she herself had no wish to go to.

'Her mother doesn't believe in pretty dresses, so she doesn't. She might have one, though, hidden away somewhere.'

'She just wears that old coat all the time.' Frances wrinkled her nose. 'It smells of mothballs and is much too big for her – or was,' she added as a thought came to her. 'It's a bit tighter now. She must be getting fatter.'

Ada Perkins heard all this and fell to silence. They'd be coming over then – her daughter and her granddaughter. They'd be coming over soon.

CHAPTER SIX

Ruby no longer regarded the hard eyes and strong faces of factory workers with apprehension. She'd learned that the way they looked at her through half-closed eyes was because they were tired. They were all working twelve-hour shifts, some more than that depending on shortages and the demand for whatever they were making.

'Ladies,' she began, 'I'm sure you'll agree that sandwiches are the mainstay of a worker's lunch. Luckily for us all, bread is not on ration just yet. But let's be fair, it isn't easy to make that two ounces of cheese per person go far when you've got sandwiches to make. This especially applies when there's more than one of you in the house working every hour in the day. So here are a few simple suggestions . . .'

'Number one,' she said, her voice resonant as she counted the first one on her finger. 'Try adding chopped onion to dripping before spreading it on bread.

'Number two: use a spoonful of chutney – home-made or otherwise – instead of butter.

'Number three: always grate cheese and, again, add a little chopped onion for your sandwich filling. You'll find it goes a lot further.

'Number four: carrot tops can be used as you would lettuce; just chop it up and sprinkle on whatever filling you're using.

51

'My only warning is not to use onion in the sandwiches you make for yourself if you've got a date that night, eh girls? Even the most hardened army veteran draws the line at kissing a mouth that tastes of onion!'

It pleased her to hear a smattering of laughter. She'd learned pretty quickly that it paid to be amusing.

'Grated white cabbage and carrot make good sandwich fillers especially when mixed with cold meat. And mince the meat to make it go further. You'll find it goes further still if you mince it the night before then press it between two plates and place a weight on top of it; that way it flattens, goes further and is easier to place between two slices of bread.'

As she spoke, her gaze swept over her audience, settling for a moment on Corporal Smith. He was sitting with his arms folded, his eyes fixed on his boots, a quirky grin on his face. His expression was like that of a boy about to get up to mischief.

'Now for the best part,' she cried, loud enough to ensure that everyone was wide awake. 'We come to the subject of pastry and cakes. We all know how difficult it is getting enough fat, sugar and basic ingredients for making a pie, a tart or a cake. But, with a little ingenuity you will find you can produce something to tickle even the most sceptical of taste buds. I use the word "sceptical" because jam isn't always real jam, cream isn't always real cream and the ingredients of mock duck pie have nothing to do with duck whatsoever!'

Once a murmur of approval ran through her audience, she knew they were really listening.

'As you may or may not have noticed, my name is Miss Sweet. There are two of us: I'm Ruby and then there's my sister Mary. You may have heard her on the BBC *Kitchen Front* programme. You may also have noted that we both advocate that every main meal should be followed by something sweet, a little luxury to keep our spirits up. To that end we have gathered together some baking recipes you may like. Sweet-tasting recipes produced by the Sweet sisters!'

Even to her own ears, Ruby thought again how very apt and wonderful it sounded. Sweet things produced by the Sweet sisters!

At the end of the talk when she'd handed out recipe leaflets, the atmosphere literally buzzed with enthusiastic conversation.

'Cakes and pastries courtesy of the Sweet sisters,' declared the factory foreman. 'Give her a hand, girls. Sweets from the Sweets!'

Titters of laughter accompanied the clapping, and then it was all over. Another talk and baking demonstration had come to an end.

Corporal Smith followed her out, the wicker hamper swinging from one hand. He was looking down at the ground and shaking his head. She wasn't fooled: he was smiling to himself. Or smirking. Either way something had amused him.

'So what were you grinning about?' she said once they were in the car. The morning had been given over to the factory audience, but the day was not yet over. She was scheduled to demonstrate the best ways to save fuel at a department store in the Georgian city of Bath.

Corporal Smith changed down a gear before sweeping around a hairpin bend. 'You were talking about onions and going out on a date.'

Ruby shrugged. 'It's called empathy, Corporal. I wouldn't want to go out on a date with my breath smelling of onions. I reckoned they wouldn't either. Empathy! See? Meaning we can put ourselves in the shoes of others.'

'I'm not ignorant. I know what it means!'

Ruby bit her lip. She hadn't meant to be patronising, but she'd obviously hurt his feelings.

'Sorry. I didn't mean to upset you. Are we still friends?'

'Is that what we are?'

He was being facetious, but Ruby knew he was only pretending to be vexed. John Smith was one of those people who invited conflict.

Ruby had taken to sitting in the front passenger seat of late. When they'd first been thrown together she'd always sat in the back.

'Like Lady Muck being driven around by 'er chauffeur,' her father had said. The comment had affected her deeply. She didn't want to be Lady Muck, and she didn't want Corporal Smith to think of her that way. Even though he was curmudgeonly, she had grown quite fond of him.

While he was focused on the road ahead, she eyed his profile. He had a straight nose, a high forehead and a strong chin. Despite his army haircut, tufts of curly hair sprouted from his neck. They looked soft. Touchable. She had to look away in order not to follow her inclination.

'So when was the last time you went on a date?'

His question took her by surprise.

'That's none of your business!'

Suddenly she wasn't so keen on touching him.

'I thought you'd say that. Keep the working man at bay . . .'

'Don't start that again!' There it was: her old self barging through just when she'd thought it safe to like him.

He shrugged. 'It strikes me that you're a right one for giving out advice that you know nothing about.'

'I beg your pardon?'

Ruby thought she had got used to Corporal Smith and his ways. In the beginning he'd been sullen verging on downright rude. Now he was only surly – not much of an improvement but better than he had been.

'A date. I asked you when was the last time you went on a date.'

'And I said it was none of your business!'

He seemed to think about her statement before shaking his head. 'A man would have to be brave to ask you out for a date.'

She gurgled with laughter. 'I haven't been eating onions if that's what you mean.'

'That's not what I mean. You're the sort who can't leave the job behind. You've always got to be in charge and people like that find it hard to relax. Laugh. Dance. Have a drink. Especially the drinking part. Bet you don't do that too often.'

He glanced at her before turning his eyes back to the road ahead, a smile twitching around his mouth.

'Are you saying I'm not good company when I'm relaxed?' she asked. He had riled her, and she knew he knew it.

'How can I say that? I wouldn't know, would I?'

'That's right. You've never been out with me. I would point out that I don't drink much and I never get drunk.'

'Never?'

Ruby chewed the inside of her mouth, a desperate habit that only served to make her mouth sore. 'Only tipsy. But as I've already said, you wouldn't know. You've never been out with me.'

'Well, I can sort that here and now. How about we go to the pictures once you've finished with this lot in Bath?'

For a moment she couldn't find the right words. She liked this Corporal Smith. Over a period of time she'd got to like him more and more. But did she want to go out with him?

She glanced at him, that curl of hair around his neck that she'd so wanted to touch. Unfortunately, she had other plans.

'I can't. Mary and Dad are expecting me for supper. Besides, I have to be up in the morning to fetch Frances from Gloucester. She's coming back for Mary's wedding, and I guess she'll stay with us now for good. She'll be fourteen next year so there doesn't seem to be much point in her going back.'

'And no longer a child. No longer an evacuee.'

'That's right. So I'm off to Gloucester first thing. It's going to have to be on the train. Dad couldn't get the petrol coupons.'

'No need. Your sister's got no speaking engagements tomorrow and neither have you, but I'll still have the car. I can go with you. We've got some unused petrol coupons from the van we sometimes use to deliver bread, and luckily the Ministry give us a very generous allowance. We'll have enough to get there and back. I know the way. We can take sandwiches and stop in a pub for a beer. No onions though.'

She saw him grin. He was definitely being a bit forward, but under the circumstances she could hardly hold that against him. What was that old saying about not looking a gift horse in the mouth?

The prospect of getting to Gloucester railway station hadn't been an attractive one. The journey was long by either train or bus, the services lengthened on account of rolling stock – both goods trucks and carriages – being diverted to war work and the ferrying of military personnel.

Ruby looked out of the window as she weighed up her objections to going with him. Still thinking it through, she faced forward again. On turning to face him their eyes met briefly. She read a challenge in that look, in the clear calm of those bright hazel eyes.

Again she looked out of the passenger side window.

Yes, no, yes, no: her fingers tapped the walnut-veneer trim of the door in time with her thoughts.

'You'll need more petrol,' she finally said.

'I've got plenty of petrol and a chitty to get more. Your sister didn't use up the allowance the other day.'

'All right,' said Ruby relaxing against the warm leather of the passenger seat. 'You can drive me to Gloucester.'

'I will. There's just one thing you have to agree to.'

'What's that?'

'You have to continue to sit in the front with me, not behind like a bloody duchess like you used to.'

Ruby agreed. 'I like sitting up front. In fact I've got quite used to it.'

As it turned out, Ruby had made the right decision. The day was fine and she'd done better than make sandwiches, she'd made pork pies with hot water pastry and the leftovers from the shoulder of pork they'd eaten for Sunday lunch. A little gravy, rolled oats and some leftover vegetables made the filling stretch further.

They left early that morning taking the A46, which would take them to Nailsworth where they were likely to find a decent pub for a break, through Stroud and thence to Gloucester.

Every so often she looked at Corporal Smith and giggled. He looked at her, frowned and asked her what she was giggling at.

'I only used to see the back of your head when you were driving. Now I can see the expressions you pull when there's something about the road or the traffic that you don't like.'

'I do not!' His face was quite taut.

'Yes, you do. Your lips move as though you're swearing at them – especially the milk cart back there. The poor horse can only go so fast you know.'

She didn't give him chance to comment, but continued to

giggle so infectiously that his lips, usually set in a surly line, broke into a smile. And then, when she least expected it, he pulled a face.

By the time they were halfway through the journey they were both laughing and feeling comfortable with each other.

They found a pub at the side of the road near Nailsworth and while Johnnie – he now insisted she called him Johnnie – went in to buy a pint of beer and a half of shandy, Ruby attended to the small basket she'd brought with her in which were the pies she'd made, two apples and half a dozen cheese straws.

At first their conversation was about their jobs, the war, the car and how late the train would have been. Once those particular subjects had been exhausted, Ruby asked him where he came from.

'London.'

'What part of London?'

'Bermondsey.'

'What's it like there?'

'Rough. It's near the docks.'

'You don't seem rough.'

He paused as though he were in two minds whether to tell her any more. 'I've been away from there for a long time,' he said in a clipped manner.

'But you still have family there?'

'Some. Some are away in the army. Some are dead. Scattered to the four winds. That's my family.'

Somehow she didn't believe him. She sensed there was another truth behind what he'd told her that he was keeping to himself.

'I know that the docks in London have been heavily bombed. Have your family been affected?'

'No. They were already dead.'

He looked away, his eyes fixed on a cow that had pushed its head between two lines of barbed wire.

'The other man's grass is always greener,' he said suddenly. 'At least as far as that cow is concerned.'

'Are you in touch with any of your family?'

'No. I told you. They're mostly dead.'

Ruby fell to silence. She felt awkward and wished she hadn't asked. It sounded as though John had lost a lot of his family either to war or disease. She had no wish to press him further. Neither did she wish to challenge him that he wasn't telling her the whole truth. Her intrusion would not be welcome.

She had to forgive him for being terse. Everyone had trouble talking about losing family members. Charlie loomed large in her thoughts, but she didn't want to talk about it. She sensed Corporal Smith didn't want to talk about it either.

Since speaking in public, she'd become quite adept at changing the subject. 'I wonder what Frances will bring with her? Last time she brought two pheasants and a brace of trout.'

'Lucky you.'

He seemed thoughtful the rest of the way. It wasn't until the tower of Gloucester Cathedral pierced the skyline that he relaxed again. She couldn't help thinking his silence had had something to do with his family. One day he might reveal more. In the meantime, he made her laugh, sometimes he annoyed her, but basically she liked him.

'Are you Ruby's sweetheart?'

Johnnie was carrying Frances's luggage and a whole Severn salmon wrapped in newspapers at the bottom of a sack. Ruby caught the blatant innocence on her cousin's face as well as Johnnie's look of amusement.

'He's my driver,' she explained in a clipped voice. 'We work together for the Ministry of Food.'

'I know that. But you've known each other for ages now.'

Ruby cleared her throat and tried not to laugh. Frances was growing up. She'd begun noticing such things. Pretty soon she'd be noticing boys a lot more, if she wasn't doing so already.

When they pulled up outside the bakery, a gang of Frances's schoolfriends awaited them. Chattering and asking Frances a host of questions, they gathered around the car, eyeing it inquisitively, sticky fingers leaving imprints all over its shiny bodywork.

The smaller kids leaned on it. The older ones commented to each other as to what make it was and how fast it might go. A shiny motor car was an object of interest to these children who were more used to the village bus, horse-driven milk carts and hay wagons, even if the car had become a common enough sight outside of Sweets' Bakery. Even before the war, with the exception of the doctor, there had been few private cars in the village.

Once Mary had opened the shop door, Corporal Smith stepped inside and placed the luggage down on the floor. He was about to do the same with the fish when Mary invited him to take it into the kitchen.

'Help yourself to a cup of tea,' she called over her shoulder as she went to welcome her cousin back with a big hug and a smack of a kiss on the cheek.

'Glad to be home?' Mary asked her.

Frances pulled a face that could have been a positive or a negative response. 'I think so.'

'You've got a bridesmaid's dress to try on. Isn't that exciting?'

There was not a trace of excitement on Frances's face, just a guarded wariness. 'It isn't pink is it? I don't like pink. I like blue.'

Mary laughed. 'You guessed correctly. It is blue. The roses in your posy will be pink, but there will be cornflowers as well.'

Frances breathed a sigh of relief. 'That's all right then.'

Mary's arm was around Frances's shoulders, guiding her towards the kitchen when she looked back at Ruby. 'I fancy wearing blue if you want me to be your matron of honour.'

'Don't worry about it just yet. I've got nothing planned,' grunted Ruby as she heaved the wicker basket containing all her demonstration equipment past them, the gap so narrow they were forced to flatten themselves against the wall. 'Nobody's asked me to marry him so it's not an issue.'

Out in the kitchen Johnnie Smith had poured himself a cup of tea and was eating one of the jam tarts Mary had set out for him.

Ruby thumped the hamper on the table. 'My sister said you could help yourself to a cup of tea, not a full-blown meal.'

He carried on chewing. 'I was starving.'

Ruby stood with her hands on her hips, eyeing him accusingly. 'So I noticed,' she snapped. 'This hamper is heavy, you know. I could have done with a hand.'

'I brought it in from the car.'

'But not into the kitchen.'

'I don't have to bring it into the kitchen and, anyway, I was gasping for a cup of tea.'

'Oh, wonderful. So you left it for me.'

Something seemed to shift in his eyes. 'You didn't have to struggle. You could have left it until I'd finished.'

He brushed a few stray crumbs from his tunic while eyeing her speculatively. Earlier today he'd thought a truce had occurred between them. She hadn't snapped at him and he hadn't made cutting remarks about her attitude. They'd got on really well at lunchtime, her making sure he had enough to eat, and him brushing away the spiders she'd noticed in the pub's outdoor lavatory. All in all it had been a grand day and he'd thought quite seriously about asking her to go on a proper date. Not now though. She was back on her high horse and all because he'd grabbed a cup of tea and a tart before bringing in her precious hamper!

'I'll be going then,' he said, already sliding his beret from his shoulder and on to his head.

'You're welcome to join us,' said Mary brightly. She threw a questioning look at her sister. Something was going on here that she wasn't quite sure of.

Ruby gave nothing away. She liked Johnnie even though she sometimes found him exasperating. What she couldn't quite come to terms with was that she was finding it hard to cope with her feelings. She didn't want to face them. She didn't want John to think he could be more to her than the bloke who drove her around to baking demonstrations.

John nodded. 'Thank you, Miss Sweet. I would love something to eat. It's a long way back to the depot.'

He had noticed that Mary was far less abrasive than her sister and he really fancied another bite before he went back to barracks. She pushed the plate of tarts in his direction. Ruby pushed them beyond his reach behind the teapot.

'Try these,' said Mary and pushed forward another plate containing small pasties. 'Pilchard pasties,' she added.

On eyeing the golden pastry, Corporal Smith's stomach had rumbled. But the moment he knew what the filling was, he withdrew his hand. 'No thanks. I don't like fish. I think it's time I went after all.'

As he headed towards the door, Mary nodded at her sister and mouthed a silent, 'Well go on. See him out!'

Ruby glowered. 'Let me see you out,' she said. 'Just in case you steal the silver.'

He threw her a surly look. 'Very funny.'

Ruby jerked open the front door. 'Just for the record, the only piece of silver we have is a candelabra on the dining-room sideboard. We're not rich, Corporal Smith, even though you seem to think we are.'

His eyes, such a delicious shade of hazel, narrowed as he looked at her, the two of them standing close in the doorway.

'I was Johnnie at lunchtime. Seems now I'm back to being Corporal Smith.'

'That was today.'

'A "thank you" would be nice.'

'Thank you.'

She didn't raise her eyes. 'And the pictures?'

She bit her lip. 'I'm sorry. Frances has just come back and I have to measure her up for the bridesmaid's dress.'

'If that's the way it is.'

He sounded angry. She wanted him to be angry so she could argue and dislike him as she once had. It was only working to a point; her feelings had definitely changed. She liked him a lot, perhaps more than a lot. But she couldn't, wouldn't, get involved, and sharp words were her only defence.

'I'll see you on Friday. Nine o'clock sharp.'

After closing the door on him she pulled down the blind, closed her eyes and rested her forehead against it.

Sitting up front with him, talking as they drove along, then eating sandwiches and drinking cool beer, had been quite wonderful.

Why aren't we nice to each other all the time? she thought. Why do we speak nicely one minute and strike sparks off each other the next?

Mary met her on her way back in. 'Is he gone?'

'Yes.'

'You weren't very nice to him.'

'He's an oaf.'

Mary looked quite shocked. 'No, he's not. He's sweet. And he's sweet on you. That much is obvious.'

Ruby dug into the hamper, taking out the dirty dishes, the paper bags, the cutlery and Thermos flask. 'He's just a work colleague who had the means of taking me to Gloucester to collect our Frances.'

'He's not just that at all. I can see it in your eyes.'

'See what?'

'I think you're getting quite fond of him.'

Ruby stopped flattening the paper bags she'd extracted from the wicker basket for reuse.

'He's just a friend.'

'I think he'd like to be more than that,' said Mary, a little warily, because she'd obviously rattled her sister.

'Well, he never will be. He's not my type. Besides, he's only a corporal. I'm off out with an officer tomorrow night. Much more my cup of tea!'

'Another one?'

Mary knew she shouldn't have said it, but once it was out there was no taking it back.

A nerve flickered just beneath Ruby's cheekbone. 'That's the way I like it!'

Mary hugged herself and bent her head. 'Just be careful. You'll be getting yourself a bad reputation.'

Ruby saw red, slamming her hands down on the table so hard she made the tea cups rattle in their saucers. Two spots of red dotted her cheekbones. 'That is my bloody business and nobody else's. I told you before that I intend to have a bloody good time. I belong to nobody and, quite frankly, that's the way I prefer things to stay.'

She stalked out through the back door, slamming it behind her. She leant against the wall of the house for what must have been half an hour or more. Thoughts of past mistakes and her probable future flew around in her mind like so many starlings, noisy and bustling, though she had never actually gone the whole way.

It could have been so easy to do so. The memory of Gareth Stead was still with her. She'd had a narrow escape and the experience had made her wary.

Why can't I be like the saintly Mary? she wondered to herself.

She almost burst out laughing at the thought of it, but there it was: Mary had attracted an offer of marriage without playing the field first. She's most certainly the saint of the Sweet family, thought Ruby, and I'm the sinner.

CHAPTER SEVEN

Mary's wedding dress was pale blue and made from the same bolt of cloth as that of her bridesmaid's, Frances. Like the length of white lace, the cloth had come courtesy of Bettina Hicks, who often popped in to see how things were progressing.

It was noticeable to all of them that their father made himself scarce when Bettina dropped in. They made a point of apologising for his absence. Bettina brushed it aside, giving the impression that she really wasn't that concerned, though it was obvious that she was.

'He needs time to himself. He probably will do for some time.'

On this particular day when she called, Mary was standing on the kitchen table while Ruby pinned up the hem of the dress. There was barely enough fabric to make two dresses, so although Mary would have preferred a full-length wedding dress, she'd had to settle for a hem that skimmed her knees.

'It looks lovely dear. I'm only sorry I didn't have white,' said Bettina ruefully. 'Though I have to say, you look quite beautiful. The colour matches your eyes.'

'I think it does. Thank you, Mrs Hicks. I really appreciate it.' Mary meant what she said. The material was lovely, but in her heart of hearts she had wanted a white wedding dress and one dress in particular: her mother's.

Ruby's fingers momentarily faltered in their task of pinning up the skirt. She knew that although Mary was thankful for the donation of lace and blue silk, deep down she would have preferred a more traditional colour.

Ruby found her father's attitude frustrating. The dress was hanging in the wardrobe upstairs, neatly wrapped, undisturbed for years. Unlike Mary, she was angry enough to want to do something drastic and had suggested that she take it and alter it to suit without telling their father that she'd done it.

'He won't even know until your wedding day and he's a man – he probably won't even notice,' she said in a throwaway manner.

But Mary, true to form, had been downright shocked by the suggestion.

'Ruby, I couldn't do that.' Her face had blossomed to a most becoming pink. Combined with her dark-blonde hair, it made her look positively doll-like.

Ruby looked at Mary, the sister who always acted responsibly, never one to rock the boat. No, thought Ruby. You couldn't. But I could.

She'd made up her mind. That afternoon, on the pretext that she was going to finish off Frances's dress, Ruby made her way up to the attic room where her brother used to sleep. His room had been kept closed up, empty of most of his possessions which had been boxed up and stuffed in a cupboard. On pushing open the door, the first thing she noticed was the smell. She could still smell Charlie, the faint odour of cigarettes and maleness.

She relished that faint odour serving to keep his memory alive, though there was nothing left in the room that had once belonged to him. The chest of drawers had been emptied of his things and he'd taken his hairbrush, comb and shaving tackle with him. All that remained of him in this room was the furniture: the chest of drawers, the single bed, the threadbare rug throwing a splash of colour on the bare floorboards, the curtained-off section of wall that had served as a wardrobe. The only addition was the small table set in front of the window on which sat a twenty-year-old Singer sewing machine.

Ruby assumed it was the furniture that still held his scent, though she'd noticed of late that it was lessening. She swiped away a tear that threatened to emerge from the corner of an eye. In time the smell of him would disappear and they would be left with nothing but a memory and a few grainy pictures.

Blinking back her tears, she shut the door behind her and went to the small room across the landing from Charlie's. A wardrobe of elaborate design and made of ebony wood was the only piece of furniture in the room. Ruby turned the cast-iron key and opened the door. The only item hanging in the wardrobe was her mother's wedding dress, covered in a mass of tissue paper.

Ruby reached beneath the folds of crispy, crackly paper, now yellowed with age. Her fingers sought and found the dress itself, a soft mixture of satin, silk and lace.

Such a shame to leave it here, unseen and unworn, though still loved, if her father's attitude was anything to go by. He'd certainly loved the woman who'd worn it all those years ago.

Ruby sighed. It had occurred to her that Mary would have been allowed to have the wedding dress if only tragedy had not struck. She was certain her father's attitude would have been different if Charlie hadn't been killed.

With brazen swiftness, she pulled the tissue paper aside so she could see the dress more clearly. Even in the gloomy depths of the wardrobe, its beauty, its whiteness, was totally astounding. It deserved to see the light of day once more. In her head she imagined her mother flashing her an approving smile, though goodness knows she wouldn't know what that smile would have been like. She imagined it would have brightened her face and made her eyes glow. Though Ruby had been too young at the time of her mother's death to remember her, sometimes in the dead of night, she was almost sure she could recollect a kind arm cradling her, a sweet voice singing her a lullaby.

The sudden creak coming from the winding staircase that led up here caused her to hold her breath, brush the tissue back over the dress and wait. She listened, her eyes on the simple pine door dividing the bedroom from the landing.

There was no other sound of footfall, at least not coming in her direction.

Nerves on edge, knuckles white on the hand that gripped the wardrobe door, she took a deep breath and realised she'd amplified the sound, assuming it had come from the upper staircase. In fact it must have come from the one below that: somebody on their way to the bathroom. Like Mrs Hicks, they had an inside lavatory and a bath.

Quietly, so nobody could hear, she took the wedding dress from out of the wardrobe and tiptoed back into the other room, the tissue paper, lace and satin rustling all the way.

The old sewing machine was made of cast iron and inlaid with mother of pearl, and was operated by hand. It dated from just after the Great War. The one they were using downstairs to make the dresses from the cloth Mrs Hicks had donated was a treadle and worked by both feet pressing down on the footboard.

Once the bedroom door was closed behind her, she laid the wedding dress out on the bare mattress of the bed. Piece by piece, she peeled away the tissue paper, which had been sealed down each side and sewn into place. Once she'd stripped off the tissue paper, carefully folding it for future use – and just in case she was discovered and forced to cover it up again – she laid the dress flat on the bed, the arms outstretched, the skirt carefully spread.

She admired it for a moment, imagining Mary wearing it, then imagining how her mother had looked in it. Under the circumstances, it seemed strangely apt that she'd laid it out flat on Charlie's bed. He would approve of that. She knew he would.

After close examination, she was satisfied that no moths had damaged the dress and it didn't smell of mothballs. The tissue paper alone had protected it.

It was too old-fashioned for Mary to wear in its present state. Changes would have to be made. The dress had sleeves that were bell-shaped as far down as the elbow then gathered into tight cuffs. A fall of embroidered lace fell from the neckline and almost reached the waist. The lace had also been made into a confection resembling a rose that sat on the left shoulder – like a corsage, though too heavy, Ruby thought, for modern tastes. The bodice was quite loose-fitting and bound with a satin sash. The skirt was fashioned from yards of embroidered tulle, falling in panels which were banded with silk, and underneath it was lined with satin. The dress had been made to hide a figure, rather than enhance it. If she was going to do this, she had to remodel the shape to accentuate the waist and bosom, not swamp them. She could do it. She knew she could.

All the same, it was worrying.

Ruby chewed at her bottom lip. There was plenty of material to play with, though the thought of cutting off layers, particularly the lacy rose, was disconcerting. It would take a lot of skill, but she was sure she could do it. What concerned her more was her father's reaction: he would be furious. Yet somehow she knew her mother would approve. All she hoped was that her father would come round. And Mary would be pleased – once she knew about it. But Ruby wanted this to be a surprise. Her sister wanted a white wedding dress and she would have a white wedding dress. Ruby could secretly adapt the blue dress into a bridesmaid dress for herself. She made up her mind: this was the dress her sister would wear to her wedding, though drastically altered. Besides, keeping her hands busy would keep John Smith from her mind. Banish him. It was best not to think about him.

The scissors sparkled like silver when she looked down at them in her workbox in front of the attic window. For a moment she hesitated, her cautious side asking her to reconsider. Her wilder, more wilful side urged her to start snipping. Her wilful side won.

'Well. Here goes.' She picked up the shears, took a deep breath and began to cut. The rose was the first to go, falling like a real one at the end of the summer. The sleeves were next. Her intention was to cut off the tight lower sleeve and re-cut the full part to form a bell-shaped sleeve that would skim Mary's elbow. The cape-type collar would also have to go. The under-bodice would need reshaping. Luckily the neckline was very similar to the modern sweetheart design and would stay. The extra layer of tulle at the front had a gap about twelve inches from the bottom showing the satin underskirt. She was undecided on what to do with that yet, although it would be nice to keep something of the old design, a little piece of her mother.

She fingered the net, surprised at how soft it felt. If she did this right, there should be enough tulle left over for a veil, a short one, but a veil nonetheless.

Her eyes settled on the fabric rose she'd cut off from the shoulder. Joined to a length of tulle it should make a very pretty headdress.

The satin underskirt would also have to be modified, but that, she decided, should be quite easy. It was just a case of removing a few panels from the skirt, especially from the train at the back. The dress would still be ankle-length, but the hemline would be at the same level all the way around except for the inverted 'V' at the front where the tulle was cut upwards and the satin underskirt exposed.

As she went along she would cut, sew and fit the dress to the person who would be wearing it, but in this case her instinct told her to keep it a secret. Anyway, she didn't need to have Mary to hand for fittings. They were of identical size so would try it on herself at each stage of making it.

Once she'd started cutting, she found she couldn't stop. It was like running downhill in high-heeled shoes: once you'd started, the speed of your descent increased until it was a headlong rush.

At last there was no dress, just the pieces that had once contributed to the whole.

With a sinking feeling, Ruby looked at all the pieces laid out on the bed, two arms, a bodice, big pieces of material and smaller pieces. The lower arms lay to either side of what remained of the main dress like truncated limbs.

'Oh God,' she murmured, suddenly struck by the enormity of it all. 'What the bloody hell have I done?'

She sat down on the bed, her fingers teasing the six pearl

buttons running up from the cuff of one sleeve. Her mother must have gasped when she'd first seen herself in it. So must her father, white suiting her mother's peachy complexion and swept-up hair, the scooped neckline emphasising the length of her neck.

'Dad will kill me!' she muttered.

Another harsh truth struck her: she now had a white wedding dress to make plus two blue dresses, one for Frances and one for herself. Would she get it all done in time?

'Well, you'll bloody well have to,' she muttered. In her mind she imagined Mary scolding her for swearing, reminding her that she'd promised not to swear now Gareth Stead was no longer around.

Mary wasn't around at present, though Ruby did have a quick look over her shoulder.

'It's enough to make anyone swear,' she whispered. 'What the bloody hell have I done?'

Mary was bent over the gas stove, the oven door open.

'Oh there you are,' she said, her voice muffled as she ladled mutton fat over the crisp pastry topping of mutton and carrot pie. 'I wondered where you were.'

'The dresses have to be finished and I'm the one who has to make them.'

Mary glanced at her sister long enough to gauge a shifty look in her eyes. She put it down to something secret about the wedding; perhaps she was making a little extra something for her trousseau.

'Do you need me to give you a hand?' Mary asked.

'Certainly not. Anyway, you're all fingers and thumbs. Are you all set for your talk tomorrow?'

Mary picked up a knife and cut into the pastry, just

73

enough so some of the mutton fat seeped through into the filling, which wasn't mutton. She'd had to use corned beef, the rest made up with root vegetables. 'As ready as I'll ever be.'

'Are you putting that back into the oven?' Ruby asked.

'Just long enough to keep it warm. I think I can turn the oven off.'

'So what's on the agenda for tomorrow's talk?'

The pie safely back in the oven, Mary picked up the precious notebook in which they wrote their recipes. 'Buns, cakes and tarts and how best to make jam from carrots.'

Ruby threw back her head and laughed. 'The humble carrot! Where would we be without it?'

'I think I shall use that line you came up with, Ruby. Sweets from the Sweet girls. It's very catchy. Is that all right with you?'

'Of course it is. It might make us famous. We might get people stopping us in the street and asking for our autographs.'

Mary paled. 'You don't think so, do you? I don't think I would like that.'

Ruby grinned. 'I'm only joking. I just can't believe we didn't think of it before.'

'So you'll use it at this talk you're giving to the women's group in Warmley at the end of the week?'

'At a school hall, that's if I can get everything finished in time. Call me when supper's ready.'

The front room where the treadle sewing machine lived felt incredibly cool after the warmth of the kitchen and Ruby was glad of it.

Her face felt as though it was on fire, though she didn't feel embarrassed, just scared and guilty and just ever so slightly selfish. She'd gone ahead and cut up her mother's wedding dress without her father's permission. He'd probably explode when he found out. Whatever had she been thinking of?

On sitting down in front of the sewing machine, she buried her face in her hands. What could she do about it now? Nothing. The deed was done. She couldn't possibly sew the dress back together. Whatever happened, whatever her father's response, she would have to deal with it. There was no alternative.

Sewing was a skill that came easily to her, the material sliding easily beneath her fingers, the blue dress Frances was to wear already shaped and half-finished. Feeding the fabric through the machine was second nature, she could do it blindfolded, and because of that she could think of other things while the machine rumbled on and on, material in one end, a garment out at the other.

At this moment John Smith was on her mind. She found herself quite looking forward to him driving her to Warmley for her talk and had already decided she would apologise for her behaviour the other day and tell him how much she'd enjoyed his company on the drive to Gloucester. I might even suggest going to the pictures, she thought to herself. There's no rule says that he should do the asking is there?

Another idea suddenly hit her. In an effort to make up with him, she could ask him to the wedding. Mary had already suggested it, and Ruby had said she didn't want to. She might question Ruby's change of heart, but that didn't matter.

That evening before supper in the warmth of the kitchen, she made Frances try on her bridesmaid's dress. Like the white wedding dress she was secretly redesigning, it had bell sleeves and a long skirt. It even had a sweetheart neckline very similar to the one on the white wedding dress.

'You made that quick,' Mary remarked. 'When will I be able to try on my dress?'

'Soon.' Ruby hid her guilty expression behind the dress she was pulling off over Frances's head. 'I knew this little madam was impatient to try it on. Isn't that right, Frances?'

'At least it's blue,' their cousin commented, pulling her day dress over her vest and knickers.

Ruby folded the dress over her arm. A stitch or two and it would be ready for pressing. She turned to her sister. 'I wondered if you would mind me inviting Johnnie Smith to the wedding.'

Just at that moment her father came in from the garden, the smell of turned soil and dusk coming in with him.

'That all right with you, Dad, if I ask Johnnie Smith to the wedding?'

Both her tone and her facial expression were blithely innocent, a classic case of butter not melting in her mouth.

Stan Sweet looked unconcerned. 'That's for your sister to decide. I don't mind much either way.'

The two sisters looked significantly at each other behind his back as he hung up his hat and coat.

Mary sighed, her eyes locked with those of her sister. 'I think he deserves to be invited.'

'As long as you don't mind.'

'Of course I don't mind. If you remember rightly, I suggested it the other day and you said you didn't want him to come.'

'I know, but I've changed my mind. It was good of him to take me to Gloucester to collect Frances.'

'I think so too.'

And so it was that, at the sound of the car pulling up to take her to the talk in Warmley a few days later, she had the wedding invitation in her hand when she opened the door. Only it wasn't John Smith.

'I'm Brenda Manning, your new driver,' said the freckle-faced redhead standing there. 'I hear we're off to a cooking demonstration. Is there likely to be any free food going at the end of it? Don't mind telling you, I'm starving.'

'Where's Corporal Smith?'

The redhead was one of those fidgety types who swayed when she spoke, as though fearing she'd be struck dumb if she didn't keep moving.

'I understand he asked to be transferred for personal reasons.'

CHAPTER EIGHT

Stan Sweet clenched his jaw so hard, his teeth ached. His eyes were fixed on the spumes of earth erupting beneath the onslaught of his garden spade. The furrow for the onions would be much deeper than was strictly necessary. The vigorous way in which he attacked the soil wasn't strictly necessary either. His muscles ached with the effort, but still he proceeded to slice, hack and stab at the soil.

Only those who knew him understood that gardening was the only way he could cope. The more gardening he had to do the better, and venting his anger and despair with a spade, a garden fork or a hoe was the only reason he still applied himself to his garden and to that of Bettina Hicks. He wouldn't come near the place otherwise. Life was utterly grey, the only brightness the vivid redness of his anger.

He used to be good company for Bettina. He'd enjoyed chatting with her over a cup of tea or something stronger. That was before Charlie had died, before his world was torn apart. After that he'd found it hard to take up where they'd left off.

Every so often she asked him in for tea. In the past he would have accepted her invitation. But not now. Sometimes he merely turned her down flat. Sometimes he pretended he hadn't heard her calling – like now. She'd go inside once it was clear that he wouldn't answer.

'Stan! Stan!'

He glanced beneath his arm. She was still there, looking prim and pretty in a pale grey dress, her hair a slightly lighter colour and in what they'd used to call pompadour style.

She kept calling! Couldn't the woman take no for an answer?

He peered beneath his arm on the upward stroke of his spade. She was hanging by one arm from the back door, her other hand resting on her walking stick.

It struck him that she was being unusually persistent today, calling and calling despite him ignoring her. He chose to believe she was just being obstinate, determined to have him in for a cup of tea and biscuit.

Leaving the spade standing proud in the earth, he went round the back of the early runner beans. Half hidden behind the seven-foot-high sticks, he thought that would be that. She would go back inside and leave him alone.

Squeezing a handful of green leaves in his hand, he peered around the bean sticks and saw she was still there, still calling him and waving, beckoning him as though she had something important to say. He thought he saw her handkerchief in one hand, or what looked like a handkerchief. Something white anyway.

There couldn't be anything important to say between us now, he thought. There's nothing much I want to hear – from anybody, not from anybody.

The dull ache in the small of his back reminded him that he'd done enough on his own garden today. Although he hadn't done much here, he judged it was time to go home. Especially now Bettina Hicks had come out to bother him.

'Stan. Stan.'

She was breathless and her cheeks were pink. He might have thought she was having a heart attack or something, but for the fact that she was so animated. With the help of her walking stick, she closed on him fast. It was then that he saw her expression; she was crying. Still sobbing his name too. All the same, he couldn't quite bring himself to acknowledge her.

'Stan.' In her free hand she held a flimsy white piece of paper, not a handkerchief at all. 'I can't believe this! I can't believe it! Dead! Dead!'

His blood froze in his veins. Mike! It had to be Mike.

'Such a tragedy! Such a terrible tragedy!' Her shoulders heaved with sobs, tears squeezing from the corners of her eyes.

'No! No.' He shook his head forlornly as if that alone would make the statement untrue. It had to be Mike.

'But there's more, Stan. There's more . . .'

'Let's get you back into the house.'

Troubled as he was, afraid of hearing the details of the death of her nephew – Mary's fiancé – he had to be strong for her. He knew – or thought he knew – how she was feeling.

He took hold of her arm, but even she tottered a bit, her unsuitable shoes slipping in the soft earth, mud gathering around her heels. She leaned on him heavily, her shoulders quaking all the way back up the garden path to the back door.

'Better take them shoes off before you go inside,' Stan said. 'I'll make the tea. You need it strong and sweet.'

'Never mind that. A little dirt never hurt anybody. What does a bit of dirt matter when such things like these can happen, terrible things . . .'

Stan felt an overwhelming desire to be doing any small thing in an effort to hold off the moment when she would tell him the full details. 'I'll put the kettle on.'

'No. Don't bother. I need something stronger than tea.' She eased herself into a chair, the letter still clutched in her hand. Her tears appeared to be drying. 'I'm amazed, Stan. Truly amazed.'

Stan frowned and briefly wondered whether she'd read things right. She'd gone from devastated to something else in a matter of minutes.

He looked at her, remembering the girl she'd once been before she'd married Alf Hicks and gone away. In a way she hadn't changed that much, just older – like all of us, he thought wryly. But today . . .?

Sadness clouded her eyes.

'Do you want me to call the doctor?'

She shook her head, sniffed then lifted her chin defiantly. 'Gilda! It's Gilda!'

'What happened?'

She handed him the letter. 'An air raid. Gilda's been killed in an air raid. I told her not to go back to London!'

Her shoulders began to quake anew. She sucked in her lips and hung her head.

Stan headed for the kitchen dresser where Bettina kept her store of sherry, port and spirits and put the letter down. 'Let's have that drink first.'

He thought about the children. Please God, not them too! He didn't want to ask. His courage failed him.

Steadying his hand, he reached for two glasses. 'Brandy?'

'Yes.'

He poured a glass for each of them, turned round and handed her a glass. 'Drink it,' he said.

'You too.'

He did as ordered while all the while his stomach tightened and churned at the prospect of hearing further details of yet more bad news. She still hadn't said anything about the children. That was why he hadn't read the letter yet, why it was there on the dresser wedged between a blue-striped butter dish and a sugar basin.

He swigged the drink down in one gulp. Bettina did the same.

She handed him her glass. 'Another. I need another.'

He poured again.

'Read it. You must read it, Stan.'

Stan took a deep breath. 'I take it the children were with her?'

'Not quite. That's why I want you to read it. There's something in it that concerns you.'

Stan frowned as he walked back to the dresser. What did she mean?

The paper was thin and crisp between his fingers. He raised his eyes to meet hers before dropping his gaze back to the flimsy sheet of paper. First he read the heading. The address was that of an adoption society in London.

He looked at Bettina, wanting to ask what an adoption society could possibly want with him, and secondly why the letter had been sent to Bettina.

Bettina read his expression. 'Read on, Stan. You need to read on. This letter is really for you, not me. It's for you Stan!'

He didn't fail to notice that she'd stressed the fact twice. Still he questioned it in his mind. The letter was for him? He turned his eyes to the page.

Dear Mrs Hicks,

Your name has been passed to us by a Mr and Mrs Jacobsen whose daughter-in-law, Mrs Gilda Jacobsen, recently died in an air raid.

Fortunately, her two eldest children were staying with their grandparents so were unhurt.

However, we have been told by Mr and Mrs Jacobsen that the third child, a boy of about nine months, was with his mother.

It appears from eyewitnesses that the mother protected the baby with her body . . .

82

Not knowing anyone in London, Gilda had stayed with Bettina when she'd first arrived in England but had gone back to London when Charlie had been killed. She had thought that her dead husband's parents had also died, but they'd managed to escape from Europe, finding their way over the Baltic Sea to Sweden and from there to England. Gilda, it seemed, had ended up staying with them, but only until they'd found out about her pregnancy.

Stan looked up from the letter. 'A third child?'

Bettina nodded. 'Read on.'

. . . We have been informed by Mr and Mrs Jacobsen that they are unwilling to take the child in as he was not fathered by their son, who, I understand, died at the hands of the Nazis. As he is not their son's child, nor of their religion, they feel they cannot accept him into the family. However, they wish him no ill and have instructed us to trace whatever other family he might have.

In this regard, they were given to understand by Gilda Jacobsen that the baby is the son of one Charles Sweet.

The Jacobsens have asked us to contact you, Mrs Hicks, as a dear friend of their daughter-in-law and her parents, who we believe are also dead, to act on their behalf in arranging that Mr Charles Sweet is told of his responsibility and makes arrangements to collect the child, whose name is also Charles, from the orphanage in which he presently resides . . .

By the time he'd finished reading, Stan Sweet felt as though every bone in his body had been ground to dust.

'Dear God!'

With his elbows resting on the table, he covered his face with his hands.

'I had known Gilda as a child before her parents moved to the Netherlands. I don't know where they are now. Her husband's family managed to escape to London. They contacted me because Charlie and Gilda used this address when they wrote to each other. They thought you didn't approve that they were lovers,' she said in response to his questioning look. 'And they *were* lovers. There's no question about that.'

'I shouldn't think there was any doubt!' said Stan brusquely. 'There's a baby!'

Once again he hid his eyes behind his hands as a whole regiment of thoughts marched around his brain, so much so that his head ached with the pressure of them. One after another they tumbled over as he tried – and failed – to analyse his feelings.

'You know, Betty, I've walked in darkness ever since our Charlie died. Nothing, not even the prospect of our Mary's wedding, helped soothe the hurt. Terrible to admit, but even going to the churchyard and telling my Sarah about it didn't help. It used to, but of late . . .'

'I know,' Bettina said quietly, reaching across and patting his hand. 'You didn't bother to come to see me either. I did miss you. Friends get fewer the older you get. And I appreciated our little chats. You must know that, Stan Sweet.'

He came out from behind his hand to see her smiling through her tears.

'Anyway,' she added briskly. 'Did Sarah say anything back to you?'

He eyed her thoughtfully. 'I'm not sure. It might just 'ave bin my imagination, but . . . I could hear what she might have said, or thought I did.'

He looked down at what remained of the brandy, pushing the base of the glass round with his index finger so that the liquid quivered in the glass.

'Gave me a right telling off, I don't mind saying. But it was no use. I couldn't snap out of it, but . . .'

'But now you have to.'

Bettina waited for him to tell her what he thought Sarah was saying to him, but when nothing seemed forthcoming she filled in the gap herself.

'One life ends, another begins. Your son Charlie presented you with a grandson. "Look after him, Stan," she would have said to you. "Look after our grandson just as you did his father and the girls. Frances too."'

'A baby! I can't believe it!' His hand fell away to hang limply between his knees.

'A grandson, Stan. He's your grandson.'

When he looked at her, she was smiling. For the first time in ages, he smiled too. It felt as if the weight of the world had been lifted off his shoulders.

He studied the high cheekbones, the coif of cotton wool hair, the way her eyes were studying him, searching for his reaction to what she'd said.

Bettina smiled. 'And his name's Charles. Charlie.'

'Charlie!' He said it with wonder, his eyes moist.

Bettina covered his hand with hers. She smiled into his face. 'You're not just his grandfather, Stan. The adoption society are asking about Charlie, but it's you who is now his legal guardian. They're asking Charlie to have him, but it's you who is next in line for the legal responsibility. Are you willing to have the baby live with you?' She paused.

Stan stared at her as he digested what she was saying. Suddenly he was no longer looking backwards, wishing things had been different. It was like when Sarah had died and he'd taken on the reins of raising his family on his own. This is what he would do again.

'Can you write back to them?'

Bettina leaned forward slightly. Her tears had dried up though her eyes were still puffy.

'What do you want me to say, Stan?'

Stan Sweet's features had drooped for far too long. He was fifty-two years old and about to take on raising his baby grandson. But he didn't feel as though he were over fifty. He felt reborn, ready again to take on the world. For the first time in months the ghost of a smile spread over his lips and brightened his eyes.

'Tell them that my son is dead but I'm coming for young Charlie. I'm coming for my grandson.'

This time her tears were of happiness and she was smiling through them. 'If that's what you want.'

He nodded profusely. 'I do. I most certainly do!'

'I'll reply right away.'

Stan clasped his hands in front of him as Bettina got up from the table and went to the writing bureau sitting in an alcove to one side of the fireplace. Suddenly he felt terribly guilty at the way he'd behaved over the last few months since Charlie's death.

'Bet,' he said. 'I'm sorry.'

She turned round and looked at him, her reading glasses perched halfway down her nose. 'Sorry about what?'

He looked down at his hands, one thumb rubbing against the other. 'Sorry I've been so offhand of late, but . . .'

'There's nothing to apologise for, Stan. You've lost your son. But now you've got to pull your socks up. You've got a grandson to think about. Your Charlie would want you to. So would Sarah.'

'You're right. Of course you're right.'

There was only one thing left to worry about. Bettina noticed his sudden frown.

'I know what you're thinking.'

He looked up sharply.

Bettina continued. 'You're wondering what Mary and Ruby will think of all this.'

He nodded. 'I am. It's going to be quite a shock.'

She couldn't stop smiling. In fact, she felt she could burst with joy.

'You're not as young as you were when they were babies, so they'll have to step in on occasion. It's just a case of a bit of give and take.'

'Yes.' He nodded resolutely. He thought he could see things very clearly.

What Bettina said next pulled him up short. 'You've neglected them too since Charlie died. You can't preserve the past, Stan. Keep his memory in your heart, not pinned on your shoulder. Your Sarah would have told you that – if she'd thought you'd been listening.'

CHAPTER NINE

Sitting at the kitchen table, Mary contemplated her list for the wedding, a pencil clutched between finger and thumb.

Booking the village hall already had a big tick beside it.

Next her pencil hovered over the list of food wished for, acquired and promised.

Tins of salmon and ham were already sitting in the larder. A pound or two of Cheddar cheese had been promised by Mrs Martin whose brother had a dairy farm between Cheddar and Yeovil in Somerset.

Ruby had made sure they had enough dried fruit and sugar for the cake. Miriam Powell had donated a packet of icing sugar.

'It's the last one.' She'd told Mary this proudly before whispering that they also had some tinned pineapple arriving shortly.

'At least bread won't be a problem,' Mary murmured to herself.

She was just ticking off the last items on her list when a blur of blue passed the kitchen window accompanied by a lot of childish tittering and laughter. Then came Frances's bragging. 'This is the dress I'm going to be wearing when I'm a bridesmaid. Isn't it pretty?'

Mary let both her list and the pencil fall, dashing outside to rescue the bridesmaid's dress. 'Frances!'

Half a dozen surprised faces turned to face her. Frances, the little minx, was wearing her blue bridesmaid's dress, showing it off to her friends.

'Frances! Who said you could try that dress on?'

Frances looked totally shocked. She'd thought everyone was in the shop. 'I just thought—' she began.

'Do you realise how much effort Ruby put into that dress? It is not for wearing in the garden. Now get into that house and take it off this minute!'

Getting this angry was alien to Mary, but during the past couple of weeks it seemed as though Ruby's feet had been welded to the cast-iron plate of the treadle sewing machine and she didn't want her sister's efforts to be ruined.

'I was very careful. And it hasn't even been ironed yet,' Frances protested. She was standing with her arms outstretched, her hands clutching the fine material to either side of her.

'You heard what I said. Get indoors and take it off now!' Mary pointed a finger at the back door. It wasn't like her to lose her temper, but everyone had been working and saving so hard to make this wedding special. Frances could be so thoughtless at times.

Defiant to the last, Francis gave one more twirl, the fragile skirt wafting out from her legs, the hem catching on the rose bush.

Frances gasped. 'Whoops!'

Seeing what she'd done, the village kids hot-footed it out of the back gate, one or two pausing to make faces at the woman who'd spoiled their fun.

'You'll get "whoops" indeed!' Mary scolded as she crouched down to untangle the hem from the rose bush. 'Stay still.'

Frances covered her mouth, her eyes round above her

hand. She'd been enjoying showing off in front of her village friends. She'd also enjoyed regaling them with tales of her stay in the Forest of Dean, embroidering some of the details in order to make them sound even more impressive.

'I was telling them about the Italian and thought I'd dance too,' Frances explained to her cousin.

Actually she'd embroidered the truth to the extent that the hungry man she'd met in the forest had been an Italian spy – which was only half a truth. He had been Italian, but she'd no idea whether he was a spy or not.

Mary slapped her arm. 'Stop telling stories and keep still!'

Her fingers seemed turned to thumbs and even toes as she attempted to disconnect the hem of the dress from the thorny stem.

Frances wasn't good at keeping still and even though Mary was careful, the material was old and thus rather delicate. There was a sudden ripping sound.

'Oh no!'

Mary eyed the tear, which was about four inches in length.

'Now look what you've done!'

Frances pouted. 'I just wanted to show them how pretty it was. I like blue. They like blue too – except for Christine. She likes pink.'

The moment Frances was out of the dress Mary shouted for Ruby. There was no response.

After putting her old clothes back on, Frances slumped at the kitchen table holding her head in her hands. She might have deserved the telling off, but that wasn't quite the way she saw it.

'I didn't mean to tear it. I didn't do it on purpose.' She wished her cousins would stop treating her like a child. She was beginning to get curves and bumps in the same places that they had them. At least Ruby had noticed and given her a cast-off brassiere. It was a little big yet, but Ruby had assured her she'd grow into it and Frances was pleased at the prospect.

'I can't wait for them to grow,' she'd said to Ruby. 'I want big ones. Do you think I might have big ones?'

Ruby had laughed and told her that anything was possible. Mary, Frances decided, was just being mean. Perhaps she didn't really want her to be a bridesmaid.

Mary ignored the hangdog expression and puppy-dog eyes. As far as she was concerned, Frances was still a child, though not a very obedient one.

'The fact is you put the dress on without telling anyone, then went outside wearing it. It's a bridesmaid's dress, Frances. You're supposed to wear it when you follow me up the aisle. You do *not* wear it out in the garden to show your friends! And that's it. And before you ask me again, no, you cannot go off with those children today. You are not going out to play!'

'I don't play. I'm too old to play.'

'Well, you're not going out anyway, and that's it and all about it!'

After another quick examination of the tear, Mary wondered whether Ruby could sew some pink silk flowers over it. There were some tiny ones in the sewing box, clipped from a dress one of them had worn as a child. She decided it was possible and went in search of her sister.

The living room was her first port of call, the room where everything for the wedding, excluding the tins of ham and salmon, was being stored. It was also the room where Ruby had been making the blue dresses, pressing Dad's shirt and suit, and the best linen tablecloths and napkins.

The chair set in front of the treadle was unoccupied and

the sewing box was nowhere in sight. The simple blue bridal dress was there, all finished and pressed. There was also a veil made from the lace Bettina had given her and some tulle Mary didn't recall having seen before. Of Ruby there was no sign. Wherever the sewing box was, there Ruby would be found.

Underwear, she suddenly thought to herself. She's making me new underwear for my trousseau and keeping it a secret from me.

She smiled and blushed at the thought of it. Underwear was becoming notoriously difficult to get hold of – especially pretty underwear, things made of silk and lace. It occurred to her that Ruby might have secretly got hold of some parachute silk and trimmed it with some of the leftover lace Bettina had given them.

Mary sighed. If it hadn't been for the tear in the dress, she wouldn't dream of spoiling Ruby's secret. But there was nothing for it. There was so much still to do before she got married and having to mend this dress was an extra burden that had to be dealt with promptly.

'Ruby,' she called again as she made her way upstairs.

Yet again there was no response. If her sister was upstairs she'd probably fallen asleep, quite likely considering all the hours she'd been spending making clothes and getting enough supplies to make a wedding cake, plus carrying on sharing the workload of baking demonstrations they'd become so good at.

She went into their bedroom. 'Ruby?'

There was no sign of her. The window was open, the yellow check curtains billowing in like sails in the soft draught. The next option was to ascend the flight of stairs leading to the attic rooms at the top of the house.

That was when it occurred to her that there was a hand

machine up in the attic, an old Victorian thing inlaid with mother of pearl. Despite its age it worked exceedingly well. And there was also quite a large dormer window throwing extra light into the room. Good light was essential to good sewing. All that sewing was bound to be making her eyes tired; in fact, hadn't Ruby said just that the other night?

The skirt of the damaged blue dress swung from her arm as she propelled herself up the second flight of stairs, the threadbare carpet deadening the sound of her footsteps.

She called out before pushing the door open. 'Ruby?'

The doorknob was made of brass, though half the size of a standard one. It was as though it had been borrowed from a doll's house, too tinny and small to get a good grip on it. It certainly wasn't opening today, no matter how hard she tried to turn it or how fiercely she rattled the door. It was obviously locked, but from the other side.

'Ruby!' She hammered her fist on the door before attempting to turn the knob again. 'Are you in there? Is everything all right?'

Muffled shuffles and whispered exclamations came from inside the room. Then her sister saying, 'Just a minute.'

The key grated in the lock before Ruby's flushed face appeared in the narrow gap. Her eyes were full of owlish surprise. The light from the dormer window streamed into the room behind her, but she kept hold of the door, keeping the opening to a narrow crack.

'You locked the door.'

'Did I?' Her voice was small. She *had* been asleep.

'Did you fall asleep?'

'Yes. I'm sorry. I did.' At first she sounded apologetic. Then her look hardened and her voice turned defensive. 'I have been busy, you know.'

Mary was taken aback and not a little hurt. 'Yes. I know

and I wouldn't have disturbed you if it hadn't been urgent. The fact is Frances decided to show her dress off. She caught the hem on the rose bush.'

She held up the blue dress, using her finger and thumb to show Ruby the damage.

Ruby groaned. 'Better give it here. That little mare . . .'

She held both hands out to take the dress. As she did so, the door she'd been holding, which always had been loose on its hinges, swung wide open.

Cool northern light fell on to Charlie's old desk and the ancient sewing machine sitting upon it.

Mary's eyes strayed beyond that to the white dress hanging from a coat hanger to one side of the window. She gasped. 'Ruby!'

'Oh Lord!'

In no doubt that she'd been found out, her sister backed into the room, Mary following on. Then Ruby sighed. 'Well, I suppose you had to find out some time or another.'

Mary crossed the room slowly, her eyes as round as her mouth, her expression one of total surprise.

Letting the bridesmaid's dress fall into a heap on the bed, she went to the window. For a moment she stared, her mouth still agape. Slowly, very slowly, she reached out, fingered the tulle and delved beneath it to touch the shiny satin.

For the sake of secrecy – at least from everyone else in the house if not from Mary – Ruby closed the door. Now she stood in the middle of the room wishing the floor would open up and swallow her whole.

'It's our mother's wedding dress,' Mary whispered.

'It was. It's yours now. I cut it to fit and made it more fashionable. I think it looks lovely.'

Ruby waited for the words of condemnation: *you had no*

business doing this; you should have asked Dad; I don't think I can possibly wear it.

'It's beautiful.' Mary's voice was like a soft breeze, hardly noticeable but very welcome.

The words were like honey in Ruby's ears, but Ruby knew very well that there'd be a price to pay. Nerves getting the better of her – at least temporarily – she bit her bottom lip.

'I know I should really have asked Dad, but the more I put it off the harder it got. And you know what he's been like of late . . .'

Mary barely heard her. 'It's beautiful,' she said again, running her fingers over the bodice that Ruby had altered to fit closely to her body.

'I think our mother would have wanted you to wear it. Under different circumstances, I think Dad would have wanted you to wear it too. But since our Charlie . . .'

Mary nodded slowly. She couldn't deny that it had been her dream to wear her mother's wedding dress, not just because it was beautiful, but simply because it had been worn by her mother on her wedding day.

'You've altered it beautifully.'

'It was a bit old-fashioned. But even after all these years, the material is so good.'

'I wonder what he'll say. Dad's been so . . .'

Their eyes met in mutual concern. Before Charlie's death their father would have been amenable to what Ruby had done. In the aftermath of their brother's death there had been no smiles, laughter or cracking of jokes. He even frowned at anyone who laughed too loud. Ruby had once remarked that it was sometimes like living in a funeral parlour, not a bakery.

Ruby shook her head. Her gaze moved overhead to the

dormer window. Through it she could see puffball clouds rolling across the sky. 'Such a waste not to use it. I'm sure Mum would have loved the idea.'

Although neither of them had known their mother, they were in agreement. Any mother would love the idea that their dress would be handed on to their daughters.

Ruby picked up a folded piece of material from a pile beside the sewing machine. 'This is so soft.'

She unfolded it and shook it out.

Mary could see it was a piece of silk about three feet long and a foot wide.

'I've got pieces left over for baby clothes, even a christening gown.' Ruby refolded the piece and put it back on the pile.

'A baby! Goodness!'

Although she should feel grateful, Mary eyed the remnant with misgiving. Oddly enough she hadn't really thought about having a baby – not actually *having* it, giving birth to it – until this moment when Ruby had shown her the piece of silk. She knew how it happened, knew what a mother went through when the baby was coming, though only by word of mouth. She'd also seen the animals in the fields around them. Up until this moment she hadn't visualised the actuality and faced up to the pain her body would be subjected to. The wedding night scared her most of all. She wasn't too sure how it all came together. The best person to ask was her sister. Ruby seemed to know everything there was to know about men. But not now, she said to herself. She couldn't bring herself to talk to her about it just yet. There's plenty of time, she told herself. Plenty of time.

'What will you tell him?'

Ruby knew very well that her twin sister was referring

to their father. 'I'll think of something. Don't worry. I've got it all in hand.'

She didn't have it all in hand, but wasn't about to get her sister as worried as she was. It had all seemed so straightforward. Carried away on a magic carpet of excitement, she hadn't been too concerned that she had not asked his permission. Now though, after the event, the enormity of what she'd done finally hit her.

'I think I should be there when you tell him. After all, I'm the one you did it for. Thank you, Ruby. Thank you very much.'

'Somebody had to.' She waved her hand as though it really was of no consequence when in fact it was far from it. 'But don't worry about it. You don't need to be with me when I tell him. After all, it wasn't your idea. You knew nothing about it. Yet again Ruby Sweet was her usual impetuous self! You don't have to hold my hand when I tell him, though you can if you like. I reckon he'll be fine if we stand together. If that's what you want to do.'

'It's me that's going to wear it – I hope.'

Mary would keep to her promise. Obviously it would have been better if Ruby hadn't touched the dress, though she had to admit to herself that the white dress was beautiful, a proper bridal gown and far superior to the simple blue one Ruby had made. She presumed that now there was a dress available, Ruby would become a second bridesmaid. It might have helped if Ruby had told her what she'd planned, but that was her sister. She'd always been headstrong.

Ruby pointed out how many clothing coupons it cost to buy a wedding dress. 'I don't mind taking the blame. I know I shouldn't have done it without telling you, but I couldn't help it. I don't regret it. Honest I don't.'

It wasn't exactly the whole truth. Only now had it finally hit her just what she'd done. The consequences they could only guess at.

Stan Sweet breezed in the back door of the building that was both his home and business premises with a spring in his step that he hadn't had for ages.

With the letter from the adoption society in his hand, and bursting to tell everyone the news, he was slightly disappointed to see only Frances in the kitchen.

'Where's our Ruby and Mary?'

Frances had decided to maintain her pouting lips and soulful eyes, a tried-and-tested method of getting her own way – most of the time. 'I don't know. Don't care either.'

Stan Sweet was old enough and knew his niece well enough to realise that she'd had a telling off.

'So what have you done? Go on. Tell me.'

Frances pouted her lips so hard that it almost hurt and sniffed – just enough to make it sound as though she'd been sobbing.

'Mary won't let me out to pl— Meet my friends.' She'd tripped over the word 'play'. She wasn't a child. She was quite adamant about that.

'So go on. Tell me. What have you done?'

She told him about showing her friends her bridesmaid's dress.

'You showed it to them? Then what happened?'

Frances fiddled with a lock of hair, twiddling it and folding it across her lips as she looked away. 'I had to try it on to show them. I had to let them see it floating around me, but . . .'

Stan raised his eyebrows. Sometimes Frances amused him with her excuses, but sometimes she reminded him of

Mildred, her mother. Though Mildred had never amused him. He'd never forgiven her for abandoning her daughter. Not that he'd regretted taking Frances into his home. One more youngster to bring up was neither here nor there seeing as he'd been left a widower to raise his own.

'But?' He raised one eyebrow as was his habit when he wanted an answer.

Frances pouted. 'When I twirled it got snagged on Charlie's rose bush,' she said.

Stan fixed her with the sort of look that made her wither away from half-baked excuses.

'I didn't mean to.'

'So. You got it caught on Charlie's rose bush.' His voice caught in his throat, not so much with sadness as a hint of surprise. He put the letter from the adoption society in his coat pocket. His hand lingered there, his fingers remaining on it in an effort to reassure himself that it was real, that it existed and was not merely a trick of the imagination. Even now the feel of the letter sent a thrill of electric current up his arm.

Frances noticed that her uncle was no longer frowning at her and seemed suddenly distracted, his gaze having wandered to the photo of Charlie on the mantelpiece. The photo had been taken on the quayside just before he'd embarked on his last voyage. It had arrived with the last letter he'd sent before going to sea.

'Never mind.' He smiled the sadness in his eyes tinged by something else.

'Can I go out now?'

He thought about it. 'I think you need to stay. There's something I need to tell you all. Something quite wonderful.'

Frances looked puzzled and was only a little disappointed that she couldn't go out to meet her friends. If he had something important to say and she was included, then she needed to be here.

Stan patted the pocket into which he had placed the letter. He didn't regard himself as a superstitious type of bloke, but the letter, the rose bush . . . one very big thing, one very small: perhaps someone was trying to tell him something.

He was suddenly overwhelmed with a great longing to walk down to the churchyard and tell Sarah all about it. Perhaps he should do that first. Good Lord, he thought, I feel that confused and excited, like a kid at Christmas!

In the process of setting his hat back on his head, he heard the sound of footsteps coming down the stairs out in the hallway.

Probably Ruby or Mary coming down to prepare supper. It was best that they were told first.

'Uncle Stan?'

Frances's voice.

'Huh?'

'You've got your hat on back to front.'

He chuckled as he shook his head at the same time as taking off his hat and his coat, hanging them back up and preparing himself to tell everyone the wonderful news.

'Can you keep a secret, Frances?' He was positively beaming.

Frances nodded. Her face was bright with curiosity.

Stan gave her the letter to read. 'Shhh!' he said once she'd finished it. 'Not a word. Promise?'

Frances, her face shining with joy, nodded. 'Cross my heart and hope to die,' she whispered. She sucked in her breath. 'A baby? Charlie's baby?'

'Shhh!' her uncle said again, placing a finger in front of his mouth.

After that he found himself straightening his tie and pulling down his pullover so it sat better over his waistband. He was even in half a mind to polish the toe of each shoe against the back of his trousers. The announcement he was about to make was extremely important and somehow his appearance had to reflect that.

Standing upright, like a newly conscripted and slightly nervous army recruit about to face his sergeant major for the first time, he took a deep breath. This was it. He was about to make the announcement. He was so excited that his breath caught in his throat. He cleared it swiftly before the door between the kitchen and the hallway opened and Ruby appeared.

Her lovely face was wreathed in smiles. Her cheeks were pink and there was something a little pensive about her expression.

'Dad. We thought we heard you. I've got something to tell you . . . Me and Mary have got something to tell, well, show you.'

Although he was bursting to tell all of them the news, something in her expression stopped him. Her eyes were bright and her heart-shaped face looked a little taut, almost as though she had something to fear.

The other thing he noticed about her was that the hair on both sides of her head was tucked behind her ears. He hoped the style would be permanent because it would mean she had at last stopped being so touchy about her birthmark, the one feature that set her apart from her sister. Whatever was on her mind had caused her to forget her self-consciousness.

'Never mind that. I've got something to tell—'

It was all he had time to say before Ruby stepped to one side as she pushed the door open. 'Dad. I hope you won't be angry.'

Stan's jaw dropped.

A vision in a white wedding dress stood framed in the doorway. On her head she wore a confection of satin bows, tulle and lace.

His hand flew to his chest. His breath caught in his throat. Sarah, he thought, though of course it can't be.

'Dad?'

Mary stepped forward, which meant he could see her more clearly.

She'd argued with Ruby about doing this, but her sister had been adamant.

'He has to see you. He has to see that we've done the right thing.'

It was hard to judge. On seeing the look of astonishment on his face, Mary wondered if it might have been better for the pair of them to tell him rather than show what Ruby had done.

Mary sucked in her breath. She loved wearing the dress but still, she dreaded his reaction whatever it might be.

'He'll be speechless,' Ruby had said. 'And anyway, even if he does rant and rave, it's too late for me to sew it all back together.'

In the absence of any ideas of her own, Mary had gone along with Ruby's plan. Now she was standing here with her legs turned to jelly.

'Dad? You're not mad are you?'

It was hard to read his expression, partly because it kept changing, his mouth hanging open as he attempted to put what he felt into words.

Seeing her sister's nervousness, Ruby decided it was down to her to apologise, to explain and to try and persuade him that it was the right thing to do.

Her stance was adamant, her back stiff, her face open and her eyes glowing with courage.

'Dad, we can't waste this dress. I'm sure Mum would want Mary to wear it down the aisle. If she was here, she'd want to see her daughter looking lovely on her wedding day. None of the bits I've cut off will be wasted. They'll do very well for baby clothes – even a christening robe – once there's a baby to make clothes for, of course.'

At the mention of baby clothes, Stan blinked. He felt as though he'd been hit on the head with a sledgehammer. His eyes went back to Mary, looking so beautiful in her mother's wedding dress. For the second time that day he felt like crying. Not just that, he felt as though the wife lying in St Anne's graveyard and the son lost at sea were very close, whispering in his ear that life is a banquet of changing courses. He certainly believed it now.

'I want to speak to you both. Best you go off upstairs and take that dress off, Mary. One ruined dress is enough for one day.' He glanced at Frances and winked. Frances grinned. Her eyes sparkled.

Both his daughters looked at him dumbfounded. He looked happier than he had for ages. Something special must have happened.

'I'll help you.' Ruby followed her sister up the stairs. Once she'd reached the top she looked back down the narrow flight with its twisting quarter landing at the end, still expecting to see her father there, face red with anger, as though what she'd done had only just sunk in. But he wasn't there and no sound came up from the kitchen.

'Something's happened,' remarked Mary softly. 'Did you get that impression?'

Ruby unbuttoned the buttons down the back of the dress, pulled it down her sister's body and carefully, very carefully, smoothed out the creases and hung it back on the hanger.

Once Mary had pulled her short-sleeved sweater over her

head and refastened her skirt, she and her sister stood facing each other, both wondering what their father would say to them once they were back downstairs.

'I feel so guilty,' said Ruby.

Mary shook her head. 'I'm not sure an apology is going to be enough.'

'I'm not going to apologise,' Ruby retorted with a toss of her head. 'If I get a ticking off, I'm going to the pub and I'll get drunk. Then tomorrow I'll chuck in the cooking job and join the navy – or the air force – not the army. Khaki isn't my colour!'

Mary was in two minds whether to laugh or cry. She did manage to smile.

'Oh well. I suppose we'd better go back down.'

'Wait while I brush my hair.'

It was odd, thought Mary, that while talking enthusiastically about the wedding dress and the wedding itself, Ruby had tucked her hair behind her ears. Now she was brushing it forward so at least half of her face would be hidden just as it usually was. Nerves, she decided. Time to face the music.

Their father was sitting at the kitchen table, tapping the dented wood with the fingers of one hand, holding what looked like a letter in the other. His face had a new vigour about it. Whatever had happened was nothing short of a miracle. Even the lines across his forehead and around his eyes seemed to have diminished.

'Frances has made tea,' he said before looking up. 'And she's found some biscuits. Oatmeal, if I'm not mistaken.'

The twins regarded their cousin quizzically. Seemingly recovered from being banned from going out to play, Frances was grinning like the proverbial Cheshire cat. Never keen on household tasks, on this occasion she seemed to be thoroughly enjoying laying out the cups and saucers on the table, setting out the milk and a small bowl of sugar.

'I'll be mother,' she exclaimed cheerfully then giggled as she poured.

Mary noticed that she hadn't warmed the pot first, but didn't bother to point it out. Something strange was going on, some secret that Frances seemed privy to.

Ruby frowned. She'd readied herself for a severe ticking off. Red-faced anger. Shouting. Perhaps even the chance of being told to leave the house. Even that was something she could cope with.

The twins exchanged worried frowns. The exchange did not go unnoticed by their father.

'Sit down.'

There was no loud voice, no angry words. Both Mary and Ruby were surprised that he seemed so calm and collected. And was that a smile they could see on his face?

Neither twin picked up their teacups, each of them gazing intently at their father's face, sensing that he had something important to tell them.

To one side of them Frances crunched her way through one half of a biscuit dipping the other half into her tea. She grinned at her uncle. He winked at her in a conspiratorial way and she winked back.

'Right,' said Stan, an odd fluttering feeling in his stomach. It was as though he really did have a host of butterflies inside him, all aching to be released. It was a thoroughly alien sensation after these long months of feeling he had a stone in his stomach, a cold, dead weight.

When he'd digested the incredible news handed to him by Bettina, Stan Sweet had felt something inside him crack – a bit like an icy puddle in the depths of winter. He had every intention of taking his grandchild, Charlie's son, under his wing. All that concerned him now was how Ruby and Mary would react to the news.

He'd instantly regretted telling Frances first. The twins should have been first to hear the news. Young Charlie – he was already thinking of him as young Charlie, not *the baby* – was their nephew.

The moment had come. He took a deep breath and pushed the letter across the table. 'Read that.'

Mary picked it up, her eyes searching his face for some idea of what it was about. He wasn't exactly smiling, but there was something different about him. The last time she'd seen him was at breakfast and he hadn't been smiling then.

'Read it,' he said again.

Mary read it.

Ruby looked from her father to her sister, waiting her turn to read while studying Mary's face for some sign of what this was all about.

Mary gasped. Her hand flew to her mouth. 'Oh my God!' She held her hand to her cheek as she read it through. The exclamation was followed by a gasp then another, as though she'd been holding her breath as she read it through.

Finally she looked up at her father. 'Charlie!'

'Charlie?' echoed Ruby, impatient to know what this was all about. 'What is it? Tell me. Is he alive?' It couldn't be true! Surely they would have known before this if he was.

Stan Sweet shook his head, a little sadly. 'Not that Charlie!'

'A little Charlie!' Frances drew everyone's attention with her excited voice and vibrant grin.

Ruby looked at everyone in turn, noting the sparkling eyes, the looks of excitement and astonishment.

Mary confirmed the news. 'It's true. It's a little Charlie. We have a nephew, Ruby. This is amazing!' Then a sad look came to Mary's face as she passed the letter to Ruby. 'Poor Gilda.' She looked at her father. 'When is he coming to live with us?'

Her father sat back in his chair, his tea untouched. He folded his hands in his lap, interlocking his fingers as he did so. 'I think that's for you two to decide. Our lives are about to be turned upside down. The future we thought we were facing has changed. Young Charlie will see to that, no doubt. Bringing up children is not an easy task.'

When she came out from behind the letter, Ruby's surprised expression was no different to that of her sister. 'A baby! Our Charlie has a baby.'

'It's incredible isn't it?' Stan Sweet mopped at his forehead with a crumpled handkerchief. 'It's as if . . . well . . . as though Charlie's been reborn.'

Ruby sat back in her chair, her eyes perusing the letter for a second time. Finally she looked up. 'I won't say I can't believe it, because I can. That night she and our Charlie . . .'

She stopped herself from going further. The night Mrs Hicks had been away, Charlie had stayed the night with Gilda. He'd declared that Gilda was nervous of being alone and that he would sleep on the settee. Everyone knew they were attracted to each other. Nature and romance had obviously run their course.

Stan felt a new sense of vigour course through his body. Nobody was going to stop him having his grandson live with him and that included the spiteful tongues of those in the village who enjoyed spreading malicious gossip. 'What happened can't be undone. I, for one, am over the moon to have a new life enter our home. Do any of you have an objection to young Charlie coming here to live?'

'Of course not.' Ruby heaved her shoulders in a casual shrug. She was as excited as the rest of them. Besides, there had been no mention yet of the wedding dress. News of the baby had superseded everything. 'He's Charlie's boy. Gilda's parents-in-law are right: since his mother has passed on, and her family have disappeared in Austria, it stands to reason he has to be with his father's family who do want him.'

'And we do want him,' her father said pointedly. 'Are we all agreed on that?'

Ruby was in no doubt that he was asking her to confirm that she could cope. After all, Mary was getting married. She was the one staying and although her father had coped with bringing up his children without a wife to help him, he'd been younger then. She was glad to see her father looking so happy, but her own life would be affected by the new addition to the family.

Mary remained silent as she contemplated the consequences for them all, her hands clenched on the table in front of her, eyes downcast. She was thinking of Gilda, and of the sacrifice she had made to protect her son.

'Mary?' Her father had noticed her reticence. He eyed her expectantly. She knew he wanted her approval quite badly.

She raised her eyes and passed the letter back to him across the table. 'Sorry. I was thinking of Gilda, buried in that rubble and protecting her son with her body.' Taking a deep breath, hands still clenched in front of her, she looked wide-eyed at her father. 'Of course he belongs here. He's Charlie's son, a little piece of him he left behind when he died. I'll help as much as I can, even after I'm married. When can we collect him?'

* * *

Stan Sweet was sitting on the pig bin, smoking his pipe and enjoying the crisp early evening. The sky twinkled with stars and the smell of rich earth and pipe smoke obliterated whatever might have wafted up from the pig bin, which was sealed anyway. It was a wonderful night and had been a wonderful day.

He heard the back door open and close, though, of course, no light fell out. Ruby had turned off the light before coming out. He was aware of her lithe figure courtesy of the stars and a crescent moon. He knew what she was out here for, could tell without looking at her that she was all at once apologetic and nervous.

All the talk over supper this evening had been about the baby. The upcoming wedding had been all but forgotten for once.

'Dad?'

'I think I'll plant some winter carrots. The more the merrier, eh?' He chuckled and puffed a ring of smoke into the air.

Somewhere a nightjar was singing and despite the profusion of vegetables that now far outnumbered flowers in Stan Sweet's garden, the scent of honeysuckle was strong. So too was the smell of the rose bush they'd given Charlie the Christmas he came home.

Rubbing her clammy palms together, Ruby plunged straight in. 'You haven't said what you thought of Mary's wedding dress. Mum's wedding dress. I know I shouldn't have, but . . .'

Ruby looked for any sign of reaction in the strong square features she'd known all her life.

Stan remained silent, his eyes still fixed on the far end of the garden where raspberry canes rubbed shoulders with rhubarb and blackcurrant. Autumn, he hoped, would be bountiful.

'I can hear it in your voice, Ruby. What is it you want to say about that dress?'

Ruby looked down at the path. At one time a few stray tufts of grass sprouted in the gaps between the flagstones, but not now. Stan Sweet spent every spare moment tending his vegetables; the path was too well trodden for grass to grow in the cracks.

'Mary really wanted to wear our mother's dress and at some time – if and when I get married – I would like to wear it too. It's second best to having her there at our weddings. When we asked, you said no, but I believed you might change your mind. That's why I altered it without telling you. I'm sorry.'

She waited for him to respond. The light from the moon lit one side of his face when he turned to look at her. Suddenly he shook his head and laughed.

'I thought about pulling you up about it when I first found it cut about up in the attic just after we heard about young Charlie. It did take me aback I must admit. But after a bit of thinking I decided to say nothing. I thought about what your mother would want and realised she would want you to wear it. In fact if she was here, she'd insist on you wearing it. Like you and Mary, I thought it only right to have Mary wearing her mother's wedding dress even if it meant having it altered. Like you've just said, it's second best to having her there. This way she'll be there in spirit, if not in fact.'

'Oh, Dad!'

Ruby flung her arms around his neck and kissed both cheeks, relishing the sweaty wholesomeness of his smell, overlaid by the tang of Old Holborn.

'And I can make romper suits with what's left. Even a christening robe.'

After she'd gone back inside, Stan got up from the pig bin, doused his pipe and rolled down his shirtsleeves.

He needed to apologise to Bettina Hicks. He also had to share with her how much he was looking forward to seeing one daughter married and a grandson coming home.

CHAPTER TEN

June 1941

'Reconstitute the egg powder, season lightly then pour into a shallow greased basin. Stand in a pan with a little boiling water and simmer gently until set. Allow to cool then mix with chopped parsley or cress if you have some. I think you'll find this mixture makes a very nourishing and tasty sandwich. Add a little mustard and milk to bind, if you prefer. Oh, and remember to dip your knife blade into hot water before spreading the margarine – or butter if you're so lucky, though I would add that this particular mixture does spread quite well over bread by itself . . .'

There were titters of approval before the applause and a queue formed at the end of the table where Brenda Manning, Ruby's new driver, was handing out leaflets.

Most of the women working at the aircraft factory in Filton where Ruby had given her talk were unskilled labour and had replaced men who had been called upon to serve their country. Despite many of the women being draftees, they were a cheerful lot, even though they had to wear shapeless dungarees made to fit a man's figure, certainly not that of a woman. Colourful headscarves wound into turbans helped to lift the dull colour of their clothes, and even though boots were available, most of the women preferred to wear their own shoes. Older women went for sensible shoes, but there was a regular flash of colour from painted toenails protruding from peep-toed court shoes.

The comments came quick and fast. 'Good job you told me what to do with that egg, love. I took one look at it and thought it was custard powder.'

'Or face powder,' chortled another.

'Or powder for my Sammy's bottom,' said another.

Ruby laughed. 'I guarantee you can use it to make custard. I don't recommend using it for the face or the baby! A spot of rain – or any other liquid – and it's likely to set to the consistency of concrete!'

The women laughed before melting away back to their work. Coming from beyond the canteen doors, the sound of machines rattled into life.

The women all had their own ideas about making pastry and cakes when fat, sugar and eggs were in such short supply. One egg per person per week – if available, was, in reality, roughly one every two weeks for each of the women who lived in the city and didn't keep chickens! At least the packets of dried egg went further, though not much, a whole packet every four weeks.

'Not a bad bunch,' she remarked as she helped Brenda pack everything into the wicker hamper and her brief case.

'Yes.'

Brenda seemed to be putting heart and soul into packing things away. Usually she chattered on about the people they'd met today, poking fun at some and saying what darlings others were, including some of the aircraft engineers who were either too old or too important to be drafted into the forces.

Today was different. Brenda had been quiet from the moment she'd picked Ruby up that morning.

Once they were in the car, and the acres of factory, aerodromes, test beds and runways were behind them, Ruby asked Brenda if anything was wrong. Brenda's gloved hands gripped the steering wheel tightly. Her expression was strained. 'I'm sorry, miss.'

'Sorry? For goodness' sake, Brenda, what have you got to be sorry about?'

'I'm leaving the RTC. I was going to tell you this morning, but I just couldn't bring myself to do it – not seeing as you've already had one driver leave—'

'Because of me? Am I the problem?' Ruby tried to think of how she might have upset her.

'No!' Brenda suddenly burst into tears. The car wobbled from the centre of the road to the kerb before it stalled. Once it did so, Brenda's head dropped on to her folded arms and she sobbed pitifully.

'Brenda!' Ruby gripped her shoulder, feeling it shaking beneath her hand. 'Have I done something to offend you?'

Brenda shook her head, her face hidden, fingers gripping the steering wheel as though afraid it might fall off. 'No. It's me. I'm the one who's let you down. I've got to leave. I've got to get married.'

Ruby sighed and looked beyond her driver to the road, the fields and the grazing cattle.

'So who is he, this young man you're going to marry?'

Brenda's forehead rested on her hands. Ruby passed her driver a handkerchief up between the spokes of the steering wheel. Brenda took it and blew her nose. She raised her head, brushing the crumpled-up handkerchief over each eye in turn.

'He said he loved me.'

They all do, thought Ruby and hoped her cynicism didn't show on her face.

'I see.'

'He said if I loved him I would let him do it, especially seeing as he could be posted at any minute.'

'So you did and now you find out that he isn't being posted just yet and you've got to marry him. You're not the first, Brenda, and you certainly won't be the last.'

'But he did get posted.' Brenda gushed into a new flood of tears.

The tears were getting in the way of the explanation and Ruby was getting impatient. Tomorrow was Saturday. Mary and Mike were getting married at St Anne's and there were still a lot of things to do. She began drumming her fingers on the lid of the wicker basket.

'Danny got killed,' Brenda said at last. 'So I can't marry him. I have to marry Ted instead. He offered and my mum and dad said I had to accept, seeing as I was expecting.'

'But you don't love him and he's not the father of your child.'

'No,' Brenda responded softly. The stiff curls at the nape of her neck were damp. Her neck was quite pink thanks to the stiff collar of her shirt.

Poor girl. She must be suffering, thought Ruby. She leaned back into the car seat and folded her arms. Brenda was yet another casualty of war even though she hadn't been injured.

'You could say no,' she said, as though being an unmarried mother was easier said than done, as though there would be no pointed fingers, no wagging tongues. It didn't matter that her sweetheart had perished in battle; she'd had the bad luck to get pregnant outside of marriage. Her reputation was ruined.

Brenda turned round in her seat. The handkerchief was now clenched in a tight ball in one hand. 'I can't say no. My mum and dad won't hear of it. They say it's either that or I have to move out. They don't want no . . . *bastard* under their roof. That's what they said.'

'And this Ted. You're sure you don't love him?'

'No.' she dabbed her nose again. 'I've known him all my life. He's a friend. That's all.'

'He seems like a particularly good friend, one that loves you enough to take on another man's child. It's quite a forgiving and kind man who would do something like that.'

Ruby scrutinised the slightly overlong face with its turned up nose and sprinkling of ginger freckles. Brenda wasn't the prettiest girl in the world, but she had a voluptuous figure and a hearty laugh. It struck Ruby that men would find those things alone attractive.

Brenda turned the crumpled handkerchief over and over in her hands. Her knuckles were white, her fingernails bitten to the quick. It occurred to Ruby that Brenda had been contemplating her future for some time. Suddenly what seemed like the right question came to her.

'What would Danny say to you marrying this man? Would he be pleased that his child would have a father seeing as he wouldn't be around to bring him up?'

Brenda gulped. Ruby could see she'd just swallowed another sob.

'It's so unfair, miss.' Brenda raised her head. Fresh tears were brimming from her eyes.

'I know.' Ruby thought about Gilda and Charlie, both dead and leaving an illegitimate child behind, though in young Charlie's case he was lucky: he was coming into a ready-made family. It was just a question of satisfying the adoption society that all was well and getting all the papers in order, which seemed to take quite a long time. Her father was boiling with impatience.

Brenda handed Ruby back her handkerchief.

'I never thought I would end up like this,' said Brenda shaking her head forlornly. 'We had it all planned, or thought we did . . .'

Her gaze wandered along the hedgerow to where a pheasant's head showed above the long grass peering at them as though waiting for them to make the first move. Pheasants had a habit of running out in front of anything that moved. If he did get hit he'd make supper tonight!

'But you didn't plan for this,' said Ruby with an air of finality.

'Not really . . . but . . .' Brenda bit her lip and placed both hands back on the wheel as though she had decided to move the car forward.

'Go on.'

Ruby watched, sensing that a whole plethora of emotions were hidden behind Brenda's freckled face.

'He did say that if anything should ever happen to him, I should remarry – for my own sake and for any children we might have.'

'Well, then . . .' Ruby smiled.

Brenda returned the smile, though more bashfully. 'So I suppose we did agree on that, marrying for the sake of the children if nothing else.'

'I suppose you did.' Ruby waited until she was certain Brenda was fully recovered. 'Are you ready to drive on now?'

Brenda nodded. 'Yes. Yes. I am.'

'Good.' Ruby paused. An idea had come to her. If she was going to lose this driver, perhaps her old one could be reinstated?

'Brenda, could you see if I could have John Smith back as my driver? Would that be possible?'

Brenda nodded. 'I could ask.'

* * *

Mike Dangerfield stared at the star-filled sky. How different it looked from the ground compared to when he was up there, the plane rattling with the sound of the engines, the flak, the explosions tearing upwards in fiery pillars.

He didn't like dropping bombs. He didn't like war. The only thing that kept him going was the hope that in time the world would be at peace once the evil Nazi regime had been destroyed.

He was still standing there when his aunt came out of the house. 'My word! Michael! You gave me a fright. How long have you been out here?'

'Only a few minutes.' He bent and kissed her cheek.

'I'll get you some supper.'

'Not yet. I'd like to see Mary first.' As he bent down to retrieve his kit bag, a thought came to him. 'I presume I am allowed to see the bride before the wedding.'

'As long as she's not in her bridal gown,' Bettina replied laughingly.

He left his kitbag inside the kitchen door.

'Rabbit pie when you get back,' pronounced Bettina.

'Can't wait,' he said, and darted off.

Mary was excited, and not just because of the wedding. She and Ruby had gathered up every scrap of blue material for the purpose of making romper suits for their nephew. They weren't sure of his size and didn't have a proper pattern, so they cut generously.

'Buttons,' said Mary. 'We need more buttons.' She finished snipping off the last ivory button from one of Charlie's old shirts. Using his shirts seemed very apt seeing as the coming baby was his son.

'I suppose it'll be my shirts next,' grumbled their father.

Mary and Ruby exchanged smiles. Both of them knew their

father was only pretending to be grouchy. He was over the moon and wouldn't care if they used every shirt he had if it meant his grandson would be properly clothed.

'Not your best shirt, Dad,' said Mary. 'I wouldn't want you giving me away in church with no shirt on. I'm not sure the vicar would approve either.'

Ruby rolled up the scraps they couldn't use inside the old shirt. The shirt itself would be useful for patching or for dusters if nothing else. The last thing they dared do was to throw it in the bin. Rumours were rife that bins were inspected in the dead of night by people employed to snoop on their neighbours. It might not be the truth, but there had been instances of big fines being levied on those branded as squanderers.

Mary sniffed. 'That pig bin's beginning to smell. I'd better empty it.'

The main pig bin containing food waste was kept in the brick shed that had once been the outside toilet.

Mary tugged open the wooden door, holding her breath as she tipped what she had into the bin. It wasn't the most pleasant job in the world, but once the door was closed she was able to breathe in fresh air.

The scent of the garden was a mix of peaty earth, vegetables and roses, the latter provided by the rose bush the family had bought Charlie the Christmas before he was killed.

Mary wandered down the path to the far end of the garden to where her father had set up a wooden seat made from pieces of apple tree branches woven in together.

She sat looking up at the stars, her hands folded in her lap. It was like looking up at the inside of an umbrella, though one spangled with stars of every size.

Her thoughts were confused. She didn't feel as though she were about to get married, but then, what should she feel like? Everyone said she was lucky to be marrying Michael. He was handsome and he loved her. But did she love him? She thought she did, but what was love anyway? Her father had once said to her that love was a tickle under the heart that couldn't be scratched. She wasn't sure she knew what that meant.

A warm breeze ruffled her hair and she sighed. 'Whoever they are and wherever they may be, please God, keep all the young men safe.'

The sound of the side gate creaking open attracted her attention. Even though there was only starlight to see him by, she knew it was Michael.

She got to her feet, wanting to shout out to him but too overcome with emotion.

He paused where he was and then began walking down the garden path to where she was standing. Halfway down he turned and looked up at the house. She heard him sigh. 'Thank you, God, for bringing me home when so many will never be coming back again. Thank you for giving me Mary.'

Her heart lurched. 'Michael!' She ran into his arms.

'Mary!'

He hugged her close as if afraid to let go. They clung desperately together.

'I'm home,' he whispered into her ear. 'I'm home.'

His cheek was damp against hers. His shoulders heaved in a sob.

'Yes. You're home, Michael. You're home.'

'Are you still going to marry me?'

She laughed up into his face. 'Of course I am.'

Their lips met for a long kiss that seemed almost as endless as the star-studded sky above them.

'I can't believe I'm here. For a while, I didn't think I would make it, and then . . .' He sighed that deep sigh again.

Mary laid her head against his shoulder, breathing in his unique scent that was made up of the smell of his uniform, his cigarettes, him. He'd been through so much. Of course she would marry him and together they would learn what love really meant.

CHAPTER ELEVEN

Mary's Wedding Day

'Are you ready?'

Mary nodded, her eyes sparkling so much that her father could see them luminous behind the veil of white tulle hanging over her face. A smiling Stan Sweet squeezed his daughter's hand before slipping his arm through hers. 'Then let's make the grand entrance!'

He nodded over his shoulder at Ruby and Frances who were wearing the blue dresses Ruby had made. The tear in Frances's dress had been mended and hidden beneath an appliquéd pink rose. Ruby was wearing the blue dress that Mary had been going to wear.

Stan was feeling happier than he'd felt in a long time. Ideally he would have preferred to have collected his grandson from the adoption society by now, but as always with such institutions there were formalities to be dealt with. He was becoming increasingly impatient with all the red tape.

Ruby had calmed him down. 'Let's get the wedding over first, Dad. At least you can smile on the day, especially when you think of what's to come.'

The wedding march struck up as Mary and her father

stepped into the church. All heads turned round to smile at the bride. Expressions of admiration were whispered from one guest to another as she swept past. The lace trimming around the neckline showed up her creamy complexion. Beneath the veil her hair was glossy and woven into a soft white hairnet studded with seed pearls. The tulle overdress floated like gossamer over the satin underdress, small seed pearls shimmering as Mary made her way down the aisle to where Pilot Officer Mike Dangerfield was waiting for her.

Standing in front of the altar, Mike looked over his shoulder and smiled. He and his best man, the legendary Guy, plus other pals from Scampton, were wearing their distinctive blue air force uniforms.

Stan Sweet whispered in his daughter's ear. 'That lot are going to set hearts racing. No girl can resist a man in uniform.'

'Are you remarking on this from experience, Dad?' Mary whispered back. Her father had served in the Great War back in 1914 to 1918, but in the army not the air force.

Her father grinned and patted her hand as he passed her over to the man she was about to marry. The vicar smiled, his pale eyes looking at them over a pair of glasses that resolutely clung halfway down his deeply pink nose.

'Dearly beloved . . .'

Decked with ribbons and bows made from off-cuts of Mary's wedding dress, the car provided by the Ministry of Food took Stan, Ruby and Frances to the village hall for the reception. Corporal John Smith drove them.

'You look lovely in blue,' he whispered as he helped Ruby from the car.

'You look pretty good yourself,' she whispered back, her

eyes sweeping over the double-breasted grey suit, the crisp white shirt and burgundy tie.

After that it did a second trip to collect the bride and groom. The rest of the guests walked from the church to the reception.

John came in from parking the car and made straight for Ruby.

'My,' she said, looking him up and down yet again. Seeing him dressed in a suit instead of his usual uniform had come as something of a surprise. He looked so different. Even his countenance was more cheerful. Although desperate to ask him how he was getting on without her, she held off. 'I'm seeing Corporal John Smith out of uniform! A rare privilege. Did you find a seat in the church? I didn't see you.'

'I stood at the back. It was crowded.'

He was right. The pews on either side of the aisle had been packed with people.

'Thank you for coming, and thank you for driving.'

'I had a free weekend and you sent me an invitation, after all,' he said somewhat flippantly. Realising his tone was falling back into his old brusque manner, he flashed a reassuring smile. 'Anyway, I quite fancied coming down to see you, if only to check on how you're gettin' on without me. Started driving yourself around yet?'

'A bit. If my sister can drive herself around, so can I.'

He didn't seem to know that she'd asked for him to be her driver again. She presumed he'd been asked but had refused. Pride wouldn't let her mention it.

'Two Sweet girls on the road. Things are getting dangerous!'

He gave her a cocky grin, his usual habit before telling her what a cushy number she had working for the Ministry of Food. Just for once he broke the habit. The words were gone, but the grin persisted.

The toast to the bride and groom plus a speech from the best man and Stan Sweet came first. After that it was help-yourself time.

'Pasty?' Taking a platter of pasties from the buffet table, she held them so they were only just under his nose. Even she thought the smell was tantalising. 'I made them.'

'Of course you did.' John frowned, and eyed her warily. 'Pilchards?'

She shook her head, wishing a lock of hair would escape and hide the mole. Her headdress consisted of a cream-coloured silk flower nestled into her hair on either side of her face. She fiddled with the one on the same side as the mole so that her hair fell forward slightly.

'It's corned beef.' She'd remembered John didn't like pilchards.

Ruby took one for each of them, and while she held on to them, John fetched a bottle of stout for himself and a lemonade for her.

They looked for a chair, but none were free, the older guests having bagged them first, some already pushing off their shoes and rubbing their aching corns.

Ruby inclined her head in the direction of the door. 'Follow me.'

There was a small area outside the main door leading to a flight of stone steps descending to ground level. The parapet surmounting the top of the wall was wide enough to act as a shelf for their food and drinks. Resting their elbows on the warm stone parapet, they held their pasties with both hands while enjoying the view: Lansdown in the distance, the road leading down the hill, the green fields and trees in the distance. The smell of freshly mown grass and warm weather mixed with that of cottage gardens, resplendent with delphiniums, dusty-smelling geraniums, stock and lavender.

Ruby was aware of the warmth of his body close to hers.

'I suppose you know that Brenda's left me without a driver.' She eyed him sidelong looking for a reaction.

'Of course I know. She's up the duff.'

'Don't let Mary hear you refer to getting in the family way like that. She thinks it's common.'

'I am common.'

'I would never have guessed,' Ruby shot back sarcastically. 'Anyway, you don't look so common today. That suit looks as though it cost you a packet.'

'As a matter of fact, I had it years. I bought it for a job I was up for only, Mr Hitler started a war and I was one of the first blokes to be called up. I've been sidelined for a while – resting, they call it. But not for long. I hope.'

She knew what he was saying, that at some point he would ask to go back on active duty. He showed no sign of being injured – not physically – but then, she thought, not all injuries showed.

Finishing off the last of the pasty Ruby took a good swallow of lemonade.

She felt his eyes on her. 'You sure you don't want something stronger?' he asked.

She grinned. 'Are you trying to get me drunk?'

'You flatter yourself. I came here just to be sociable.'

'I don't believe you. Hang on while I get us some more pasties.'

She returned with two more wrapped in a linen napkin.

'Glad I'm wearing a suit. Couldn't come here wearing my khaki when I knew all the boys in blue would be here. Do you know how many DFCs and DSOs are among that lot? And from all over too. They might be Royal Air Force, but besides Mike there's a few with a flash on their shoulders; some Canadian, some Australian. An elite lot, them. Not the sort the army mixes with.'

'You met Mike.'

He nodded. 'Yeah. I like him.'

The noise from inside the hall drifted out on to where they were finishing off their food and drink. A few people emerged, fanning their faces and complaining about the heat.

John ran his fingers around his shirt collar. His face, like hers, was beginning to glisten with sweat. The sky glowed with the shining blueness of summer. The fields reflected the heat. Over to the east a speck in the sky swooped and dived leaving a trail of smoke behind it.

'I want to go back in there.' He jerked his head at the hall behind them.

'You could get us two more drinks and then we could go for a walk. There are some nice paths at the sides of the fields, and nice lanes brimming with wild flowers – and shade!'

'Sounds good to me.'

They'd only got to the bottom of the steps when she looked down at her blue dress and the pretty white shoes with chunky heel and lots of straps. 'On second thoughts I'm not really dressed for hiking.'

'Neither am I. But I'm game if you are.' Giving into the heat, John took off his jacket, folding it neatly over his arm. He loosened his tie and thrust his trilby on to the back of his head. 'All right. We'll keep to the lanes.'

The lane running behind the village hall was shaded by ancient elm trees. Pimpernel, speedwell, primroses and anemones peeped from between ground-covering ivy. Foxgloves, their purple flowers heavy with pollen and bees, nodded from among clutches of ragged fern growing against the fence bordering the railway line.

The sound of the bees got louder as they approached a field of hay. Because of the wonderful weather, the hay was already being harvested, an army of land girls and older men using pitchforks to get the hay into bales. A tractor bumped its way around the edge of the field, scraping the hay into handy stacks with some contraption it was dragging behind it.

Ruby frowned. The bees were getting even louder, much too loud to be ordinary bees. On turning to remark about it to John, she saw that he had stopped, his hands resting on the top rail of a five-bar gate and was staring skywards. An aircraft was approaching the field of hay, a plume of smoke trailing out behind it.

'It's a plane!' he said. 'A fighter plane! And it's coming down.'

Ruby saw that he was right. The plane was coming down, its nose pointing downwards, the rest of the craft smothered in thick, black smoke. Everyone in the field began to scatter to the edges watching as the aircraft, its insignia hidden in smoke, grazed the treetops on the other side of the main road to Bath and headed straight for the trees at the far end of the field. There was a loud bang. Everyone gasped as a plume of flames and smoke erupted from the other side of the trees.

'Poor bastard,' she heard somebody murmur.

One of the land girls burst into tears.

'Look!' Johnnie pointed skywards to where a parachute was floating gently downwards. It was coming straight for them. There was a shared gasp of surprise before everyone in the field began running towards it.

In a billowing surge of white silk, the parachute spread over the close-cropped stalks of wheat.

John leaped over the gate. Clutching her skirt around her thighs, Ruby followed him. 'Stay away,' he shouted, waving his arms as he ran. 'Stay away in case it's an enemy pilot. He might shoot.'

The people with the pitchforks got there just as the pilot hit the ground.

Parachute silk billowed in big fluffy lumps until finally falling in upon itself to lie in a massive white sheet like washing left out to dry.

The pilot emerged from the midst of it beaming from ear to ear as he unbuckled his harness. 'Good afternoon,' he said in heavily accented English. He gave a stiff bow from the waist and clicked his heels. 'I am very pleased to meet you.'

'Good afternoon? Good afternoon? You bloody Nazi bastard. I'll give you good afternoon!' The speaker brandished a pitchfork at the unfortunate pilot. 'Somebody go for the police,' he shouted. 'You!' He indicated one of the more athletic-looking land girls.

'No need.' John was standing between the pilot and the man with the pitchfork. 'He's not a German. See the uniform? He's Polish. There are two Polish squadrons in the RAF, or so I've heard. Air Field Marshal Dowding won't easily forgive you if you put holes into one of his fighter pilots.'

The rotund man with the pitchfork eyed Johnnie sceptically. 'Are you sure about that?'

'Positive. If you don't believe me, there's a whole team of Brylcreem boys up at the village hall. Ask them.'

They decided to take Johnnie's word for it. The pitchforks were lowered.

'I'm sorry,' Ruby said to the pilot. 'It was your accent, you see. We don't get to hear many foreign accents round here.'

'I am sorry too. My name is Ivan Bronowski. I need to learn better English,' he said to her. He had golden eyelashes and the bluest eyes she had ever seen – either that or it was just the way they lit up when he looked at her.

'That might be a good idea,' she said, feeling her face turning red.

He beamed at her. 'Will you teach me? If I am to be taught, I would very much prefer to be taught by a pretty lady like you. With a beauty spot.'

The question was unexpected and took her by surprise. So did the flattery. So did the mention of her mole – the beauty spot, as he put it.

She touched her mole nervously and gushed, 'I would, if you happened to be close by.'

'Whitchurch,' he said. 'I am at Whitchurch airfield. That is not too far, yes? I am very hungry. Do you have more food?' He rubbed at his stomach.

'Have one of these. Both if you like.'

She ignored Johnnie's scowl as she handed the Polish pilot the napkin holding the two pasties. She snatched the bottle of lemonade from Johnnie Smith. 'I expect you're thirsty too.'

She would have preferred offering him the beer, but Johnnie was hanging on to it for grim death. And he was still scowling. Not that she cared. She was mesmerised by the pilot's eyes, his smile and the charm he exuded like falling rain.

'I'm Ruby Sweet and these are from our family bakery. This here is Corporal Smith. I give cookery demonstrations to aid the war effort. Corporal Smith is my official driver.'

Johnnie nodded a welcome to the Polish airman and scowled once Ivan had turned his attention back to Ruby. Ruby threw him a warning look.

'Ruby, I think we should be getting back to the wedding. They'll be looking for us.'

'You are getting married?' asked the Polish airman.

The spell he'd cast over her broke long enough for her to explain that Johnnie was referring to her sister's wedding.

'If you're that hungry you can come with us,' she suggested, a comment that brought a scowl to Johnnie's face. 'There's plenty of food.'

'Do they have a telephone? I need to contact my base and let them know where I am.'

'There's one at the police station just along from the village hall. You can telephone from there.'

She knew Corporal Smith was still scowling probably because she was gushing with enthusiasm. It was those blue eyes, or perhaps the accent, the uniform – all manner of things.

Once the golden man standing in front of her had finished the pasty – she couldn't help thinking him golden – he brushed the crumbs from his uniform, clicked his heels and saluted her. 'Flight Officer Ivan Bronowski. At your service, lady. That was very delicious. Now I must get back to my base. I have some explaining to do. And I need a new Hurricane. Could you please direct me to the police station?'

John got in a response before she could.

'Yeah. We can arrange that pronto.' He sounded hyper-efficient, or merely just in a hurry to get rid of him.

Ivan walked beside her on the way back, Johnnie lagging behind somewhat.

Ruby chose to ignore him, instead paying rapt attention as the Polish pilot told her where he came from and how he'd come to England.

'I was studying in Holland. The moment I heard that the Germans had marched into my country, I came to England.'

They parted at the police station, Ruby telling Pilot Officer Ivan Bronowski that if he had the time he would be more than welcome to come along to the village hall and fill up on food. 'It's not as sumptuous as a peacetime spread, but it'll fill you up until you get back to Whitchurch.'

Once Ivan had gone into the police station, Johnnie suggested she'd been a bit too forward.

Ruby was having none of it. 'I was just being friendly. He's an allied airman. I can hardly refuse to speak to him.'

'It was more than that. The things women stoop to when there's an RAF uniform around!'

Wedding guests trooped down the stairs of the village hall, throwing home-made confetti over Mike and Mary. Ruby ran forward. 'Almost missed you,' she said, kissing her sister on the cheek. 'You looked lovely,' she whispered.

'Thanks to you,' Mary whispered back.

Ruby whispered into Mike's ear as she kissed him on the cheek. 'Take care of my sister or you'll answer to me.'

He grinned. 'I can't always tell you apart – until you talk like that.'

Mary threw her bouquet and although she aimed it in Ruby's direction it was Lilly Martin who caught it.

Ruby lowered her voice and whispered to the bride. 'She's got longer arms than me, plus I wouldn't dare push in front of her. She's built like a tractor.'

'Are you coming to help me change?' Mary asked her. 'I don't think I've got the strength left to do it by myself.'

Her voice was shaky, but then, thought Ruby, all brides are nervous.

She smiled reassuringly. 'Of course I will. Someone has to make sure you look good enough to eat. Tonight's the

night and that silky nightdress . . . Well . . . once he sees
you in that there'll be no stopping him.'

Ruby thought it might have been her imagination, but
just for a moment she thought she saw Mary's features
tighten as she forced a smile.

'Oh dear!' Ruby said chirpily. 'You *are* nervous. Well,
it's too late now, dear sister of mine. You've made your bed,
so to speak, and you'll definitely be lying in it. In Clevedon!'

She laughed. Mary's laugh was more restrained.

Ruby helped her get out of the wedding dress and into
a powder blue costume, an A-line skirt, a jacket with a
peplum over the top of a silk blouse with tiny pearl buttons.
Her handbag and shoes were a soft shade of beige.

'There,' Ruby said, eyeing her approvingly. 'You're all
set, Mrs Dangerfield.'

The twins stood looking at each other in the room they'd
shared for so many years. Now Ruby would only have
Frances for company.

'It's going to seem strange,' said Ruby.

Mary nodded, the nervous smile returning to her mouth.
'I'm looking forward to getting back . . . what I mean is,
I'm looking forward to my honeymoon too – being with
Mike – but I also mean . . .'

'I know.' Ruby interrupted. 'You're looking forward to
meeting little Charlie. It's going to be quite amazing.'

Mike's voice calling for Mary was the signal for the
sisters to hug each other before the sound of his tread on
the stairs preceded the opening of the bedroom door. His
body half leaning into the room, hand clasped around the
edge of the door, he smiled. His glance went from one to
the other before settling on Mary.

'Luggage pick up for Mrs Mary Dangerfield,' he
exclaimed.

There was no mistaking the pride and happiness in his face. If an expression could be termed hungry, he would have eaten her up there and then.

'I'll be right behind you,' said Ruby as Mary followed Mike out on to the stairs. 'I just need to freshen up a bit.'

Mary paused in the doorway. 'Ruby. I must say your hair looks better like that, brushed back from your face. You look stunning.'

Then she was gone.

Mike and Mary were ahead of Ruby, a crowd of wedding guests behind all insisting they would accompany them to the railway station. The train would take them to Temple Meads Station in Bristol. At Bristol they would change for the train to Nailsea then the branch line train to Clevedon where they were having their honeymoon.

Ruby hung back from the crowd of well-wishers, glancing intermittently at the police station as they passed by. There was no sign of her handsome pilot. There was only Miss Hunt, a sweet old lady of no more than five feet tall. The moment Miss Hunt spotted her, she explained that one of her cats was missing but there was nobody in the station at present.

'Has the Polish airman left yet?' Ruby asked her.

'That's just it, my dear,' she said in her high squeaky voice. 'Apparently they've got nobody at the airbase to collect the airman, so the constable has to drive him there himself. It's very inconvenient,' she said shaking her head. 'I so wanted to give him a description of my missing tabby. I would hate to think that something's happened to her.'

Ruby wasn't really listening. She was feeling disappointed not to have caught the airman before he left.

Before joining her sister and brother-in-law and the rest of the merry throng on their way to the railway station, she glanced across the road. Johnnie Smith was leaning against the driver's door of the car provided by the Ministry of Food. He was smoking a cigarette, a self-satisfied grin on his face.

She walked over the road and stood beside him. 'You look very pleased with yourself.'

'I am.'

'What's happened?'

He nodded. 'I'm afraid you've got me again. Though not for long. Only until my foreign posting comes through.'

'Oh well,' she said chirpily. 'There's always Ivan Bronowski to fill the time.'

Johnnie scowled. Ruby refrained from laughing. She didn't really mean it, but Johnnie could be so insufferable at times. On the other hand, she'd seen the way Ivan Bronowski had looked at her and had felt a fluttering response inside.

CHAPTER TWELVE

Because Mike only had a two-day pass, their honeymoon was to be spent in a guesthouse in Clevedon not far from the pier and overlooking the sea.

The landlady, a Mrs Rees, welcomed them cordially. She had a round face, plump hands and smelled of lavender. Her dress was flowery and shapeless, trimmed with lace and almost reached her ankles.

'Right. Mr and Mrs Dangerfield isn't it?'

She didn't mention them being there on honeymoon and Mary wasn't going to enlighten her. The woman need only to look at her flushed face to see she was a newlywed and nervous as hell.

As she led them up a wide staircase to their room, Mrs Rees told them all about the house. 'It was built around 1803 in the French style, which is why you've got French doors that open out on to a lovely veranda with all that wrought-iron work. And you've a fine view of the sea of course.'

A smell of seaweed and salt came in from outside when she opened the doors leading out on to the veranda. Mrs Rees placed her portly body to one side of the window.

'You can just about see the islands of Steepholm and Flatholm if you look carefully,' she said waving her hand vaguely to where salmon pink clouds were sinking with the

136

sun into the sea. A pale moon was already throwing silvery light over the water.

Mike and Mary nodded respectfully when she told them that breakfast was from eight until nine and that she only cooked an evening meal on request and they were a bit late for that now.

Mike's smile was warm. 'That's fine, Mrs Rees. We ate earlier,' he said courteously.

'I see you're in the RAF, Mr Dangerfield.'

'That's right, ma'am.'

'A fighter pilot?'

'No. Bomber Command.'

The smiling eyes turned hard. 'Pray God you stay safe and that your bombs kill as many of the enemy as possible, wicked people as they are.'

Mike flinched at her comment. There were times when he and his colleagues did feel the enemy should be blasted to hell. But there were other times when they fell silent as they contemplated the civilians caught up in the mayhem. Nobody liked war.

Once the flowery dress had disappeared and the door was firmly closed, Mike placed both hands on Mary's shoulders and turned her to face him. His hands dropped from her shoulders to clasp her hands.

'Well, Mrs Dangerfield.'

'Well, Mr Dangerfield.' Her voice wobbled. She couldn't help it.

A soft breeze blew in through the window, disturbing the lace curtains lying inside the heavier drapes, and blowing wisps of hair across her face. Mike stroked them away, bent his head and kissed her. She shivered. His lips felt cold and he tasted of beer. He hadn't drunk that much, but the taste had lingered.

'Happy?' he said to her once the kiss had broken, his hand cupping her face.

Even though she wasn't sure, she said yes because that was what was expected of her. Every bride was happy on their wedding day and she'd pretended all day that's all she was. No one had had any idea of how she was feeling inside, that she'd had second thoughts about marrying Mike.

Was it right to marry somebody just because you thought time was running short? Ruby had asked her if she loved him. She said she thought so, but did she really? They'd known each other for only a very short while before he'd proposed.

Marry in haste, repent at leisure; that's what Mrs Powell had said to her. She reminded herself that Gertrude Powell was a dried-up old woman, lines of bitterness sketched all over her face. She pushed the comment to the back of her mind. Mike was her husband now and this was their wedding night. She would be happy because he was happy – and he needed her. He needed her very much.

He rained kisses on her face, his ardour intensifying as his hands covered her breasts. His fingers went to the buttons of her blouse. His loins pressed tight against her and she felt his pulsating hardness.

'Damn,' he said as one of her buttons popped off. It rolled off the rug and beneath the dressing table. Mary sprang after it, getting down on her knees to fish it out.

It crossed her mind to stay there under that dressing table. A silly idea, as though she could hide under there or, better still, suddenly become invisible. Her fingers curled over it, but still she stayed there, running her free hand over the floor as though still seeking its whereabouts, putting off the dreadful moment when . . .

'Is it that important? It's only a button.' He sounded impatient.

Her fingers tightened over the button. This was stupid. She could hardly stay under here for ever.

'I've got it.' She backed out and got to her feet. Her face was flushed. She held up the button between finger and thumb. 'It rolled away.'

She placed it in a small glass dish on the dressing table. She caught sight of their reflections in the dressing-table mirror, a large mirror in the centre flanked by two smaller ones. Three Michaels and three Marys were reflected back at her from three different angles.

He reached out to finish where he'd left off.

'Let me.' She reminded herself that she was a wife. She was his. She managed to smile, but something within her wasn't accepting this. It was hard to put it into words. If she'd been able to do that she would have confided in her sister. But she couldn't. She was emotionally tongue-tied.

Her fingers trembled as she unbuttoned her blouse.

His head was bent over hers. She kept her eyes lowered, concentrating on the buttons of her blouse. She felt his hands around the waistband of her skirt. The zip being undone set her teeth on edge. She tensed as his hands pushed the light-weight skirt down over her hips.

She pushed his hand away. 'I'll do it!'

'Okay.' He sounded surprised, even hurt as he stepped back from her and there was a puzzled look in his eyes as though he were seeing her for the first time and trying hard, very hard, to understand. Seeming to come to terms with her behaviour, he took off his jacket, one finger hooked in the loop, his other hand tugging at his tie and unbuttoning his shirt.

Even though he had a vest on beneath his blue shirt she averted her eyes. A single curl of hair sprouted over the top of his vest, under which were the contours of his well-developed chest muscles.

Her face felt as though it was on fire. The calves of her legs tensed in readiness to run away. It was suddenly difficult to breathe.

'I'll just get my things . . .' She spun swiftly away from him, reaching for the small brown case he'd placed on a chintz-covered chair.

'Things?' He sounded surprised and she knew that if she did dare look at him, he would probably look quite astounded too.

She pulled out the white silk and lace nightdress she'd brought with her, scattering rose petals over the floor as she did so.

'Frances put those in there.' She laughed nervously and for a moment stood very still holding the silky nightgown with both hands. 'They're from Charlie's rose bush.'

A wave of sadness flooded over her. If there had been no war Charlie would still be alive and perhaps, just perhaps, she would never have met Mike and therefore she wouldn't be here now.

Mike frowned as he watched her place the silky nightwear on the bed, rearranging its folds again and again, fussing and pulling at the lace with nervous fingers.

She turned her attention to his kitbag. 'Do you have your pyjamas?' She kept her eyes averted as though unpacking was the most important thing in the world.

Mike stood silently watching her, his jaw firm, his mouth set in a straight line and his eyes narrowed. His shirt was totally undone now fully exposing the white vest that clung to his muscles, enhancing his well-toned body.

He pointed at the nightwear she'd pulled from his kitbag. 'Mary, do you seriously think we're going to wear these things?'

Mary hugged his striped pyjama top against her body. She

couldn't bring herself to look at his face. 'I'm shy,' she said softly. 'I didn't think I would be, but I am.'

For a moment they said nothing to each other. She wondered whether he too was now realising the enormity of what he'd done, marrying an inexperienced girl he hardly knew. From the very first there had been an extreme sense of urgency in his pursuit of her. Why hadn't they waited?

The answer of course was always the same: because of the war, the bloody war!

She felt such a fool. Here she was on her honeymoon and feeling more like running out of the room rather than leaping into bed.

She heard Mike sigh as he reached for his shirt. 'Tell you what. I'll head along the landing while you undress. I'll take these with me.' He picked up a packet of Craven A and headed for the door where he stopped, his hand on the doorknob. His expression was grim. 'Take your time.'

Then he was gone. She heard his footsteps stomping along the landing and then off down the stairs. The front door down in the hallway opened and then slammed shut. He was angry. That much was obvious. He had good reason to be.

Discarding the pyjama top, Mary slumped down on the bed and threw her hands over her face. 'What have I done?'

A shiver ran across her shoulders and she hugged herself.

Everyone had been so happy at the wedding, the day that should have been the happiest of her life. Her father had laughed, chatted and smiled with and at everybody. His daughter was getting married.

She raised her head and swiped at her nose, her gaze falling on the silk nightdress. Perhaps she wouldn't have reacted as she did if he hadn't suggested it was stupid to wear night-clothes. That part of it was his fault. He had to be patient with her. He had to understand.

She checked her watch. He said he would only be gone for a few minutes. He'd been gone for fifteen already. She felt guilty she'd upset him. He really didn't deserve her treating him like that.

The sun had set and the room was getting darker; a shaft of moonlight highlighted the shape of the silky nightdress on the bed.

She got up from the bed, reached for the bedside lamp, an extravagant bronze lady holding up a marbled globe of orange and white glass, and turned it on. The room was lit by a muted amber glow. Tentatively she touched the soft material of the nightdress, sucking in her bottom lip as she thought things through. Somehow she had to make amends to Mike. Somehow she had to accustom herself to being a wife.

Taking a deep breath she turned off the bedside light, took off what remained of her clothes and reached for the nightdress. The room remained lit by moonlight.

A glimpse of her body in the dressing table mirror surprised her. Her nightdress bundled in one hand, she stood still for a moment looking at her reflection, her body bathed in the silvery glow filtering through the window. The material of the nightdress felt cool and soft against her skin. The material was so sheer that her nipples and the patch of dark hair between her thighs showed through it.

This, she thought, is the vision that Mike, as a husband, would see and of course he would want her.

She closed her eyes and took deep breaths, willing herself not to be frightened.

Pretend to be somebody else.

The thought seemed to enter her head from out of thin air. Her eyes flicked open just in case there was somebody else in the room. There was no one except the moonlight and the sound of the sea sucking at the rocky shoreline. But the idea had taken root. There was only one person she would choose to be at this moment in time, one person who could deal with this situation without fear and probably with the greatest enjoyment. Ruby!

Mike Dangerfield sucked on the cigarette he was smoking, his face turned towards the sea. A warm breeze toyed with his hair sending tendrils of it across his face. His narrowed eyes were fixed on the dancing water, the path of moonlight running over it.

Usually he enjoyed a quiet smoke, but tonight, tonight of all nights, the taste of the cigarette was bitter. What the hell was she playing at?

He'd expected her to be shy; after all, she was a virgin and he deeply appreciated that she was. He'd thought he'd known how to proceed – slowly and gently. It hadn't worked and he was damn sure he hadn't made a wrong move. He was the one with the experience. Not that he'd disclose to her just how many lovers he'd had, it just wasn't done. He was a man. It was expected that he was the one with the experience and that was the way it should be. As for her, she was exactly the kind of woman he'd resolved to marry, the total opposite to what his mother had been.

He scowled at the memory, her first marriage, the affairs, the second marriage, yet another stranger in her bed. As a young boy it had sickened him. As his aunt Bettina, his father's sister, had said, 'Some people can't help gambling, some can't help drinking. and in your mother's case, she can't stop taking different men into her bed.'

The moment he'd seen Mary he'd known she was the one for him, self-assured, yes, but untouched, virginal.

Taking the cigarette from his mouth, he eyed it briefly, considering whether the tobacco had been contaminated by something and that was the reason it tasted so bitter. His jaw tensed, eyeing it accusingly as if it were more than just a half-smoked cigarette. On deciding the taste was off he flicked it between finger and thumb. Faint sparks trailed from its red glow as it flew down on to the rocks between the promenade and the sea.

He shoved his hands in his pockets feeling both disconsolate and disgruntled. What to do next? He could go back and force the issue, but Mary would never forgive him if he did, and besides, it wasn't his way. Or at least, he didn't think it was unless there was another man lurking deep inside him, a different man to the genial person everyone knew so well. It had surprised him that he'd felt so angry, so let down. He'd imagined things being so different – her acting so differently.

The breeze strengthened as he walked back along the promenade, tousling his hair and numbing his cheeks. The sea air dried his lips. He badly wanted a drink.

Halfway back to the guesthouse, he heard something creaking away to his right. Buildings of various ages and sizes lined that side of the road. By virtue of the blackout, no lights shone from either windows or doors, though nobody could black out the moon. The buildings shone like silver.

Thanks to the moonlight, Mike spotted a wooden sign depicting a bewigged man wearing a patch over one eye and a sign saying *The Nelson.*

He was an aviator, a member of the boys in blue, the Brylcreem boys, as some called them, and the RAF boys knew a pub sign when they saw one. Mike was no exception.

Yes, he thought, I could do with a drink, in fact more than one.

His toe stubbed against a pebble lying on the pavement in front of him. With one angry kick he sent it flying over the railings of the promenade to join his unfinished cigarette. Then he was off, across the road and into the pub.

Once she'd changed into her nightdress, Mary brushed her hair, telling herself with each stroke that she had to go through with this and that there was nothing to be afraid of. Once that was done she got into bed, shivering as she slid her bare feet down between the cotton sheets.

The night was warm, but still she found herself shivering. Her eyes began to flutter, but she didn't want to fall asleep, not until Mike was back. She wanted to apologise for acting like a foolish girl. She was his wife and would start acting like one.

The breeze rustling the curtains, the clear beauty of the moonlight and most of all, the fact that it had been a long hard day finally took their toll. No matter how hard she tried to keep her eyes open, Mary fell asleep.

It was late when, his shirt newly unbuttoned, Mike entered the room where his wife was sleeping. His hair was awry, he'd had too much to drink and he was too tired to think straight.

The moment he saw her, he knew she'd believed he was only going to be gone for a few minutes. He wished now he'd kept his word. She looked so lovely lying there.

She'd pushed the bedclothes down to her waist. Her arms were flung above her head and she was facing the window. The moonlight caused the thin material of her nightdress to become transparent.

He could see the darker colour of her nipples, the spherical contours of her breasts rising and falling in time with her breathing and all touched with a silver light.

Instead of taking her in his arms and showering her with

demanding kisses as he had planned, he sat himself down in a tub chair, the sort that had been fashionable back in the twenties. Like the rest of the room it was dated, but it didn't matter, certainly not to him.

The crowning glory of this room was the iron work of the veranda, which framed the seascape on the other side of the road. Or it had been. The best view was now Mary, sleeping soundly, her body clearly visible beneath the flimsy gown.

He sat there watching her for some time as he gathered his thoughts, made bleary now by the amount of drink he'd consumed.

The landlord of the pub had been a convivial host, proud to serve an honest-to-goodness Royal Air Force bomber pilot. Once all the other customers there heard he flew bombers, they all wanted to buy him a drink, and now . . . his head ached.

He frowned to himself, unsure of what to do next. One thing he was sure of was that Mary would not welcome a man stinking of booze into her bed. Plus he was tired. He hadn't told her he'd dashed down the night before immediately after landing his plane, fresh from bombing the enemy. He hadn't wanted her to know how tired he was.

Thoughts blurred by drink came and went and he almost fell off the chair when he pulled off his boots. It was something of an achievement that he actually managed it.

His head drooped as he lay back in the chair, telling himself he would be fine soon. A few minutes and he'd be full of beans.

I'll just close my eyes . . . His chin sank to his chest. A few minutes' sleep and he'd be right as rain.

The faint light of early dawn flooded the room with a pale grey light. On hearing the sound of snoring, Mary believed she was lying in her bed back in Oldland Common. She snuggled deeper into the pillow telling herself that it was either her father or Charlie snoring. For that moment at least she was back in her old room at home. It came to her suddenly that it couldn't be Charlie. Charlie was gone. And Dad . . .?

Her eyes snapped open. She took in the unfamiliar surroundings, the curtains billowing into the room from the open doors and the smell of the salty Bristol Channel.

Her eyes alighted on the man slumped in the chair, head lolling over his shoulder, mouth wide open.

Mike!

Last night, their wedding night, had not been the wondrous experience she'd been told to expect and she blamed herself.

She looked at him, her big Canadian with the strong chin and tough-looking body, a man who could cook and bake and didn't mind admitting it. He seemed so vulnerable sprawled in the chair like that, too tired to notice she was awake. It couldn't have been a comfortable night in that chair, for a start it was much too small for his muscular frame. He should have been in bed, beside her. That's what married couples were supposed to do. Normal couples, anyway. So why couldn't she? The very thought of what they were expected to do terrified her. It didn't terrify him. She'd felt his need – that hardness had scared her most of all. It couldn't be possible that a woman could possibly endure being penetrated by that . . . that . . . thing!

She closed her eyes and took a deep breath. Other women must be different than she was, otherwise why would they end up getting married and having babies? If her marriage was to endure, she had to go through with it. Now! Right now before her courage failed her.

'Mike.' She said his name softly.

He stopped snoring but didn't stir.

147

'Mike.' A little louder.

His head rolled off his shoulder. He winced, rubbed his neck with one hand and slapped his other hand against his forehead. It went some way to bringing him round. He groaned and leaned forward, his arms falling between his bent knees, his head hanging over them.

'Oh, God. I've got one hell of a hangover.'

'Mike,' Mary said again, swallowing her fear though her heart was beating like a drum. She was ready for what had to be done. 'Come to bed.'

He rubbed his eyes with finger and thumb, palm over the bridge of his nose before looking at her bleary-eyed.

'Sorry,' he mumbled. Using the chair arms for support, he got to his feet, staggering as he pulled off his trousers. He tried to take off his underclothes, but gave up, crashing on to his side of the bed where Mary had had the foresight to turn down the bedclothes.

His beery breath fell over her as his head hit the pillow.

'Sorry,' he said again, then closed his eyes and was dead to the world.

Once he had woken up, they spent the rest of the day walking along the seafront, though they hardly spoke, each attending to their private thoughts. Arriving back at the guesthouse at around midday, Mike was given a telegram.

'Back to base. It's a special mission,' he said gravely, his eyes failing to meet hers. 'I have to go.'

Mary guessed otherwise. If he'd really wanted to stay, he could have protested that he was on his honeymoon. But he didn't. It was hard to say whether he was embarrassed to try again or merely disappointed. Nobody liked rejection.

They barely spoke to each other on the journey back except to make comment about the view, how long the journey was taking and when they were likely to get back.

There was a parting of the ways when they got into Temple Meads Station in Bristol. Mike was changing trains to go eastwards back to the airbase. Mary was catching the branch line train to Oldland Common.

'I'll write,' he said to her.

'Telephone, if you can. I'd like to hear your voice . . .' She looked down at the small suitcase containing her lacy underwear and pretty nightdress. Her fingers tightened around the frayed handle. What was the point of such pretty things if nobody saw them?

She looked up at him. He appeared to be looking over the heads of the crowds towards his carriage, as though he was anxious to get away. She couldn't blame him. 'Wedding-night nerves,' she said plaintively. 'I'm sorry.'

The tension left Mike's face and he managed a weak smile. 'And I got drunk. And then the job got in the way. Never mind.' He kissed her forehead. 'Another time, another place.'

He turned to go. 'No.' Mary grabbed his arm, then the nape of his neck bending his face down to hers so she could kiss him.

The kiss was breathless. She never wanted it to end and she felt his urgent need, hard against her belly.

'I love you,' she whispered once they'd broken apart.

He nodded. 'I know.'

Somebody blew a whistle. The train was about to move out.

He gave her one last wave before melting into the crowd. She committed the look in his eyes to memory. Would he be back?

The thought seemed to have come from nowhere, slamming into her mind. He was off to do his duty for King and country, flying over enemy terrain, dropping bombs and being shot at.

She prayed then, prayed as she'd never prayed before. 'Bring him back. Please, God, bring him back home safe.'

The station platform was shrouded in steam as the train pulled out. She watched it until the guard's van had cleared the end of the platform, tears streaming down her face. He was off again and that in itself saddened her, but more so that when she'd told him she loved him, his only response had been, 'I know.' He had not said that he loved her.

CHAPTER THIRTEEN

Dawn was a long way off when Stan Sweet swung his legs out of bed and went down to the bakery. The bread oven was up and running in no time, its comforting warmth pervading the whole house with the smell of fresh bread. Mary and Ruby weren't far behind him, and neither was Frances, even though she was knuckling her eyes and yawning.

'Go back to bed, Frances. We can manage,' said Ruby.

Frances took no notice. 'What time are you going?'

Mary was packing sandwiches for the trip to London where they would collect the baby from the adoption agency. 'As soon as we can.'

'I want him to call me Auntie Fran,' Frances declared emphatically after loading her toast with a day's butter ration, which Mary promptly scraped off and returned to the butter dish.

'You're his second cousin, not his auntie. Charlie was your cousin,' Ruby reminded her.

Frances frowned. Being a second cousin didn't seem half as exciting as being an auntie.

Stan Sweet had been standing in the doorway, taking in the scene. He was like a dog with two tails, his face crinkled into good-humoured amusement. 'I don't see why he can't call you Auntie Fran. In fact, I think it's heaps better than calling you second cousin Fran.'

Frances burst into smiles. 'Oh good!'

After Mary and her father had gone, Ruby headed out into the back garden. She was hot and sticky and the yeasty smell of baked bread had steamed throughout the house and into the back garden. Loaves of crusty bread, golden and hot from the oven, had been set out to cool before being placed on the glass shelves behind the bakery counter.

Ruby leaned her head against the back wall of the house. The morning air smelled sweet and fresh, an antidote to the heat of the baked bread and the retained heat of the oven. Her gaze fell to the soft pink petals torn from the rose bush by a sudden breeze and rolling over paths and earth alike. They were falling from the rose bush, Charles Stuart, the only one left in a garden that was now given over to growing vegetables. It was funny how often rose petals entered her life nowadays, some scattered among Mary's things in the suitcase she'd taken with her on honeymoon – Frances had seen to that. As though Charlie was telling them that he wasn't far away.

Charlie had been a keen gardener, the rose bush bought for him as a present the Christmas before his ship had been torpedoed. The bush was planted among a whole bed of vegetables, mostly potatoes that gave it shade. So far the rose bush seemed to like the arrangement and the potatoes weren't complaining.

It had become her habit to check the bush. She liked to know how many buds and fully blooming roses the bush had.

'One, two, three . . .'

She smiled. Seven blooms and twelve buds, an appropriate quantity on a day like today.

For Charlie, she thought. For little Charlie, her nephew, her brother's son.

'Ruby. We have to open the shop.' As today was a special day Frances had been allowed to stay home from school.

Ruby could see her out of the corner of her eye hanging on to the open back door. The light of excitement shone in her eyes. She couldn't wait to see the baby and had wanted to go to London to collect the child. As the baby's grandfather, Stan Sweet was the one who had to sign the papers and had to go. He'd also thought it a good idea that as a married woman, Mary should go with him.

'I shall need a hand with setting the bread on the shelves. They won't get there by themselves,' said Ruby.

'I've done some,' said Frances. 'Two at a time, one in each hand.' She held up her hands expressively.

Ruby smiled. It was usual for a whole tray of bread to be taken out into the shop, but it was a bit cumbersome for Frances, so she'd compromised by carrying two loaves at a time.

Once the loaves were set on the shelves, Ruby added the 'specials': pasties, cakes, pies and tarts, all from her and her sister's recipes. They baked just enough so that none were left on the shelf and besides, their ingredients were rationed.

The morning dragged. Ruby kept glancing at the clock. Frances fidgeted, torn between wanting to go out and see if any of her friends had been kept home from school. A lot of families in the village kept their children home when there was work to do in the fields, especially in the autumn when there were lots of apples to be pressed. Because they were at war there was more work to do and not enough hands to do it. A few, like Frances, missed a few days at school because they weren't far off leaving anyway.

Frances decided to stay put just in case she missed something, though as Ruby pointed out to her travelling to and from London took some time.

'It's not a flying carpet. It's a train they're on.'

Frances pouted. 'I'm not stupid. I know that!'

For the sake of peace and quiet, Ruby let her serve in the shop.

'I want to serve somebody all by myself,' Frances declared.

'Are your hands clean?'

Frances held up both hands. 'I've already washed them. You told me to earlier.'

Ruby had to admit she had no excuses not to let her serve and besides she did have some recipes and demonstration notes to write up before starting back to her war work once the baby was settled in.

'Will you go back to work straightaway?' asked Frances while counting the fairy cakes Ruby had whisked into being from the things she happened to have to hand.

'Tomorrow. I have to.'

'But you'll miss all the fun.'

Ruby had set her mind on not getting too attached to the baby. After all, she was considering her options. She fancied herself in a uniform, and then there was Johnnie Smith, still waiting for his posting to come through. Not much of a romantic, he admitted he didn't like dancing, and was downright cantankerous at times.

Bettina Hicks was one of the first customers to come into the shop.

Frances pushed herself against the counter in front of Ruby, her pert nose lifted as though she were trying to make herself look taller.

'Good morning, Mrs Hicks. What can I get for you?'

Usually Mrs Hicks's complexion was quite pale, a little powder enhancing her cheekbones and just a hint of lipstick. Today her cheeks were flushed with excitement.

'I had to come in. I'm so looking forward to seeing the baby.' She addressed Ruby. 'How was your father this morning?'

Annoyed because Bettina didn't seem to want to buy anything, Frances rested her chin in her hand and her elbow upon the counter, not that Ruby and Mrs Hicks appeared to notice.

'I don't think he slept a wink all night and this morning I caught him rearranging the bedding on the cot. He brought the cot down from the attic weeks ago when he first heard about Charlie. It used to be our cot – Mary at one end of it and me at the other.' Ruby frowned suddenly. 'I do hope we've got everything the baby will need. I'm still not sure Dad remembered to get a feeding bottle.'

'Any bottle will do in an emergency,' said Bettina. 'I used to use a cleaned out coffee bottle for mine. You can still buy the teats separately. It didn't do him any harm.'

Just for the slimmest of moments a look Ruby could only regard as regret flashed into Bettina's eyes and was gone again. It was a pity Bettina Hicks's son was so far away, but at least he was away from the war doing munitions work in Canada.

'Thruppence,' Frances said suddenly thrusting forward a cone-shaped paper bag she'd made from a sheet of paper. There was something in the bottom.

'Oh!' Bettina regarded the bag appraisingly. 'Now what on earth have I bought?'

Ruby looked at her cousin disapprovingly. 'Frances! Mrs Hicks has already said that she doesn't want to buy anything. Give me it this minute!'

Ruefully, Frances handed it over. Ruby looked into the bag. During their talk about milk bottles Frances had slipped a fairy cake from the shelf and into the bag.

Bettina looked up from rummaging in her purse. 'Is it something really nice?'

'A cake,' stated Frances.

'Lovely,' said Bettina. 'A celebration is in order. I think I'll eat that with my mid-morning cup of tea.' Smiling broadly, all hint of regret dismissed from her countenance, Bettina handed over a threepenny bit.

Before opening the shop door, she paused, the paper bag clutched in one hand and a great longing in her eyes. 'Let me know when I can see the baby. I don't want to intrude, but . . . well . . . I was very fond of Charlie and very fond of Gilda. The things that girl went through . . .' Her voice trailed into the same sadness reflected in her eyes. The German army had marched into Austria where Gilda lived with her husband and children. They had experienced the Nazi regime's brutality first hand.

'I'll send Frances over the moment they arrive. You'll do that, won't you, Frances?'

Frances promised her cousin Ruby that she would.

The shrill sound of the telephone ringing was easily heard from the hallway separating the baking area from the kitchen. 'You're in charge,' Ruby said to Frances, dashing off to answer it. She knew who it was. Her father had promised to telephone the moment Charlie was in his arms.

Halfway there, Ruby turned and threw Frances a stern warning. 'But no pressing cakes on people unless they genuinely want to buy. Is that clear?'

'Yes. I heard you, cousin Ruby,' Frances shouted back in a cheeky singsong tone.

Ruby cradled the telephone to her ear and said hello.

She heard the sound of pennies dropping into the box and the garbled sound of the station announcer at Paddington Station.

'We've got him!'

Ruby instantly wanted to know more. 'What's he like? Does he look like Charlie?'

'He's wonderful. Not the same colouring, but our Charlie all the same.'

She heard the trembling in her father's voice. He wasn't usually a man of few words, but on this occasion he most certainly was. The sound of the station announcer disappeared. She guessed the door of the telephone box was now closed behind him. She imagined Mary sitting in the station buffet with the baby on her lap, perhaps having a cup of tea. As for her father, well, she knew that he would be overcome by emotion.

The stilted conversation – one way for the most part – was interrupted by the sound of the pips indicating the end of the call.

'Bye, Dad,' she said softly although she knew they'd already been cut off. The telephone clicked as she returned it back into its cradle.

Getting out her handkerchief, she swiped a tear from each eye before telling herself to get a grip. The shop would get busy soon; in fact, it sounded as though somebody was already in there. She could hear Frances talking to somebody on the other side of the door connecting the hallway to the shop. Best get in there, she decided. Just in case Frances was trying to get them to buy something they really didn't want.

Wearing a smile to placate the surliest of customers, Ruby pushed open the door.

Frances was chattering away as though she were thirty not thirteen.

'We're having a baby today. My cousin Mary has gone to fetch it with my uncle Stan. Me and Ruby had to stay here to run the shop. That was probably my uncle Stan on the phone. They're on their way. I can't wait to have a baby. Neither can my cousin Ruby; can you, Ruby?'

Ruby was speechless. She hadn't moved from the door. On the other side of the counter stood a man of average height with the deepest blue eyes and a familiar smile. He was also wearing an RAF uniform. On the shoulders were the insignia of the Free Polish Air Force. Ivan Bronowski was becoming a habit.

His grin almost split his face in half. An infectious grin. His hair was like ripe corn.

'Have you any more pasties?'

He had a quirky glint in his eyes that made her think he might be teasing her. Not that she cared. He was here and she was glad that he was here.

Seeing as Ruby was standing there speechless, Frances carried on talking to the Polish pilot as though she wasn't there.

'We don't have enough flour to make cheese pasties *and* fish pasties today. Sometimes we've got rabbit pie but not today. Or we might have pheasant or pigeon pie but that all depends on Mr Martin running over a pheasant or shooting a pigeon. Quite a few pigeons sometimes . . .'

Frances was chattering on like a train rattling on the rails.

'Shut up, Frances,' Ruby said.

'But all I was saying—'

'Here. Take this sixpence and buy some sweets at Miriam's shop. There's enough there to cover your week's rations I don't doubt. Don't forget your book.'

The prospect of buying bull's-eyes and any other sweet she fancied might once have appealed to Frances. But that was when she was younger. She was not far off fourteen, and not so easily swayed by sweets, besides which adult conversations were becoming increasingly attractive.

'Now,' snapped Ruby.

Frances sighed with an air of disconsolate boredom. 'All right.'

'She is your sister?' Ivan asked once the door had banged shut behind Frances.

'My cousin. Her name's Frances. She's thirteen years old and thinks she knows it all.'

He rested one arm on the counter, one ankle crossed over the other. By doing that he was slightly lower than she was, his face looking up into hers.

'She did not want to leave us alone?'

Ruby blushed. 'She's at an awkward age. She wants to know everything I'm up to and listen in on every conversation I have.'

'Are you up to anything at present?'

His eyes sparkled. Her heart leapt. She had no doubt as to what he was *really* asking her: did she have a regular boyfriend.

Ruby rested her folded arms on the counter so her face was level with his and there were only inches between them. She loved the way his flesh crinkled at the side of his eyes, the way he smiled as though he knew the biggest and best secrets in all the world. He made her skin tingle. He made her heart beat faster and her pulse race.

She smiled beguilingly. 'I could be. Depending who I was with.' She said it huskily, just like a film star when out to get her man.

'How about I take you out tonight?'

Ruby smiled at the same time as wishing she'd renewed her lipstick after answering the phone. It had to be smudged by now. She only hoped her eyes weren't too red from her earlier tears or the lipstick hadn't left smears of red on her teeth.

'How could I resist?'

'I have a motorbike. I will collect you at seven?'

It could have happened then and there, the lightest of kisses, but it didn't. Perhaps it was the uniform, perhaps it was the cheeky grin or the glint in those sparkling eyes, but Ruby wanted to wait for that kiss. Waiting until this evening would heighten her excitement and thence her enjoyment. Kissing Ivan, she decided, was worth waiting for.

The shop door closed behind him.

Too late she remembered baby Charlie's imminent arrival. Flicking the thumb of her nail against her mouth, she weighed up whether she should run after her Polish pilot and arrange another time for their date but she didn't want to put him off. She wasn't expecting her father and sister to be back until later, though she guessed they'd likely be tired after the journey. Were they expecting her to take charge? Coping with a baby was something her father hadn't done for years and her sister had never done, after all Frances had been a toddler when their father had taken her in.

Be here for them or out with her newfound beau? The choice was perilous. It was her duty to be here awaiting their arrival. On the other hand, she had been left to run the business. I'll be tired too, she told herself. I'm here all day looking after the store, even mixing up a fresh batch of dough this afternoon and setting it out to prove by the time they get back.

Anyway, Frances would be here and there was always Bettina who couldn't wait to see the baby. Besides the baby wasn't going anywhere.

She made her decision: Ivan Bronowski was too good a

chance to miss. She deserved to go out and enjoy herself. She vowed not to be too late home. It didn't matter if the baby was in bed by the time she got back – she could volunteer to get up for him during the night. She'd be there for him and for everyone else later.

CHAPTER FOURTEEN

The train pulled out of Paddington on time, but the journey was ponderously slow and the carriages packed with people, most of whom were in uniform.

Baby Charlie was asleep in Mary's arms. She kept looking down at him, humming a little tune, smelling the sweetness of him, feeling the warm weight of him in her arms. His eyes flickered open.

'Give him here,' said her father. 'Let me hold him.'

Reluctantly she passed the sleeping child to her father, though her eyes stayed fixed on the round, pink-cheeked face.

The moment she'd set eyes on young Charlie, she was smitten. As for Stan, he couldn't stop cuddling the little boy while telling him all about where he was going and what a lovely life he would have in the village.

The other people in the carriage looked on with amusement.

Mary leaned closer and whispered. 'Dad, he's a baby. I don't think he understands a word you're saying.'

'It doesn't matter. He likes the sound of my voice, don't you Charlie my boy.'

A pair of dark brown eyes looked up at them from beneath a thatch of black curly hair. Young Charlie's looks took after his mother rather than his father, but Stan Sweet didn't care.

This little boy was a victim of war as much as his parents. He was his grandson and he loved him already.

Mary had been a little down on the journey up, but occupied with keeping Charlie amused, fed and changed helped her forget about her wedding night. Mike had promised her that he would write but he'd managed to telephone her just twenty-four hours after he'd left.

The sound of his voice and what he'd said made her feel guiltier than ever about their disastrous honeymoon.

'I've no wish to force myself on anybody,' he'd said, 'I can wait, though only because I love you.'

She hadn't argued with him. She desperately wanted a second chance, to put right what had been so wrong.

'So when will I see you again?'

'That's why I rang. Because I was called back off our honeymoon early, they've given me extra leave.'

'That's wonderful.'

God bless the RAF, she thought. He was coming home. This would be her chance to make amends.

'Yes. Wonderful!' He sounded edgy, almost evasive.

'What's wrong?'

'This is special leave. There's a chance I might be posted to a different outfit. I'll tell you all about it when I get there.'

On the journey to London both she and her father had pondered where Mike might be posted.

'In his last letter he talked about applying to be transferred to fighters just to vary his experience. He thought it might be useful.'

She suspected it might also have something to do with getting posted to a base closer to the West Country. The bomber bases were in the east of the country where the land was flat and closer to the bombers' targets. The West Country, being further away, had mostly fighter bases.

'Well, let's hope it won't be too far,' her father had said, giving her hand a quick squeeze.

He knew nothing about their wedding night and she wasn't likely to tell him. She couldn't even tell her sister in case Ruby laughed and told her she should have considered becoming a nun instead. Mary would be mortified if she did that, but perhaps Ruby was indeed the right person to ask. Her sister was so much more experienced – or willing – whichever the case might be – than she was. It wasn't even that she knew that Ruby had already lost her virginity; it was more that she clearly liked men and was so much more at ease with them than she was.

The train groped its way along railway lines cloaked in darkness, the driver easing his way forward. Every so often, he left the fireman stoking up the fire bed with coal while he hung out of the cab, using a railway issue storm lantern in order to see the signals telling him whether it was safe to continue. There had been instances of trains colliding, the driver unable to see whether the signal arms at the side of the track were up or down. They'd be best lit, but the dictates of the blackout banned this.

The journey took twice as long as in peacetime so by the time they got home Mary was using the torch to see their way ahead while carrying the baby's few things – milk, bottles, nappies, etc., in a canvas knapsack given to them by the adoption society. Her father carried Charlie, the baby's head resting on his shoulder, eyes closed in deep slumber.

'He's been so good. Good as gold,' her father whispered, his voice full of pride.

It was almost ten o'clock by the time they gingerly made their way home from the station. Because of the blackout the bakery, like every other house and shop in the village, was in darkness.

The jangling of the bell above the shop door sounded before the weakening beam of her torch reflected off the glass. Mary made a mental note to seek out new batteries.

Frances was calling to them from the open door and just for once she'd remembered to turn off all the internal lights. The ARP warden – Malcolm Chance, their postmaster and one time member of Oswald Moseley's blackshirts – wouldn't hesitate to shop them if a light showed.

'Uncle Stan! Have you got the baby? Can I see him? Can I?' Frances didn't attempt to keep her voice down.

'Shush,' Mary called back. 'You'll wake up the whole village.'

'We've got him,' said Stan Sweet, sounding as though he'd won a million on the football pools, though to his mind his grandson was a better prize than that. 'Where's our Ruby? Go and tell her we're back.'

A figure loomed up behind Frances, smothered in darkness.

Stan presumed it was Ruby. 'Ruby! He's here. He's a right little corker!'

'It's me, Stan.' Even before the torch caught her face, both Mary and her father recognised the voice of Bettina Hicks. 'I couldn't wait to see the little chap. Now come on in and get your hat and coat off. I've made a stew for your supper and the kettle's boiling.'

'Bet, you're an angel. I could murder a cup of tea!' Stan exclaimed.

Once they were inside, the door was closed against the darkness, the blackout curtain drawn across covering both the beige blind and the shop door.

Mary and her father blinked as the lights went on. They'd got used to the darkness and also to the gloominess of the lighting in the railway carriage.

On clapping her eyes on the baby, Bettina Hicks clasped

her face in her hands. 'Oh, my! Isn't he beautiful? So beautiful. May I hold him?' She looked pleadingly at Stan.

For a moment Stan Sweet tightened his arms around the child as though loath to let him go. 'He's a bit of a buster,' he proclaimed. 'Might be a bit heavy for you.'

'I'll sit down,' said Bettina firmly once they were in the kitchen. 'Mary can pour the tea and Frances can dish up the stew. It's rabbit stew and I made dumplings. Please,' she pleaded. 'It's been such a long time since I held a baby.'

Stan Sweet couldn't ignore the tone of her voice or the imploring look in her eyes. She was a good sort, was Bettina, and he'd treated her badly during the past few months. Anyway, it was thanks to her that young Charlie had been born, seeing as it was at her house that Charlie and Gilda had made him – so to speak.

'Well?' Stan shrugged off his coat. 'Go fetch our Ruby to come and see her nephew. She's missing out. Where the devil is she?'

Bettina didn't look up from cooing at the baby and stroking his soft pink cheeks. He was still sleeping soundly. 'She's not here, Stan. She had a date.'

'Had a date?' His expression clouded as he looked around him as though half expecting her to leap out from playing hide and seek.

Frances piped up from counting Charlie's fingers and feeling for the tiny toes in the canvas boots he was wearing.

'She's gone out with a man on a motorbike. I saw her go.'

Stan's face clouded over. 'What man?'

Frances chattered on, unaware of her uncle's angry expression, too wrapped up in baby Charlie. 'His name's Ivan. He's that pilot from Poland. He bailed out from his plane in the middle of Clancy's field when everybody was at our Mary's wedding. Ruby stopped them from sticking him with a pitchfork.

166

And she gave him a pasty. He was very hungry, though I expect he would be after shooting down enemy bombers, don't you think?'

Stan Sweet prided himself on supporting anyone who had the guts to challenge the people who had killed his son; however, the fact that Ruby was not here to greet them and the baby overrode anything else. Her first duty should have been to her family. It didn't occur to him that his daughter might not be as engrossed in his grandson as he was. He expected everyone to feel as he did; in fact he couldn't imagine them thinking any other way.

Just as he was about to put his feelings into words, some of which would be downright angry, the sound of a motorbike engine came from outside, then fell to silence as it stopped outside the bakery.

The women showered attention on the baby rather than acknowledge Stan's bad mood.

Stan glowered at the clock. It was half past ten. Hard to credit how much time a baby snatched from your life, he thought. Half past ten and they'd only just got back from London and Ruby was just getting home.

'She should have been here! Damn it! She should have been here!'

'She's here now, Stan.' Bettina could see how agitated he was because this was a special day. However, Ruby had only missed their arrival by minutes.

Face flushed with anger, he was just about to rush out there and give both Ruby and her young man a piece of his mind, when Bettina suggested, quite forcefully, that it was time young Charlie was put to bed.

'It's been a long day. You're tired and so is this child. Now then. Are you going to take him up, Stan? Or do you want Mary to do it?'

Her eyes met his in warning. He knew what she was silently advising him: leave them be. Ruby had come home and the baby wasn't going anywhere. There were tough times ahead and he'd need both of his daughters and his niece to give a hand. Her too, she hoped.

The tension in Stan's shoulders lessened. Up until then he could have been described as hard as a block of wood or a wedge of cheese. He nodded and gruffly agreed. Bettina smiled and turned to Mary.

'Do you mind if I go up and give you a hand, Mary?'

Ruby had enjoyed a lovely evening, one full of sweetness, conversation and shared thoughts and reminiscences.

They'd driven to a small country pub at Upton Cheyney, no more than a hamlet of old stone houses and cottages situated up a turning off the main road. The pub bar was divided into small rooms, most unable to take more than eight people at a time.

Ivan and Ruby had one to themselves.

Ivan had told her about learning to fly when he'd been studying law in Holland. He also spoke about the horror of his country invaded by a foreign power, and as he did, he clenched his hands in front of him, his eyes staring into distant scenes only he could see.

'We were helpless. Our army still had horses; our air force was out of date. The Germans had tanks and modern aircraft, Stuka bombers that made a screaming noise as they dived to bomb their targets. I went back to Poland only for a few weeks. When I saw what was happening I got out as quickly as I could, back to Holland, and then I came here. I have been very happy here. Very happy.'

It was impossible to read the look in his eyes, but she caught something there, something that he wasn't telling her.

She presumed it was about Poland and what it had been like to be enslaved.

When he kissed her goodnight, she promised she would see him again and he gave her the telephone number at the base.

'I like you,' he said in his matter-of-fact way.

'And I like you!' She meant what she said.

'And I like your cooking.'

'I'm glad.'

He touched her mole with his fingertip. 'And I like your beauty spot.'

They kissed again, his lips warm and soft as velvet. She wished the night could go on for ever. A clinch with him was nothing like being in a clinch with any of her previous dates or even, God forbid, Gareth Stead. Ruby shivered at the very thought of Gareth's hands on her and the way his lips had seemed to suck her into his mouth. Ivan was different: she loved his accent, his romantic ways, a kiss on the hand, the clicking of heels. So very different.

His lips only reluctantly left hers.

'I'll write to you,' she exclaimed breathlessly. He retained his hold on her, holding her tightly against his body. He wanted her and she wanted him. Perhaps this was the one she would give into; after all, he had swept her off her feet.

'I will write to you,' she said again. 'At the base. Would that be all right?' She wasn't sure what the form was, whether he could receive telephone calls.

'I would like that, but my writing is not good . . . my English . . .'

She thought his English was fine. 'Whenever there is a word you don't know, call me, or write to me. I'll explain. I promise I will.'

'You have a telephone?'

'Yes.'

'I telephone you.'

Ruby almost fainted at the thought of him ringing her, of that lovely accent speaking to her over the telephone.

'I will telephone you,' he whispered, his warm breath tickling her ear. 'There is a dance at the base soon. You will come?'

She liked the way he said, *you will come,* a command rather than an invitation. It made her feel cherished, especially the way he said it. She loved his accent.

'A dance? Lovely. Just try and stop me.'

She glanced in the general direction of her father's shop. The building itself wasn't easily seen except for the outlines of the chimneys and rooftop against a sky that glowed indigo at its outer edges.

Due to the thickness of the blackout curtains it was hard to tell whether anybody was still up, though she guessed they were. The baby would see to that. At this very moment somebody might be peering out at her through a window. She couldn't tell.

She tucked her fingers beneath the collar of Ivan's jacket, tilted her head back and playfully kissed his chin.

'So smooth,' she whispered.

Her tilted back head was enough of an invitation to receive more kisses and a closer pressing of bodies.

It was as if their lips had become magnetic, unable to resist meeting and not letting go. They clung together like that until Ruby pulled away.

She glanced again at the bakery. Her father would be livid. She hadn't been there for the homecoming, and him so engrossed in everything and anything to do with her brother's baby.

'I have to go,' she said.

He groaned as she drew away from him. He had been about

to kiss her again, and although she wanted that, it was getting late. It was time to go.

She touched his mouth with her fingers, felt them purse under her touch. 'I'm all kissed out, and besides, I think I can see my father looking out of the window.'

It was rubbish. She couldn't see a thing, but that didn't mean her father wasn't looking out of the window and more than ready to give her the dressing down she deserved. The guilt she'd put to one side for the evening slowly resurfaced.

Ivan was, of course, ignorant of this.

'Saturday,' he said. 'I will see you Saturday. For the dance. That is when it is. We always have dances on Saturdays. Not every Saturday. But often.'

Unwinding his arms from around her body, Ruby gave him one last kiss, nothing more than a quick peck.

'I have to go.'

Her voice was breathless and her heart was singing and it was so terribly difficult to turn her back and walk away. Even then she threw him a smile and a wave, though he wouldn't have seen it, not in that incessant blackness.

The bell above the shop door jangled as she pushed it open. The smell of bread wafted out along with what seemed to be a rich stew, the one Bettina had promised to make. And there would be tea, of course; there was always tea.

Ruby grinned. Very weak tea nowadays, the leaves used more than once. There was still some sugar left in the sack she'd purloined from Gareth Stead, but not much. Mary's wedding and the delicious cakes they sold in the shop saw to that.

Pushing open the kitchen door, Ruby was met by the warmth of the gas stove and an atmosphere. Her father's face looked as though it had been carved from stone. He was not pleased; not that it was going to stop her from being full of vim and vigour.

Frances was there too. Ruby ruffled her hair. 'Hi, poppet.'

'The baby's here,' Frances exclaimed. 'He's here and tomorrow I'm going to take him out in the pram. Do you want to come?'

'If I can, I most certainly will,' Ruby replied while feeling her father's eyes cast sternly in her direction.

Mary was looking distracted. 'I've put him to bed. He was tired out. As we all are.'

'So am I. Run off my feet today.'

Mary didn't seem to have heard her. Ruby didn't bother to repeat herself. Mary was like that a lot of late.

'He's a lovely baby,' added Bettina Hicks.

'I don't doubt it,' Ruby responded. 'He's Charlie's, so is bound to be lovely. I'd like to see him as soon as possible, right now I think would be a good time.'

'We've just put him down. You should have been here earlier,' growled her father.

'I had a date.'

'So I noticed.'

'He's Polish.'

'So I hear.'

'He's a flier. Just like Mike, though he hasn't asked me to marry him and live happily ever after like Mike did Mary. Well, not yet he hasn't. I just don't seem to have your luck, Mary. You must tell me your secret some time.'

A red flush appeared on Mary's neck spreading fast up on to her face.

'He flies Hurricanes,' she declared proudly. 'Did you know that there are more Hurricane fighter planes than Spitfires? Apparently they're easier to repair than Spitfires and no pilot has managed to tear the wings off a Hurricane. It has happened to Spitfires when the pilots got a little overexcited.'

She held her bright expression even though everyone was eyeing her silently.

'Very interesting.'

The speaker was Bettina Hicks. She was sitting at the kitchen table, both hands resting on the handle of her cane. Out of all the people in the room, Bettina was the one who, with one look, seemed to read what you were thinking. That's how it felt now, as though Bettina knew exactly what Ruby had been up to and what was on her mind.

Her father's face was like stone. 'I expected you to be here when your nephew came home.'

'Sorry. But I can see him now, can't I?'

Smiling as though she didn't have a care in the world even though nobody had actually replied to her question, she felt the teapot. 'Oh lovely. It's still warm. I could just do with a cuppa. Would anyone else like one? Dad?' She poured herself a cup before waiting for an answer.

'I expected you to be here,' her father repeated. His iron-grey brows beetled so they met just above the bridge of his nose.

Ruby stood holding her cup and saucer with both hands. The warmth was welcome after the ride back on the motorbike, her hands clinging to Ivan's body.

'I'm sorry. I promised Ivan I would meet him and I did. I'm seeing him again. On Saturday.' She looked tellingly at Mary. 'Tonight he told me how dreadful it was in Poland before he managed to escape and come here. The Germans just marched in. He's very brave. I felt I couldn't turn him down.'

'What about Johnnie?' said Mary.

'He's not here. Ivan is.'

Nobody made comment and despite her father's displeased expression, she was determined not to back down.

Bettina Hicks attempted to struggle up from her chair, but didn't succeed. Her arthritis was getting worse of late. 'She's young, Stan. Just like we once were.'

There seemed just a beat when a pin could have dropped and been heard as though it were a hammer striking the floor.

Ruby maintained her buoyant attitude. 'So! Where is he?'

Bettina smiled. 'Where all babies should be at this time of night. In bed. How about you and me go up and see him? I'd love another look at him. If you don't mind giving me a hand up from this chair . . .'

Bettina reached for Ruby's hand.

'Right,' Bettina said resolutely as they headed for the stairs. 'Let me have one more look at the lovely child.'

Ruby helped Bettina along, conscious of her father's eyes dark with disapproval. At the bottom of the stairs Bettina let go of her arm.

'I'll go first shall I?'

Ruby watched as Bettina climbed the stairs. Suddenly the stiff joints didn't seem as pronounced as they'd been in the kitchen. Ruby followed her up.

The baby was in her father's old room, which had been turned into a makeshift nursery. It smelled fresh and clean and also of something else, something warm and milky and quite indescribable; it smelled of baby.

Stan Sweet moved up into Charlie's old room up in the attic. The twins and Frances had helped turn what had been their parents' room into one fit for a baby. The floorboards were painted blue and a yellow, beige and green rag rug lay beside the cot.

There were new yellow curtains hanging at the window behind the blackout curtains, cut down from an old pair that used to be hanging at the living-room window of Stratham House. When it came to fabrics, Bettina Hicks appeared to have an Aladdin's cave of riches!

The cot was set against the wall next to the small cast-iron fireplace. It was made of beech and although its original colour had glowed like honey, it was now darkened in places thanks to the sticky hands of the children who had once slept in it.

The light shining into the room from the landing was just enough to see by. Bettina stood at the head of the cot, her smile beatific, and her surprisingly small hands resting on the rail.

'Take a look,' she said softly. 'Isn't he beautiful?'

The moment she set eyes on her nephew, Ruby was dumbstruck. For the first time that day all thoughts of Ivan flew from her mind and she felt regretful that she hadn't been here the moment he came through the door.

She couldn't drag her eyes away from the pink cheeks, the downy soft head of hair, the plump fists clenched as though he might take a jab at the people who'd killed his parents. And who could blame him? she thought to herself. Something changed inside her then and something fierce was born, the kind of fierceness a tigress acquires once she's given birth to her cubs. Ruby was not the mother of this child, yet the fierceness was there.

She stroked each little fist in turn and then each flushed cheek, amazed at the softness of his skin, the creamy freshness of his complexion. And the smell. That beautiful smell.

'Please God. Once this war is over, please don't ever let there be another.' The words had welled up inside her and were out before she knew what she was saying. She didn't want this Charlie to go to war and die as her brother had.

Gradually she sank to her knees and put her hand through the bars of the cot, touching his hands again, feeling how soft and warm he was beneath her fingers. So fragile. So vulnerable. Suddenly a tear squeezed out from the side of one eye.

'Dear Charlie. What a pity you're not here to see this.'

She'd almost forgotten Bettina was there until she felt her hand on her shoulder.

'I'm sure he knows.'

Ruby nodded. She had to believe that he did – wherever he was.

'Was he awake when he arrived?' Suddenly she had to know what she'd missed.

'No. At this age babies sleep a lot and he's a good baby. He was sound asleep. Mary put him to bed. I helped her – well, not physically. I just gave her advice.'

'Please forgive me. I wish I'd been here,' Ruby whispered, addressing the child. 'I wish I'd been here to say hello.'

Bettina smiled. Ruby was talking to the baby. There would be no falling out between father and daughter. Whatever happened they would remain a tight-knit family. She was glad of that.

CHAPTER FIFTEEN

The day before Mike came home on leave, Bettina Hicks made herself scarce, on the pretext of visiting an old friend named Grace. Mike and Mary were left with the run of the house.

'Does she really have a friend called Grace?' Mary asked.

Mike confirmed there was indeed such a person though had never met her. 'Though I understand she wants to meet me – when I'm ready – whatever that means.'

Just after supper, they'd eyed each other. It was almost bedtime. An unspoken message passed between them: Mary needed more time. Mike gritted his teeth and proclaimed his intention to check on the chickens.

'You can go on up,' he said to her. 'I won't be long.'

She knew what he meant: he was giving her time to get undressed before he came up. So far he had not seen her naked and she could not bring herself to let him see her.

She visited the bathroom before finally undressing and slipping her nightdress over her head.

Even once she was under the bedclothes, she couldn't stop shivering. Perhaps if she closed her eyes? If she couldn't see him come into the room, if she couldn't see his naked body, perhaps then things might happen. She got out of bed and turned off the light. There! She couldn't see him even with her eyes open. That might help.

The bedroom door creaked open; Mike was back. She heard him sigh. He probably didn't like the fact that the light was off. It was further confirmed when he hit his toe against the end of the bed. She heard him swear.

She felt him slide into bed beside her. His torso felt warm though the rest of him was cool on account of having been outside.

His breathing moved closer.

She lay on her back unable to move. He kissed her cheek. His hand caressed her jaw, turning her face. She didn't flinch when he kissed her lips, but her heart was pounding. She suspected his next move. He would place his hand on her breast next, and then slide it beneath her nightdress. She could just about bear that. She could also bear him rolling up her nightdress to expose her thighs.

'Take it off.' His demand was unexpected.

'No.'

She clung to the rolled-up material even though it was now above her breasts and his penis was throbbing against her thigh.

She heard him sigh – an angry sigh – a frustrated sigh.

'Okay. Okay.'

He spoke to her softly, as he might to a wild creature that he wished to tame. Only he didn't wish to tame her. He merely wanted to make love to his wife. He stroked her breasts and her belly in an effort to calm her, to prepare her for what would come next. She relaxed until the moment he attempted to stroke between her legs.

'I can't do it!' She clamped them tightly together.

He sighed, still patient but still persistent. He followed the same movements all over again, his touch gentle and slow, casually stroking, kissing her cheeks, her forehead, her mouth and her breasts.

Slowly, she released the tension in her thighs. She gasped when his hand stroked her, arched her back and closed her eyes. The moment was pleasurable.

Mike responded to her arousal, mounting her, his knee forcing her legs apart. She froze. The pleasure died, her legs moving tightly back together.

He threw himself off her turning the other way, ramming his head into his pillow.

'Like making love to a block of wood!' he muttered to himself.

He never mentioned it the next morning or the next night, talking as though everything between them was normal, if not wonderful. He made no attempt to touch her. He told her he had plans for them both and it was all to do with them having their own place.

'It's a cottage. Guy said we could have it as long as we liked. You'll love it – roses around the door, thatched roof, black and white walls . . .'

Mary was lying beside him, flat on her back, one hand fluttering over the shoulder of her nightdress. Her body was tense, her tone of voice brusque. 'Half-timbered. It's called half-timbered.'

'What? Okay. Half-timbered. Anyway, a real pretty place.' He didn't mind her correcting him. It meant she was listening.

Mary was filled with alarm. The cottage was being offered as married quarters close to RAF Scampton. It meant her moving away from her family to Lincolnshire.

As he talked he began to trail his fingers through her hair, teasing it back from her forehead in silky rivers. She loved her head being caressed. It made her feel sleepy. Baby Charlie loved it too. When she caressed his head, his eyes fluttered before he fell asleep.

He'd been teething, waking in the middle of the night, hot tears running from his squeezed-up eyes. Caressing his scalp soothed him to slumber.

'I'm not sure,' she said to him. 'Not at this moment in time. There's Charlie to consider now.'

Mike sighed and kissed her ear. 'You could bring the baby with you.'

A sense of panic immediately enveloped her. She shook her head, her hair fanning out over the pillow. 'I'm not sure Dad would like that.'

Mike drew away from her, turning on to his back, staring up at the ceiling with his hands behind his head. There was a space between them in the bed yet she could feel the heat of his body, anger simmering just beneath the surface. This was his second night back. The first night had been bad enough. Tonight he'd hoped for better.

Nothing was going right for them. He wanted her to move so she was closer to him, even though she still couldn't bring herself to let him make love to her.

Tonight he'd tried a different strategy. Tonight he'd told her about the cottage in Lincolnshire.

'Ruby can look after him. She's the one who's still single, for God's sake!'

For his part, Mike figured he'd been patient for long enough. How many other brides refused their husband their rights? Not that he saw making love to her as his right. He loved her, he wanted her, and it had seemed she loved and wanted him, but when it came down to it, she froze. Forcing her was the last thing he wanted to do, but he was tempted. If it went on for much longer he just wouldn't be able to help himself.

Propping himself up on the pillows, he reached for his cigarettes, opened the packet, took one out and lit up. There wasn't much else to do except smoke and look around the room. The bedroom they were in at Stratham House was square-shaped and the ceiling fairly low.

Mary was distraught. She'd told herself she would stop this stupidity and really try being a wife. Alas, she'd made that resolution before. Tonight she had done the same as before, undressing alone before he was in the room.

Tonight he hadn't attempted anything other than to kiss and caress her, to run his fingers through her hair as he told her about the cottage.

She kept apologising. 'I'm sorry, Mike. I can't help it. Please,' she said pleadingly, turning her head towards him. 'Give me a little time. Just a little time. That's all I ask for.'

Mike expelled a smoke ring, watching it curl and sway as it floated gently upwards. 'I suppose we rushed things. I'm sorry. It's my fault.'

'No, Mike. Not just yours. Mine too. I'm just not that worldly wise with men. I've never . . . well . . . you know. I've not even had a boyfriend. Not a proper one. I never seemed to have time. And then you came along.'

He held the cigarette as far away from her as possible and kissed her cheek. His lips were cool.

'I do love you. I wouldn't have married you if I hadn't. I would still have been Mary Sweet – or Mary Sensible as some people used to call me.'

'Mary Sensible?' He laughed. 'That's what drew me to you. I thought you'd understand how I was feeling, the need to want to live every moment because it might soon be my last. But . . . well . . . I should have slowed down a bit. It's my fault. I rushed things. But moving into this cottage might help. It'll be just the two of us, no outside interruptions. I think we need to get to know each other better, and we can't do that with all these miles between us. We need to be together.'

Mary hid her rising panic and spoke very carefully. 'I've lived in this village all my life. My father is here, my sister too, and then there's Frances and the baby. My family and my friends . . .'

'You're my wife. I want you near me. I want us to be as happy as your father was with your mother. Do you want to hear more about the cottage, or what?'

Although his words were softly spoken, she sensed they were merely a velvet coating for the stronger, harsher emotions he must be feeling, the frustration as he tried to ease her into making love but all to no avail. She knew she was being unreasonable and going on like this could end in divorce. Divorce! The idea was abhorrent, but she couldn't help the way she felt. Looking back at Mike's proposal the last thing she'd expected was to discover she was frigid the moment she was married. She knew she should confide in Ruby if no one else. Her sister might be able to give her some advice that would help.

'Yes. Tell me more about the cottage.' It took a lot of effort to sound intrigued, even enthusiastic.

Mike leaned over to the bedside table stubbing out his cigarette in the glass ashtray so determinedly he looked likely to make a hole in it. Slumping back on to the bed, he lay flat on his back, his arms behind his head, staring at the ceiling. As though he were dead – or just not here any more.

Seeing him like that she had a sudden urge to touch him, to stroke his chest. Would that be too forward? The truth was she didn't know what to do. She studied his armpits, curiously aroused by the sight and smell of them, a masculine smell. It would appear to him that her eyes were lowered. She was glad of that. She didn't want him to know she was studying him – getting to know him, though furtively – just in case it was the wrong thing to do. The one thing she could study with impunity was his voice; she loved the sound of his voice, the way the words seemed to reverberate in his larynx before he said them – like a deep echo though it occurred when he spoke not after he'd spoken.

'You can see the airfield from the back windows,' he said finally. 'We'd see each other every day – more or less – except when I'm on Ops. Can you imagine that?'

His voice had become suffused with boyish excitement. Yes. She could imagine herself staring out across the flat fields of Lincolnshire at a wide expanse of sky full of black shapes flying eastwards and wondering when – and if – they were all likely to come back.

'I could throttle back my engine and flash my navigation lights as I flew over the cottage roof so you'd know it was me. Not for long though. We turn our lights off once we near the coast.'

Mary was touched. What he was saying sounded so very romantic.

She rolled on to her side. His hair was tousled. His skin glistened. He'd lit another cigarette and was blowing more smoke rings into the air, his eyes following each one as they rose to the ceiling. She guessed smoking helped him cope with everything – including her.

'When does your friend want an answer?'

She thought she saw his profile stiffen, his eyes narrow. 'I've already said I would take it. I thought you'd be pleased.'

Mary lowered her eyes just in case he looked into her face suddenly and saw the depth of her dismay. She didn't want to go. She didn't want to leave Oldland Common or her father and family. The old saying, home is where the heart is, sprang to mind. Was it so very wrong that her heart was with her family not with her husband?

'I need to tell Dad. It's going to be hard for him, what

with looking after Charlie and the bakery. Unless Ruby gives up giving talks and demonstrations and she won't want to do that. She is a bit of a gadabout and poor little Charlie needs a mother—'

Mike's chest heaved with a monster sigh. 'For Christ's sake, Mary! You're not Charlie's mother! You're my wife! Love, honour and obey, in sickness and in health and all that. Your place is with me, and before you again mention looking after your nephew, the idea is that we have our own babies – though at present there seems to be little bloody chance of that happening!'

Mary rolled away from him, lying on the other side, her fists gripping the corner of her pillow. Squeezing her eyes shut she bit her bottom lip so hard she was sure she could taste blood.

She felt him roll to face her back, which he proceeded to stroke with softly tickling fingers.

'I'm sorry.' His voice was heavy with emotion.

Mary closed her eyes. 'It's me that should be sorry. I just can't seem to . . .'

Her eyes felt sore and heavy behind her lids. She loved him, but she couldn't make love to him. Generations of women had been virgins on their wedding night. She was hardly the first and knew she had to get over it. The right thing to do would be to face him, kiss him, caress him and give in to the inevitable. On his part perhaps he should be more forceful, but Mike wasn't like that. He was kind and gentle.

'Mary. I didn't mean to upset you, but we have to do *something*. We can't go on like this.'

She grimaced at the touch of his fingers kneading her shoulders, a comforting gesture, but one that now made her tense. How far would his hand go? Down over her body following her spine then to the deep indent of her waistline, the upward flare of her hip, or down over her shoulder to cup one of her breasts?

'It might not be straight away, but it won't be too long. Frances will be fourteen soon.' In her mind she had a plan, enough of one to fend off moving to Lincolnshire, at least for a little while. 'She'll be starting work in the bakery and I know she loves looking after Charlie.'

The front of him was slap bang against her back, his lap cupping the curve of her backside. In deference to her he was wearing pyjama trousers but she could still feel his desire like a hard bone pressed against her buttocks. She closed her eyes and bit her bottom lip hard. She had to get over this, but how?

'I can sleep in the spare room if you like.'

She didn't answer him at first, not until he made a move to get out of bed.

She reached behind her and caught his arm. 'No. Just give me time, Mike. Just a little more time.'

He rolled back into bed, facing away from her, his eyes blinking into the darkness. He couldn't bring himself to say that there might not be enough time, but he couldn't. She had to come to it in her own time, even though his time, as a bomber pilot, might be running out.

CHAPTER SIXTEEN

Andrew Sinclair arrived to take Mary to do a *Kitchen Front* broadcast for the BBC in Bristol. She'd tried to get out of it, citing the fact that her husband was home, but Andrew had been adamant.

'You're scheduled to go on air and the BBC is not in the habit of distributing broadcasting slots only to be let down. We all have to make sacrifices, my dear.'

Because it was Mary's turn to do her bit, Ruby was stuck in the shop, though hardly upset by having to stay behind. Her face was flushed and she was doing a kind of foxtrot while humming dance tunes, mostly those by Glenn Miller, the American bandleader.

Ivan had invited her to the dance on Saturday and she was looking forward to it. She wanted something different to wear and Mary had just the right dress, something really special.

She'd meant to ask her the night before, but she'd got in late, tiptoeing up the stairs, taking two stairs at a time in places just to avoid the ones that creaked. It had been a wonderful night and Ivan was wonderful, so wonderful she couldn't stop thinking about him all night. And dreaming about him.

There was just enough time to ask Mary before she left for the broadcast.

A sharp knocking on the door heralded the arrival of Andrew Sinclair who had made it his job to take Mary into Bristol even though she'd told him that she could drive herself.

She was wearing a blue flowered dress and a navy blue jacket trimmed with white piping.

Ruby caught her arm just as she came into the shop from the family kitchen. 'Mary, I've got a hot date on Saturday.'

'I take it you're going with the man on the motorbike.'

'Yes. He's invited me to the dance at his base in Whitchurch.'

Mary pulled a rueful expression. There was a sad look in her eyes. 'Pilots of aeroplanes are becoming quite a habit in this family.'

'Yes, well. I don't want to wear the same dress I wore last night, so I wondered . . . do you think I could borrow your green dress?'

'My. You sound as though you're smitten.'

Ruby pulled a face. 'He's nice, plus he's far from home. I mean, such dreadful things happened over there in Poland . . .'

'And you're going out with him because you feel sorry for him?'

Mary smiled. It was obvious from the sparkle in Ruby's eyes that this wasn't about feeling sorry for him.

'I like him,' Ruby admitted. 'I want to look gorgeous. Do you mind?'

'I don't mind. It's hanging in the wardrobe over at Stratham House. I wore it out with Mike the other night. I hope it fits you. You did take it in for me, remember?'

Ruby grimaced. 'Well, you have lost a few pounds since getting married. I'll try it on. I'm not that much bigger than you.' Ruby paused and considered Mary's weight loss. It wasn't the only thing she'd noticed about her sister. There were dark lines under her eyes as though she wasn't getting enough sleep – and not just when Mike was home. Something was worrying her and she was acting in a more introverted manner, which for Mary was very out of character. Yes, she'd always been the responsible one, not as outward-going as Ruby, but very much in charge when things needed sorting out. Whatever was troubling her she was keeping close-mouthed about it.

Sooner or later she'll tell you, Ruby told herself. In time all will be revealed and it might be . . . She smiled at the thought that her sister might be expecting. Two babies in the family! Now wouldn't that be something?

She ventured to ask. 'Are you sure you're not pregnant?'

'No!' Mary's sharp response was accompanied with a deep blush that gathered in her cheeks before fanning out all over her face. 'I have to go.'

It wasn't the first time she'd asked, but Ruby couldn't help wondering.

Mary made a sharp exit. Deep down she wanted to tell her sister what was wrong and ask what she could do about it. As regards the dress, she didn't give it a second thought.

The BBC had moved the light entertainment division to Bristol at the beginning of the war, plus some news and public information bulletins. The majority of programmes on food and general home-front economy were still broadcast from London to Bristol, with popular programmes such as *ITMA – It's That Man Again*. With regard to *Kitchen Front*, Mary's contribution as a local girl was very much appreciated.

Andrew Sinclair was the kind of man who tended to concentrate on whatever he was doing so spoke very little as they drove into the city. Once they got there he smiled at her and asked how her family was doing. In return she asked him about his mother who he lived with despite him being in his mid-thirties.

'The sound of exploding bombs wearies her, but I find it impossible to get her into a shelter. She stubbornly refuses, is sure that the moment she does either a bomb will come down through the roof or we will be burgled. So she stays sitting in her favourite armchair knitting socks for our boys overseas. That way she insists the bombs will always fall on somebody else and nobody would dare break into a house that is occupied.'

'So she just sits there in the dark and silence?'

'Oh no. She keeps the radio on especially if it's Ambrose and his orchestra playing. She loves Ambrose.'

If Mary remembered rightly, Ambrose played at the Savoy. Or was it the Ritz?

It turned out that they were a whole hour early. The producer maintained that Andrew had known that; Andrew insisted he had not.

'Never mind. We can have a cup of tea in the canteen while we're waiting. Would that be all right?' Andrew sounded very happy about the situation, beaming so broadly that Mary was convinced he had got the time wrong on purpose. He wanted time alone with her over a cup of tea. The prospect unnerved her, but this was work; this for her country, or was it? She didn't want to be alone with him.

To her great relief, the canteen was full of chatter and the clink of teacups in saucers. One of the waitresses, a cigarette dangling from the corner of her mouth, was rubbing something off a blackboard advertising what food they had available. The list was getting shorter. They passed somebody grumbling that there were no custard creams left, only rich tea. The ashtrays on the tables were overflowing; it looked as though they'd had a busy morning.

Andrew found an empty table, recently wiped down, cleared
of dirty crockery and still damp from the waitress's cloth. The
ashtray had been emptied too, but that didn't stop Andrew
from placing it on another table. He'd only recently given up
smoking, so he'd told her. His mother had thought it was a
good idea and he always did his best to comply with her
wishes.

He left her there while he went off to get them a cup of
tea. Mary declined a biscuit. When he got back, he made a
big fuss of placing the cup and saucer in front of her, as
though it had to be set just right in case she couldn't see it.
To her surprise he'd managed to get two rich tea biscuits.
Again she declined.

'Are you sure?'

'Yes.'

'Never mind. I can manage two quite easily. Only a slice
of toast at the boarding house I've been staying at. Not enough
to set a grown man up for his job! Are you nervous?' he asked
suddenly.

She shook her head. 'I was when I did the first broadcast,
but not now.'

He grunted amiably before dunking a biscuit into his tea,
nibbling the soft bit away before dunking it again and popping
the lot into his mouth. 'You're married now.'

'Yes. You know I am.' She frowned. He'd declined her
wedding invitation, so knew she was married.

'But you still live locally, not with your husband?'

'He's in the air force. In Lincolnshire.'

He concentrated on dunking and eating the second biscuit
before speaking again. 'You could do better, you know.'

'What?'

She presumed he meant Mike and was about to admonish
him for his rudeness.

'You've done very well down here with your broadcasts and demonstrations and suchlike, but I think you could do better. To that end I was wondering if you fancied giving a talk, perhaps more than one, to selected guests at the Savoy Hotel. All expenses paid, of course.'

'Well . . .' Mary held her hand against her forehead. Mike had asked her to move to Lincolnshire and now Andrew was asking her to give at least one talk in London.

'There's a fair chance of it being broadcast,' he went on while dabbing at the corners of his mouth with his handkerchief. 'Just imagine. Mary Sweet at the Savoy!'

She'd noticed his handkerchief before, neatly pressed into a perfect triangle, part of which protruded from his breast pocket.

'I'm not Mary Sweet any longer. I'm Mary Dangerfield.'

'Mary Dangerfield doesn't have the right ring to it,' he said with a wave of his hand. 'Mary Sweet sounds *so* much better.'

Mary's finger tightened into the handle of her teacup. 'I'm not sure I can do it. You see, I may be moving to Lincolnshire. My husband—'

'Ah yes. Of course. Your husband.'

Andrew had the ability to undermine her confidence. She didn't quite know how he did it, just that he did.

'I won't be going for quite a while. Not until my cousin Frances begins work. We have a baby, you see . . .'

His pale eyes, made larger thanks to the thickness of his spectacle lenses, flickered with surprise. 'You have a baby?'

'Not mine. It's my brother's baby. My nephew. Our Charlie died at sea. Torpedoed.'

'Ah! Of course.' He hit his brow with the palm of his hand, relieved it seemed that she didn't have a child. 'How silly of me. I forgot. I didn't know that he was married.'

'She died too. In London. A bomb dropped on the house

she lived in. The baby survived. We took him in, baby Charlie. He had nowhere else to go.'

She purposely skirted his statement about the marital status of her brother. Andrew was not a friend as such, though from their very first meeting, she sensed he would like to be more than that, despite her being off limits.

Brow furrowed with sympathy, he nodded over interlocked fingers, his elbows resting on the table. 'The baby is very lucky to have a family willing to take care of him.'

Concerned he might press her for more information, she changed the subject. 'Will they be long now do you think?'

With a flourish of his fine, long hands, he brought out a watch from his waistcoat pocket. He often wore waistcoats. And bow ties. A dickie bow as her father called it.

'Never trust a man who wears a dickie bow during daylight hours. They're for wearing after sunset – or not at all.'

He frowned at his watch. 'You stay here. I'll go and check.'

His manner was oddly protective. *Stay here. This is where you'll be safe.*

Andrew was the first man she'd ever come across who wore a dickie bow during daylight hours. Today it was mustard-coloured. His waistcoat matched his suit – pinstriped, just like the doctor wore, though the doctor's was shinier than Andrews. Andrew, she'd realised from the start, was not short of money.

He came stalking back through the canteen, skirting the tables and chairs and brushing aside the smoke of cigarettes with a flutter of one hand, an admonishing look thrown at those who could eat while surrounded by a thick blue haze.

A few who met his gaze mouthed silent admonishments of their own. Mary hid her smile behind her teacup. Andrew had seemed a likeable enough man at first, but he had a high-handed way about him at times. At present he was focused on getting her on air, but there was an odd motherliness in his attitude, perhaps his mother's influence?

Mary put her chunky white cup back into its equally chunky saucer, looked up at him and smiled. 'Are they ready for me?'

'They are now, once I told them it wasn't fair to keep you waiting seeing as you had a baby at home.'

Mary's eyebrows arched skywards. 'They don't think it's mine . . .' She stopped herself from continuing. What was it about her wanting people to have a good opinion of her? Perhaps she should have been a nun!

'Ten minutes.' He sat back down, fetched out his pocket watch and laid it on the table. 'And they'd better not be late. To the minute and not a second later.'

Mary couldn't help giggling. 'What will we do if it does go over ten minutes?'

'Leave,' he said with an air of finality. 'Employees of the Ministry have not got time to waste. Wasting time is like wasting food. It is not in the national interest.'

For a moment Mary thought he was joking, but the expression on his face said otherwise. He meant it!

'Let's talk about you, the happily married woman. I take it you are happily married?'

She felt her cheeks reddening. 'I think that's a little personal.'

'Yes,' he said, nodding not so much as though he'd been rude to ask, but more so that he'd put it rather clumsily. 'What I mean is that I hope he's treating you as well as I would have. You're the only woman I've ever considered suitable wife material. You have that stiff-upper-lip quality that I like. You're a good organiser and it also strikes me that you're not given over to unnecessary hysteria or physical demands like some women I've met. And of course, so many women consider a marriage isn't a marriage unless there are children

193

– lots of children. I think a marriage of two people alone without children is eminently satisfying. A partnership. That's what I regard as an ideal marriage.'

Stiff-upper-lip quality!

She hardly knew what to say, but felt if she did say anything her words would be angry. As it turned out, she was saved from having to answer when along came a little bespectacled man who asked her to follow him to the recording studio.

It took a lot of effort to put Andrew's words to the back of her mind and concentrate on how best to reconstitute dried egg, not to overcook it, how to sweeten it for puddings . . . it was harder to concentrate than usual.

Once the broadcast was over Andrew's comments sprang straight back to her mind. How dare he call her stiff-upper-lip material? As for his ideas about marriage, well, it sounded as though all he really wanted was a housekeeper! Someone to take over from his mother. Whereas Mike . . .

She walked so briskly back to the car that even Andrew with his long, spidery legs, could barely keep up with her. Once there she stood waiting for him to open the door.

Inside she bristled. Outside her face was still pink and she was clamping her jaw together so hard her teeth were hurting.

She saw the studio buildings in Whiteladies Road reflected in his spectacles and had a great urge to pull them off and throw them away. His words had stung her as physically as though he'd slapped her face. Was she really the sort of woman who would suit him and not the Mike Dangerfields of this world, the sort of woman who kept a pristine house where nothing dirty or sinful ever got past the front door?

'Are you all right?' His tone and expression gave no sign of him regretting what he'd done.

'Yes. Take me home, will you? To the bakery please.'

Mike must be back at Stratham House by now, but she

wanted to see her family first. She wanted to see Charlie and she badly wanted to speak to Ruby.

Without knowing it, Andrew had opened her eyes to how she was seen by those around her. It made her even more amazed that Mike had seen beneath the surface to what she could be. He'd had to have done. Why else would he have been so determined to marry her?

As usual Andrew drove silently, hands grasping the steering wheel, eyes narrowed as he traversed the darkening road ahead. He said not a word until they were outside the bakery.

'I'll let you know about the broadcast from the Savoy. Shouldn't be more than a few days.'

As if she would want to go to London with him! What did she care about giving a talk at the Savoy? Nothing. Well, almost nothing. The fact that Ruby and she had landed the job had pleased their father. He hadn't wanted them to move away from home to work in the forces or in a factory. Ruby was better at it, loved meeting and talking to people, demonstrating their latest dishes, advising on how best to eke out the weekly ration in order to conserve enough ingredients to make a simple cake or pie. Perhaps Ruby was the one who should go to London, though she guessed Ruby wasn't what Andrew wanted.

Andrew had given no sign of realising that she was angry with him, but then he wouldn't, she thought. He was too absorbed in his own little world: his job as a civil servant, his mother, London and everything connected with the privileged upbringing he'd had.

'How about I take you to lunch on the way home?'

Mary declined. 'I have to get home. I promised Ruby I wouldn't be long.'

He gave no sign of disappointment, just a slight shrug of his shoulders.

'Of course you did. We should have made arrangements before we left your village. Remiss of us not to think ahead.'

It astounded her that he proclaimed this in the plural, as though she wanted to have lunch with him as much as he did with her.

'My sister's waiting for me. We have important things to discuss.'

CHAPTER SEVENTEEN

That day, once her sister had gone, Ruby made her way over to Stratham House. The house had no back door as such, having been blocked off years ago when the shop on Court Road had been sold off and divided from the main house. Entry was always through the front door, which opened out on to a large garden with an orchard at the far end. Like most houses in the village, the door was left unlocked during daylight hours.

Once the bakery was closed, the housework done and Frances was home from school to help her uncle look after Charlie, Ruby made her way along the high street, down Court Road and along the lane to Stratham House. Once through the door, she went upstairs to the room presently occupied by her sister and brother-in-law.

Mike, she'd been reliably informed by one of the village kids on her way here, had gone up to one of the farms where a land girl had been chased by an escaped pig. The pig was still roaming free and Mike had gone to help catch it. She'd have the house to herself.

Feeling a little apprehensive on entering the bedroom of a newly married couple, she paused in the doorway. The room smelled of her sister's scent, a mix of Wrights' Coal Tar Soap and Evening in Paris, the only perfume still available. She also detected the smell of a man, that salty mix of fresh sweat, Brylcreem and tobacco.

A sudden movement disturbed her reverie, a shock of whiteness from one side of the room. No ghost but the billowing of white net curtains. The wind had risen suddenly. The blue sky that had promised a day of sunshine had turned to a rolling mass of grey, navy and black. The day outside had grown darker and so had the room.

Ruby didn't hesitate to slam the casement window shut and tidy the curtains before the first drops of rain began to fall.

As the house was built of stone with small windows and thick walls, the rooms were inclined to be dark. Even if it hadn't been late afternoon the square room was never filled with light. Thankfully there were no alcoves a dull day could make even darker.

A splash of mint green hung from the wardrobe door. Such a beautiful shade of green. For a moment she just stood there admiring it. She so loved that dress, the simplicity of its softly falling skirt, the slightly puffed sleeves and her favourite sweetheart neckline.

Before the war the skirt would have been fuller, but as fabric was in short supply, war, not fashion, dictated how many yards of fabric a dress should take, the length of the hemline, just below the knee, the suggestion that sleeves should be short rather than long. Ruby had even read an article on how to lengthen suspenders on corsets rather than buy a new pair, how to cut down men's shirts to make children's clothes, to make baby napkins from old Turkish towelling, coats from blankets and how to weave hats from straw.

The material felt soft between her fingers. The dress looked as though it were made of silk, but was in fact made of an American man-made fabric called rayon. Mike had brought it over for Mary as a wedding present. This was why the skirt was fuller than current fabric rules allowed.

Ruby sucked in her breath and pressed her hands to her mouth. 'Oh my word!'

The words came out in a whisper. What was she waiting for?

In her haste to try it on, she forgot to undo the fastening on the plain navy blue dress she wore on shop days. Tugging it off, her hair became tangled in the button and tumbled forward on to her face.

'Drat!'

After bringing the dress back down to her shoulders, she untangled her hair from the button and tried again. This time the dress came off though she'd messed up her hair in the process. Not that it mattered that much. On Saturday it would be just as she liked it and would look wonderful. Ivan's eyes would shine with admiration and he'd tell her she was the prettiest girl in the room. He'd also told her she was the prettiest girl he'd ever met.

'And I bet you've met lots,' she'd said to him.

He'd laughed and thrown back his head, the veins in his throat like stiff twigs. 'Lots! Yes. Lots! I love girls, I tell you. I love girls!'

Because he laughed, she took it that he was only joking about having known lots of girls. He'd said she was the prettiest and made her feel like a queen. That was good enough for her.

Taking the dress off the hanger, she carefully undid the tiny pearl buttons that fastened it at the front and slid it over her head. 'Please let it fit,' she muttered.

Ruby crossed her fingers as she slipped the dress over her head, uncrossing them so she could button it up. Once it was on she opened the wardrobe door to observe her reflection in the full-length mirror attached to the inside of the door.

The sight took her breath away. The dress fitted perfectly and made her feel like a film star. The skirt fell in a vaguely bell shape and ended just below her knees, and the soft material floated around her.

The only light in the room came in from the window, dimly reflected in the wardrobe mirror. The room had turned unnaturally dark for the time of day. There was just enough reflected in the mirror for her to see herself. She ran her hands down over her hips. Her hair fell luxuriantly around her face and over the mole she had once hated, but no longer, not since the day Ivan had called it her beauty spot.

Satisfied that she looked fabulous, she began pulling it off over her head. Yet again she'd forgotten one button and ended up with it stuck halfway over her head and covering her face.

'I thought you'd gone.'

Startled at the sound of Mike's voice, she turned round, the wardrobe door crashing shut when she let go of it. The room turned even darker until she managed to pull the dress down enough to see.

She stammered for the right words through the material clinging around her mouth. 'I didn't . . . hear . . . I mean . . . you mustn't . . .'

'Of course I mustn't. Do you want me to give you a hand with that dress?'

'No!'

'It's okay. I'm not going to touch you. I promised I would wait until you're ready and I will. I'm off to check on the hens. Then I'm off back up to the farm. They need a hand.'

Then he was gone, leaving Ruby standing there, the dress still stuck around her head.

If he had lingered, perhaps she would have laughingly informed him of his mistake, that this was Ruby not his wife, Mary, and that Mary had gone into Bristol as planned.

Ruby stared at the closed door. What was that he had said?

I've promised to wait until you're ready and I will.

Was she correct in what she was thinking? Perhaps it was rash to jump to conclusions, but it sounded as though this married couple weren't yet married in every sense of the word. She could hardly believe it. Was there something wrong with one of them? She knew that her sister had been nervous, but to have not made love yet! No! It couldn't be true. She must have misunderstood.

Once the dress was back on its hanger, Ruby stared anew at her reflection. Even though her sister had lost a little weight, it could almost be Mary standing there; they were identical twins after all. She swept her hair back from her face.

Sucking in her bottom lip she considered what to do next. Should she go downstairs and wait for Mike to come in from collecting eggs and tell him he'd been mistaken? She visualised laughingly revealing his mistake. Somehow she guessed he wouldn't think it a laughing matter. He might well be mortified. She made a decision. She had to speak to Mary, the only person she could share it with.

Quickly, before he returned from the hen house, she was back in her own clothes, the green dress taken down from the hanger and rolled up under her arm, her shoes off so she wouldn't be heard descending the stairs.

The front door was open, the smell of wet cabbages coming in from the garden and bird droppings from the hen house. Looking out of the door, she spied Mike's broad back. He was bent over, changing soiled straw for fresh; the hens preferred to lay their eggs in clean straw and they needed all the eggs they could get.

Judging the time was right, she was out of the door and through the garden gate before he could see her. Once outside the garden, she clambered back into her shoes and headed for home, not stopping until she was at the top of Court Road.

Taking a breath, she decided to speak to Mary the minute she got home, preferably the moment she alighted from the car. It was best if she warned her of what had happened before Mike had chance to speak to her and realise that she had gone to Bristol. Seeing as he was up at the farm all day, he wouldn't know otherwise and it might be best if he didn't.

Decision made, she dashed round to the back door of the bakery and into the kitchen where her father was sitting with Charlie on his lap. Charlie was chomping on a Farley Rusk, his few sharp baby teeth nibbling tentatively all around its outer rim. Her father looked up, his eyes shining with pride. 'That's his second Farley's Rusk. He's going to grow into a strapping lad is our Charlie.'

'Just like his granddad,' Ruby called over her shoulder as she ran up the stairs, the dress tucked under her arm. Once the dress was safely hanging in her wardrobe, she dashed back down again.

'I'm going to fetch Charlie's National Dried from Powells'. I'll make a cuppa when I get back. We can have a fancy cake too. Even you, young Charlie,' she added, tapping her nephew's nose as she passed.

Charlie tried to grab her finger but missed.

It didn't take a minute to fetch the tin of National Dried Milk, concentrated orange juice and cod liver oil, all of which young Charlie was entitled to. Because the clinic was all the way up in Kingswood, the district nurse brought it in the pannier of her bicycle and left it at the Powells'. Mrs Powell had been her usual offhand self and Miriam hadn't been around. Ruby had asked her where she was.

'Behaving herself as a good Christian girl should,' she'd responded, fixing Ruby with a pair of accusing black eyes.

Ruby gathered up what she'd come for, tossed her head and stalked out. She loitered between the shop and the lane leading to Stratham House, trying to guess which route Andrew would take: would he come down California Road or come along the main road and up the hill? No matter which way they came, she was likely to miss them. She couldn't keep her eyes on both routes. There was nothing for it but to head for home, for the bakery. That's when she had the sneaking suspicion she was finally going in the right direction. Something told her that Mary would head for home. She didn't know why, she just knew.

'I know that things aren't right,' said Ruby as she marched alongside her sister.

Andrew had left, the sound of the motorcar gradually fading into the distance.

'No. They are not,' said Mary, presuming she was referring to Andrew Sinclair. 'I swear I will drive myself everywhere in future. I will not be swayed.'

'Whatever did he say to upset you?'

'It's something I have to deal with.'

'Look,' said Ruby keeping pace all the way to the back door. Once in the lee of the back wall of the house she grabbed her sister's elbow, forcing her to stop and face her before they went in. 'I know something's wrong, Mary. Just talk to me about it. I'll listen. I promise. Are you staying for supper?'

'I'd like to. Mike will know where I am if he wants me, and anyway, I'd like to see Charlie.'

'And we need to talk,' Ruby said firmly.

'I know.' Mary's eyes were averted. Because of the blackout there was little light to see by, but to Ruby it looked as though her sister was churning thoughts over in her mind.

'Mary,' she said, taking a deep breath. 'There's something

I have to tell you. I was in your room over at Stratham House trying on your green dress and Mike came in. He thought—'

A pink blush spread over Mary's cheeks. 'Ruby, can we talk about this later? I need to think things through and, well, there are personal things . . .'

'I know.' Ruby's eyes locked with those of her sister. There were certain times when they seemed to communicate without the use of words. This was one of them.

'Later?' Mary's chin jutted forward in the old way, a sign she was going to face whatever was wrong.

'Later,' Ruby agreed. 'After supper.'

'And in private. Perhaps we could both put Charlie to bed and talk then.'

Ruby nodded.

Mike joined them for supper. Ruby noticed how tense he was, how he kept showering her sister with furtive glances as though waiting for a kind word or some sign that everything was going to be fine between them.

Frances diverted Mike's attention with imaginative details of her job prospects while there was a war on, though everyone knew she was too young to be allowed to do war work. Frances had not as yet accepted this, or the fact that she was needed at home to work in the bakery and look after young Charlie.

There had been talk of the school leaving age being raised from fourteen to fifteen, but although the law had been passed it wasn't likely to be implemented until the end of the war.

'I think I would like to join the Royal Air Force,' stated Frances loftily. 'I like the uniform and I think I would be very good at flying an aeroplane.'

Everyone laughed. Stan took the opportunity to inform her where she would be working once she'd left school.

'Ain't it occurred to you that I'll need an extra pair of hands here? Your sister won't be around for ever you know.' He jerked his chin at Mary who looked down into her lap. She hadn't said a word about going to Lincolnshire.

Frances didn't look too happy until he pointed out that she'd also be looking after her cousin most of the time. 'I think Charlie's dad would appreciate it,' he added.

Everyone noticed his misted eyes and sad smile, weak but sure signs that his time of mourning was over. His son Charlie would live in his heart, but there was a new Charlie now, a little boy who Stan determined would be a credit to his parents.

Well-fed and tired, young Charlie had fallen asleep.

'Come here, little man. Time for bed.' Gently, so as not to wake him, Mary unclipped the harness that kept him fastened to his high chair.

Ruby also got up from her chair. 'I'll come up with you.'

Once Charlie was undressed and snug beneath his blanket in his cot, the twin sisters, mirror images of each other except to those who knew them well, stood looking down at the rosy-cheeked child.

'He looks the picture of contentment,' Ruby observed. She looked tellingly at her sister. 'Which is more than I can say for you. What's the matter, Mary? And don't say nothing is wrong, because we both know it's not true.'

Mary stiffened, her fingers tightening over the bar of the cot, her knuckles angular with tension.

Ruby went over to the window, trying to appear nonchalant as she waited for her sister to decide whether she was going to deny anything being wrong or pour all her troubles out there and then. In the meantime she chanced opening a chink in the blackout curtains, just enough to see that the only light in the blackness were the myriad stars shining from an indigo sky. God, she reflected, did not respect the laws of the blackout. The moon and stars shone on regardless.

Along with these thoughts came more pressing ones concerning her sister's marriage. If Mary denied anything was wrong, was it right for her to persist, to make her reveal her problems?

Smoothing away the gap in the curtain, she turned back to face her sister, saw the tension in Mary's shoulders and heard the strangled sobs, which she was trying to make sound as though they were heavy sighs. Ruby was not fooled.

'Mary!' Ruby threw her arms around her sister. Mary's head landed heavily on her shoulder. 'Let it all out, Mary. For goodness' sake, let it all out.'

The sighs turned into the sobs they really were. 'Ruby, I feel such a fool! I shouldn't have married him. It wasn't fair. On either of us. I know nothing. I know absolutely nothing about men!'

Ruby closed her eyes and soundlessly cursed those that had started a war that had turned the world upside down. 'Tell me about it,' she said softly, mindful of the sleeping baby.

Mary raised her head while reaching into her sleeve for a handkerchief. She blew her nose quietly. Her eyes stayed fixed on Charlie as she voiced her fear, her foolishness and her regret.

'You see, I was never like you Ruby. You've always been at ease with men and although I tried to be like you, I never was.' She shrugged. 'I kept my distance. I was Mary Sweet, the dutiful daughter who always wanted everyone to think well of her. I was always standoffish with men, the girl who would remain a virgin until the day she married, the girl who never invited gossip or wicked rumours.'

'Definitely not like me then,' giggled Ruby.

Mary laughed quietly. 'I scared them away. You see, I just

never knew . . . about things . . . you know . . . what men and women did to make babies . . . not really . . .'

'How did you think babies got made?' Ruby couldn't help sounding amazed and if the room had been better lit, Mary would have seen her surprised expression.

'I guess I knew on some level . . . the mechanics of it but not the reality. I just didn't have any direct experience.' Mary shrugged again. 'I knew nothing, and once faced with having to do it . . .'

Ruby didn't know what to say. Even though her preliminary suspicion had proved right, it still took some believing. But there it was. Mary and her husband had never consummated their marriage.

'The thought of it scares you?'

Mary kept her eyes lowered as she nodded, her handkerchief scrunched into a tight knot between her tense fingers.

Ruby frowned. Living in a village on the edge of countryside, it was always assumed that nobody needed to be told the facts of life because it was there all around them. And how often had they heard their father speak of taking the sow to the boar, and a few months later hearing of a load of little suckers being born.

Most people worked things out for themselves what happened between a bull and a cow, a sow and a boar, a man and a woman, though obviously not Mary. There'd always been naughty comments in the shop and elsewhere, but Mary, it seemed, had been above all that, knowing what they were saying but somehow managing to distance herself from it.

'I've let Mike down,' Mary was saying. 'Our honeymoon was a disaster and I still can't . . . though I have to . . . I must!'

Ruby gripped her sister's shoulders. 'Now look here, Mary. I've got something to tell you.'

She went on to tell Mary what had happened as she was trying on the green dress. 'He thought I was you and said that he would wait until you were ready. He didn't realise it was me and I don't think we should tell him. Do you?'

Mary lifted her head and raised her eyes which were still moist, though she was no longer sobbing. 'It's all come to a head today. Andrew Sinclair more or less told me that I was frigid and that suited him fine. He would have married me like a shot. He doesn't want a physical relationship with a wife. He doesn't want children, all he wants is a companion.' She laughed weakly. 'Anyway, I don't think his mother would have approved of him sleeping with a woman. He's still her baby, I think.'

She looked down at the sleeping child, her expression more serene now and certainly less troubled. In fact, thought Ruby, her eyes are full of love.

Mary turned back to face her sister, her eyes shining with a new resolve. 'But I don't want to be that woman. Facing up to what marriage really involved was such a shock. I knew what I was expected to do, but couldn't bring myself to do it.' She shook her head. 'I feel such a fool. Such a big baby. Then today I realised just how much I love Mike and how awful it would be if . . . if anything happened to him before we'd actually . . .'

'Made love.'

Mary looked at her as though she'd made a great revelation.

'Yes,' she said, her voice barely above a whisper. 'Made love. Yes. We need to make love and perhaps . . .' Her gaze travelled once again to the sleeping baby who was making snuffling noises in his sleep. 'Make love and make one of those. Now wouldn't that make Dad happy?'

* * *

Before they had dinner that night, Mary took two glasses and a decanter of brandy upstairs. She didn't tell Michael she'd done it, not until they were undressing did she point it out.

'A nightcap. Isn't that what they call it?' Her heart was hammering in her chest. She'd never done anything like this before.

Michael looked surprised. 'Am I getting this right? You're plying me with drink in order to take advantage of me?'

She felt herself blushing. This was so unlike her, and yet she felt that once she'd done it . . .

'I think I could do with it. I love you, Mike, but I'm a silly goose who—'

'Not you are not!' He hugged her tightly to him, felt the tension in her body ease as he kissed her forehead, her head, her ears. 'Would you like me to pour?'

She nodded.

He loosed her from his grasp and poured them a measure. 'Here's to us,' he said. 'Always and for ever.'

The brandy left a burning sensation on her tongue. It left her feeling a bit light-headed. It also helped her relax.

Suddenly she was seeing how gaunt his features had become since the first time they'd met. He'd been close to death so many times, yet didn't go into much detail, but now she didn't need him to. She could see it on his face and almost feel it, as though she had been there with him.

'Michael!' She buried her head against his chest, her tears wetting his shirt. 'I don't want to lose you!'

He wrapped his arms round her. 'I don't intend that you should.'

To her surprise she didn't need any more brandy. An unfamiliar need seemed to explode deep inside. Her blood hammered in her head. Their kisses were passionate and taken between great gasps of breath and words of love.

Unlike their wedding night, their clothes were discarded hastily, left in crumpled heaps on the floor. There was no pretty nightdress laid out and none was needed. Mary wanted to feel her husband's bare flesh against hers.

The bed sheets were cool against her back. His hands were sometimes rough and sometimes gentle and she welcomed each different kind of touch. She wanted him. She wanted him inside her. Her body was no longer under her control. It was his, just as his body was hers. There was surprisingly little pain, just a lingering feeling afterwards that it wouldn't be long before she wanted him again, that she never wanted him to leave her side.

After that first time they lay stroking each other's bodies.

'What was it really like?' she asked him.

'Wonderful!' He kissed her.

Mary laughed. 'That's not what I mean. I mean up there, flying over enemy territory?'

The beech trees at the edge of the churchyard creaked in the strong south-westerly wind. It had rained overnight and although grey clouds rolled across the sky like ghostly sheep, the rain held off though the grass was still damp.

Stan Sweet went down on one knee beside his wife's grave, pulling out weeds as he told her what was going on. 'I've had to do a bit of apologising of late. I got a bit down after our Charlie was killed and, well, I put my friendship with Bettina Hicks on hold, ignored her, in fact. I felt I didn't deserve to be happy once our Charlie was gone. Then everything changed. I found out that our Charlie had a son with that Jewish girl Gilda. You may recall I told you all about her, how her husband got executed, accused, so she said, of printing anti-fascist leaflets. Poor girl. Now she's gone, killed by the same people who killed her husband. They've been dropping bombs all over. She was in London and her house was bombed. Anyway, I think I've already told you much of this already, but I just had to say what a joy the baby has brought into my life. Our grandson!' He chuckled. 'Would you believe it? It's like having a ray of sun shining through after a very dark storm. New hope, I suppose, something special for the future. Life goes on and we must go on too.'

The whole family had breakfast together on the day Michael was scheduled to return to base.

Michael and Mary were sitting together directly opposite Ruby. What was more they couldn't seem to stop smiling and touching each other.

Ruby noticed the lingering looks, their fingers intertwining and Mary brushing her husband's hair back from his forehead. Something had changed – for the better – and she could guess what it was.

It appeared nobody had seen the change in the two of them except for Ruby.

'Right,' said Stan Sweet. 'Let's all go with you to the train station and give you a good send off.' He was in the process of making his way to the hallway when Ruby headed him off.

'No, Dad.' She said it quietly and firmly.

'No?' He eyed Ruby dubiously, puzzled until she whispered to him that his daughter and new son-in-law might want some time to be alone together. Nobody knew when Michael was likely to get more leave. They escorted Mike and Mary halfway to the station, then left them to walk on alone so they could share their goodbyes in private.

Although she was happy for her sister, Ruby also felt envious. They might have got off to a rocky start, but her sister had undoubtedly found the love of her life.

'All's well that ends well,' she whispered as she waved them goodbye along with the rest of her family plus Bettina Hicks.

Only Bettina, lately returned home from visiting her friend, heard what she'd said.

CHAPTER EIGHTEEN

The Sweets' home had changed for the better since the baby's arrival, and so had Stan. His world revolved around the smiling little chap who had dropped like a bomb into their lives.

'Nothing's too good for my grandson,' he'd declared loftily insisting that Charlie should have the best of everything and nothing second-hand. He had given in on the cot once used by his own children, seeing as it was already there on the premises and in good condition. He hadn't taken the wartime government's rules and regulations into account when it came to actually getting everything new.

Gilda, quite rightly, had used up the rations allocated to her as an expectant mother and purchased what was needed, including a pram, all of which had been destroyed on the night the bombers came. There was a scheme in existence for those who had lost their belongings in the blitz. It didn't apply to the grandparents who were taking the child in, after all they had not lost anything. Not that it worried Stan Sweet. As he never failed to remind everybody, they'd gained something very precious.

Mary and Ruby took turns with regard to cooking demonstrations and looking after the baby. Frances had also become a willing nanny to young Charlie, playing with the little fellow as he edged towards becoming a toddler. Life revolved around the little chap's needs, though the bakery carried on and so did Ruby's affair with Ivan Bronowski.

Mary wrote a letter to Mike every other day. Ruby had stopped looking for letters from John Smith, though every now and again his surly smile crept into her thoughts. Ivan helped her cope.

Three months after Charlie's arrival, just two days after his first birthday, the wicker hamper was filled. Yet another cooking demonstration was on the horizon and it was Ruby's turn. Everything was ready. All she had to do was wait for her driver – whoever that happened to be this morning.

'I just hope whoever it is, isn't late,' she grumbled. The last driver she'd had had got lost. 'A few more like that and I'll drive myself.'

When the shop bell jangled it came as something of a surprise to see that it was dead on nine o'clock. On time!

John Smith was standing on the doorstep. 'Reporting for duty.' He stood to attention and saluted stiffly as he might for an officer, certainly not for a woman about to deliver a talk on menu planning using basic ingredients.

'John! You're back.' She couldn't help sounding surprised. He'd hinted he might be, but also hinted he might ship out to seek more active service. Now he was back. She guessed it might not be for long.

Although the urge was strong, she resisted throwing her arms around his neck.

He didn't smile, but there, that was his way, a brittle shell hiding a humorous interior.

'There was nobody else available to drive you around, just in case you were wondering.'

'I wasn't wondering. Not really. Anyway, I thought you were off to where the war is really going on.'

'In time.'

'Goodness. What am I going to do without you?'

His grin widened. Although John had been her driver since the very first, she'd avoided studying his features to any great extent, only on a very perfunctory, need-to-know basis. Now she looked at him more closely. He had a bump in the middle of his nose as though it had been broken at one time. It looked hooked when viewed in profile. One side of his mouth was tilted upwards, the other down, almost as though he hadn't made up his mind whether to smile or scowl.

For the past few months since Brenda's departure, there had been a number of other drivers, all of them men who had moved on to more active service. The exception was Doreen who had been hospitalised with suspected appendicitis, which actually turned out to be a baby girl. Nobody knew who the father was and that seemed to include Doreen. Two female drivers, both of whom had fallen pregnant. Who would credit it?

Ruby hadn't seen John since her sister's wedding, which was also the day she'd met Ivan Bronowski – her very own RAF pilot.

'Well,' she said smartly, handing him the familiar wicker basket that had seen better days. Still, they soldiered on. 'We'd best make a start.'

It didn't wind him when she slammed the hamper against his chest. He just smiled knowingly and she found herself smiling back.

On their way out, Bettina Hicks begged a lift into Kingswood. 'I need to see my solicitor.'

She didn't elaborate as to why she was going to see him and nobody asked. When the conversation turned to young Charlie, John fell unusually silent.

Today Ruby's demonstration would be given from a dark green caravan provided by the Ministry of Food. It was a big square old thing located in Kingswood High Street, with a drop-down hatch held up by chains. It was lit by gas and boasted a decent-sized cooker, a sink and cupboard space. Originally she was supposed to have one for her sole use, but the Ministry had run out of funds.

'You have to share,' Andrew Sinclair had said to her. 'I'm so sorry. They're in short supply.'

'Hardly news,' grumbled Ruby. 'Everything's in short supply.'

It turned out she had to share it with eight other regions from Gloucester to Taunton. On the plus side the caravan was already in situ so they didn't have to tow it.

At first nobody took much notice of it, that was until the flap was down and Ruby shouted for their attention. Curious, a host of women out shopping – which consisted of queuing for even the basic necessities – gathered round, all glad of a diversion from the daily grind.

As usual Ruby began her talk by saying how British merchant seamen were doing a dangerous job, how she herself had lost a brother to enemy action.

'It's up to us to help them in their work. We have to leave space free on our ships for weapons with which we can defeat the enemy.'

Once that was over, once the crowd was on her side, she began talking food starting off with the Sunday joint.

'Depending on whether it's a joint of brisket, a breast of lamb or offal, a little imagination and you can make it go a long way while still providing a tasty meal.

'Beginning with brisket, which is a piece of beef within everyone's price range – depending on availability of course – roast in the oven in water rather than lard or any other

216

fat. It's simply not needed. In order to save gas or whatever other cooking fuel you use, place your vegetables around the joint rather than cooking them in separate pans on the top of the stove. Every little bit of gas you save means less coal having to be burned.

'Once your joint is done, remove it from the roasting tin and leave to rest on a suitable platter. Place your vegetables around the meat. Allow the juices left in the pan to cool, that's after you've taken some out to be mixed with cornflour to make gravy. The rest can be used to make stock for soup, but only after you've scraped the fat from the top. You'll find that fat forms a nice crust on water and is quite easy to scrape off. You can use the fat for making pastry.'

A buzz of approval went through the women gathered around the van.

'For those of you who queued for hours only to end up with a bullock's heart, my sincere commiseration: a heart-less task indeed!'

Ruby paused to allow for the expected titter of laughter. She wasn't disappointed. Those crowded around the van were a down-to-earth lot, the type of women capable of rustling up a meal from a few vegetables and a pound of pork bones. They'd managed all through the desolate thirties when the dole queues had been long and many had gone without food in order that their children didn't starve.

'I usually stuff mine,' said one woman. Although she had few teeth and wore a hat with a wilted feather, she spoke proudly, her chin held high.

Ruby nodded and agreed with her that was the way most people roasted a bullock's heart.

'However, with an eye on gas consumption yet again, how about slicing it up and mixing it with sliced onions and any bits of fatty bacon you might have? Or even getting hold of a few bacon bones from the grocer? Even the fatty bits some members of the family leave on the side of their plates can be used. Bacon keeps the offal moist and adds extra flavour. Finish off with seasoning and pour over some stock. That should keep it juicy . . .'

Out of the corner of her eye she saw John looking at her. In the past he'd stood to one side shaking his head and eyeing her as though she didn't have a clue what she was talking about. It wasn't the best time to analyse what change had occurred to make him look at her that way, the way that made her blush. When had it happened? Asking that question brought on a second one: why had he chosen to return to his position as driver to a home economist?

After taking a sip of cold water, she cleared her throat and went back to her talk, hauling her gaze away from John Smith and refocusing on the job in hand.

'And of course all offal can be minced and mixed with other more fatty meats. Offal is full of iron, so it's very good for you.

'Finally we come to my favourite bit. Cakes, pies and pastries. Everyone has a sweet tooth, and we all love a cream bun, a slice of fruit cake or a spicy pastry. My name is Ruby Sweet. I can't help but like sweet things!' The comment had the desired result: laughter followed by closer attention.

On the drive home John Smith purposely went to the front passenger door. She'd sat in the back in the early days of their acquaintance and had done the same when she'd had other drivers. John was different. Mrs Hicks wanting a lift into Kingswood had resulted in Bettina sliding gratefully into the back. Ruby had sat at the front. John had already placed the wicker basket on the back seat. She slid in next to him.

'So. How have you been getting on?'

'Fine.'

She didn't know how she knew, but there was something just a little bit different about his manner. He was holding something back.

Another long silence ensued.

She glanced at his profile. 'You didn't write.'

A shorter silence this time. 'Neither did you.'

'But you said . . .'

'I hardly thought you'd want a letter from me after you met the bozo from the RAF.'

'Bozo?'

'The Polish flier.'

'He is not a "bozo", as you put it.' She spat the words, she was that indignant.

He grunted in a disparaging manner that left her in no doubt that he held her flier in contempt.

'All right. Not a bozo. A charmer. Prince Charming in air force blue.'

'He is not!' Arms folded, face rigid, she turned her eyes to the passing hedgerows.

Silence reigned again. She presumed it would be that way all the way home, but Corporal John Smith had other plans. All of a sudden, he pulled in front of a farm gate where the earth was packed hard and no grass grew. He switched off the engine and pulled on the handbrake. 'Right. Let's talk.'

'Why?'

She turned to face him, her eyes blazing.

In a split second his arms were swiftly around her and she was devoured in the most voracious, passionate kiss, so intense that she was left breathless.

'Well!' Her chest heaved as she fought to catch her breath. What a kiss that was!

He nodded. 'That was good. Shall we do it again?'

He didn't wait for her answer, not that she was likely to protest. John Smith kissed her again. Again she was breathless, though not quite so breathless as with the first kiss.

'I want to take you out tonight.'

'I do have a boyfriend . . .'

He nodded. 'Yes. I know. The Polish pilot.'

A sullen look made both ends of his mouth turn down, but there was a determined look in his eyes. Usually they were bright blue, but today they seemed darker, as though the thoughts behind them were darker too.

'Ye . . . sss,' she said slowly. 'The Polish pilot.'

'Is it serious? Do you see him on a regular basis?'

'Whenever he can get leave. About every two weeks depending on . . .' She heard the evasive rambling in her voice and stopped. Why tell him? He was only her driver!

'Look, I don't think it's any of your business . . .'

She said it despite herself, despite the fact that she wanted him to kiss her again.

'Pilots are like sailors,' Johnnie proclaimed. 'A girl in every port, or as is the case with the boys in blue, a girl for every night of the week – or for every night when they're not flying . . .'

'Now look here!'

Suddenly she regretted those kisses, though only on account of not seeing Ivan the way Johnnie saw him. Ivan had told her he loved her, that she was the only girl he was seeing, despite days when she heard nothing from him.

'I'm being posted.'

His bald statement brought her up short. He was looking beyond her to the fields, the trees, the swooping birds diving after insects. 'I'm just filling in driving you around this week. I might as well tell you I'm off to fight this bloody war pretty damned soon.'

Ruby swallowed the angry comments she'd been about to make. His expression was vague, almost sad.

Suddenly she felt guilty that she'd been thinking of Ivan. 'Where are you going?' Somehow John seemed to matter more.

He looked at her then over her shoulder to the field beyond the farm gate. It was the end of September. The harvest had been brought in. Flocks of crows and other birds pecked and fluttered around the remaining stubble.

'Malaya. Singapore. The bastion of the Orient, they call it. Should be safe enough. Plenty far enough from Germany anyway.'

Despite his confident tone, her heart fluttered. The only thing she knew about Singapore was that it was on the other side of the world. 'It's a long way away.'

He shrugged. 'I have to go where they tell me to go. I applied for a posting and I got one.'

'But . . .' She'd been going to mention family, but remembered that John Smith didn't seem to have a family. She wondered whether John Smith was really the name his parents had given him or had been given by somebody else, an orphanage perhaps, a simple name, the most basic of names for a child with a basic beginning.

'So,' he said, turning to her suddenly, his expression intense and his blue eyes turned to grey. 'Will you come out with me tonight?'

Despite her involvement with Ivan, she agreed to go out with him. 'Though not tonight. It's my turn to look after Charlie. How about we go on a picnic tomorrow once the shop's shut?'

His eyes lightened and he managed a tight smile. 'Can I kiss you again?'

She nodded, presuming he meant tomorrow, but he didn't.

Yet again he took her by surprise, not just with the speed of his reaction but the intensity of that kiss, its sweetness, and the way she was instantly aroused.

It seemed natural to respond to him, to reflect his passion and not to protest when his hand slid on to one breast. Her own desire surprised her. John intrigued her like no other man had ever done, not even Ivan. He hadn't fallen easily for her charms: he'd needled her, he was exasperating, and totally, totally beguiling.

There was still Ivan to consider, of course, but he had slipped from her mind so easily. Anyway, he would never know any different.

John called for her the next day, dead on time. She'd already put a picnic together; a few white cabbage, carrot and chutney sandwiches and a small chocolate cake made with cocoa and the little bit of sugar she had left down in the cellar.

Thanks to the time of year, it was too damp to picnic in a field, so they compromised by taking their picnic down to the station where they could sit on a bench and watch the world – and the trains – go by. They wore warm coats.

'Do you like trains?' asked the stationmaster. That was after he'd eyed them up myopically, just in case they were strangers and working for the enemy. Recognising Ruby as being Stan Sweet's daughter went some way to dispelling his fears. On top of that the young man with her was in uniform, though of course that didn't mean anything. He narrowed one eye so that it was almost shut. Young Ruby had been a bit flighty in the past, but she was more responsible now. She ought to know the genuine article when she saw it.

'Enjoy your picnic,' he said to them, disappointed when

they failed to offer him a bite. The chocolate cake looked exceedingly good. 'Back to the bread and dripping sandwiches,' he muttered to himself as he made his way back to his office, no more than the size of a pantry cupboard, but his very own domain.

'I take it your brother-in-law's gone back to Scampton,' said Johnnie once he'd taken a generous slice of chocolate cake.

Ruby eyed him with mock disapproval. 'You're not supposed to broadcast where he's based. Careless talk costs lives. Haven't you read the pamphlets or seen the public notices at the cinema? Mr Hitler might be listening.'

She laughed and was surprised when he didn't laugh. Corporal John Smith looked to be in one of his serious moods.

There were two benches on the station, one beneath the canopy that served as a waiting room and the other two-thirds of the way along the platform. Both were empty. It seemed the only travellers that day were likely to be four hutches of rabbits and three of pigeons. In peacetime the pigeons would have been sent travelling by train, released at their destination to race back to their lofts. Now they were most likely being sent off for the table. Pigeon pie had become quite common in wartime whereas before it had been a delicacy reserved for a rich man's table.

'Will you write to me? When I'm in Singapore, will you write to me?'

His hands were clasped in front of him and his gaze fixed on the embankment opposite the platform.

She gave him a wry smile. He didn't smile back as she'd expected him to, but then she should have known better. When John Smith adopted a serious expression his eyes became intensely penetrating as though he were spearing her to the spot until she gave him an answer.

She decided to keep her voice light and cheerful. 'If you want me to. I'll even throw in a few recipes so you can impress your mates in the mess, cook them up a decent meal when they're far from home and their mum's cooking.'

'Don't toy with me.'

Her smile faltered. 'I'm not toying, I was merely suggesting . . .'

'Don't write to me unless you want to. I don't like being pitied. I don't want you to write because you feel sorry for me.'

'I'm happy to write to you.'

For a moment he stared at her silently. She assumed he was contemplating her sincerity. She meant it. Of course she did. While waiting for him to speak, she tossed a mental coin as to what his response might be. Heads he would smile, tails he would get huffy, get up and walk away.

It surprised her only momentarily that he did neither but sat with his elbows resting on his knees, his gaze returning to the barbed-wire fence separating the railway embankment on the other side of the tracks from a field of Jersey cows.

The wind blowing towards them brought the smell of manure and the rich peatiness of fertile earth from the field beyond the cow pasture.

The rich gold and russet of early September had faded to moss green and grey.

Ruby silently contemplated the scene. Soon all the leaves would be gone, and so would John Smith. John's silences could often be intimidating, just as they were now. Ruby found herself disliking, almost fearing, the length of this one. She wanted to go on talking, eating sandwiches and cake, drinking the elderberry wine her father had made last autumn.

It was usual with John to expect a terse, even a sarcastic response. She could cope with those. The silences were harder to endure.

'I've got nobody else to write to me,' he said suddenly. 'No family. I was brought up in an orphanage for bastards.'

She guessed he wanted her to be shocked, not at his background but because of the word he used. He wanted her to know the names he'd been called as a child and to share his bitterness. He wasn't to know that she'd already guessed.

'How about friends? Do you have friends?'

She guessed the answer even before it came.

'There's no point in making friends in an orphanage. People move on. Friends come and go.'

His jaw seemed to clam shut over the last sentence. She didn't need him to confirm it had happened to him on a number of occasions.

Ruby studied him as he maintained the same pose, studying his profile, the firmness of his jaw, the redness around his neck because his army issue collar was too tight. His shoulders were broad and when he was standing, they were laid-back and straight, a direct consequence of him having joined the army some time before the outbreak of war.

'You've no family at all?'

She tried not to say it too softly. John was not a man to be pitied. He was just lonely.

'No family.'

'No friends?'

'Only in the army. It was the best decision I've ever made. I made some good mates in the army, some of them from a similar background to me.'

She could tell by his tone that he wouldn't elaborate. It was enough that she knew where he stood and where she stood. There had been no loving family in his childhood, even though he'd once hinted that there was – a rough and ready family from the East End of London.

Ruby took a deep breath. 'I'd like to write to you.'

His gaze left her and returned to the fields beyond the barbed-wire fence. 'Only if you want to.'

'I said I did, didn't I? You should know me well enough by now to know that I mean what I say. I'm going to write to you.'

When he turned and looked at her, she fancied his features were less rigid. In fact, she discerned a look of relief in his eyes. Even gratitude, though God knows he wasn't likely to admit to that!

He nodded thoughtfully. 'I'd like that.'

Ruby smiled. 'Well, that's settled then. Would you like another sandwich?'

'No. But there's something else I'd like.'

She would have been disappointed if he hadn't kissed her again. Kissing him was such a natural thing, spontaneous, not forced. The kiss lasted until she was breathless, but still she found it hard to break away.

She pressed her hands against his chest so that a bigger gap opened up between them and tried not to think of what she wanted next, of suggesting that they go into that field opposite, away from the cows in the brush and the long grass, and make love there until it was time to go home.

Instead all she said was, 'That was nice.'

She fancied he was as breathless as she was. Even as surprised as she was. She had to remind herself that he was a man who had arrived with a chip on his shoulder and become a friend. That's what she kept telling herself, though the feel of his lips on hers still lingered; as sweet as wine, as soft as velvet. She found herself licking her lips as though she wanted to relive the sensation again and again.

She jerked her head towards the stile next to the cow pasture. 'There's still some grass in that field.'

He frowned at first, unsure of her meaning.

'Enough to lie down on. I have a blanket.'

He didn't need to say anything. She could see by the look in his eyes that he would follow her when she got up from the seat, and he did.

The stile was cramped between overgrown bushes. They'd had to cross the railway line to get to it, which was no doubt the reason why the hedges were overgrown. Great swathes of cow parsley snuggled for shelter close to the hawthorn hedge. Wheat grass, untouched by the plough, grew among it.

They lay the blanket on the ground close to the hedge and took their coats off before lying down. Tall heads of cow parsley and spear-headed grass formed a barrier between them and the field.

'We might get cold,' said Ruby, pulling her coat over her.

'It's not that cold.'

'It will be,' whispered Ruby as she unbuttoned her blouse.

Although they were not completely naked, it was enough to be half undressed, to feel at least some of their flesh meeting beneath the warmth of their coats.

Their lovemaking was spontaneous, sweet and extremely satisfying. When it was over, Ruby lay on her back watching the clouds roll by. It wasn't that she was inexperienced, but fear of pregnancy had always curbed her going so far as to make love. At the last moment she had considered what her father might say, how disappointed he would be. Perhaps it was because she was wary of men like Gareth Stead, or perhaps it was because Johnnie was unlike most of the men she knew, honest to a fault. Had she been reckless to give in now? What guarantee did she have that she wouldn't get pregnant? None at all, but somehow she knew beyond doubt that Corporal John Smith would not let her down.

'I wish we could capture moments in time, don't you?'

'Hmm,' he grunted. 'Now wouldn't that be something.'

'I think so. Then we could relive that moment over and over again. I think I would like that, wouldn't you?'

'You're right,' he said, pulling her back towards him. 'I can't be sure but I think I can feel a captured moment coming on. I'd better do it one more time – just to make sure.'

It was an hour later when they finally walked silently back to the bakery, both engrossed in their own thoughts. It was hard not to feel perplexed. She'd thought she was falling in love with Ivan, but perhaps she was not. She'd thought it would just be a picnic with a friend, but it had not. She'd also thought it was just a kiss, just a tumble between a man and a woman, making love in a field.

But you should fall in love with Ivan, she thought to herself. He'll be here. Johnnie is going back into battle, on the other side of the world.

It wasn't until they were halfway home that she realised they were holding hands. Confused by mixed thoughts and feelings, she swiftly disengaged, shoving both hands into her coat pockets. John looked disappointed.

'My hands are cold.' A pathetic excuse, but the only one she could come up with. What was happening to her? How come things happened so easily between them? When had such things started happening?

Once they were outside the shop they faced each other. John took hold of both her hands. His palms were warm around her cold fingers. 'You will write.'

He didn't ask as such. Neither did he plead. He sounded as though he were giving her a chance to change her mind.

'Of course I will.'

'Remember to tell me the latest recipes. Army food isn't all that special.'

She smiled. 'I will.'

'And mind how you drive.'

Ruby smiled and shook her head. She'd voiced her complaints about her drivers. He'd told her it was time to drive the car herself.

'I'll be fine. Shame I won't have an assistant any more. Still, if the Far East needs you . . .'

There was bound to be a goodbye kiss. When it came it was warm and along with the hug he gave her, quite memorable.

'Take care,' she said finally.

'Don't cry.'

'I'm not.'

He touched the corner of her eye with his finger and brought it away wet. She hadn't realised her eyes were that moist. She would miss him. Of course she would.

She was still thinking of that kiss on Saturday night when she was getting ready to go to yet another dance with Ivan. On checking the mirror, she admired again how Mary's dress fitted her perfectly, clinging provocatively in all the right places. Her eyes were bright, her hair brushed and bouncing around her shoulders. Her cheeks were flushed.

Tentatively she touched the mole on her face.

Ivan had referred to her mole as a beauty spot and she'd loved him for it. Funny, but John had never mentioned her mole. It was her he'd noticed above everything else. He saw the woman behind the face, the human being who interested him.

She touched her lips. She could still feel John's mouth

on hers. She'd expected him to kiss her but certainly hadn't envisaged ending up in a field on an October day. The picnic had turned into something quite special.

She'd miss him, not just the surly countenance that hid the gentle man beneath, but his sarcastic wit, his protests when she dragged him up to assist in her baking demonstrations. On the whole he was the most honest man she'd ever met – a bit like her father, in fact.

Sighing she turned away from the mirror and reached for her coat. She took a deep breath. The smell of face powder and the rose water she'd made herself from Charlie's rose bush was strong.

Downstairs the kitchen was warm and cosy. Her father was sitting in his favourite chair at the side of the fireplace. 'Looks like we're going to have the first frost of the year tonight,' said her father without looking up from his newspaper.

'Never mind. I've got my coat.'

Stan Sweet looked up at his daughter. 'You look very nice, love. I take it your Polish flier is going to pick you up on his motorbike.'

'He is.' She waved a headscarf at him. 'Hopefully I won't look as though I've been dragged through a hedge backwards when we get there.'

'Good for you, girl. Give the young man my regards.'

Her father went back to reading his paper.

'I will,' Ruby said softly, so softly it didn't appear her father had heard her.

The sound of a motorcycle heralded Ivan's arrival and Ruby's heart leapt with joy. Forget about John, she told herself. It was Ivan she was going to the dance with tonight. It was Ivan she was in love with. Wasn't it?

'By the way. Corporal Smith left that here.' Her father

nodded to a brown paper bag on the mantelpiece. 'He said it's a going-away present. I understand he's been posted.'

'Yes. He has.'

Ruby frowned as she reached for the paper bag. It came as a complete surprise. John hadn't mentioned leaving her a present.

On opening it she found a notepad and envelopes. She smiled. John was holding her to her word. Not that she minded. She'd meant what she'd said. She would write to him.

The night air stung her face with its crispness. Ivan and his motorcycle were only barely discernible in the darkness. Without giving her time to swing her leg over the seat, he hugged and kissed her.

'My goodness,' she said once she'd managed to grab a breath. 'Being hugged by you is like being hugged by a bear!'

'We have bears in my country,' he laughed.

'Not all of them are still in Poland,' she responded, giving him a playful push on his shoulders. 'Now. Are you taking me to that dance or what?'

'Of course I am. You look wonderful,' he said to her. That was before she put on her headscarf.

'I won't do without this,' she said laughingly. 'Come on then, Prince Charming. Take Cinderella to the ball and don't spare the horses.'

The ride to the dance at the base was a whirlwind of frosty air that reddened her cheeks and stung her eyes. By the time they got there she was holding on to Ivan with one hand and her headscarf with the other.

'Your hair looks wild,' he said to her once she had both feet back on the ground.

'Like a witch?'

He shook his head. 'No. Or perhaps, yes. An enchantress. Is that what you call them?'

Ruby said that she wasn't sure and anyway, once she'd visited the ladies' powder room, a comb and a lick of lipstick would make her presentable again.

She wasn't exactly unaware or immune to the admiring glances she received as she joined him. Attracting men had never been very difficult; it was sorting out the good guys from the bad eggs that she'd found more difficult; the horrendous Gareth Stead was the worst of them, but then, that was at the beginning of the war. A lot of water had flowed beneath the bridge since then.

'You look wonderful,' Ivan said to her again, his lips brushing against her ear. 'See? All my friends adore you too.'

She laughed but made no comment. She was the belle of the ball in a dress that wasn't home-made, her hair glossy, her eyes gleaming with excitement. She felt as though she were floating on air. That was before one of Ivan's friends, a bull-necked man with a pockmarked face, made a comment that, although it was in Polish, Ruby instinctively felt was derogatory.

Ivan caught hold of her arm and guided her swiftly away. Catching the hint of a scowl on his face, she asked him what had been said. Just a beat of a pause, but enough to set alarm bells ringing before he told her the man had commented how beautiful she was. He said it laughingly, but with an edge that Ruby didn't like. Whatever it was the man had said, Ivan hadn't liked either. It couldn't have been that she was beautiful. She suspected Ivan was lying to shield her feelings.

She watched Ivan closely that night. Purely judging him on first impression, John Smith had said he was a charmer. Perhaps he was. Tonight he absolutely doted on her, fetching her something to drink, something to eat and absolutely refusing to allow any of his colleagues to dance with her.

'You are mine and mine alone.'

His words were soft in her ear, his arm firmly holding her to his side. Every dance she danced with him. He wouldn't have it any other way.

Telling herself that John must be mistaken, she pushed aside her unease and told herself she was mistaken about the Polish airman's tone of voice. Ivan was the sort of man who could make her forget anything. He treated her like a princess; as though there was no other woman in the room, in the world, who was as beguiling as she was.

They danced all night, their bodies tight against each other as they glided through the waltz, laughing and giggling when they attempted the latest American craze, the jitterbug.

It was halfway through a waltz that he whispered in her ear about going outside. Ruby felt herself tingling all over. They'd already had some pretty hot moments on previous dates. His loins pressing against her, she'd felt his hardness. She counted it lucky that the waltz called for some pretty close contact.

Something in her responded even though she knew what the consequences might be, besides which John was still there in her mind, that magic afternoon among the cow parsley.

'You've danced me off my feet,' she said to him as he guided her towards the set of double doors that led on to a concreted area at the rear of the hanger where the dance was being held. 'I need to cool down.'

Thanks to the blackout the outside area was in total darkness. Shrouded in camouflage at the edge of the runway, fighter aircraft vaguely resembled hump-backed monsters, even their propellers hidden.

Somewhere in the distance an owl hooted. She was aware of whispers and muted gasps close by, couples in clinches hidden by darkness. To her right she saw the red gleam of a lit cigarette, the smell of tobacco on the night air.

She also smelled Ivan, felt his closeness, his hand firmly cupping her elbow as he guided her to a private place where they would be hidden by darkness.

'Step carefully,' he whispered. 'I won't let you fall.'

She didn't know where they were going, but was aware they weren't too far from the doors they'd come out of. She knew what he had in mind. At the beginning of this week she might have considered giving in, but not now. She had to get her feelings in some sort of order. She'd thought she loved Ivan, but following John's visit, she wasn't quite so sure.

They kissed passionately, his hands roaming down her back until they were cupping her buttocks as firmly as he'd previously cupped her elbow. He was nothing if not persistent.

'I want you.'

Shielded by darkness, his hands travelled over her, firstly covering a breast, then sliding above her stocking tops. Perhaps she might have gone further if she hadn't already lost her virginity to Johnnie Smith so recently, persuaded perhaps by him leaving and the smell of damp grass.

She pushed him away. 'I don't want to get pregnant.'

'Ruby. Sweet Ruby.'

'Ruby Sweet actually,' she snarled, pushing him away for a second time.

'My precious Ruby . . .'

His lips clamped to hers. His hands began to ramble over her body.

'No.' Her voice was hushed and although she said no, her body was screaming otherwise. She wanted him, but wasn't sure it was he whom she really wanted. John was still in her mind. If she'd been drinking she might have weakened, but she hadn't been drinking. She'd kept her wits about her and was glad.

'Ruby! Please . . . you have to understand—'

She put her hand over his mouth. 'Don't say it.'

'Don't say what?'

'You know what,' she whispered back, desperately trying to be firm with him while keeping her voice down.

'No,' he whispered. 'No, no, no. I do not know.'

Each word was delivered on his breath directly into her ear or against her cheek while his fingers trailed through her hair, smoothing it back from her face.

Ruby kept her hands pressed against his chest and the soft wool of his RAF tunic.

'You were going to say that you might be dead tomorrow, almost as though it's my duty to give into you. But I'm sorry, Ivan, I can't. I won't.'

'Then you cannot love me.'

He sounded both dejected and angry. It did make her feel guilty and perhaps she might have gone ahead, but he'd chosen his time badly.

'It's the time of the month,' she murmured as an excuse he might accept

She felt him tense. 'Are you sure?'

'Of course I'm sure.'

Resting his chin on her shoulder he made a sound that was vaguely like crying.

'Oh my darling Ruby. I need you so much. Soon. We must make love soon, my darling Ruby. Soon before time marches on and we are far away from each other. I need to know you will be waiting for me. Whatever happens I need to know that.'

The words seemed to fall on to her shoulder and from there find the pathway to her heart. He loved her! Ivan Bronowski loved her. He really meant what he said. She couldn't get John Smith out of her mind, but he was gone. He might never come back. Ivan was here.

If she let down her guard or if she truly wanted to, she would give in to Ivan Bronowski. It was just a question of when.

CHAPTER NINETEEN

December 1941

By Monday morning there were only two topics of conversation among the women coming in to buy bread.

The first was that the Japanese had bombed an American Naval Base at a place called Pearl Harbor. Not everyone was quite sure where it was until Frances, always top of the class in geography, informed them it was in Hawaii which in turn was in the Pacific. The Americans had entered the war.

The other topic of interest was that Miriam Powell, who had been putting on weight consistently enough to convince gossips she was in the family way, now didn't look that way at all. In fact somebody commented that she looked like a scarecrow.

'And a bit mad,' that same person added.

Frances helped Mary to serve the customers, who were taking longer than usual to complete their purchases.

'I reckon she's miscarried,' one of their regular customers exclaimed to another.

'Do we know who the father is?'

'The vicar – sorry – the Methodist vicar. That young man with the round face and the cheeky laugh. The one who looked like Mickey Rooney with acne.'

'So where is he?'

'Gone. I heard from a cousin of mine who attends the mission in Hanham that he's enrolled as an army padre.'

'She might not have been in the family way. Perhaps it was just fat.'

There were loud chuckles at this remark.

'Yeah, perhaps it was too much bread,' Mrs Telford, the village gossip remarked with a knowing nod of her head. 'Mark my words, that girl had a bun in the oven.'

More chuckles.

'Then where's the proof of the pudding?'

'You mean where's the bun that was in the oven,' said somebody else.

Yet more laughter before everyone agreed that if Miriam Powell had been pregnant, there would have been a baby by now.

It was remarked that she hadn't been away to have it as girls did if they were led astray. She had been seen around the village, serving in the shop and attending various religious services with her formidable mother, though there was a gap of a few days when the shop was closed, a note pinned on to the door that they'd gone to visit Miriam's grandmother, Ada Perkins, in the Forest of Dean.

Mary smiled sadly to herself. The puzzle would remain a topic of conversation in the village for a long time. Poor Miriam. She'd had a thing about Mary's brother, Charlie at one time, not that Charlie had been interested. She recalled finding slips of paper with prayers for Charlie's safety written on them. She'd watched Miriam from her bedroom window, surprised to see her creeping into their backyard and stuffing the prayers into a gap in a crumbling brick wall.

At first she'd thought the prayers were to the Virgin Mary.

It turned out that they were actually written to some pagan deity that nobody this side of the River Severn knew anything of. But Frances had known. Frances who had been evacuated to the Forest of Dean for a while with Miriam's grandmother, Ada Perkins. It was there Frances had seen people posting notes into the hollows of old trees, prayers to a pagan goddess of the forest.

'One step at a time.'

Parking the pushchair at the gate, Stan Sweet had taken his grandson into his arms and took him into the churchyard. On deciding the long grass looked a grand place to explore, young Charlie kicked his legs and made demanding noises.

'All right, my boy,' said Stan recognising what he wanted. 'You want to walk.'

Charlie had taken his first steps and now was keen to try at every opportunity with varying degrees of success. Stan clutched the plump little hand in his as Charlie tottered forward into one step after another before landing on his bottom. Undeterred, up he got, clinging to his grandfather's hand as he fought to regain his balance.

Bit by bit, the distance along the path covered partly by a tottering walk and partly being carried, they finally came to the grave of Sarah Sweet.

It wasn't the first time Stan had brought Charlie's boy to visit his grandmother's grave though on previous occasions he had remained in his pram or pushchair, either asleep or eyeing his surroundings, especially the birds and the butterflies that frequented a nearby buddleia.

After tottering for a few steps, Charlie once again landed on his bottom. Entranced by Michaelmas daisies nodding at the side of the headstone, he sat there plucking at them, chuckling in triumph when he finally managed to pick one.

Content that his grandson was enjoying himself, Stan took off his hat and got down on one knee.

'Here again, Sarah. As you can see our Charlie is growing fast. What's more he's starting to walk already. Isn't that marvellous?'

Stan beamed. It was true. His female customers, and Bettina Hicks, had all confirmed that he was a very forward baby. He'd ignored the advice of one customer who insisted that if a baby walked too early it would end up bow legged. This was his grandson, Charlie, and he would grow up to be the handsomest man alive!

'I have to tell you, Sarah, that the Yanks have entered the war. One of their bases was attacked by the Japanese. They weren't best pleased, I can tell you! So they're in the war now too. I only hope this means a quicker end to things. Nobody wants this war spreading and dragging on. What was it we were promised back in 1914 – it would be over by Christmas? Well, we were promised that this time too . . .'

Stan looked up as a sound came to him, carried on a breeze that was blowing his way. It was like crying – wailing, more like. The only sound he'd heard up until this moment had been the cawing of crows from the tall beech trees shielding the church from the slope and the lane.

After preventing his grandson from eating a particularly large dock leaf, he gathered him up into his arms and looked over to where withered grass rustled and rattled against the stone wall. All the rest of the grass in the churchyard had been cut at the end of October. The long grass at the edge of the churchyard remained, a place where slow worms lurked and stoats burrowed beneath the wall.

Somebody was crouched over, only their head and shoulders visible, their attention absorbed in whatever lay in front of them. Whoever it was seemed suddenly to become aware of his presence, stiffening at first before popping up like a Jack in the Box. He almost laughed, until he saw it was Miriam Powell, back from the Forest of Dean.

He held up his hand in acknowledgement more so than a wave. 'Miriam!'

Her face was pale as death in contrast to her black coat. Always black, he thought. A young girl like her. It just isn't right.

He'd obviously taken her by surprise. She looked scared. 'Miriam. Are you all right, love?'

She gave no sign that she'd heard him, though she'd definitely seen him. Her face was as pale and still as a plaster saint, her hooded eyes fixed on Charlie.

'Poor girl,' whispered Stan. He'd always felt sorry for the girl, having a mother like Gertrude Powell. Not that it was any of his business and Mrs Powell had always been friendly enough, or at least neighbourly.

As for Miriam, well, she had always been kind to Charlie when he was in the shop, kicking his legs in his pushchair, enjoying all the attention he received from the customers. Normally she merely smiled at him, tickling him under the chin, running her fingers over the backs of his hands. But she'd never spoken to him. Not a word. Not directly to the baby, just stared at him with round, adoring eyes.

'She makes the same comment every time she leaves,' Mary had told him. 'He's Charlie reborn. That's what she always says. He's Charlie reborn.'

'Deacon told me that people can get reborn as rabbits or deer,' Frances had added.

'Better not eat them then.' Ruby grinned as she said it.

Frances had tossed her head. 'I don't believe silly things like that. I'm not a child. I was just saying. That's all.'

Now in the cemetery, Stan was perplexed, not sure quite what to do. 'I'm going back home, but if you want me to see you back to the shop—' he called.

'No!'

Suddenly she was running out of the long grass, weaving between the gravestones and heading for the far gate that led over a stile and in entirely the wrong direction for her mother's shop.

Stan stared at the space she'd occupied, amazed at how quickly she'd disappeared.

'Well, I'll be blowed!' He turned to look at his grandson's chubby face. The little lad was engrossed in crushing the head of a Michaelmas daisy between finger and thumb. 'One thing you'll learn as you get older, little man, is that women can be funny beasts. But I expect you already know that, don't you.'

It was two weeks before Christmas when Stan Sweet picked up the post from off the doormat and took it through into the kitchen where the family was having breakfast.

'Well, look at you,' Ruby declared to her nephew. Charlie's face was smeared with porridge. Most of it Ruby had fed him but, being a determined child, Charlie had folded his chubby fingers around the spoon and attempted to feed himself. Unfortunately his sense of coordination was such that he was having trouble getting the spoon into his mouth.

Mary laughed. 'He's growing up so quickly, though I think we still have a year or so to wait before his table manners improve.'

Believing his grandson to be the most advanced baby ever born, Stan Sweet leapt to his defence. 'Not that long. He's a very forward baby is our Charlie. Not many babies started walking when they were only ten months old. Our Charlie did.'

Ruby and Mary exchanged smiles. They were used to their father's pride in his grandson grabbing every opportunity to praise the little boy. They never contradicted him. Charlie had been the miracle that had changed their father's life, theirs too.

'Besides which he's a toddler, not a baby. He can toddle. Walk. He's a growing boy,' Stan added, his face glowing with pride.

The twins hid their smiles. They knew very well that their father was totally besotted with his grandson.

After wiping Charlie's hands and face, Frances unstrapped the little boy from his high chair. She also offered to change him before taking him for a walk in his pushchair.

Mary and Ruby, grateful to their cousin, turned to the letters addressed to them. Mary recognised Mike's handwriting and the official paper. The letter Ruby had been sent was on similar paper; it had to be from John Smith.

Mary took a deep breath before reading her letter. She was missing Mike dreadfully, especially having him in bed beside her. They'd made a new start and things could only get better. Things had most definitely changed in that department. The thin paper crackled which in turn seemed to set her fingers tingling.

Darling Mary, Mary, my darling . . .

She smiled at the repetition, which proved he was missing her as much as she was missing him.

He went on to describe how the sunlight lit up the rooms of Woodbridge Cottage, of flying over its thatched roof, imagining them living there, eating breakfast together, sharing a bed more often than they did at present.

Mary broke into a smile. Since his last leave she too had

often thought the same. She'd gone from lying beside him stiff as a wooden plank to a creature of longing, her body responding to his. However, there was still this fixation of his about the cottage. Much as she wanted to, how could she leave her father and family at a time like this? There was the bakery, the baking demonstrations, not to mention her father was getting older and now there was Charlie. She reminded herself that Mike had suggested the baby live with them. They could adopt him. But she knew her father would be heartbroken if Charlie was taken away from him. She couldn't do it. She had to think. She had to sort something out.

Her expression stiffened as she reread the paragraph relating to the cottage offered to them by Mike's friend. She didn't know what to do.

Stan Sweet noticed the consternation on his daughter's face while pretending to peruse yet more directives from the Ministry of Food. She didn't see his smile of satisfaction, his gratefulness that his daughters were at home, though still doing their bit for the war effort.

She caught his smile when she looked up. 'Everything all right with our Mike?'

'He's fine,' Mary said quickly.

Stan Sweet wasn't fooled. His daughter's response was a little too curt for his liking. Something was wrong. Not that she'd tell him unless he asked and he wasn't going to do that. His daughter was a grown woman and a married one at that.

Ruby laughed at something in her letter. 'John's waiting for the troop ship to leave. He's not saying in so many words where he's going, only that he hopes to drink a gin sling at the end of it. He'll be halfway there by now. This was posted just before his ship sailed.'

Mary took advantage of Ruby's interruption. 'Isn't a gin sling something to do with Singapore?'

Ruby grinned. 'I think so. I heard it mentioned in that film with Sydney Greenstreet. That's our Corporal Smith for you! A man who knows how to flout orders without appearing to. Anyway, he said that's where he thought he was going. How stupid. First he was free to tell me where he was going, and now he's not allowed to put it in writing. Ludicrous!'

'What on earth's the difference between telling us and putting it in writing,' asked Mary.

'In case it gets intercepted,' said Stan. That to him seemed the most logical answer.

Ruby laughed again. 'Listen to this. "*Can you send me a thousand and one ways to make a meal with bully beef? Rice might be one ingredient you'd care to consider.*"'

Just like her sister, she omitted to read out the last paragraph of her letter. It was all about getting together after the war was over.

'*I'm missing you.*'

Ruby read the last words again and again.

Funnily enough, I'm missing you too, you awkward, cantankerous . . . She smiled. John Smith always managed to stir up her feelings and being far away from each other didn't seem to have made much difference. Every time she thought of his caustic remarks, his reluctance when she'd first dragged him into assisting her with her demonstrations, a smile crept on to her lips.

He knew about Ivan, had warned her against him, but she was having fun. John was far away, and she could see herself falling for Ivan. The fact was she was torn between the two of them. Only time would tell which one of them would win through. John was on the other side of the world;

Ivan was on the doorstep. Besides, she was missing the passion they'd shared and Ivan was putting on the pressure for her to give in. Was the fact that she was deliberating proof that she had stronger feelings for John than her Polish pilot, despite the fact he was so far away?

'Is John well?'

Ruby looked up from the letter, her eyes meeting those of her father. 'He seems to be. At least he's a long way from Germany.'

Stan Sweet turned his attention to Frances who was guiding Charlie's arms into his jacket. 'I'm off to Powells',' she said brightly as she tied the strings of his knitted cap beneath his chin. 'We're nearly out of cod liver oil.'

Charlie's happy little face creased and he began to cry.

'He knows the words,' Frances said. 'He's beginning to know a lot of words. He doesn't like cod liver oil.'

'Never you mind, my boy,' he said, cupping Charlie's chin in his hand. 'He doesn't have to have it, does he?'

'Yes. It's good for him,' said Mary. 'We can mix it with jam.'

Ruby tickled the little boy's chin. 'Never mind, Charlie. Your auntie Mary will give you a spoonful of jam afterwards.'

Charlie retrieved his curled bottom lip and flashed his two front teeth in a gummy smile. It was followed by a happy chuckle.

'That child understands too much, Dad,' said Ruby. 'What do you say to him when you take him to see Mum?'

'Just a few pearls of wisdom,' Stan replied. 'Like how to cope in a world increasingly ruled by women!'

He shoved the pile of official pamphlets to one side. His thoughts went back to the day he'd seen Miriam – and heard Miriam – crying in St Anne's graveyard. What was that all about? He hadn't mentioned it to anyone. There was enough gossip going around the village as it was. Miriam deserved some time to herself and if it happened to be in St Anne's graveyard, then so be it.

CHAPTER TWENTY

'Hey! Sweetie!'

Frances knew very well that Paul Martin had seen her turn down into Court Road on her way to Powells' shop but had pretended she hadn't. Paul brought a flush to her face, though not such an intense flush as Deacon, the boy she had met when living with Ada Perkins in the Forest of Dean. She had turned fourteen, and having left school she was now too old to be evacuated under the children's scheme, but she had promised herself to go back there for a visit and Uncle Stan said she could once he had enough petrol coupons.

Frances slowed so Paul could catch up with her.

'You coming to the Sunday School ramble? We're walking to Lansdown.' He sounded desperate for her to say yes.

Frances kept her chin up and her eyes straight ahead. She considered herself too old to go on rambles with the Sunday School. 'No. I don't think so. It's just for kids, isn't it?'

Paul latched on to her mood and matched his own to suit. 'Yeah. Just for kids. That's why I'm not going either.'

Frances knew he was lying. He didn't want to be thought of as a kid.

'How about the Christmas party? We'll have jelly and blancmange and Mum's saving some cream from Fat Polly.

Fat Polly always gives creamier milk than any of our other cows so the milk people won't notice there's a pint or two short here and there. And my brother's got a gramophone. We can dance.'

Frances sighed. 'Of course I'm coming to the Christmas party. Ruby's made a cake. A sponge. She used dried egg to make it. Mary's made a Christmas crumb cake. It's got nuts and fruit in it.'

'Yummy. Bags me a piece.'

Frances was under no illusion that Paul didn't have a clue what a Christmas crumb cake was. Basically the Sweets had enough fruitcake ingredients to make one cake and that was for the family to consume at Christmas. All baking ingredients were in short supply but Mary had enlisted the help of a few other women whose children were looking forward to the Sunday School Christmas party. Without much persuasion they'd all scrimped and saved enough ingredients from their rations to make a Victoria sponge, but that wasn't going to provide enough cake for all the kids in the village.

The idea for the Christmas crumb cake had been Ruby's. The main ingredient, rather than flour, was stale cake and breadcrumbs. Frances had watched as Ruby had wetted the crumbs, most of which had been gathered from the bread baskets that lined the shelves, some from the counter, some from the stale end of a loaf or any stale cakes they had left over. The rest of the crumbs came from stale crusts. Nobody dared waste crusts nowadays. It was rumoured that inspectors from the Ministry of Food came round in the middle of the night to inspect the bins. There had been reports in the newspapers that those who wasted food were fined.

The Sweets were not ones for wasting food and were creative

in their use of leftovers. After all, the Sweet sisters gave lectures on how to make the best use of food.

'This is a bit experimental, but I'm sure it will work. What I need you to do is to write the ingredients down,' Ruby had said to her.

Frances had studiously found a pencil and paper.

'Right,' said Ruby. 'A pound of breadcrumbs – more if possible. A pound and a half might be better. No. Wait. Seeing as we're making this for the Sunday School kids, let's say two pounds of crumbs.'

'That's a lot of crumbs,' Frances had remarked.

Ruby had agreed with her and decided to settle on getting as many crumbs as possible.

'Mix with three tablespoonfuls of sugar. Two ounces – no – four ounces of fat. Any fat.'

Frances had duly written the instructions down while wishing they could find enough butter to make the cake – not likely, of course. Butter was rationed and when a joint was roasted or meat fried – even bacon and sausages at breakfast time – the fat, once cooled, was collected and used in baking. It didn't matter whether the baked dish was sweet or savoury, fat was fat and always made full use of.

'Nuts. I think we have enough hazelnuts left over from the ones we gathered in the autumn to crush and mix with the mixture. I've also got some dried blackberries. Luckily for us they were quite sweet this year.'

'And treacle,' Frances had suggested.

Ruby had stopped stirring the mixture while she considered the rightness of her cousin's suggestion.

'I was thinking honey, but perhaps you're right. A good dollop of treacle. That should make it sweet enough.'

And so Ruby's Christmas crumb cake was created.

'You'll love it,' Frances stated in a superior voice. Of

course she wouldn't be divulging the ingredients. They were a secret between her and her cousin Ruby, a person she considered to be the greatest cake and pastry maker in the world. Along with Mary, of course. Mary was a super baker too and her cakes were mouth-wateringly good.

Paul gave Charlie a little wave. 'Hello, Charlie.'

Charlie looked at him with a puzzled expression on his face.

'He's not all that friendly.'

'Of course he's not. He doesn't know you,' remarked Frances with an air of self-assured tolerance.

'If you didn't have him with you, I could show you the piece of bomb shrapnel my cousin Eddie gave me. He got it in Bristol. That's where he lives. A bomb fell on a house in his street. Everyone plays on the bombsite – not me, of course. It's just for kids. Still, it's a great place for making dens like when I was a kid. Do you want to see my shrapnel?'

Frances endured a sudden conflict between the child she had once been and the adolescent in waiting. A piece of real shrapnel harvested from a genuine bombsite had an almost magical connotation about it. Paul was quite tempting too; in fact, boys were becoming more interesting all the time.

'Is it at your house?'

'The den. The one we call the Dingle. Down in the Pit. I know I'm not a kid, but it's a good place to hide if the Jerries ever invade.'

It amused Frances to hear Paul trying to be a man one minute and sliding back into being a boy the next. It didn't occur to her that she was doing the same thing.

The Pit was a copse of young willows and birch down the bottom of the hill next to the brook. It was where the boys made dens in the summer, some of them in the centre of thick bramble bushes well hidden from view.

Frances was sorely tempted. The fact was that if she collected the cod liver oil and then took Charlie back home, the twins or her uncle Stan would find her something to do. What was to stop her taking Charlie with her? He'd love it!

'I'd like to see it, but I've got to get Charlie's cod liver oil first. Can you wait out here and look after him while I do that?'

Paul screwed up his face and looked as though he were considering the matter, which wasn't really the case at all. He liked Frances and wanted to show her his most treasured possessions. And the den was the ideal place to take a girl when you wanted to be alone with her. Nobody could call him sissy and anyway, most of the other boys who used the Dingle were at school. Nobody would know. Nobody would see him kiss her and that is what he very much wanted to do. He reckoned he was ready and it excited him. It also scared him. In the meantime he was out to impress her.

'I'll wait.'

Paul beamed with satisfaction as the shop door clanged shut behind her. His stomach felt as though it were tied into knots. He'd never kissed a girl before – not in the way he wanted to kiss Frances, the way he'd seen his sister kissing her soldier boyfriends. Still, he'd started work and was a man now. Kissing a girl – Frances in particular – would make him more of a man.

He looked down at his long trousers and wondered if she'd noticed them. No more short trousers and long grey socks for him! No more grubby knees either.

Absorbed in thoughts of Frances, he didn't at first notice Charlie helping himself to a carrot, the brightest of vegetables on the display to the side of the shop door.

'Charlie. That's stealing,' he hissed once he had noticed.

When he tried to take it from the baby's tightly clenched fist, Charlie began to cry.

'No. Don't cry,' Paul whispered, glancing towards the door in case Frances had heard; if she had, it would ruin everything.

Preferring to placate Charlie rather than have Frances angry with him, Paul let go the carrot and Charlie stopped his yelling. If Charlie wanted to steal a carrot, that was fine by him. The last thing he wanted was for Frances to think he'd hurt the child in some way. He certainly wouldn't get a kiss if that happened.

'All right, little 'un. All right. It won't be missed.'

Charlie chuckled before shoving the carrot into his mouth, his sparkling white incisors biting cheerfully into the bright orange vegetable even though it still had a crusting of dirt.

Paul went back to his plans for getting Frances alone and kissing her. He reckoned mentioning the shrapnel was a great idea. Everyone was interested in seeing bits of metal that had exploded from bomb casings and Frances was no exception. She'd be impressed; at least he hoped she would. But what if she wasn't?

The knot in his stomach tightened. What would he do if she laughed in his face and told him only little boys thought shrapnel was interesting?

Focusing on the prospect of Frances ridiculing him before he had chance to kiss her, brought on a severe case of cold feet. Never mind the shrapnel; kissing suddenly became as frightening as facing a whole battalion of enemy troops. Worse still, it also brought back memories of Sunday teatimes with his father's sisters, spinsters one and all. His aunts used to coo over him, kissing him and ruffling his hair. He could still feel their papery lips on his cheek, their spidery fingers in his hair.

'Yuk!' He shook his head in an attempt to dislodge the memory of those cold lips and skinny fingers. The memory refused to shift and because of that the whole idea of kissing Frances was no longer palatable. It wasn't so much that his feet were cold, he was cold all over. He no longer wanted to kiss her or attempt any of the other things that kissing led to. He knew this from watching his sister when she and her boyfriend thought they were all alone. He was growing up and figured he had to attempt those things too; it was expected of him. And anyway, it excited him.

He'd even been looking forward to those things beyond kissing, those things that you had to suggest after using sweet words. His sister went all soft and silly after Percy, the name of her latest boyfriend, whispered sweet nothings in her ear when he thought nobody was looking.

It was no good. He'd initially wanted to try all those things, but didn't now. The idea had excited him, but he no longer felt the urge to ask her to show him her knickers or unbutton her blouse, feel her chest to see if her boobies were beginning to grow. He'd learned all this stuff from the men he worked with, men in reserved occupations. They talked about 'it' all the time: how far they'd got, how they lied to girls, telling them they were off to war and might never come back. Anything to persuade them to do all the things he dreamed about at night that made his bed damp in the morning.

When I'm called up, I can say things like that too, thought Paul. In the meantime he just wasn't up to the job. He couldn't stay.

'You stay there, Charlie,' he said. As if the baby was likely to go anywhere. He was strapped into his pushchair.

A quick glance at the shop and he was gone.

Charlie didn't notice him go. Charlie was absorbed in

chewing on his carrot. It wasn't until he was lifted from his pushchair by a pair of strong arms that he became aware that something had changed. The new person smiled and he smiled back before his sharp little teeth bit once more into the carrot. As long as he had that he was quite happy.

Inside the shop, Mrs Powell was heaving a big box up on to the counter. 'It's only just come. It came by van today. The district nurse couldn't carry it all. I haven't opened it yet. You'll have to wait.'

Mrs Powell delivered short sentences in a flat monotone. She never smiled and nothing she did was done gladly. It was almost as though customers were supposed to give her good service, speak to her politely without her having to treat them well at all. She wasn't at all like her mother, Ada Perkins, a woman Frances had grown very fond of.

'I need scissors to get this undone,' Mrs Powell declared before disappearing into the back of the shop.

Frances fidgeted. She was looking forward to seeing Paul's piece of shrapnel and perhaps being alone with him for a time in his den. She wasn't fooled by him suggesting he was going to show her a piece of shrapnel, in fact she was more than a little excited as to what he really had in mind. Charlie could come too, of course. The entrances to dens were kept small in order to keep adults out. Charlie would have no trouble crawling in – in fact he could probably walk right in – or toddle, at least.

Growing more and more impatient, she tapped the countertop with her fingers, her gaze fixed on the door Mrs Powell had gone through. Surely it didn't take that long to find a pair of scissors? In the end, she grew resigned to waiting. She turned slowly round until her back was against the counter and her elbows resting on it.

The shop was small and dark, the only light courtesy of

255

a bare bulb above her head. The shop windows were narrow and cluttered with items for sale so not much daylight was let in.

The counter formed the bottom part of a letter 'U' at one end of the shop. A bacon slicer, a big red thing, stood on the left-hand side next to a wooden board on which sat half a truckle of Cheddar cheese and a cutting wire. To her right a few jars of sweets, possibly pre-war if their faded colour was anything to go by, jostled for space with cabbages, leeks, tins of Brasso, Colman's mustard and Bird's custard powder. There had most likely been more of everything before the war, but even now because the shop was so small it didn't really notice.

The handle of a silver-coloured tea shovel peeped out from a sack of loose-leaf tea. The whole area to her right was covered with chicken wire so no prying hands could steal the stock when Mrs Powell or her daughter weren't looking.

She noted there was no bacon in the slicer; there hadn't been since before the war. Only the butcher could secure stocks of that and a queue formed when word got round that he had some. People even got excited when he had tins of corned beef from Argentina for sale or Spam – tinned sausage meat – from the United States.

Frances turned back to face the counter, her fingers resuming their impatient tapping. Paul must be getting impatient too.

Craning her neck, she looked over her shoulder and through the shop door. If the door hadn't been covered with notices about ration books and other official notices, she might have seen Charlie and Paul too. As it was all she could see was the handle of the pushchair.

Mrs Powell came out as though having a customer in the

shop was the most inconvenient thing that could ever befall her. She was brandishing a pair of large kitchen scissors in her hand. Her expression was as severe as her hairstyle, brown hair streaked with grey pulled back into a bun. No jewellery. No colourful clothes. Mrs Powell always wore black.

Frances tried smiling at her, and brought up the subject of Ada Perkins. 'I really enjoyed staying over there. I didn't think I would, but I did. The forest is really quite wonderful and I liked Ada – your mother – very much.'

Mrs Powell looked at her as though she'd taken leave of her senses. 'The forest is not a Christian place. In time my mother will see the error of her ways and return to the fold.'

Frances presumed her reference to the fold meant Oldland Common. 'It would be lovely having her back here.'

Mrs Powell looked at her as though she had materialised from thin air. 'Why?'

Seeing nothing wrong in what she'd said, Frances maintained her wide smile even though it was hurting her cheeks to maintain it for so long. 'She knows such a lot about the forest and everything. The forest is full of magic.'

'Are you all there?'

Frances was taken aback. 'All there?'

'All there. Are you a little touched in the head? People who smile all the time are sometimes a bit touched in the head. Head in the clouds. Not quite with it. The forest is not magical. It's wicked. Evil.'

'Rubbish! It's full of birds and animals and plants. Ada uses the plants to heal people when they can't afford to go to the doctor.'

Mrs Powell's eyes narrowed and glittered. 'She's like you. Not all there.'

'I'm fine, and so is Ada. And I'd much appreciate you get on with giving me the cod liver oil for Charlie. The government says he has to have it. And while I'm here I might just as well take the orange juice he's entitled to and the National Dried Milk. Two tins please!'

Mrs Powell scowled. 'That's in other boxes. I haven't unpacked them either.'

'Then perhaps you should,' Frances said tartly. 'There's no point leaving it in boxes is there, not with babies needing it.'

'There wouldn't be so many babies in need if people controlled their wicked urges,' snarled Mrs Powell. Leaning forward so her scrawny breasts were resting halfway across the counter, her face loomed large in front of Frances. 'The godless are taking over this world,' she pronounced, her eyes round as tea plates, unblinking as their black-button brightness glittered into Frances's face. 'People having babies without bothering to get married. It's a slight to God, it is. A sign of the evil encompassing the world. All children should be born in wedlock. Children not born in wedlock are imps of the devil. Imps of the devil, I tell you!'

Frances felt her face growing hot. She was having none of it. 'Our Charlie is not an imp of the devil! He's a lovely little boy and his father was lovely too.'

'Ah! But what about his mother? She was foreign.'

'Austrian. She was from Austria!' Frances didn't care that her voice was getting louder. She would defend those she loved and those she had loved. They didn't deserve such talk from this stupid woman.

'That's what I said,' snarled Mrs Powell. 'She was foreign with foreign ways. And I didn't see her in church. Not any church.'

'She was Jewish.'

'Ah!' Mrs Powell exclaimed, her face tense with the bitterness of her own beliefs. 'That explains everything. An evil woman from an evil race!'

'That's stupid. Jesus was Jewish!'

'How dare you say such a thing?'

Frances's patience was at an end. 'I said it because it's true! Now can we get back to business? I'd like what's due for Charlie please. Now!'

Mrs Powell faltered on seeing the determined look on the face of the young girl in front of her. In the past, Frances had endured Mrs Powell's ill-tempered comments. Up until now she'd kept her own counsel. Referring to Charlie and his kind as an imp of the devil was too much. There was no childish respect in her upturned face, no weak trembling of her jaw. On the contrary, she had every intention of telling Mrs Powell what she thought of her – once she had what she'd come for.

Each box, the one containing the bottles of cod liver oil, the one containing concentrated orange juice, and lastly the one containing tins of National Dried Milk, were opened. Regretting she hadn't thought to bring a bag, Frances wound her arms around the two bottles of cod liver oil, one bottle of orange juice and a two tins of National Dried Milk. She would just about be able to open the shop door, but first . . .

Her stance was defiant as she stood in front of the door, her fingers shaking slightly on the door handle while clinging on to the supplies she'd come for with the other.

'Jesus Christ *was* a Jew.' She repeated as a parting shot.

'Blasphemer!'

The word hurtled through the air. Instead of arguing or telling Mrs Powell that she was talking rubbish, she began to laugh. This was so totally absurd. 'You stupid, stupid woman!'

Mrs Powell gripped the edge of the counter with both hands, her elbows held at acute angles. She leaned forward, like a hawk about to land on a sparrow. 'How dare you, you wicked girl! You're as bad as the rest of your family. As bad as Bettina Hicks and that other child of the devil, the one she calls her nephew. But I know the truth. I know the God-given truth!'

As her voice climbed from decibel to decibel, Mrs Powell's face turned a deep shade of puce.

Lingering in the doorway, Frances shouted back. 'No wonder Ada doesn't come to visit you too often. Even when she does, it's only to see Miriam. Not you. I wouldn't come either if I had a daughter like you. You're a dreadful woman. A wicked, dreadful woman!'

'Get out of my shop,' shrieked Mrs Powell, her pointing finger quivering like a twig in the breeze. 'Get out of my shop and never darken my door again!'

Frances had grown up a lot of late. Besides that, little Charlie was the apple of her eye. She'd do anything for him and that included making sure he had his designated rations. He was a growing boy and would be denied nothing. She stood her ground, resolved not to be ordered out but clinging on to the door handle until she chose the moment to go.

'I have to darken your door again, as you put it, Mrs Powell. You're my family's designated supplier of items our Charlie is entitled to. If you don't supply us, then the Health Authority will want to know why and they'll probably take your licence away.' Her angry voice rang around the little shop, joining forces with the jangling of the rusty bell above the shop door as she dragged it open with a forceful yank.

She opened the door just wide enough to escape, laughing quietly as she slid sidelong through the gap, her arms firmly holding the items against her chest. Feeling this triumphant she felt she could fly all the way home, pushchair and Charlie too.

There would be room in the pushchair for the bottles and

tins. She had it all planned and Paul would help her – only Paul wasn't there.

Neither was Charlie. His pushchair was empty except for a few carrot crumbs on his pillow. She whirled round, her whole body shaking with fear. Where had they gone?

'Paul! Paul, where are you?'

Court Road was empty, the only sound that of cattle lowing in the nearby fields which lined each side of the road. The only buildings were the cottages and houses at this end of the road where it swooped down towards the brook and the valley before the land sloped up again towards St Anne's Church and California Road where there used to be a coal mine. It had been called California Pit, the owner hoping that by calling it that he'd become as rich as the men who'd flocked to the California Gold Rush.

Unfortunately the coal mine referred to had flooded in 1902. Luckily none of the miners had been inside. It had never reopened. But the area could be treacherous. There were still tunnels beneath the surface, sinkholes into which a child could fall, never to be seen again. The pit the children referred to was the hollow amongst the trees where they built their den and lit camp fires.

Paul hadn't mentioned taking Charlie off anywhere. Was this some sort of game? If it was it angered her. She ran out into the middle of the road, looking up the street towards West Street and the High Street.

'Paul! Come out wherever you are. This is silly.'

Of course it was silly. It was also silly of her to think he would play such games. He was older now, almost a man, she reminded herself. And who played hide and seek with a baby in tow?

Frances unburdened her arms of the bottles and tins, tipping them into the empty pushchair. All the while, her

261

eyes searched up and down the road, turning on her heels this way and that just to make sure she hadn't missed them. They had to be close by.

She placed a restraining hand over her stomach. It felt as though the bottom had fallen out of it.

She strained to hear the sound of Charlie crying; he would cry if he was taken by a stranger.

A stranger! Surely not. Everyone knew everyone else in the village. Besides, she'd left Charlie with Paul. Nobody would take him and there wasn't a soul in sight.

The most logical explanation she could think of was that Paul had taken Charlie to see the cows, but she could see nobody hanging over the fences on either side of the road.

Leaving the pushchair where it was, she dashed up the road, diverting into a hedged lane, which dissected fields on the same side as the shop.

The smell of damp grass and cow dung hung heavily in the air. A fine mist rolled knee high among the cows, making them look as though they had no legs.

She turned and ran back down the lane out on to Court Road. Her own legs were shaking as she ran up and down the road, peering into the fields on both sides. Her heart was beating wildly, her hair growing damp in the mist and clinging in tendrils around her face.

'Paul! Charlie!'

Cud-chewing cows looked dolefully in her direction. She could hear and see nothing.

Shaking her head in disbelief she asked herself what Paul would want with a baby – if he'd taken Charlie that is.

'No. No,' she kept repeating, kept shaking her head.

It was silly to think Paul had gone off with the baby, but if he hadn't, who had?

She looked over her shoulder at the shop door. Should she go in and ask Mrs Powell whether she'd seen anything? She shook her head again. No. It was quite impossible. She'd left Charlie with Paul outside while she'd gone inside to get what she'd had to get. If Mrs Powell hadn't taken her time unpacking the boxes and let her have what she wanted, she would have been heading home by now, or on her way to inspect Paul's piece of shrapnel.

It wasn't easy to overcome the state of panic she was in, but she did her best to think straight. What would Mary do? What would Ruby do?

She eyed the small frontage of the village shop. It might probably be a waste of time, but she was going to do it anyway. She was going to go back into the shop and ask Mrs Powell whether she'd seen anything. It wasn't at all likely, but at least it was a start until she'd calmed down, until she could think straight.

'One, two, three.' She counted the cracked flagstones that bordered the front of the shop. Counting to ten was calming, so she'd been told. 'Four, five, six . . .'

On spotting a familiar figure walking towards her along the lane that divided Stratham House from the adjoining field and Mrs Powell's shop, she stopped counting.

'Mrs Hicks! Mrs Hicks,' she shouted.

Bettina was dressed in her outdoor coat, a warm hat pulled down over her ears and stout boots on her feet. As usual, she was using a stick to walk because her hip gave her such pain. On seeing Frances she quickened her pace, a querulous look on her face.

Much to Bettina's surprise, Frances threw her arms around her.

'There, there, my girl. You nearly hit me over. Whatever's the matter?'

'I've lost Charlie,' said Frances, and immediately burst into tears.

'Now, now, child.'

Bettina reached out and gently patted Frances's shoulder. At the same time she thought how much she resembled her mother. Hopefully it would only ever be in looks. Bettina shuddered at the thought of her having the same reckless personality as Mildred Sweet.

'Have you considered he might have climbed out of his pushchair and toddled off somewhere? He's found his feet very quickly.'

Bettina Hicks was a cool-headed woman in an emergency and her comments were reassuring. She also knew better than to tell a young girl like Frances to control herself and mop up her tears.

'I didn't think of that.'

'Well, you should have,' said Bettina forcing a smile. 'He's a very strong little boy. Though he can't have got far.'

'I didn't think he could get out. His harness was fastened. I didn't think he could undo buckles.'

Bettina shrugged and smiled. 'I wouldn't put anything beyond that little lad. Right,' she went on. 'Now let's get down to business.'

She went on to suggest that they wander around the immediate area, Frances going off in one direction and she in the other.

Frances retraced her steps up the lane then down over the hill towards the church, peering into the cottage gardens to either side of the shop. A few people asked what she was looking for and she told them about Charlie.

More than one person offered their help in the search. 'Let me get me coat and I'll help you.'

Bettina hadn't walked very far, but her mind was working

logically. First things first: she needed to trace Paul Martin who might indeed have taken the child with him.

Frances came back with a group of people around her.

Tom Shepherd, who had once been the village policeman and was now retired, took it upon himself to get his neighbours organised. 'We'll go look down the bottom and up in the fields, though it seems a bit far for a little lad of his age to walk.'

Her heart in her mouth, Frances watched them saunter off down the road, some with the spaniels they used when they went shooting at their side, the animals' noses tight to the ground, stumpy tails wagging with excitement.

Bettina watched them go too. Her heart was heavy: strong boy as he was, she didn't really believe that Charlie would have gone very far. He could walk, yes, but only just. He wasn't that steady on his feet for that great a distance.

She was about to send Frances to search out Paul Martin, when there he was, larger than life sauntering down the road.

There was a sheepish air about him, the way his hands were shoved into his pockets and his shoulders hunched. He frowned on seeing the state of Frances's face and the formidable presence of Bettina Hicks. He thought the fact that he'd sloped off might have something to do with Frances looking so distraught, but would have preferred Mrs Hicks not being involved.

'No needs to take on like that,' he said to Frances. 'I only went to check on something.' It was a poor lie and too vague to be a viable excuse but he could hardly tell her that he'd planned to kiss her, had thought better of it and ran away. Now here he was again, his courage renewed.

Frances carried on sobbing.

Paul nodded at Bettina. 'Hello, Mrs Hicks.' Again he glanced nervously at Frances. 'Is something wrong?'

'Charlie's gone!' Frances sounded frantic and her words were punctuated by loud sobs.

Bettina took over. 'Paul, did you leave Charlie here all alone?'

An embarrassed flush coloured Paul's sallow complexion, so deep it made the white of his shirt collar look a dirty yellow.

Paul shuffled from one foot to the other. 'Well . . . yes. But he didn't mind. He was here in his pram.' He grinned. 'He nicked a carrot from the box. I tried to get it off him and put it back, but he was having none of it. Determined little bug— devil he is . . . was . . . um . . .' His words stuttered to a full stop.

Bettina sighed. 'He is little more than a baby. It wasn't long ago he started walking.'

Paul looked down at his feet, toeing the ground while chewing the inside of his cheek. It was a bad habit, but he always did that when he felt awkward or guilty about something. Earlier he'd thought himself quite the man with all his ideas about Frances. Now he felt like a schoolboy again.

All three pairs of eyes turned to the carrot crumbs. Bettina sighed. 'I suppose your uncle Stan will have to be told.'

Frances immediately erupted into a fresh torrent of tears.

Bettina patted her shoulder. 'Now, now. Calm down. Let's think this through carefully.' She turned to Paul who was looking more than a bit sorry for himself. The boy's eyes kept flickering in the direction of young Frances. He was sweet on her, that much was apparent. She wondered if Frances knew that, then pushed the thought from her mind. There was no time for things as trivial as adolescent romance when a baby was missing. Charlie was top priority.

'Paul,' she went on. 'Think back. Did you see anyone

else around when you were outside the shop with Charlie? Anyone at all?'

Paul frowned as he tried to remember. 'The kids from up the Barton were playing with a kitten, though not for long. It ran off up the lane and they ran after it. And Mr Harris looked over the wall and asked me what day it was and what time the Kaiser was expected.'

Bettina closed her eyes and wiped her perspiring forehead with the back of her hand. It was quite a cold day but she couldn't help feeling hot and very exasperated. All down to worry, of course.

The prospect of anyone having seen anything wasn't great. The children would have been engrossed by the kitten and although Mr Harris had come back from the Great War in the physical sense, his mind was still out there. Judging by his ramblings the Germans had won the war and the Kaiser was travelling around his new domain checking up on all those who had fought against him.

The poor man, she thought sadly. She also felt sorry for his wife; it couldn't be easy. Thankfully he did bring in a small wage, bending his brawny back doing causal labour for a few farms and suchlike; that and a small pension was a tiny bulwark between getting by and total poverty. She'd noticed he was one of those accompanying Tom Shepherd in the search for the child.

Bettina looked thoughtfully at Frances who was dabbing at her red-rimmed eyes. 'How long were you in the shop?'

'Quite a long time. Twenty minutes at least.' Frances dabbed again with her soggy hankie. 'Mrs Powell hadn't unpacked the boxes. I had to wait.'

Bettina nodded thoughtfully. 'How about Miriam? Was she there?'

Frances shrugged. 'I don't know. I didn't see her.'

Bettina swallowed a lump in her throat but couldn't stop her mind focusing on basic fears. She'd heard stories of babies being snatched – in her young days it was always the gypsies who were blamed. She had no idea whether it was true or not. Nobody was sure whether Miriam had had a baby. Perhaps she had and it had been given up for adoption. Or perhaps it had died.

She knew she was only surmising, but nobody knew for sure whether Miriam had been pregnant or not. A lost baby had turned the mind of many a grieving mother.

Her rambling thoughts were interrupted.

'Can I do anything to help, missus?' Paul was looking at her with a mixture of fear and pleading.

If she'd been able to read his mind, she would know how he was feeling: if only he hadn't run scared at his intention of kissing Frances, the only girl in the whole village who really interested him.

Bettina instructed him to fetch the baby's grandfather. 'Run like the wind and fetch Mr Sweet. Tell him what's happened. Tell him I'll wait for him here. And hurry!'

Taking his hands out of his pockets, Paul broke into an instant run, his legs kicking behind him, his arms powering him along like engine pistons as he raced for help. By and by his figure became smaller before vanishing altogether as he turned into West Street.

Bettina turned back to the snivelling Frances. 'Pull yourself together and wipe your eyes. You stay here. I'll go in and have a word with Mrs Powell and Miriam.'

When rationing had come in, Bettina Hicks had purposely avoided registering with Gertrude Powell. In fact, she purposely avoided having anything to do with the woman. Her reasons were numerous, but there was one above all others, one she kept strictly to herself.

The devil himself would have had trouble dragging her into Gertrude's shop, but on this occasion she had no choice. Charlie was missing and no stone must be left unturned.

CHAPTER TWENTY-ONE

The old iron bell above the door jangled in warning as Bettina Hicks entered the dingy shop tut-tutting loudly at the lack of light. Mrs Powell was not one for throwing money around. There was nothing generous about her; there never had been.

The glass in the door between the shop and the living quarters rattled loosely in its frame as the dark-clad figure of Mrs Powell came out from the back.

On seeing Bettina Hicks, Mrs Powell visibly stiffened, her jaw seeming to clamp hard on something in her mouth that was too bitter to swallow.

'Bettina.'

'Gertrude.'

The two women faced each other like fighting dogs, each assessing the best chance they had of biting the other.

To say that Mrs Powell had a hostile attitude towards Bettina Hicks was putting it mildly. Gertrude's features took on a superior look that held more than a pound or two of sanctimonious zeal.

Bettina held her head high. She knew Gertrude's opinion of her. She wouldn't have held the views she did if it hadn't been for the careless comment of a midwife many years ago just after the men returned from the war – very few men, as a matter of fact.

The two women sized each other up.

'So the devil's spawn has gone missing.'

Bettina sighed. 'Don't be so melodramatic, Gertrude. He's just a baby and could be in danger. And Charlie Sweet was hardly the devil was he? Just a sweet boy who lost his life in this blasted war. That's beside the point anyway. Frances said she was in here waiting for you to unpack when he went missing. I know it's not likely, but did you see anything?'

'As you said, I was here minding my own business. Unpacking. I wouldn't have seen anything, would I.'

Her tone was as sharp as her features; deep-set black eyes, streaks of grey running through hair that had once been chestnut in colour, dulling to brown over the years. Her aquiline nose flared at the nostrils like an angry horse.

'I only asked. How about Miriam? Do you think we could ask her?'

Gertrude's bony fingers gripped the edge of the counter. 'She didn't see anything.'

'But she might have done.'

'Perhaps the Sweets might not want him back.'

Bettina's jaw dropped. 'Really, Gertrude, you always were a bit insensitive, but to say that . . .'

'The child was born out of wedlock. Better if he hadn't been born at all. Do you still visit Evelyn?'

Evelyn was a friend in Stroud who she visited on a regular basis.

'That is none of your business!'

Bettina found herself boiling with anger at both the words and the way they were delivered. She would have dearly loved to wipe the evil look off Gertrude Powell's face with the back of her hand. But she wouldn't do that. She wouldn't rise to the truth Gertrude thought she knew but couldn't prove.

Nobody even suspected that Mike Dangerfield was not her brother's child.

She felt her heart pounding but told herself it was just the cold she was coming down with, the fever she was feeling. If she hadn't felt so unwell she might have given Gertrude more than a piece of her mind. As it was, she stood her ground. 'I need to speak to Miriam. Would you call her please?'

'She's upstairs.'

'Please.' It almost choked Bettina to plead like this, but swallowed her pride.

Gertrude's black eyes held no shine. Her look varied from sheer malice to disinterest. She turned her back on the shop, pushing the door open to her living quarters, the thin glass in the upper half of the door reflecting her sour expression.

Bettina pursed her lips. It was difficult to keep her temper under control with Gertrude. They'd known each other all their lives. As a child Gertrude had been precocious and doted on by her father. Her mother, Ada Perkins, had been a gem of a woman. It was noticeable that mother and daughter didn't seem to like each other, yet although Ada did visit the village occasionally, it struck everyone as odd when a few days ago a note had been pinned on the shop door stating they'd gone to visit Ada Perkins, Gertrude's mother; Gertrude did not visit her mother. There had to be a good reason for it, though nobody would dare ask her what it was.

Gertrude had adored her father and replacing him with another father figure was perhaps why her husband, Godfrey, a deeply religious man of great charm and firm belief, had taken over her life.

Godfrey Powell had taken the fundamental line in Christianity, firmly believing that no woman could enter heaven and be considered a true Christian unless she was married. He also adhered to a rather puritanical version of religion and held to himself that his way was the right way and no other counted. If one had known Godfrey Powell it was understandable that both his wife and daughter attended church a great deal – and not just one church. Methodist, Baptist and Church of England: there they were every Sunday without fail and sometimes during the week if there was a good fire-and-brimstone speaker expected.

God help the speaker if Mrs Powell thought the sermon wasn't full enough of fire and brimstone. Godfrey Powell might be dead but his spirit lived on in his wife. Like a frightened dormouse, their daughter Miriam went along with it all because she had to.

Out of sight of Bettina Hicks, a woman she despised, Gertrude Powell stood looking around her living room. The room was predominantly brown, the curtains thick Victorian velvet, the lighting dim. Religious tracts and pictures hung on the walls. The furniture was Edwardian and polished every day. The room smelled of beeswax. There was no fire in the grate. Fires encouraged laziness. Gertrude's creed was that if you kept moving and kept working, you didn't need a fire.

At no point did she attempt to shout for her daughter or go upstairs to her room. There would be no point. She wasn't there. She wasn't in the cellar where she'd left her either. Somehow or other she'd managed to get out, though not for long. She'd be back and then she'd go back in there and stay in there until she'd mended her ways. A few hours a week of that kind of treatment and she'd be pliable again, her timid, innocent daughter – no – not innocent. She would never be that again, Gertrude thought grimly.

She fixed her gaze on the wall clock, counting the times the pendulum moved from side to side. Time itself was evil, taking minutes, hours, years from one's life, and taking other things too. Her husband was dead and as for her daughter – well – she was no longer the little girl she'd melded to her will. She'd been touched by the devil. Gertrude blamed her mother for that, her and those wicked people in the forest who didn't go to church, who'd turned her head with their pagan ways. As for Stephen Briers, the Methodist minister who had called himself a Christian . . . ! Her lip curled at the thought of him.

Deciding a suitable amount of time had passed, she let herself back out into the shop. Bettina Hicks was standing straight and tall despite her arthritic hip. Gertrude had always envied Bettina her height and the thick head of hair she'd had when she was young – a kind of apricot colour back then. Off-white now of course and not nearly so glossy.

Her face was without emotion. 'I'm sorry. She's asleep. I'm reluctant to wake her. She's not been well.'

'Is that so?'

Bettina noted the sharp lines radiating from Gertrude's pursed purple lips. Only lips long used to being held in abject disapproval could look like that. They certainly weren't so prevalent in people who smiled a lot. It came to her that Gertrude never smiled – not in her presence anyway.

Gertrude's eyebrows arched in thin dark lines. 'Are you calling me a liar?'

Bettina almost smiled. 'I could call you a lot of things, Gertrude. Liar might very well be one of them. Sanctimonious, certainly. Bitter and twisted, yes. No wonder you have to go to church so often. You need to pray for forgiveness. You need to be forgiven more than anyone else I know!'

Bettina turned abruptly, clamping her lips together, though heaven knew it was too late now. She had said more than was prudent. But there it was, she thought as she jerked open the shop door; Gertrude Powell brought out the worst in her. She'd never liked the woman even when they'd been children, but later on she'd come to dislike her even more.

She pushed the memories of that time behind her. Mike was happy now and would never know the truth, not if she had anything to do with it. However, Gertrude Powell was the weak link, the woman who would hurt them all if she could.

CHAPTER TWENTY-TWO

Outside the shop Paul stood with his hands in his pockets, his eyes flickering in Frances's direction.

'I'm sorry, Frances. I shouldn't have left him. I didn't think. I mean, people don't steal babies, do they?'

Frances glared at him. 'Are you totally stupid?'

Paul's face took on a flat look as though she'd hit him hard with the base of a frying pan.

'I said I'm sorry.'

Frances shook her head and looked away.

'How about if we walk down to California Pit? The boys might be down there, or will be soon when school comes out. They'll help us look for him. They can go faster than grown-ups, and so can we.'

Frances threw him another icy glare. 'I am not a child, Paul.'

'Neither am I.' Paul could feel his face getting hot. He'd so wanted to impress Frances at how grown up he was, but every so often he slid back to being a boy again, thinking the way he always had, doing the things that were so familiar. 'Fran, I feel so bad about this. If you don't want to come with me, I'll go by myself. I'll look for him. If it takes all night, I'll find him. I swear I will!'

He started to walk away, hands shoved back into his pockets, head bent. He looked totally dejected.

'Wait.'

Frances fell into step beside him. She couldn't help blaming him for this. It was silly of him to slope off, but then it was hardly the first time she'd left Charlie outside the shop. He'd always been there when she'd come back out. Always. Except for today.

'How many boys will be in the den?' She'd finally stopped sniffing and stuffed her handkerchief in the pocket of her dark red coat. The well-worn coat had belonged to Ruby and was a little big for her. Ruby had offered to cut it down a bit but then reconsidered. 'It might have to last until this war is over, and goodness knows when that's likely to be. I think we should leave it alone,' she'd said. 'Yes. I think we'll leave it alone. Anyway, you'll grow into it.'

Frances had taken advantage of the fact that the coat was too big for her and worn thicker jumpers, though the shoulder pads were still too large for her frame, sagging a bit down her arms.

They hurried down Court Road and up the other side, following the lane at the side of the church and the old manor house. The path across the field was uneven and there were sharp rocks sticking out between mounds of dug earth. Trees, their roots barely holding on to the earth, leaned over each and every ditch, chasms that might once have been firm ground. The deep ditches were ideal for making into a den by enterprising youngsters. They'd been making dens here for generations.

The path down to their particular den, the one they called the Dingle, was steep and stony, a definite asset in dry weather, but treacherous when the ground was covered in frost or when it was damp as it was today.

Frances took small, careful steps, her arms held out on either side of her like a tightrope walker. Paul followed on behind with trudging steps, automatically grabbing her upper arm when it seemed she might slip.

'I never used to slip,' she said indignantly.

'You never used to wear shoes with heels,' returned Paul.

Frances noted his tone. She'd noticed that men often adopted a tone like that when women were talking about shoes and clothes, subjects that obviously bored them. The shoes belonged to Mary who said she could borrow them for special occasions. Frances counted taking Charlie for a walk as good an occasion as any.

The thorny bushes to either side grabbed at the hem of her coat. The coat had been made before guidelines had been passed on how much material could be used. Coats these days were a lot skimpier than they had been.

Finally they were on level ground, high stony banks and foliage rising to either side of them.

A mist swirled around the roots of the trees and lumps of rock pierced the dark earth where whole sections of farmland had sunk down into the old mine shafts. The corridor it formed was a dead end. That's where the Dingle was situated. Nobody could recall who had first decided to build a den here. It seemed as if it had been here for ever, refurbished and redesigned in consecutive summers by a new generation of kids.

Formed over a large ditch about four or five feet deep, the twisted roots and spindly trunks of dead trees formed a framework for a roof of corrugated iron and tarpaulin. Various pieces of old carpet and linoleum covered the dirt floor and there were bits of wood laid on bricks to form benches. An old chair took precedence at one end of the room, the preserve of the gang leader – whoever that happened to be at any specific moment in time.

'You used to be the gang leader,' Frances said suddenly, shaking him from his thoughts.

'Yeah. When I was a kid. It's Billy Tanner now.'

Billy Tanner was the son of the porter down Bitton Railway Station. Frances guessed he might be a popular choice on account of all the railways bits and pieces stored at the back of the signal box just a quarter of a mile down the line. Dens were only as good as the material they were made from and Billy had access to broken and disused railway sleepers.

The darkness intensified the further in they went, the stringy branches interlocking overhead like so much woven raffia. Even though the branches were bare, they diminished the daylight into twilight and shadows into darkness. Anyone who didn't know the den was here would never find it.

A bird flew from a low hanging branch at their approach. Something scuttled into the undergrowth. By virtue of the rock and earth strata on either side, no wind disturbed the peaty air.

Frances suddenly stopped in her tracks, aware that she'd heard something, but not quite sure what it was.

'Singing,' she said softly. The sound made her tingle all over. 'I can hear somebody singing.'

Paul looked terrified. 'Is it a ghost?' His eyes were round as the marbles he used to roll along the gutter.

Frances frowned. It was a woman's voice singing softly. She recognised a lullaby the twins used to sing to her when she was smaller. *Hush! my dear, lie still and slumber.* All at once it stopped. The voice that had been singing was now saying something, though Frances couldn't quite make out what it was. And then it came to her. Cooing. Baby talk. Somebody was talking to a baby!

She looked at Paul and pointed in the direction of the den. 'Someone's there,' she whispered.

The sound ceased. Whoever was inside had heard them. For a moment there was silence, and then . . .

'Hello! Is somebody there?'

'Yes. Is that you, Miriam?'

'Yes. Yes, it's me.'

The voice seemed to fall away as though Miriam regretted having spoken.

Frances pressed on. 'It's Frances Sweet. I'm looking for my nephew. Have you seen him?'

There was the sound of movement, things bumping. There was also the unmistakable sound of Charlie chortling good-naturedly between sharp cries and unintelligible sounds that weren't quite words.

'Charlie!' Before she had chance to get down on her knees and crawl forward, there was Charlie, his face beaming with smiles and arms outstretched as he toddled towards her. Feeling relieved and too excited for words, she bent down so he could run into her arms. 'Charlie,' she shouted again.

Charlie didn't hesitate. Gurgling and laughing, he started towards her, tottering along on legs that were becoming stronger every day.

'Thank God for that,' she heard Paul say.

Hugging her nephew to her breast, she squeezed her eyes shut and offered up a prayer of thanks. Charlie hadn't been taken by the gypsies or fallen into a stream and drowned and neither had he been spirited away by the fairies; he was here, in her arms, happy as could be.

On opening her eyes she espied the figure of Miriam Powell, her black coat dragging in the dirt as she crawled out from the entrance to the den.

'I found him,' said Miriam once she was on her feet. Her smile was hesitant as were her movements. She took a step or two forward, wringing her hands, then stopped before taking two more. 'He was lost. But I found you, didn't I, Charlie? I found you.'

She reached out to stroke the chubby hand that lay on Frances's shoulder.

Frances glared at her. 'I don't want you touching him.'

'But I found him, and Charlie likes me. Don't you Charlie?' Totally disregarding Paul, she turned back to Frances, her face shining with delight. 'I think he thinks that I'm his mother.'

Frances fancied she could smell coal dust. Miriam's hands were dirty, her fingernails black. Her face was streaked with black dust and so was the funny old hat she was wearing which resembled a tea cosy. What had she been doing? Frances wondered. Living in the coal shed?

'Where did you find him?' Paul asked.

Joyful at finding her nephew, Frances had almost forgotten about Paul but was grateful to hear his voice, glad he was asking a sensible question. In other circumstances, she would have asked the same question, but her nerves were still on edge. Things could have worked out so differently.

'In the churchyard. I found him there. He goes there with Mr Sweet sometimes. I've seen them. Mr Sweet talks to his wife. I know she's dead, but that's what he does – talks to her as though she were alive. He's not mad, mind you. It's easy to imagine somebody you love and to talk to them. Very easy.'

'I know,' Frances said quietly. 'Why did you bring him here?'

'The Dingle is a safe place, just for kids,' said Miriam, half turning and glancing at the makeshift structure with something approaching affection. 'I used to play here when I was a child. We all did. We had fun here. It was better than home. When I could get away,' she added. She looked this way and that as though half expecting to be discovered and dragged off home. 'My mother didn't like me coming here. She stopped it. She didn't like me going to stay with Gran either. She stopped me doing that too.'

Resentment briefly flashed in Miriam's eyes, but it didn't last. Miriam was in the habit of bowing to her mother's dictates. Nothing was going to change that. Her face, then her whole body, seemed to crumple.

Frances turned to Paul. 'I think we should go. They'll be looking for us, and everyone's worried enough as it is without it looking as though we're missing too.'

Paul agreed with her. Carefully, so as not to slip especially now she had Charlie in her arms, they wound their way back along the path, away from the tangled roots and branches of the copse and back into the open field.

As they picked their way, Charlie waved at Miriam and muttered what sounded like 'mum' but could just as easily have been 'mmmmm'.

'He was ever so good,' Miriam called out as she followed on behind, picking her way along the path.

'He is good,' snapped Frances.

She hugged Charlie tightly against her chest, extra careful now not to slip.

Miriam tried again to make polite conversation.

'I think Charlie is looking after his son. He's an angel. Angels can do anything.'

Frances quite liked the thought of her cousin Charlie being an angel, but didn't want to be drawn into a conversation with the woman who had found her nephew. She was feeling bad enough about it as it was. And somehow she didn't believe that Miriam was entirely telling the truth.

It seemed Paul was having the same doubts. 'Seems a long way for a baby to wander in that time.'

It made Frances wonder. She might have wondered some more if she hadn't heard Miriam let out a loud yelp.

Both she and Paul turned round to see Miriam's hat had been pulled off her head by an overhanging branch. There it was, swinging from a twig. What was even more surprising was that her hair was cut very short and not glamorously so. It stuck up all over her head in short tufts. Here and there were brown patches – scuds. Frances had grazed her knees in the past enough times to know what they meant. Blood. Miriam's hair had been cut short and whoever had cut it had not been gentle.

Looking despairingly distraught, Miriam snatched the hat from the twig using both hands to pull it firmly down on her head. Her eyes fluttered and her face turned pale.

'I'm not supposed to be out.'

'Then you'd better come on back with us,' suggested Paul. He was standing with his hips thrust forward, shoulders back as he tried to work out what was going on here.

Somebody suddenly called out from a point between the church and the manor house. It was Tom Shepherd and a few of the others.

'We've found him,' Frances shouted, intent to get back and tell her uncle Stan that all was well. 'He's all right. Miriam said she found him.'

Whatever her reservations with regard to Miriam's story, it was as near the truth as they had at present. Charlie was safe. She turned meaning to acknowledge Miriam, but she wasn't there.

'Off towards the church by the looks of it,' said Paul.

'And I'm off home,' murmured Frances, exhausted by all that had happened and concerned what her uncle's reaction might be.

'I'll come with you.'

Her uncle Stan was waiting for them with Bettina Hicks. The moment he saw Charlie, the anxiety left his face. 'You've found him!'

Too choked up and relieved to reply, Frances beamed and nodded.

Her uncle went down on one knee, arms outstretched. Charlie willingly went into his grandfather's arms.

'He was with Miriam Powell in our den at California Pit. She said she found him there, but . . .' Frances chewed her lips backwards and forwards.

'Miriam Powell found him?' He sounded amazed.

Frances nodded. 'She smelled of coal and her head was covered in blood. Whoever cut her hair didn't do a very good job.'

Stan mentioned this fact to Bettina that evening. They were sitting in her front room with a small glass of brandy each.

'She was in a right state,' Stan said to Bettina. 'And she smelled of coal dust and her hair was shorn – not just cut – shorn!'

'Stan, you're making me shiver. I sometimes think that Gertrude isn't all there, but with this happening . . .' She waved her hand despairingly. 'I wonder what Miriam did to make her mother cut off her hair.'

Stan looked at her. 'Are you implying what I think you are?'

Bettina sighed and looked down into her glass. 'For a while Miriam was wandering around the village looking as though she might be in the family way. Then suddenly she disappeared and when she reappeared her figure appeared back to normal. Something happened to make Gertrude cut off her daughter's hair. I can't help thinking . . .' She paused, unable to speak the terrible truth she couldn't help suspecting.

'That Miriam had got into trouble and Gertrude had taken matters into her own hands.'

Bettina nodded. 'Gertrude certainly won't own up to it.'

The two of them sat silently, both contemplating the same thought. It had been noticed that Miriam had put on weight, but had never reached the stage where she was undeniably pregnant. Could it be that she had never reached full term? The question had to be asked whether she'd miscarried naturally, or otherwise. If the latter then Gertrude Powell had committed a grave crime that could land her in prison.

'Nothing can be proved,' said Bettina. Stan had to agree.

CHAPTER TWENTY-THREE

Andrew Sinclair phoned to speak to Mary about the radio broadcast she was doing the following day. 'Seeing as the Americans have entered the war, I thought you might like to mention doughnuts. I presume you can make them, can't you?'

Mary almost choked. 'Yes. Of course I can make them, Mr Sinclair.'

'Plea . . . a . . . se,' he said, drawing out the single word, a sign that he was quite hurt. 'I've told you before to call me Andrew.'

Mary sighed and rolled her eyes. Ruby noticed and mouthed Andrew's name. Mary nodded.

'Look . . . Andrew. Doughnuts require a lot of sugar and a lot of fat both to make them and deep-fry them. They have to be deep-fried or they don't fluff out as they're supposed to.'

'Oh dear. I didn't know that.'

Mary wondered how on earth he'd landed his job at the Ministry of Food. It certainly wasn't down to his baking expertise or even cooking in general. It had to be a friend of a friend. Someone from his schooldays, perhaps.

She decided on an alternative suggestion. 'How about straightforward apple pie? Americans love apple pie.'

'Do they?' Andrew sounded quite surprised.

Obviously you don't go to the cinema very much, thought Mary, or you would know that.

'As American as apple pie. That's what I've heard said in American films,' stated Mary, then rushed on, just in case he used any silence to ask her out again, regardless of the fact that he knew she was married.

'There's also pumpkin pie, of course, but that's a bit too American. And anyway it's a bit late for pumpkins and they're not that plentiful in England.'

There was silence on the line as he paused to think before conceding that apple pie was a distinct possibility.

'It's traditional to us both. Going back to the same roots,' Mary offered. 'And apples are plentiful.'

'Yes. Yes, of course they are. Now on another note, I believe Ruby is off to give a demonstration at Colman's in Bath today, or are you doing it?'

Mary explained that it was Ruby's turn and that it was her turn to look after the shop and the baby.

'Ah yes. Of course. Your brother's baby.'

He always said 'your brother's baby' as though needing to reassure himself of the fact. As with her marriage, he simply couldn't seem to grasp that she quite liked babies.

He went on to outline the events he had lined up for her and Ruby. 'I have been asked to arrange a demonstration at RAF Locking just before Christmas, not specifically for the RAF catering staff, but for all interested parties in the area. By that I mean those involved in voluntary work such as the WVS. It would be quite a large audience and will take place in the evening. It would also be something of a morale booster. Would you be interested?'

Mary frowned. 'RAF Locking? I have heard of it, I think. Where exactly is it?'

'Not far from you. Well, not terribly far. Weston-super-Mare, in fact. By the seaside. Quite bracing at this time of year I shouldn't wonder.'

There was something about his tone that made Mary suspect he had an alternative motive. Weston-super-Mare was a train ride away. She could drive the car, but there was of course the petrol issue. Train journeys nowadays took a lot longer than they used to, plus he had specifically stated it would be an evening event.

'Andrew, thank you very much for the opportunity, but I really don't think—'

'You could stay overnight! All expenses paid. I would be there to chaperone you – if you feel the need, that is—'

'No, Andrew!' Mary felt her face colouring up. 'I couldn't stay overnight. I've got Dad to think of; the bakery, the baby . . .'

'I'll do it.' Ruby snatched the telephone from her sister's grasp. 'Andrew. I would love to cheer up the catering corps,' she said in her cheekiest, cheeriest voice. 'Who knows, they might know some short cuts in baking that I don't know about.'

Silently she mouthed the words sugar, flour and fat to her sister. Everybody knew the forces got a bigger share of rations than the civilian population. Even dried egg, and goodness knows that had taken some getting used to.

Ruby sensed the hesitation on the other end of the phone. Andrew still hankered after her sister. Even though Ruby and Mary were almost identical, Andrew had not transferred his desires from the married twin to the unmarried one.

'Well . . . If Mary is sure she can't do it . . .' He sounded seriously disappointed.

'You have her willing sister,' Ruby declared, her voice ringing with both amusement and enthusiasm. 'Right. Now as I'll be speaking to people who cater to the masses, I'll be thinking simple baking enhanced with a few extra things to make them more interesting. I also think I too should bake an apple pie in honour of our American cousins entering the war. Now about that accommodation . . . it won't be with some doughty old landlady who doesn't allow dogs, babies or visitors will it?'

Andrew confirmed that she would be comfortably accommodated in a seafront chalet.

'What's it like? Room for two, is there?' She winked at her sister.

Andrew cleared his throat. 'I understand it has two bedrooms and is extremely comfortable. It is also heated. I believe it belongs to a professor boffin who used it for holidays before the war. He's too busy to use it now so lets it out to Government departments.'

All this was delivered in a dour, straightened tone. Ruby guessed he'd wanted Mary to himself even though she had made it clear that she wasn't interested in him – even as a friend.

'Oh, and I won't need a chaperone. Just give me the date.'

Once he was gone, she blew a raspberry into the mouthpiece of the telephone and laughed. 'Well, that's his little plan well and truly scuppered.'

Mary shook her head. 'He just won't take no for an answer.'

'Never mind. I'm game to do it. All those lovely RAF types. Catering corps, but lovely all the same.'

In her mind it wasn't the catering corps she was looking forward to. Johnnie was far away and she had to face the fact that he was not terribly romantic. There was that moment in the field of course, but he'd not referred to it in his letters. Neither had he asked her to wait for him, suggested an engagement or anything else. In all probability she would never see him again. The thought saddened her, but war changed people.

It also parted a great many. She had to hold on to what she had and at present her beau was Ivan. Up until now she'd held him off, but now she told herself that she might as well give in. Who knows what tomorrow might bring? They could all be dead. It was a grim thought but one that stayed with her. Yes, she would sleep with Ivan and maybe they might get married and have a baby like Charlie. Now wouldn't that be something!

She had to let Ivan know about this tremendous stroke of luck. A whole night away in a chalet fit for two.

Feeling Mary's eyes on her she looked up, just about managing to wipe a triumphant smile from her face. Nevertheless, it still shone in her eyes and Mary saw it.

'You're up to something.'

Smiling enigmatically, Ruby sprang to her feet. 'Of course I am. Just for a change I'll be talking to an audience comprising mostly of men. What could be better?'

She hung on to the kitchen door as she went out, kicking one leg behind her Betty Grable style.

Mary couldn't help smiling. Her sister was incorrigible, but who could blame her? Yes, she would have a great time with all those men and all eyes would be fixed on her. But a seaside chalet to herself? Despite the time of year it could prove quite cosy – for two.

Still, that was Ruby's business. She was old enough to know her own mind.

Her own thoughts turned to Mike. He was still pressing her about joining him in Lincolnshire, but added that he understood she had war work what with her broadcasts and baking demonstrations. He also told her about the midnight meals he cooked up for his colleagues when they came back from a bombing raid. *'Only after we're rested up of course. Then we eat and drink and generally let our hair down . . .'*

He didn't elaborate on what letting their hair down meant. It could mean other women, but somehow she wasn't taking that thought too seriously. It had to be his way of exerting extra pressure on her to join him. But as he'd said, it wasn't easy to get away, to drop everything while so much was going on.

'Wait and see,' she said quietly to herself. 'Wait and see.'

On Thursday of that week Ruby found herself giving a baking demonstration at a factory near the aerodrome where Ivan was stationed. It had been easy to persuade her sister to swap, to take advantage of some decent weather to take Charlie for a walk. From here she could get to where Ivan was stationed and tell him about the event Andrew had scheduled, an overnight stay and accommodation included.

'And you're looking a bit peaky,' Ruby had added.

Strangely enough Mary had agreed and willingly swapped.

Ruby was in her element.

'In peacetime we could use whatever fat we wanted to rub in with our flour or bake our cakes. That luxury is not available to us at this moment in time. It is therefore imperative that every bit of fat that sizzles off a roast joint, off fried bacon or skimmed from the top of a saucepan of boiled mutton or soup, is allowed to cool and used for baking . . .'

She'd grown used to churning out the same advice over and over again. It was hoped that repetition would take root in people's minds so that following advice designed to make food go further would become second nature.

'However, things have changed drastically since December the seventh. We are no longer alone in this war against Nazi oppression; our American cousins have joined us. We have a war in common, but also we share similar food tastes. Today, my friends, we turn our attention to the humble apple pie . . .'

She went on to advise on the most economical way of baking a pie, using an upper crust to cover the fruit and not bothering with a base. 'Rather than sweetening with a table-spoonful of your precious sugar ration, add honey or a saccharin tablet, crushing it and dissolving it in a little of the juice. Add a handful of sultanas or currants, or any other fruit you have available just to make it a little more interesting. For that special occasion, an added flavour to stir your man's appetite, soak the apples in beer or cider. Take the apples out of the liquid . . .' She demonstrated this with the aid of a colander. 'Place the apple slices into the pie dish adding a sweetener of your choice, or perhaps no sweetener at all, then . . .'

There was a murmur of approval as she poured the liquid used to soak the apples into a beer glass.

'There you are! What could be better than a slice of apple pie and a beer?'

The apple pie was placed into the hot oven behind her while she got on with the regular advice covering all kinds of cooking. Although both her and Mary's speciality was baking, the Ministry of Food required her to cover just about everything to do with cooking and that included how best to save the precious fuel they cooked with.

At the end of the day, she headed swiftly for the dark green van supplied by the government. Since Johnnie's departure, fed up with being supplied with one driver after another, she'd grabbed the bull by the horns and drove herself around, though at first Mary had driven around with her just until she'd gained confidence.. The only drawback was having the car exchanged for a van.

The van rattled as she drove. Putting the red brick factory behind her, she headed for the aerodrome.

The rounded roofs of the aircraft hangars were outlined

against a grey sky. It looked like rain. She didn't mind if it rained today as long as it didn't rain when she gave the demonstration at RAF Locking. A day at the seaside should be full of sunshine, not rain. Not that the day concerned her that much. It was the night she would look forward to.

At night the bombers were likely to come, though there hadn't been any raids for quite a while. The battle termed by Churchill as the Battle of Britain, when so much had been owed by so many to so few, had been won. The worst, they hoped, was over, though there were still skirmishes now and again. Though not tonight, she hoped. Tonight she wanted to tell Ivan the good news, that she would shortly have the opportunity to stay at a seafront chalet in Weston-super-Mare. And he was welcome to share it with her.

Her heart raced at the thought of her decision. If she was going to do it with him, it had to be in the right place at the right time and the promise of a seafront chalet was too good to miss. Johnnie Smith crept into her thoughts; but he's not here, she reminded herself. You might never see him again. In the meantime you have to live.

The guard at the barrier stepped out smartly, asked for her papers and who she wanted to see.

'Pilot Officer Bronowski,' she said briskly, her heart dancing against her ribs. She knew her cheeks were flushed and her eyes sparkling. If his knowing smile was anything to go by, the guard had noticed the excitement in her face. She only hoped he wasn't able to read her mind. If he did she was likely to blush even more.

'I'll ring the mess and let him know you're here.'

Her fingers drummed the van's steering wheel as she waited, peering into the basic brick structure to see what the sentry was doing. She could just about see him inside the brick built guard post, the telephone clenched against one side of his face. His back was to her. She perceived a sudden rigidity in his shoulders and heard him say, 'I see. I see. Right. I'll tell her, sir. If you say so, sir.'

He was wearing a stern expression when he came back out. She was instantly reminded of the vicar when he was about to deliver a sermon he knew nobody would like.

He stood over her, looking down at her with an odd expression on his face. 'I'm afraid he's not here.'

There was something oddly furtive about the way he glanced from side to side as though expecting more dangerous incursions to take advantage of his time dealing with her, plus his tone was brusque when before it had been friendly.

Something was wrong. She could feel it in his tone, in his stance. She automatically thought the worst. An iron band seemed suddenly to constrict her breathing. 'Oh no. Please don't tell me he hasn't come back. Or he's injured. Please . . .'

Her voice faded away. The odd look on the sentry's face intensified, though was as unreadable as it had been before. 'Nothing like that, miss.'

'So where is he?'

'I hardly think it's my duty to tell you . . .'

'Please. I have to know. Please.' Never had she poured so much pleading into her voice. She wasn't the pleading sort. Not the type who begged for anything really. But this – she could tell something was wrong and she had to know – whatever it was.

The guard cleared his throat and for the first time met her eyes. 'I'm afraid he's at the hospital.'

A little gasp caught in Ruby's throat. 'Is he hurt badly?' He had to be hurt. Why else would he be in hospital?

The answer was like a hammer smashing through glass.

'He's at the maternity hospital with his wife. She's just given birth to their first child. That's where he is. Sorry, miss.'

A feeling of despair travelled from her neck and over her shoulders. It was all over. The romance had never really been, and indeed Ivan was the charmer John Smith had said he was. She didn't need him to tell her that Ivan, her handsome, exotic Ivan who kissed her hand and clicked his heels together when they met, had a reputation. He loved women. He also left broken hearts all over the place. Why hadn't she seen it?

But she had seen it. She'd just chosen to ignore it.

Her hands shook as she heaved the steering wheel to the left, the back wheels squealing as she did a quick turn before heading for home.

Home! How could she go home right now?

Blinded by tears she headed for the outskirts of Whitchurch village. She pulled into a layby, no more than an indent in front of a farm gate. To one side of it the bare branches of an elm tree creaked in the wind. The field on the other side of the hedge was almost as dull as the sky, the earth ploughed up into evenly spaced rows.

Still gripping the steering wheel, Ruby rested her head on her hands. She told herself not to cry and that there were plenty more fish in the sea. That it was more her pride that was hurt than her heart. It did nothing to ward off the tears. They came anyway.

Mary was taking the Christmas cake out of the oven when Ruby got home.

'I think it looks good. What do you think?'

Absorbed in admiring her handiwork, Mary hadn't noticed Ruby had not bounced into the kitchen as she normally did after a demonstration, demanding a cup of tea and taking out of the hamper whatever food hadn't been devoured by her audience.

Ruby didn't want Mary to notice how upset she was. It

suited her to admire the cake. She tapped it with one finger. 'It sounds right. Looks good too.'

'I used the eggless recipe. The honey should help it keep just like sugar does.'

Ruby entertained a violent urge to pick up the cake and throw it out of the window – not because it wasn't a fine cake, because it was. And Mary was a fine cook and would be heartbroken if she did that. So would everyone else. They'd been saving up coupons for weeks, setting aside what they could to celebrate Christmas. The cake, along with a cockerel Mrs Hicks had earmarked for slaughter, would form the centre of their Christmas celebrations.

'I expect it'll be fine,' said Ruby, turning her back on her sister, the kitchen and her inexplicable urge to explode. All because of Ivan Bronowski. Why was it she always fell for the wrong man, the scoundrel, the man who had to have more than one woman in his life?

'I've written the recipe down. I thought you might want to use it when you go down to RAF Locking. It was quite easy.'

Ruby took the small notebook in which Mary noted down every recipe they could use when one of them gave a talk, or in Mary's case broadcast on the wireless. The BBC in Bristol was very encouraging.

Ruby stared at the recipe and the instructions accompanying it. 'How ridiculous.'

The comment came without warning.

'I'm sorry?' Mary looked hurt.

Ruby tried laughing it off, but her voice even to her own ears sounded brittle and insincere. 'I meant about the carrot. Who would have believed back before the war that we'd be cooking a cake made from carrots? Carrot cake. Still, you never know. Plaster the top with icing and it might catch on.'

The following day Mary received a telegram informing her

that Mike would be spending Christmas with them. The back bedroom over at Stratham House was immediately earmarked for their use. On this occasion Bettina would be staying there too and everyone would be eating Christmas dinner together.

Mary was overjoyed. Her heart raced every time she heard reports on the wireless of bombing raids over Germany. The announcer always sounded upbeat and very matter of fact when he reported of planes and lives lost. All the same it was worrying and Mary always felt that her heart was in her mouth until Mike phoned her to say that he was home safe and sound.

On the same day Ruby received a letter from abroad. It wasn't hard to guess that it was from John.

Stan discreetly looked away from his daughter, concentrating his attention on his beloved Charlie.

'Here. Have a bit of my breakfast. I know you think your granddad's breakfast tastes better than yer own.'

That said, he cut his breakfast sausage in half. It wasn't often they had sausages for breakfast and he couldn't help noticing the girls never ate them themselves but made sure he had one.

Charlie wrapped his little fist around the cooled sausage, his eyes bright with joy. 'Sozzy.'

'That's right,' said Stan, who glowed with pride every time a milestone was reached in the little lad's life. 'It's a sausage. A bit of Granddad's sausage, so I suppose "sozzy" is the right word for it. Only a bit of the word and a bit of the sausage.'

Ruby sat staring at the letter. The paper was light and crisp, a bit like tissue or tracing paper. Judging by the fact that the envelope too was very light, the letter had come by air rather than the slower sea route.

Stan Sweet noticed her face looked as though it were set in stone. Her eyes flickered over what she was reading. She read it more than once. He could see that by the way her eyes kept going back to the top of the page.

He was about to ask how John was faring in the Far East when Ruby spoke.

'Listen to this. *Dear Ruby. Many thanks for the recipe for Victoria sponge. Hopefully I will get around to making it, though rock cakes seem to be the order of the day out here. They're all over the place in the place where we're stationed, falling from the sky in fact. All I have to watch is that one doesn't land on my head. I'd never get over it.*'

Ruby looked up at her father. 'It's dated the eighth of December. The day after Pearl Harbor.'

'No it isn't,' piped up Frances. 'It's the same day.'

'No, you little know it all. Pearl Harbor was bombed on the seventh of December.'

Frances shook her head more vehemently. 'No it wasn't. It's the same day. Hawaii is one side of the International Dateline, and Singapore is on the other. That's where John is, isn't he?'

Her tension mounting, Ruby turned to her father. 'Is that right?'

Stan Sweet nodded.

Mary poured her another cup of tea.

There had been rumours that a Far Eastern garrison had been bombed but that everything was under control. The BBC had said so.

Stan Sweet voiced what was on all their minds. 'Is he saying that they've been bombed quite heavily?'

Ruby nodded. 'Rock cakes. That's what he means about the possibility of being hit on the head by a rock cake. It's his way of saying they've been bombed without the censor striking it out.'

Mary slumped into a chair, eyes downcast, her lips clenched

in a sullen line. They'd heard rumours about Malaya, the country of which Singapore was the capital, being bombed, though only lightly. For Johnnie to mention it suggested otherwise.

For some reason all eyes turned to Charlie who was demanding more of his grandfather's breakfast. Charlie was guaranteed to help them forget about the bad things going on. His antics and his cheery disposition never failed to make them smile.

'I hear they've got big guns in Singapore,' said Stan Sweet in an effort to reassure his daughter. 'They call it the fortress of the Far East.'

Ruby smiled weakly. 'I hope it lives up to its name.'

'Oh, I'm sure it will,' declared her father. He wasn't sure at all, but his daughter needed reassuring and whether she knew it or not, she cared about what happened to John Smith. Never mind her Polish pilot. Ivan Bronowski was just a flash in the pan as far as he was concerned. He only hoped the corporal would survive whatever happened and come home to where he belonged.

Stan turned his attention back to his grandson though his disquiet about John's position and Singapore itself remained. 'My, but you're going to grow into a big lad I'll be bound,' he said.

Ruby threw him a wry look. 'He will if you keep on giving him your breakfast, Dad. Do you want more toast?'

'No. I don't. But perhaps . . .' He looked at Charlie. The chubby hand was already held out in anticipation of something else to eat.

'Dad!' Ruby's voice pulled him up short.

'I know. I know.' He leaned closer to the little boy. 'We don't want you being sick now do we?'

Frances began wiping Charlie's face. 'There you are,

Charlie. Wait until ten o'clock and I'll take you for a walk. I have to help open the shop first, but you can wait, can't you?'

It occurred to Stan that Frances would make an extremely good mother. Not that his daughters wouldn't also, but for Frances to become a good mother would be a great relief. Her mother, Mildred, hadn't been very good at all, taking off once her husband Sefton had died. Stan was left to bring Frances up. Not that he regretted it. She was a headstrong girl but good at heart, a tomboy most of her life, though he sensed things were changing. Frances was becoming quite pretty. She was even beginning to help Ruby take down and enhance her old dresses, even to adding buttons and bows and bits of lace. Oh, yes, he thought to himself. Time is marching on.

He was just about to ask Mary for another cup of tea but noticed she had taken her apron off and was putting on her coat. She noticed his enquiring look and informed him she was popping along the village to see Bettina Hicks. 'She had a bit of a cold. I thought I would take her some of that curried parsnip soup left over from yesterday.'

'Tell her I'll be in to see her.'

Mary said that she would.

Once she was gone, Stan asked Ruby if there was anything wrong with her sister. 'She just seems a bit tired,' he added.

'Oh, I think she's just a bit tired trying to sort out Christmas what with Mike coming home. Mind you, Bettina's been a good help. Stratham House is like Aladdin's cave; you never quite know what else Bettina has stored away in her cupboards and attic.'

She said it laughingly, anything to throw her father off the scent of the real problem.

Last night she'd confided in Mary the fact that Ivan Bronowski was married and she didn't want to see him ever again. In turn, Mary had confided in her about the cottage close to where Mike was stationed. Mary's face had been taut with indecision and regret. 'I can't go. Not yet anyway.'

Ruby pointed out to her that her first obligation was to her husband not to her family.

Mary had bent her head. Even though her hair fell forward like a thick veil, Ruby didn't need to see the anguish on her sister's face because she could hear it in her voice. 'I know,' she said softly. Only two small words, but so heartfelt. 'And then there's the work with the Ministry of Food.'

'You could still work for them, only in Lincolnshire.'

'You'd have more work to do here.'

Mary had brushed her hair behind her ears. Ruby had reached out and tucked back a strand she had missed. She said she didn't mind having more work. Up until now they'd divided the load between them, Mary concentrating on the BBC broadcasts, taking turns to do talks and demonstrations in factories, shops, offices and women's groups. Ruby couldn't bring herself to speak into a microphone; she had to have real people to talk to. Mary could do both.

Sworn to secrecy, Ruby had no intention of letting her father know about Mike wanting Mary to move up to Lincolnshire. If anyone was going to tell him, it had to be Mary.

This morning neither of them had mentioned the conversation. It was Ruby's opinion that Mary should be with her husband; she would be if she had a husband.

'But I don't,' she mumbled to herself as she opened the cupboard beneath the stairs and dragged out the carpet sweeper.

She was just about to attack the runner in the hallway when Frances came in from the shop wearing a cheeky grin. 'It's him,' she said. 'Ivan.'

Ruby couldn't believe it. The humiliation she'd felt on finding out he was married, flooded her face with anger. 'Is it now!'

Her temper was up. What a nerve! Coming here, no doubt straight from the birth of his baby. She was tempted to get Frances to tell him that she wasn't at home, but then her father would suspect something was wrong. He was very adept at pretending to read the newspaper but actually noticing everything that went on around him.

Frances followed her to the door. 'He's very handsome. Are you going to marry him? If you are, can I be a bridesmaid?'

'I doubt it,' said Ruby under her breath.

He was standing with his back to her. Sensing her presence, he spun round, the quirky smile she had loved immediately apparent.

'Ruby. Are you free tonight? I thought we could go to the pictures.'

He didn't know she'd visited the airfield! Nobody had told him!

'No. I don't think so.' Her words were clipped. Her lips tight across her teeth.

He didn't seem to notice. 'How about tomorrow night? I could swap duty and then we could—'

'What did you have? A boy or a girl?'

At first he laughed as though he thought she was joking. When he finally realised that he wasn't joking, the laughter died in his throat and his smile froze. 'I can explain.'

Ruby raised one eyebrow quizzically. 'Can you? Quite how do you explain away a wife and baby? Come on. Let's see you try!'

Ivan shook his head, all pretext of innocence absent. 'I was lonely when I first came here. She trapped me . . .'

'An English girl?'

He nodded. 'Yes. English.'

'You mean you got her pregnant and married her.'

She heard Frances gasp.

Ivan persisted. 'But I don't love her! I love you!'

'You have a wife and child. Look after them. Goodbye, Ivan.'

She turned her back on him, retracing her steps to the living room behind the shop counter. She was seething.

'You can't mean that!'

'Goodbye, Ivan,' said Frances, taking great delight in repeating what her cousin had said and in the same tone.

Ruby slammed the door behind her. She stalked through the kitchen and out of the back door, aware of her father's eyes on her. She didn't look round. She needed to be alone with her thoughts.

There wasn't much to look at in the garden; the sprouts, winter cabbage and carrots were doing well. Beyond them the spear-like leaves of leeks and onions trailed over the hard earth. The overnight frost still lay on the ground.

Normally she might have shivered standing out here even though her cardigan was knitted from double knit wool – unpicked from her brother Charlie's old jumper.

She looked at the sombre sky thinking how greyness affected one's mood. Winter was like that.

The throaty roar of Ivan's motorbike faded into a distant rumble as he drove away. One half of her wanted to rush out after him and beg him to come back. The more sensible half knew she had to let him go. It was over. She would do the demonstration at Locking, but stay overnight in the chalet alone.

The sound of the back door opening heralded her father stepping out. One quick glance and she could see he was wearing his gardening clothes. He took out his pipe and with a practised eye surveyed the sky then the garden beneath it. 'We need some air in the ground to give the worms a chance.'

What he meant was that he was off to fetch his gardening fork with which he would stab the iron-hard ground.

She watched him amble off down the garden, the brim of his brown trilby hat pulled low over his face. He hadn't asked her about Ivan, probably because he'd guessed she'd ended the relationship. If he didn't ask it meant he approved. He'd done the same with Gareth Stead until war had broken out. That was when he'd asked Gareth to marry Ruby, just so she wouldn't be forced to work in a factory far away from home or even to join the forces.

Ivan was history. For the moment she would content herself with her job, the family and diversionary things – like writing to Corporal John Smith. Yes. John would appreciate it and it would suit her to do so – at least for now.

CHAPTER TWENTY-FOUR

The whole family went to church that Christmas of 1941 including Mike Dangerfield and his Aunt Bettina.

The vicar mentioned the greater might of the allies now the Americans had joined in the fight. 'Let us pray that their joining means a more rapid end to this terrible conflict.'

Everyone said a hearty amen to that!

The air outside the old church was crisp with the promise of yet another frosty night.

'I'm fed up of bringing in stiff washing from the line,' stated Mrs Martin. 'My Reg's combinations were stiff enough to stand up by themselves. Unnatural, it is.'

There were smiles at her remark along with shouts of Merry Christmas. Everyone began heading for the path leading down to the brook and the upward slog up Court Road to the heart of the village and the Christmas dinner everyone was looking forward to. Except for Stan Sweet.

'Won't be a minute.' He reached for the bouquet of winter jasmine and Christmas roses that he grew especially for this time of year, which he'd left in the church porch. He also reached for Charlie's hand. 'Let's go and see Grandma, shall we?'

Not really understanding, but wanting to be with his beloved grandfather, Charlie slipped his small hand into Stan's.

The twins, Frances, Bettina Hicks and Mike Dangerfield continued to head for home, though not before Mary called out to remind her father that dinner would be ready soon and not to be late.

Stan Sweet made his way over the frozen ground to his wife's grave, Charlie toddling unsteadily at his side.

After cracking the ice in the urn, he put the flowers in there, arranging them carefully in the way he'd seen her do all those years ago. Charlie attempted to ape his grandfather, patting each bloom into place.

'Carefully,' said Stan. 'We don't want to squash them. Your grandmother wouldn't want that now would she?'

The little boy giggled and began to collect sticks and stones – in fact anything that attracted his attention, most of it seemingly for no real reason.

As was his habit, Stan went down on one knee.

'Sarah my dear. It's Christmas, that time of year when it's supposed to be peace and goodwill to all men. Unfortunately the war still rages, although, as I've already mentioned, the Americans have joined in, late but not too late, not as late as in the last lot anyway. Let's hope for a speedy end to this carnage.

'Mike's home on leave and Mary seems very happy that he is though there does seem to be something going on between them that they're keeping to themselves. I'm hoping they're having a baby, but I can't say for sure.

'On another note, our Ruby has finished with her Polish flier.' He frowned pondering his thoughts. 'Ruby is the one I'll always worry about. She's not a good judge of men. Whatever happened between her and this Ivan, I don't know and she isn't saying. I promise I won't pry,' he said in answer to what had sounded like Sarah warning him in his head. He smiled. Sarah had been such a wise woman. Beautiful too.

'Frances is growing up. I'm glad to say she's nothing like her mother. She's bright too, especially in geography. I think it was her favourite subject at school. Not that she's likely to need it much serving in the bakery, but after the war? Who knows?

'As for our Charlie's boy.' He turned his head, smiling proudly at the growing toddler. 'Will you just look at him? Little Charlie. I thank the Lord that he was born.

'Right,' he said, getting stiffly on to his feet. 'I'm off to have my Christmas dinner and young Charlie here is off to play with his presents.'

Slamming his trilby firmly on his head, he turned to go when he remembered there was somebody else he wanted to mention.

'Another young man our Ruby knows is in the Far East. She's writing regularly. He used to be her driver. He's a down-to-earth sort, the kind that would suit her, though I wouldn't dare say that,' he added before he imagined her warning him not to interfere.

He turned back just in time to find Charlie toddling off across the short cropped grass towards the retaining wall where rust-coloured stalks and dried grass mingled with a bramble bush. 'Oh no you don't young man!'

His hand landed on Charlie's soft woollen hat, enough of a diversion to bring him to a halt.

'Mum! Mmmm! Mum!' cried Charlie, pointing at the desolate patch of tangled growth.

Was he shouting 'mum' or was it really just the letter 'm' drawn out to make a similar sound?

If only his mum was here, thought Stan. If only his dad was. Stan visualised the last time he'd seen his son's smiling face: early spring 1940. Charlie had come home just after Christmas following the sinking of his ship. The whole family had been relieved that he'd survived, and all thanks to an enemy captain who had scuttled his ship rather than suffer any more loss of life. Rumour had it that shortly after the Battle of the River Plate the captain had taken his own life rather than have his family suffer at the hands of Adolf Hitler for his shame.

Having had such a lucky escape, he'd never expected his son to be taken from him just a short time after he'd been spared. He didn't believe that all was fair in love and war. Life itself was unfair.

Thank God for young Charlie, he thought closing his eyes. 'And God bless Gilda,' he added. 'She's with you and our Charlie now, Sarah. I think you'll like her.' Squeezing his eyes shut to hold back the tears, he got to his feet. 'Come on Charlie,' he said to his grandson. 'Our Christmas dinner'll be waiting on the table. And then there's cake. Would you like cake, Charlie?'

Charlie didn't show any sign that he'd heard. He was looking at the brambles and was making the same sounds as before and pointing with his mittened hand.

Stan went down on one knee and touched Charlie's rosy cheek. 'Well, if you're not going to walk home, I suppose I'll have to carry you.'

Charlie didn't protest when he was lifted in the strong arms he'd grown to know and trust. He didn't protest at being carried, probably because he could see much more once he was above the sight of adult knees, but he did twist his little body so he could lean over Stan's shoulder and keep his eyes fixed on whatever it was that interested him.

Stan talked and chuckled to his grandson as they made their way to the gate. Once there he stopped to grapple with the latch, Charlie a weight on his shoulder. Out of habit he turned to take one last look at the church and the

quiet spot where his wife was buried, when a sudden movement among the brambles caught his attention. He might have
put it down to a badger or a cat out hunting for birds and
rodents if a head and shoulders hadn't suddenly popped up.

The figure was wearing a black hat and coat, her face a
ghostly white, her eyes too big for her face. Even at this
distance he knew who it was: Miriam Powell always wore
black to church. But what was she doing among that rough
patch of ground half-hidden from view? The obvious thought
came to him that she might have been relieving herself, but
surely she could have got home in time to do that.

He turned away feeling embarrassed and also slightly
disgusted – that was until it struck him that Miriam just
wouldn't do that. Her mother was a stickler for conformity,
a pillar of sanctimonious respectability and Miriam had had
a strict upbringing.

He thought back to the day she'd found Charlie, the open
innocence of her expression when he'd thanked her, her
mother's evil frown.

'I looked after him!' she'd declared when he'd spoken
to her about it.

'I believe that you did,' he'd said to her. At the same
time he'd thought how defensive she'd sounded, as though
half afraid he might believe otherwise.

His daughter Ruby had refused to believe Charlie had
wandered so far. 'He's too young. And besides, Frances
insists that his harness was fastened securely.'

'He learns things quickly, and that includes unbuckling
his harness,' he'd said, not without a flash of grandfatherly
pride.

Neither his daughters nor niece, Frances, had contradicted
him. The baby, young Charlie, was the apple of his eye and
the best thing to have come out of this ruddy war! As regards

to Miriam, whatever the truth was, there was no harm done. She would never harm a baby, and certainly not Charlie's baby. Even though there were question marks about whether Charlie really had wandered so far, or that she taken him there herself, he preferred to believe the best of her. Having a mother like she had was pain enough in her life.

He was just about to call out to her, when she emerged from the hedges, straightening her hat and running towards him, her ugly black coat flapping around her, her heavy black shoes clopping like the hooves of the milkman's horse. Her complexion was as pale as ever, but the chill day had pinched her cheeks and made them rosy. She greeted him cheerfully. 'Merry Christmas, Mr Sweet. Merry Christmas, Charlie.'

She shoved her hands into her pockets, though not before Stan had noticed how dirty they were, her fingernails choked with dirt.

Stan returned her Christmas greeting, not that she seemed to notice. Her attention was firmly fixed on Charlie, her eyes shining with joy, her face bright with enchantment. He'd heard from his daughters and Frances that Miriam couldn't seem to bring herself to speak to Charlie when he was in the shop. She could look at him and touch him, but the words never seemed to come. She just stared, her mind elsewhere.

He sighed. Poor Miriam. He couldn't help feeling sorry for her. Look at her clothes. He was no judge of women's fashions, but a girl of her age shouldn't be wearing such dowdy clothes. And what he could see of her hair was a few lank wisps showing from beneath a close-fitting hat. He vaguely recalled his mother wearing the same sort of hat many years ago.

Frances had told him about seeing Miriam's hair was cut

close to her scalp and that whoever had cut her hair had not been gentle. He omitted mentioning the discussion he'd had with Bettina, his mind recoiling from the fact that it was probably her mother's doing.

'Have you heard from your grandmother?' he asked her. Ada was totally different to her daughter, a free-thinking woman with a mind of her own.

Miriam looked sad. 'No,' she whispered softly. 'I don't think so.'

It was an odd answer but told him a great deal. If a card or message had come from Ada Perkins, Miriam's mother would have thrown it in the fire before Miriam had chance to read it. 'Wouldn't you be happier living with your grandmother?'

Her face lit up. 'Oh yes. I would love it, but my mother . . .' The glow that had lit her face was soon extinguished.

Stan felt a surge of anger. 'How old are you, Miriam?'

'Thirty.'

'Old enough to make up your own mind,' he said sternly. 'I'm surprised you haven't been called up to work in a factory or join the armed forces.'

Most likely a factory. She didn't strike him as able enough to put on a uniform. 'My mother told them I couldn't go. She told them I was . . .'

Stan raised his eyebrows, dreading what he guessed she might say.

'Spastic,' she said. 'That's what she told them. But I'm not,' she said frantically. 'It's just that since . . . but then . . . before that. She told them before that.'

Stan frowned. 'Before what, Miriam?'

Her mouth clamped shut and she looked down at her shoes. Whatever she'd been about to say was swallowed.

'You don't need your mother's permission to live somewhere

311

else,' he told her. 'You're old enough to make your own decisions.'

She didn't look up. 'I know, but my mother . . .'

'Won't let you.'

'Unless I marry, but . . .'

Miriam Powell was a bundle of nervous indecision. She'd been downtrodden by her mother and there seemed precious chance of her ever escaping Gertrude Powell's domination. There was little he could do about it, except give a moment's solace. 'Would you like to carry Charlie? He's getting a bit too heavy for me.'

'Can I?' She sounded ecstatic, her eyes like great dark pools in her pale face.

'If he'll go to you.'

Stan half expected Charlie to kick up a fuss, after all, Miriam was not that familiar to his grandson, but to his great surprise he didn't.

Charlie broke into chuckles holding out his arms and uttering half-formed words including the mmmm and mum ones, over and over again.

He handed Charlie into her arms, not liking the feeling of emptiness in his own. Charlie grinned at her, tugged her hair and patted her hat.

'No,' she said to him, pulling his hands away from her hat. She held him tightly and never once did her gaze leave his face.

'He likes you,' said Stan.

Miriam's expression was like a burst of winter sunshine. 'He thinks I'm his mother. I don't mind him thinking that. Really I don't. I really *want* him to call me mother, even though I'm not. Not really.' She sounded quite delirious about the fact that he might.

Stan reconsidered his decision to let Miriam hold his

grandson. He'd been overcome by seasonal goodwill, but now he suddenly found himself regretting it. Frances had heard singing then words like mum or mmmm when she'd found Charlie. It occurred to him that Miriam had been *teaching* Charlie to call her mum.

His fears were suddenly confirmed.

'Mum,' he heard Miriam say. 'Mmmmm . . . um . . .' She was beaming into Charlie's face, wagging his little arm, rubbing his nose with hers.

He was suddenly panicked into demanding him back. 'I'd better have him now,' he said firmly once they were halfway up the hill. 'Time for his dinner.'

'Not yet!' Her arms gripped Charlie more tightly. Her beaming expression was replaced by a startled look – worse than startled. 'You can't take him yet! I haven't held him for long enough! He likes being with me. He needs me.' Both her voice and expression verged on hysteria.

A warning bell sounded in Stan's brain, though all the same, he wanted to treat her gently. 'Miriam. It's Charlie's dinnertime. Mine too. It's Christmas. Remember?'

He couldn't help feeling that Miriam wasn't quite with it. In fact he was half wondering whether her mother was telling the truth and she was just the slightest bit deranged. He didn't want to believe it.

'He's not yours, Miriam. You're not his mother. Come on, Charlie. Come to your old granddad.'

Miriam stared at Stan accusingly as if the child was hers, as if she were indeed Charlie's mother. For a dreadful moment it seemed to Stan as though she wasn't going to let go. Carefully he plied her arms from around his grandson. Finally she stood there, staring at her empty arms.

Wrapping his arms protectively around his grandson, Stan

saw a figure in black standing at the door of Powell's shop. He recognised Gertrude Powell, her face as white as the marble urn sitting on his wife's grave.

'Go home, Miriam,' Stan said gently. 'See? Your mother's waiting for you.'

He didn't much care for Miriam's mother and couldn't help blaming her for how Miriam had turned out. However, on this occasion he was extremely glad to see her.

'Merry Christmas, Mrs Powell.'

He hadn't called her Gertrude since they were children together. Anyway she wouldn't thank him for being so personal. Since becoming an adult she kept friendship at a distance. Even arranging for Frances to be evacuated to the Forest of Dean with Ada Perkins had been done when Ada was visiting and had offered to take the girl. Funnily enough, Gertrude hadn't seemed so hard then. He wondered what might have happened to change her. Perhaps she'd been ill, but then, if she had somebody would have said so.

Stan recalled the talk he and Bettina had had about Miriam. She had only gone away for a few days with her mother to the Forest of Dean. Unless . . .

He didn't bother to speculate further. The girl needed to get away from Gertrude and if the factories or forces wouldn't take her, the best place for her to be was with her grandmother.

Stan walked on, aware that Charlie was leaning over his shoulder waving goodbye. 'Mmmmmm. Mum. Mmmmm.'

The door of the shop slammed shut on the two women. He didn't tell anyone about his encounter until Christmas dinner was over, the dishes put away and the wireless turned off once the King's speech was over. After he'd told them what had happened, he shuddered. 'Never leave Charlie alone with her. She's besotted.'

'Just as she was with Charlie,' Mary pointed out.

'She scared the living daylights out of him,' added Ruby with a laugh. 'Do you remember when he used to hide from her?'

They all did. Stan didn't laugh. Why were Miriam's hands so dirty, he wondered? And why was she spending so much time in the churchyard?

'She's mad,' added Frances. 'I've seen her hanging around in the churchyard.'

'And what were you doing there?' asked Ruby.

A pink flush invaded Frances's cheeks. 'I went for a walk. I go for a walk there a lot. I like the trees.' She didn't mention Paul and that he'd finally kissed her. She'd known he wanted to, but had held him at a distance. And her family mustn't know. She'd know they would say she was too young.

Ruby eyed her sidelong and not without misgivings. 'With whom?'

'None of your business! I can go for a walk there by myself or with any of my friends. I do have friends, you know.'

It was obvious to them all that Frances was getting more than a little bit hot under the collar. Ruby didn't mention that she'd seen Frances hand in hand with Paul Martin. At least she thought it was Paul. There was a very wide choice of Martin brothers. It seemed that Mrs Martin had spent much of her life giving birth – mostly to boys.

The fact that Frances was growing up wasn't lost on Stan. The years kept rolling past and he often wished he could turn back the clock and they could be children again. He sighed at the prospect of getting old and his children getting older, contemplating that it wouldn't be long before his daughters and Frances would flee the nest. Hopefully one would stay around until his grandson was grown – if not in this house, then close by.

'So you've seen Miriam Powell in the churchyard.' Stan directed the question at Frances. He had a suspicion of why Miriam's fingernails and hands were so dirty.

'I have,' said Frances. 'I've seen her there and heard her wailing as though she's lost something. A bit like when she was with Charlie in the den. Singing and talking to somebody. There was nobody there though. I would have known if there was.'

'Sounds like a mystery,' offered Mike in his usual affable way. 'Like a detective novel that you feel you have to solve before the detective actually does it.'

Mary laughed. 'Mike, this is Oldland Common. Nothing happens here. Now help yourself to another piece of cake.'

'I'll burst.'

'Take some.'

Gazing at Mary in abject adoration, he obediently took another slice of cake, took a bite, chewed and swallowed his thoughts on what to him still constituted a mystery. He saw no wrong in voicing those thoughts. 'You'd think nothing happened in those places in the detective novels either, but they do – well, they do when that Hercule Poirot character is involved!'

Everyone laughed except for Stan Sweet. He was a straightforward man who didn't like mysteries. If Miriam was deranged, and he didn't think she was, something had to be done about it. He'd already decided to write to Ada Perkins, the only person who might do something helpful.

'Where exactly in the churchyard did you see her?'

Ruby glanced up from cutting the last slice of Christmas cake before putting the remainder into the cake tin. Although her father sounded calm and casual, she wasn't fooled. His probing was so gentle that Frances wouldn't suspect a thing. Not that it mattered if she did. It was Miriam who had to be worried.

'She was hiding,' said Frances. 'At least I think she was hiding. And singing. I heard her singing just like she was in the den.'

Stan frowned. 'Is that so? A hymn I suppose.'

Now it was Frances who frowned as she fought to remember. 'No. Not a hymn as such. I think it was a lullaby. I heard her singing the same one down in the Dingle – in our—' She corrected herself. She was too old for childish pursuits. 'The kids' den.'

Her face brightened. 'I can tell you what lullaby it was. It's the one Mary sings to Charlie when he's got a new tooth coming through. *Hush! my dear, lie still and slumber, Holy angels guard thy bed.* That one. The same one I heard her singing down in the den.'

Bettina Hicks who had remained silent up until now, cupped her cheeks with both hands, her finely arched eyebrows knitted in concentration.

Assuming she'd been about to say something about Miriam, Stan leaned forward, both elbows resting on the table – a practice he abhorred in others. His expression was intense. 'Bettina? Are you all right,' he said when no comment was expressed.

Bettina looked away, pushed her hands down on the chair arms and struggled to her feet. 'I think it's time I went home. It's been a lovely day. Thank you for everything,' she said, showering everyone with her beaming smile. She turned to Stan. 'Do you think you could see me home? I'm feeling a little stiff after all this sitting down and rich food.'

Mike got up from his chair. 'No need to trouble, Stan. I can go with you and come back for Mary,' he offered.

She held up her hand like a policeman directing traffic. 'No. I insist you stay. The night is young and so are you. Anyway, we have things to discuss. You don't mind, do you, Stan?'

Stan didn't hesitate. Ruby retrieved Bettina's walking stick from the side of the fireplace while Stan fetched her hat, coat and knitted navy blue scarf that the cold evening called for.

Mary and Ruby exchanged worried glances. It was only just gone teatime and everyone had expected Bettina to stay longer. She didn't usually tire easily, although of course she had been ill before Christmas with a severe cold.

After fetching his own coat and hat, Stan accompanied her to the door, and opened it, his arm arched protectively around her shoulders as he ushered her out.

The night sky was full of stars and a bright moon was turning everything silver. Chimneys and the tops of trees showed starkly black against the sky. The air was crisp and they could see their breath.

'Another frost tomorrow,' Stan proclaimed.

Bettina made no proper comment. In the blackout proper he wouldn't have been able to see her expression, but thanks to the moon he could see her face clearly. He sensed her apprehension and guessed there was a specific reason she'd asked him to see her home.

'So. What's on your mind?'

She didn't attempt to prevaricate, but then Bettina wasn't the sort to do that. That was what he liked about her.

'I can't help but think of that conversation we had not long ago.'

Stan nodded. 'Yes. It's been on my mind too.'

'You know that there were rumours about that young Methodist Minister, the one that shot off to join the army as a padre?'

Stan frowned. Bettina Hicks was one of the shrewdest women he'd ever known, just as shrewd as his Sarah had been. He should have known she'd jump to the same conclusion as he had.

'So you think we were right: she might have had a baby and her mother might have pressured her to give it away?'

Bettina fell silent. 'Or Gertrude could have done worse, I wouldn't put it past her. And I wouldn't mind betting that that poor girl has been punished beyond endurance. If there's one thing her mother cannot cope with, it's what she regards as the sins of others – especially the sins of the flesh.'

'We know she's a bit overzealous for the church. Hard to believe she's Ada's daughter.'

'Humph,' grunted Bettina. 'She changed the minute she fell for Godfrey Powell. Sometimes I think that man thought he was God; Gertrude worshipped him, that's for sure. The only thing Gertrude wanted from him was a child. It was the only time he gave into her wishes. I think he also thought it behove him as a Christian to be a family man. I believe once that was done, they never slept with each other ever again. That was when Ada left. She couldn't stand her son-in-law and he never let her visit the child unless he was there.'

'Stupid people.'

'Nasty people.'

Stan tried to read the look on her face. 'What is it you're trying to say?'

Bettina folded both hands on to the top of her stick and breathed deeply, the cold air sharp in her chest. 'I think you should take your spade to the graveyard.'

The ground stayed solidly frozen during those first weeks of 1942. When he went to St Anne's to visit Sarah, he made a point of wading through the long grass and thistles to look at the spot where he'd seen Miriam.

'Even though he visited Sarah's grave at least once a week, he never saw Miriam once and wondered why. Perhaps she'd got over her loss – if indeed there had been a loss. He couldn't know for sure.

There was no sign of any disturbance among the long grass, no sign of the earth being turned over and something – a baby – buried there. Stan concluded that in all probability Miriam had miscarried over in the forest, perhaps with her grandmother's assistance. Yes, it was illegal to perform such operations, and he had no proof that she had done. But to his mind it was the obvious conclusion.

The only thing he did find were screwed up pieces of paper made crisp by the frost, the writing made illegible by virtue of those days when the temperature had risen above freezing and the ice had melted.

He reported his findings to Bettina in the cosiness of her living room.

'As long as you're sure,' she remarked as she passed him a cup of tea and a slice of what remained of the Christmas cake.

He nodded. 'I'm sure there's nothing buried there. I'm not saying there wasn't a baby. There might very well have been, but . . .' Brow furrowed with thought, he sipped his tea.

'Ada,' said Bettina.

Stan's eyes met hers. 'My feelings exactly. Ada is the only person who can help. After all, it is her granddaughter.'

CHAPTER TWENTY-FIVE

'January brings the snow, makes our feet and fingers glow. February brings the rain, thaws the frozen lake again . . . Not that you'd notice, eh, Charlie! Never mind. I'll just have to walk faster. How about that?'

Charlie gurgled a happy response. Frances loved taking him for a walk even in February. The rain that was supposed to thaw the frozen lake hadn't arrived. The wind was bitingly cold and a crisp layer of ice covered the ground.

Although Charlie could toddle along quite efficiently, he soon got tired so she still made a habit of bringing the push-chair with her. Just as she'd guessed, by the time they'd got to the bottom of Cherry Garden Hill he was asking to be picked up and placed in his pushchair.

'You've only got short legs and they've got a long way to grow before you can walk everywhere you want.'

Frances sighed with satisfaction. She liked to think that Charlie loved her more than anyone else in the family. He certainly did when she took him out for walks and especially if she had enough money to treat him to a lollipop at Mrs Powell's shop.

She'd bought one this morning though had peered between the chequered notices on the shop door beforehand checking that Miriam was serving behind the cramped counter before pushing open the door. Mrs Powell had forbidden her ever to cross her threshold again because she'd been cheeky. Frances had considered her cheekiness justified. Mrs Powell had made some pretty mean remarks about Charlie and his parents.

Miriam looked pleased to see her, especially with young Charlie hanging on to her hand, his little feet carefully negotiating the high sill that separated the inside of the shop from the street outside.

'Charlie!'

Miriam's voice had been no more than a hushed whisper. Her eyes shone with delight but every so often she glanced furtively over her shoulder, terrified her mother might appear and explode with anger.

'Your mother won't eat you,' said Francis.

'No,' whispered Miriam. 'But she might lock me in the coalhouse again. In the dark. I hate the dark . . .' She shuddered before changing the subject. 'Are you going somewhere?'

'Only for a walk.'

Frances thought back to the smell of coal and the smattering of dust on Miriam's coat. She did not know what to say in response to the older girl. Shutting Miriam in the coalhouse was wrong – very wrong.

Miriam bit her lip. 'I wish I could come with you.' Her eyes glistened as she regarded the little boy. 'If you ever need anyone to look after him . . .'

Miriam was the last person Frances could ever leave Charlie with, though the poor girl didn't seem able to accept that.

Frances had given up feeling guilty about leaving Charlie the day he went missing. Nor could she believe that the little boy had managed to undo the buckles on his harness. Deep down she was sure it was Miriam who had taken him as well as 'found' him.

Once Miriam had handed over the lollipop and put the

money in the wooden box on the shelf behind the counter, she held her finger up to her mouth. 'Shush. I'm going to run away,' she breathed, her eyes fluttering from side to side as though afraid somebody might hear her.

Frances was dubious as to whether Miriam could actually plan anything without her mother finding out. 'Will you go to your grandmother's?'

Miriam had stared at her. 'You mustn't tell. Promise you won't tell.'

So that was it. Miriam was going to run away and live with her grandmother in the Forest of Dean. Frances decided that if she was in Miriam's position she would do the same.

'I lived with Ada for a while,' said Frances.

Miriam sucked in her breath. 'You mustn't call her that. My mother says I must call her Grandmother – even Gran, but never Ada – even if Grandmother insists.'

'Why? She's not my grandmother,' Frances said gently, before wishing Miriam good luck with her plan and promising to keep it to herself. Now, far away from the shop at the bottom of Cherry Garden Hill, Frances thought about how much she'd enjoyed living with Ada Perkins in the Forest of Dean. One day she would go back there, but that depended on her uncle having petrol for the car and the prospect of her old friends still being there. Deacon, Ralphie, Merlyn and the rest of them. What fun they'd had and what a lot she'd learned. She didn't think any of them had been called up yet – none of them were quite old enough. But if the war went on much longer they might be.

'Time to go home,' she said to baby Charlie. Getting a good grip on the handle, she turned the pushchair around so they were pointing back up the hill. 'Sounds like thunder,' she said to him. Not that Charlie understood what she was saying. He was still sucking his lollipop.

Although the sky was dark grey, it didn't seem warm enough for a thunderstorm.

The rumbling sound got louder and louder, rolling towards her from some way along the road that connected Bath with Bristol. Holding tightly to the pushchair, she peered to where the road snaked over the railway lines that dropped down the slope from Bitton Railway Station. The actual village of Bitton was some way further on towards Bath, a place of stone cottages and substantial houses belonging to people of note – land owners and business people. All of the houses were quite old, some dating back to Jacobean times. There was also a pub, the White Hart.

However, there were few houses lying in the direction of Bristol, but there was something there. She detected humps of blackness moving along the road towards her.

Grabbing the pushchair handle more tightly to her chest, she flattened herself against the hedgerow behind her, curious to see what this noise was about.

Gradually the shapes she'd interpreted as black humps took on recognisable forms. The sound of engines, metal and wheels grinding along on gritty tarmac became louder. The first hump – some kind of vehicle – appeared, followed by more vehicles of differing shapes and sizes, though all of the same shade of khaki, army vehicles sporting a white star on the doors of the drivers' cabs.

Lorry after lorry and open cars with canvas canopies rumbled past. The curious faces of soldiers peered out from the open ended trucks from beneath a covering of tarpaulin. There were wolf whistles and waves.

Frances felt quite breathless, both flattered that she was deemed old enough – and pretty enough – for such attention and embarrassed.

'Hi there, honey.'

The voice of the soldier who'd shouted out to her was joined by other voices, more whistling; more waving.

The cavalcade slowed suddenly as though the vehicles heading the column had ground to a halt. There, right in front of her, was the rear end of one lorry from which a sea of youthful faces grinned at her and eyed her in a way nobody had ever eyed her before – certainly not in such large numbers.

'Hey, doll,' said one of the GIs.

Her eyes sparkled. Her face glowed with pleasure. First she'd been honey. Now she was a doll. She loved it.

'Hello.' Even to her own ears she sounded nervous, yet she didn't really feel that way. She felt excited. She also thought she knew who these young men were.

'Is that your baby?'

She shook her head. 'He's my nephew. His name's Charlie.'

'Want some chocolate?'

Chocolate? These young men had chocolate? Sweets were on ration and chocolate had become a luxury. The young man was offering her a whole bar. She could see it in his hand. She nodded avidly, her eyes fixed firmly on the chocolate.

After a quick glance to see that nobody in charge was looking, the young soldier leapt over the tailboard of the lorry, his boots making a loud thudding sound as he landed.

He was grinning at the same time as chewing something, his teeth glowing white as he tossed it from side to side in his mouth. He was holding the bar of chocolate at shoulder level. Frances assumed there was a price to pay for that chocolate, though wasn't too sure what it would be.

'So,' he said, still grinning and still chewing gum. 'What's your name?'

'Frances. Frances Sweet.'

'Frances. That's a pretty name. Pretty girl too. You live around here?'

His grin was infectious. And he was tall. She had to crank her neck back to look up at him. She liked him immediately.

'Up in the village.' She pointed back up the hill. 'My uncle has a bakery and my cousins bake cakes and things and give talks and demonstrations for the Ministry of Food. I live there. And work there,' she added, just in case he thought she was a kid and still at school.

She became self-conscious about her skirt. It was an old one, navy blue and cut down from a school gym slip. And she was wearing socks. If only she had stockings; even lisle stockings, thick and black and itchy. But she didn't. She was wearing grey socks.

The young man in the uniform didn't seem to notice. He kept smiling and chewing, his teeth showing brazenly white even when he nodded. She couldn't help fixing her eyes on that grin, those white teeth. Didn't he ever stop grinning?

Charlie hated it when they were stopped or when he wasn't tottering alongside the pushchair or off on his own improving his walking. If he had to be in his pushchair, he had to keep moving. Gradually, with snuffles, snorts and a curled up lip, he began to grumble his disapproval.

'Hey little guy. How about some chocolate?'

He broke off a couple of squares holding it in front of Charlie's face. Charlie looked entranced. His chubby fist shot out and took it. Without glancing at his benefactor, Charlie proceeded to demolish the chocolate, sucking at it until it was soft enough to swallow.

'Hey EB! Get back here. We're moving.'

The convoy of army vehicles had indeed begun to move.

'Here. Take this,' said the golden-haired young man she now knew as EB.

He handed her the remains of the bar of chocolate.

'Your name's EB?' she shouted as he took off, running towards the back end of the lorry.

'Ed Bergman,' he shouted back. 'See you around, sweetheart, and if you're ever in need of extra ingredients for your baking, you can call on me. Ed Bergman. US Army Catering Corps.'

He waved frantically as he dashed off. Even from a distance his teeth seemed to glow in his sun-burned face. And he was so tall. And broad-shouldered. And he had a dimple in his chin just like . . . She tried to think of the name of the actor she had in mind, but decided it didn't matter. Ed Bergman was head and shoulders above the actor whose name she had forgotten. He was handsome, big, and brave and on top of all that he'd insinuated that he could get some extra ingredients for their baking recipes. Well, they could certainly do with that. The cupboard was running pretty bare, what with trying to help local people with family celebrations, birthdays, christenings, wedding cakes and the like. If anybody was celebrating anything and needed something special, it was the Sweet girls they went to.

'Ed Bergman,' she whispered. 'Ed Bergman.'

Even the sound of his name made her tingle.

Like a long line of khaki-coloured beetles, the stream of American army vehicles moved forward, though not for long. Somebody shouted something from up front. Relayed from the front of the convoy all the way along the line, the shout became louder.

'Reverse! Back! Back!'

One by one, starting from the very back of the convoy, the vehicles began moving. Instead of eyeing the middle part of the convoy, she found herself level with the very first vehicle.

A man in the passenger seat stood up and yelled over the head of the man driving.

'Hell. Doesn't anyone here know how to navigate? Warmley, then Siston. That's where we've got to go.'

'That way,' shouted Frances, pointing up the hill. 'You need to go that way.'

The man who looked to be in charge doffed his cap and thanked her. He was quite plump and obviously not on rations. 'We know that now, miss. Though really appreciate you confirming it.'

With a screech of tyres, the whole column began moving forward, the front vehicles turning into Cherry Garden Hill. The route would take them down Cowhorn Hill, through Warmley and up on to the common.

There were more catcalls and whistles from other young soldiers, but Frances couldn't get EB, Ed Bergman, out of her head.

She stood there until the very last vehicle had gone up the hill and disappeared from sight.

Even then she stood there, staring after them, her heart beating like a drum. The Americans had arrived and they were beautiful! So beautiful!

Before going home, she broke off some more of the chocolate. It was so rare to have chocolate nowadays and it tasted delicious. She closed her eyes and murmured her appreciation. On opening her eyes she looked down at Charlie. Although he'd eaten most of the chocolate he'd been given, some of it was plastered over his face.

'Hmm,' said Frances with a grin. 'I don't think we're going to keep this chocolate much of a secret are we?'

By the time she got back to the bakery it was lunchtime. The whole family, plus Bettina Hicks, was seated around the kitchen table and the smell of stew and dumplings lay heavy on the air. Nobody was speaking and even when they noticed Charlie's chocolate-covered face, nothing was said. Everyone seemed too quiet, too still. She presumed it was her fault and that they were just priming themselves for telling her exactly what they thought.

'It wasn't my fault,' she said. 'It was an American soldier. He gave us a whole bar of chocolate. Look!' She took the remains of the chocolate from her pocket and held it up.

Her uncle Stan was the first to speak. 'You saw an American soldier?'

'Not just one soldier. Lots of them. They were in lorries – I think they were lorries – and they were going along the road at the bottom of Cherry Garden Hill. Then they stopped and reversed and went up Cherry Garden Hill.'

Although his face was sombre as though not quite engaged in what she was saying Stan Sweet nodded in that knowing way of his. 'I heard them go past. The whole building shook. They're being billeted at Siston. No doubt we'll be seeing a lot more of them.'

He didn't seem much impressed; in fact he looked very concerned.

Frances began breaking off pieces of chocolate. 'Does anybody want some of this?'

Mary got up and fetched a flannel from the kitchen sink. 'Let's get you tidied up young man.' She turned to Frances. 'You shouldn't have given it to him. It'll spoil his dinner.' Her tone was unusually clipped.

'I didn't give it to him,' Frances protested. 'Ed Bergman gave it to him.'

'Ed Bergman?' Mary stopped wiping Charlie's face. She glared at Frances. Her cousin's expression was somewhere between a smirk and a blush.

The words tumbled out of Frances's mouth. 'They called him EB, but that's just his initials. His name's Ed Bergman. He's the American soldier I met. It was him who gave Charlie the chocolate and then he gave some to me. When I told him we baked bread and did baking demonstrations for the Ministry of Food, he said that if we needed any extra ingredients he would get them for us. He's with the catering corps you see. A cook, I suppose.'

She looked at all three of them. Nobody was smiling. Surely giving Charlie chocolate wasn't that serious. Was she in for that serious a telling off?

'I'm sorry. I didn't mean to spoil Charlie's dinner.' Her voice was timid, not something she often sounded or felt.

Stan Sweet lowered his eyes and Mary looked as though she were about to burst into tears. Ruby seemed distracted, a faraway look on her face before she buried her face in her hands.

'It's not you, love,' said her uncle. 'There's been news. We heard it on the radio. The Japanese have taken Singapore. It's a disaster. A total disaster.'

Frances's excitement at being the first in the family and possibly in the whole village to meet the Americans vanished. Young as she was, she could only guess at the gravity of the situation, but she could hear it in her uncle's voice, see it in her cousins' faces.

'Oh.'

She couldn't bear to say anything else. Like the rest of them her spirits plummeted. She remembered Ruby saying that John Smith was in Singapore. She didn't like to ask if her cousin had news of him, good or bad. It was something they'd likely face in the days to come.

'Go and wash your hands,' Mary said to her.

Frances obeyed.

Once she was gone to the bathroom, Stan Sweet regarded his daughters and Bettina Hicks. His mouth was dry. His heart was heavy.

Mary began to cry. Ruby sat as though she had turned to ice.

Stan Sweet exchanged a look with Bettina Hicks before stating what was on his mind.

'That's all we tell her,' he said quietly. 'Say nothing of the atrocities likely to have been perpetrated in Singapore to that young lady. Nothing at all.'

'Do you think it might be as bad as Nanking?' Bettina asked quietly.

Stan nodded. Bettina noticed he was clasping his hands so tightly together, his knuckles were turning white.

Bettina said nothing. The Japanese had slaughtered over one hundred thousand non-combatants plus soldiers back in 1937 – a year of horror it had been called. It was hard to suppress the shiver that ran down her spine. She feared for all those caught up in the surrender of the Far Eastern fortress.

CHAPTER TWENTY-SIX

Although they had a telephone at the bakery, it wasn't often it rang and when it did, Stan Sweet fully admitted to the darn thing scaring the life out of him.

Resigned to being the bakery telephonist, Ruby breezed through, a pile of pillowcases over her arm that she'd just made from some old sheets that were beyond repair. Buying new was out of the question. 'I'll get it, Dad.'

'Thank God for that,' he grumbled, settling back down in his favourite chair, tea and a slice of cinnamon cake balanced on his knees. The tea leaves were being used for a second scalding; the thin sliver of cake was left over from a recent demonstration Mary had given in a church hall in St George, a suburb of Bristol. There was just enough sugar in the tea to make it palatable. It went some way to making up for the weakness of the brew.

Stan sighed. No point in moaning. There are worse things going on in the world, he thought to himself, especially with regard to Singapore and the Malay Peninsula.

The paper he was reading reported that things in the Far East had been a complete and utter disaster. Although they did try to hide the truth, it was pretty obvious that too little had been done too late. The huge guns installed in Singapore only a short time before faced seawards where it was thought the Japanese attack would come. As it turned out the Japanese army had attacked from the north, pushing through thick jungle with their bicycles. Bicycles, for God's sake! Stan swore under his breath. Some of the old duffers in charge would still be using mounted cavalry given half the chance.

The paper cracked as he shook it fully open, with indignation rather than anything else. He heard Ruby calling Mary and guessed it was Mike on the phone.

'Give him my regards,' he shouted through.

Ruby came back into the room with Charlie hanging on to her skirt. He heard Mary say hello before the door closed between the living room and the hallway.

'Cake,' exclaimed Charlie, let go of Ruby's skirt and headed for his granddad's plate.

Stan's eyes flickered between his paper and his grandson who was picking the edges of the cake he'd been about to enjoy.

'How's Mike?'

'Fine, as far as I can tell. You know Mike. Everything is fine, except . . .'

'What?'

Stan left his paper and managed to claw back half his slice of cake, not that he was likely to get to eat it himself, but it would prevent Charlie from stuffing the whole slice into his mouth. He couldn't possibly eat it all at once and there would be crumbs everywhere. The girls had enough to do without extra mess.

Ruby pulled a face and although she attempted a smile, it didn't quite happen. 'He was a bit short with me – odd for him.'

'Odd indeed.'

Stan Sweet gave up on reading the newspaper and eating the cake, holding the plate so Charlie could dab his finger on the last of the crumbs. He'd eaten the rest.

When they both fell to silence, each knew that the other was straining to hear Mary's voice. If they couldn't catch the exact words, they could at least get some idea of the conversation by the tone of her voice.

The call lasted for only a few minutes, so what with the shortness of the call and the closed door, they'd learned nothing from listening and made every effort not to look inquisitive once Mary opened the door and came into the room. 'That was Mike. He sends his love.'

She said it abruptly. Both Ruby and her father were in no doubt that a lot of other things had been said. It was up to Mary if she wanted to divulge them.

'Was there any post?' she asked Ruby. 'Have you heard from John?'

Ruby shook her head. 'The only news I have is from the papers and the wireless.' She paused, her head bent. Many people had been killed. The newspapers were cagey about how many, but it was hinted that a lot of civilians had died. 'The best we can hope for is that he's a prisoner of war. Let's hope he's treated well.' She wasn't sure he would be, but she had to believe it.

Mary noticed a concerned look on her father's face and knew immediately what he was thinking. She'd read of the terrible atrocities inflicted by the Japanese on the Chinese people when they'd invaded China. Thousands were massacred, including anyone who wore a uniform. Hopefully the soldiers of the British army would be treated fairly and John would survive. Her father, always an avid follower of world news, met her own worried gaze. The only way she could describe the look in his eyes was fear. Suddenly she needed a breath of fresh air.

'Seeing as Frances is looking after the shop and I'm finished cleaning and tidying the house, I thought I might go over and see how Bettina is. She still hasn't got over that bad cold she had.' It all came out in a rush.

She said it brightly in an effort to glaze over her conversation with Mike, to make it seem as though everything was sweetness and light. To some extent it was, and in time they would be party to her news, but first she had to see Bettina.

Pulling on her thick boots and putting on her coat also helped hide the inner turmoil she was desperate not to disclose. He was still badgering her to move up to Lincolnshire. The exchange of words still rang in her mind.

'So! When are you coming up?'

'Mike, I can't.'

'Can't? Why not, you silly goose?'

'Because!'

'What's that supposed to mean?' His loving tone had changed when she appeared immovable to his request.

'Because I have responsibilities. I have Dad. I have Charlie to think about and I also have my job with the Ministry of Food. Ruby and I work at this together. We have a duty—'

'Duty! Women on duty! Given half a chance you'd both be in uniform I suppose.' He sounded totally exasperated.

'And why not?' Her tone had turned as indignant as his.

When she heard his heartfelt sigh, she was half inclined to give in and wished desperately she could touch him, run her fingers over his furrowed brow and assure him that soon, very soon they would be together. It was just a case of waiting until this war was finally won or at least until she felt her father could cope without her. Deep down she knew Mike wouldn't accept that, so she had to give him something to hope for. She had just the thing to placate him. She took a deep breath. 'Mike. If you could just wait until the baby comes. I think that would be wise. Don't you?'

She heard his intake of breath. 'Baby? Are you telling me . . .?'

'Yes.'

She imagined his face and felt her own eyes brimming with tears of happiness. She hadn't meant to tell him yet, not until she'd been to see the doctor and got it confirmed.

'September,' she said. 'If you count from Christmas . . .'

'September!' The excitement in his voice was palpable, so full of joy that she had to swipe the wetness that had gathered at the corner of her eyes. Finally his voice was there again, crackling with happiness.

'I can't believe it. Does anyone else know yet?'

'No. You're the first.'

There was silence on the other end of the phone. She guessed that he was too emotional to speak, too occupied in digesting the news she'd just given him.

'Can I ask you a special favour? Can I ask you not to tell anyone until you've told my aunt?'

Mary nodded into the phone, smiling through her tears. 'I take it you'll write to your parents?'

He said that he would. His parents lived in Canada.

'How about the cottage? Will Guy be willing to hang on to it?'

'Oh yes.' All the tension and anger had gone from his voice. 'He'll be even more determined to see us living there once I give him our news.'

He went on to ask about John Smith. 'Terrible news about Singapore. I hear they've got Hong Kong too.'

'Ruby wrote to John a while back when she still had a BFPO address. So far there's been no response. The War Office has told her not to worry. The Japanese wouldn't dare treat them badly, not if the Germans are anything to go by.'

She half expected him to say that no news is good news,

336

but Mike would be aware of what the Japanese had done in the past. Just because the Germans were adhering to the Geneva Convention didn't mean the Japanese would do the same. After all, she'd read somewhere that they had not signed the Geneva Convention, but surely that didn't mean they would treat John badly, did it?

'John's a survivor,' he said breezily.

'Yes. Of course he is.'

Bettina showed Mary into the living room, a square cosy space furnished with chintz-covered furniture and rugs that had once been thick enough to bury your shoes in. Though a little threadbare now, their jewel colours still remained.

Mary declined a cup of tea.

'Oh. Just a short visit then.' Bettina sounded disappointed. 'Are you staying long enough to sit down?'

'Yes.' Mary looked down at her gloved hands, willing herself not to blush or blurt out her news in an excited rush. She had it in her heart to cherish this moment, drawing it out so time couldn't snatch it away too quickly. She wanted to remember it for ever. 'I've got something to tell you.'

Despite her best intentions, the excitement was too much for her. The news came out in a rush. 'I'm having a baby. I haven't been to the doctor, yet but I'm sure. I thought you would like to know.'

Having noticed Mary's flushed face, Bettina had guessed at what she was about to say but had no problem expressing her delight, clapping her hands and breaking into excited laughter. 'Wonderful! Your father must be over the moon. First Charlie's son and now this.'

'I haven't told him yet.'

Bettina looked at her in amazement.

'Mike asked if I would tell you first. Before anyone else.

337

He said that he would very much like you to be the first to know – even before his mother.'

Slowly, Bettina lowered her raised hands on to her lap. Obviously she was very touched, but Mary sensed there was something more, something in Bettina's eyes too difficult, too secret to be privy to.

'He's very fond of you,' she stated.

Bettina nodded.

He'd told Mary that Bettina had been like a mother to him all his life, even though he'd lived so far away. Her letters had been vibrant and kind; describing life in the village and how things had been around the time he was born.

Bettina had always struck Mary as a strong-minded capable woman. She'd never seen her with tears in her eyes and looking so emotional. Normally she took things in her stride, was pragmatic and practical.

'Are you all right?' She reached out and touched the older woman's hand, a strong hand, even though wrinkled and spotted with age.

'He . . . um . . .' Bettina hesitated. 'He always was a dear boy. Such a dear boy. Just like his father.'

'Your brother.'

'Yes. Yes. That's right.'

It was odd, but to Mary's ears it sounded as though Bettina wasn't quite certain about what she was saying. Yet it had to be right. She had been Bettina Dangerfield before she'd married and become Bettina Hicks. Her brother was a Dangerfield.

Suddenly she shook her head. 'That dear boy. Despite the miles between us I'd always regarded him like a son, even though I've got one of my own. They were both born around the same time . . .'

Her voice faded and the loose flesh hanging beneath her

chin seemed to lengthen. For a moment it seemed she was locked in thought and couldn't find the way out.

Mary was concerned. 'Is something wrong?'

The flesh beneath Bettina's jaw went from slack to firm in a matter of seconds.

'No,' she declared. Her eyes shone once more with the glowing confidence that Mary was used to. 'So when are you going to tell your father?'

Mary smiled. She'd quite relished holding off the delicious moment, all the while imagining how he would react; how happy he would be. 'As soon as I get back. Right after supper I think.'

'And you are happy about this? Even though there is a war on?'

'The baby? Oh, yes. I can't wait . . .'

Mary found herself gushing, though her voice had an edgy quality. Bettina noticed she was also avoiding eye contact. In her experience people only did that if they had something to hide – either in their thoughts – or in their heart.

'Then what is it? What's troubling you?'

Mary clasped her hands together. She'd been quite secretive about the cottage and Mike had asked her to promise not to tell anyone – including his aunt – until they actually signed their name on the lease.

'Mike wants me to move up to Lincolnshire.'

Bettina bobbed her head. 'He would do.'

'I don't want to go. At least, not until I've had the baby.'

'And you don't want to go even then. Is that what you're saying?'

'I've never lived away from home before.'

Bettina straightened up. Her expression was stiffer than the tight lace collar she always wore. 'This isn't your home, any more. You're a married woman.'

'But what about Charlie? What about my father?'

'You're a married woman with your own baby on the way. Ruby is still single and dotes on the child. She'll be there for him. So will Frances. And your dad will look out for him.' She leaned forward and took Mary's hands in hers noticing how cold they were. 'Mary. You're not a child. You have responsibilities and Mike loves you. You have to go with him. You have to get used to living apart from your family. *Far apart.*'

The way she said those last words were very telling. Mary immediately knew what she meant. Once the baby was born, she would have to go to Lincolnshire, but it wasn't just that Bettina was really hinting at. After all, she had married a Canadian Airman, and once the war was over she would be making her home far away from her family, on the other side of the Atlantic in Canada.

CHAPTER TWENTY-SEVEN

The arrival of the Americans had set a lot of female hearts racing, and not only the younger ones. Everyone wanted to do something to make them welcome.

'It was the vicar's idea,' stated Mrs Clements, a widow who lived with a houseful of cats in West Street.

Despite being in her fifties, Ruby had perceived a definite twinkle in Mrs Clements' eyes when she'd come into the shop along with a number of other ladies who frequented the vicar's tea parties. 'We thought it would be a good idea to welcome them into the village. Not all of them of course. The village hall couldn't possibly cope with a whole camp of young American soldiers. I've seen one or two and noticed they are particularly strapping young men. Some of them quite handsome.'

Despite her age, Mrs Clements blushed and laughed nervously behind her gloved hand.

Bettina remarked to Ruby after she'd gone that she hadn't seen Meg Clements blush like she did since the Great War. 'She was a bit fast was our Meg, but you can't really hold it against her. She gave Bert Clements a bit more than a good send off before he left for the Western Front. Just as well seeing as he didn't come back. Not that it stopped there. A few others were grateful for her affection,' Bettina added after taking her second sip of tea.

Ruby laughed. Bettina knew everything about everyone in the village, some of it they'd prefer her not to know.

'So it's a dance. I take it there'll be food and drink?'

Bettina nodded. 'Everyone is going to bake something or make sandwiches for the dance. The cider will come from Farmer Martin, of course. If anyone wants beer, they'll have to bring their own, though the landlord of the Three Horseshoes has offered to bring a barrel and run a cash bar.'

Ruby was already scribbling down what ingredients she had available and what she could make from them. 'I've got a lot of carrots. I think everyone in the village now has their own recipe for carrot cake.'

'And parsnip cake, and how to make icing or mock marzipan from potatoes. Mary's wedding cake had a lot to do with that. Generous of you both to share the recipe,' said Bettina.

'We help out where we can.'

'So,' said Bettina putting down her cup in line with the spout of the teapot, a sure sign that she would like a second cup. 'What glorious goodies do you have in mind?'

Mary came in from putting Charlie down for his afternoon nap. She told them how he'd stripped off his vest and insisted she tickled his belly. It wasn't long before he was fast asleep.

'How far have we got?' she asked, smiling while pouring a cup of tea for herself and a second one for Bettina Hicks.

Bettina outlined what was arranged and when it would take place.

'Everyone's agreed to pull out all the stops and make it a night to remember,' explained Bettina. 'I presume you'll bake one of your famous cakes? I can spare some of my rations.'

Bettina peered over Ruby's shoulder at the written down recipes.

'We think the end of March or beginning of April would be the best time to hold the dance. I've already asked your father to drive me over there to deliver the invitation by hand to the commanding officer. He said he would as long as he's got deliveries in that direction.'

'Apple pies,' said Mary.

Her sister and Bettina noticed her rueful grin. Ruby got her meaning and laughed.

'Because all Americans love apple pie!' laughed Ruby and went on to explain. 'That creep, Andrew Sinclair, instructed Mary to concentrate on apple pie just after Pearl Harbor in honour of our new allies.'

They all decided that apple pies were a good idea as long as there were enough apples in storage – both fresh and dried. It shouldn't be too much of a problem. If there was one fruit they'd always had in abundance around here, it was apples.

'Americans also like doughnuts,' said Bettina. 'I know that because Mike likes them and he's Canadian. Is it possible to make them too?'

Mary confirmed that it was. 'It is now. The young man Frances knows gave her a recipe. It seems more simple than I expected – given our rations, that is.'

'In that case I'd like to try making some if you could give me a decent recipe.'

'Easy.' Mary took Ruby's pad and stub of pencil and scribbled down a recipe. 'Flour, mixed spice, margarine or cooking fat, dripping from the pan if you don't have either, two ounces of sugar, dried egg, milk, plus jam. I think that should work. What about you, Ruby?'

Ruby had been thinking things through. It would be difficult to cater for two hundred people – assuming half were villagers and half soldiers – even one hundred would be a lot to cater for with the slim rations they had. She frowned. Dividing the workload among the village had to be the best way forward.

'It makes sense to keep things simple. Let the other women in the village make the apple pies and sandwiches. You can do the doughnuts and I'll do . . .' She looked up at the ceiling as she thought about it. Mary waited, pen poised in hand. 'Carrot cookies. I've heard the Americans like cookies – biscuits to you and me. We've agreed we have a lot of carrots, so carrot cookies will go a long way with a cup of tea – or whatever else is offered to drink.' She grinned. These young Americans weren't used to tea. She understood they preferred coffee. However, the local cider might just suit them and biscuits were good with anything.

Ruby outlined the ingredients and method while Mary wrote it down.

'One tablespoonful of margarine, two tablespoonfuls of sugar plus some for sprinkling on top, a few drops of vanilla essence – as much as it takes,' she said in answer to Mary's probing look. Her sister did like to be precise whereas she was usually a test-it-and-see person. Giving into Mary's look, she worked out the precise details.

'Four tablespoonfuls of grated raw carrot, six tablespoons of flour plus half a teaspoon of baking powder.'

'I'm sorry to interrupt.'

They looked up to see their father, Stan Sweet standing in the doorway. 'This just came by special delivery.' He raised his hand. He was holding a small brown envelope. 'It's stamped "RED CROSS".'

All thought of recipes gone from her mind, Ruby felt sick.

'It's not a telegram,' her father said on seeing her face. Using finger and thumb he fingered the contents. 'It feels like some kind of card.'

The colour returned to her cheeks, but she remained seated, her legs too weak to stand and her fingers trembling as she tore beneath the gummed seal. There was no message inside just a name and an address: Corporal John Smith, First Wiltshire Regiment. Prisoner of War. Changi Jail.

That was it.

Silently she passed the card to her father.

He read it and sighed. 'Thank God.'

Mary read it and passed it to Bettina.

Bettina placed her hand over her chest and uttered a silent prayer. Mike had been scheduled to join a Canadian squadron in Singapore and then some place in Java. He'd changed his mind, preferring to stick with his RAF friends in Lincolnshire and loyal to his squadron leader friend, Guy. But this poor young man had gone to Singapore and was now a prisoner of the Japanese.

'Thank God we know he's still alive,' she said aloud.

Stan grunted in agreement but avoided meeting her eyes. The atrocities the Japanese had perpetrated when they'd invaded China had been appalling. He couldn't help feeling that they would be just as harsh towards their allied prisoners.

'So where is this Changi Jail?' Ruby asked him.

'Singapore,' he replied. 'It's in Singapore.' Then he took his pipe from its place above the fireplace and went outside.

Ruby thought it her duty to write to John that night. She'd promised she would write and she still thought of him often. She had enough of an address now to do that through the International Red Cross. It was them who would pass the letter on to John.

She wanted to ask him lots of questions but thought better of it, instead asking after him, and then keeping her tone light, she wrote to him about their latest recipes and the talks they'd given.

Mary and I did a talk together at a factory in Somerset making boots for the army. We were required to stay

overnight which was why Dad insisted we go together.
Frances, Mrs Hicks and our Dad were left to run the
shop and look after Charlie.

We had a bit of a problem with the rock cakes we
were taking as samples to the talk. Charlie had watched
us take them out of the oven. He'd also noted where
we'd put them to cool. That evening, while we were
cooking supper, we turned round to find Charlie missing.
The little tyke had not only eaten three of the rock cakes,
he'd sprinkled crumbs outside the back door for the
birdies.

We could have been angry, but he's got such lovely
dimples when he smiles and yes, he can wind both of
us around his little finger. The thing is it is now an
offence to feed crumbs of any description to wild birds.
A woman in Taunton did just that and was fined ten
pounds!

Did I tell you that Mary is expecting a baby? Dad
is over the moon. First Charlie's baby and now Mary.
She's happy about it and Mike wants her to move up to
Lincolnshire. She said she will once she's had the baby.

In the meantime I am still the spinster of the family,
lucky in a way. Both Dad and little Charlie need me.
Besides, there's no man on the horizon who I feel
remotely interested in. Not in England anyway.

She raised her head from the writing paper, the pen nib
poised just above the paper. *Not in England anyway.* It
occurred to her that she was giving him unqualified hope. He
wasn't in England. Should she add that the American army
had moved on to Siston Common? All those handsome young
men to turn a young girl's head.

She reread what she had written and asked herself whether

it was right to raise John's expectations that they could become sweethearts. On reflection she decided that John needed something to hang on to and if she gave the impression she would wait for him, then so be it. The words could stay as they were.

CHAPTER TWENTY-EIGHT

It was early in April when Mary drove Bettina to the US Army base at Siston in the van provided by the Ministry of Food – the only one with enough petrol to get her most places. She was feeling good, the early morning sickness behind her now, not that she'd been that badly affected. Her father had told her that she looked blooming beautiful.

On this particular day Frances was looking after the shop and Ruby had taken it upon herself to look after Charlie while also measuring him up for some new clothes she intended making him from the least worn bits of adult garments.

Earlier that morning Mary had caught her twin pacing up and down the hallway, waiting impatiently for the letterbox to rattle and letters to fall on to the floor.

So far there had been no reply to the letter she had sent to John Smith. Mary reminded her that it had been less than two months since she'd written.

'I still don't know how he is, and anything could have happened by now,' Ruby sighed.

Charlie was sitting on the bottom stair banging two bricks together. Every so often he stopped, his bright eyes shining with amusement as he waited for Ruby to clap. Ruby never failed to give him what he wanted. She knew she spoiled him, but Charlie was the bright spark who took her out of herself, who helped her cope with being alone.

'You don't know how long the post will take to get to him.'

Ruby had agreed that she was probably right and went back to cutting and sewing, singing to Charlie and keeping an eye on him as he tired of his bricks, toddling around the room shaking a floppy bunny rabbit; his favourite toy that he called Bunz.

'You're looking well,' Bettina remarked as they drove along the empty roads, stopping off at village shops to deliver Sweets' Best Bread and any other items they wished to sell. People said it was a miracle that the Sweet Sisters made such delicious treats in such desperate times. A few, not from their own village, suggested they were getting more rations than most people. In a way they were. The Ministry of Food gave them extra rations in order that they could carry on their important war work.

'I take it you're getting plenty to eat,' Bettina added, as she admired Mary's curving stomach. 'Is that steering wheel uncomfortable? It looks as though it's resting on your bump.'

'Of course I am, and my bump is fine,'

It was quite true. She ate well. She also managed to save a little something from all the rations she received. Her thoughts were on the time when there would be no war. There would be no extra things or salaries from the Ministry of Food then. The shop would have to stand or fall on what it sold. Hopefully it would continue to be a bread and cake shop, the hot oven behind the shop still baking bread in the same old-fashioned way. There was a rumour going round about a new mechanised bakery being built in Warmley. According to gossip, the plans had been put on hold for the duration of the war but in peace-time it could change the need for a local bakery.

Mary smiled. 'I'm feeling well. I'll be only too pleased if my pregnancy goes on like this.'

She resisted the urge to pat her stomach. Despite there being no traffic except for the odd horse-drawn farm cart, she was a stickler for keeping her eyes on the road.

On arriving at the base and explaining their mission, the guard picked up his phone, turned a handle and spoke to whoever was on the other end.

They were shown into a smart office that smelled of new paint and a brisk cleanliness. The young man in uniform behind the desk told them that his name was Lieutenant Lehman. He addressed them politely and said he would deal with whatever it was they wanted. He got up to shake their hands and get them chairs. 'Please sit down, ladies. I'm afraid the colonel's a bit busy right now, but rest assured I can place any matter you raise on his desk for his urgent attention.'

His eyes were cornflower blue and he had the palest eyelashes. His hair was no more than a frosted white crust over his head such was the shortness of the regulation army cut. His smile had a fixed quality about it, as though it were part of the uniform he was wearing and just as much at the behest of the army.

Mary took the lead before he had much chance to study her, explaining that the village would like to put on a party welcoming the American army to the area.

'We realise your boys are a long way from home and thought a friendly gesture might make them feel more at ease.' She gestured at the invitation in Bettina's hand.

It had been written on ordinary notepaper, addressed to the commanding officer and placed inside a plain brown manila envelope.

'Like a bill,' Ruby had commented. 'Only bills come in manila envelopes.'

'The only decent envelope we're got,' Mary had responded.

Bettina slid the envelope across the desk so its edges touched Lieutenant Lehman's fingertips.

His smile stayed immobile on his face. 'Well, that's very kind of you. I'm sure the colonel will be very interested indeed.'

He reminded Mary of some of the civil servants she had to deal with, efficient but far from sincere. His tone of voice hinted that he really didn't want to be bothered.

Actually she was quite right about him being condescending. Lieutenant Ira Lehman had already indulged another group of local people from some other village with his attention; they too had it in mind to arrange a party to welcome the mighty US army. Unfortunately for them their interest only served to feed his inbuilt arrogance. Yes, he was flattered by their interest, but he'd felt obliged to impress on them that the US Army did not need to be mollycoddled. Anyway, he didn't like these people with their high-handed attitude, their crisp voices and shabby clothes. Some of the clothes they wore looked as though they'd been made from blankets and old curtains. Peasants, the lot of them, and he should know. His father owned a number of high-quality dress shops in New York so he knew quite a bit about fabrics, ladies' fashions and quality sewing.

He had to concede that these two women, especially the younger one, looked well dressed, not that he cared that much. He had other things – more important things – to do.

Wanting only to get rid of them as quickly as possible, he glanced at the wall clock. They'd only been here for two minutes. He'd give them five. He'd given the women from the other village five, so it was only fair.

It was only on taking another look at the younger woman that he thought he might make it more. Seven for luck, he thought, once he'd taken in her pretty face. That was until he saw that she was pregnant.

'Okay,' he said, leaning back in his chair. He shuffled the files on his desk and fiddled with the triangular woodblock that bore his name, smiling until his jaw ached. 'Well, the colonel is all in favour of firming up relations between our two nations. He's also aware that some of our guys are feeling pretty homesick. Still, they have to get used to that. They're here to fight not to enjoy themselves.'

He swivelled his eyes to rest on Mary again. Each time he did that, his expression changed.

Bettina Hicks never missed a thing. 'Mary's telephone number is on that invitation,' said Bettina as she pushed it across the desk. 'It's the village bakery. Her father might answer. But you can always leave a message once you've had a word with your commanding officer.'

She'd adopted her no nonsense voice, her expression totally bereft of warmth and a cutting look in her eyes.

'Right,' he said wishing the old girl wasn't here and he could have the younger one to himself. 'Sounds good to me. Might even come along myself.' His smile settled on Mary. 'So how many of our guys would you like to attend this dance?'

'The village hall can take no more than two hundred people,' Mary replied.

'So one hundred men and one hundred villagers?'

'One hundred and fifty at the most, plus fifty villagers – or perhaps one hundred, but that would be a bit snug. It's not that big a village hall.'

He scribbled something down on the corner of the envelope containing the official invitation they'd all agreed on. Mrs Webster, who lived in West Street, used to be a secretary to a company director, had typed it out on her old Imperial typewriter.

'That's fine. You can count on me,' he said on rising to his feet, the chair legs scraping the floor with a high-pitched screech.

Mary and Bettina accepted they were being dismissed and weren't exactly unhappy to leave. Bettina had taken an instant dislike to this young man and Mary also wanted to put as much distance between them as possible.

'Allow me,' he said. He helped with their chairs and led them to the door. 'If the colonel okays it, we'll put something up on the notice board. The guys can do the rest. We can't force them to attend, but if they want to they just write their names on the list. Oh, I presume we're talking about just white guys. No blacks.'

Mary frowned. 'No, not at all. Everybody is welcome regardless of colour. After all they've all come over here to fight, haven't they?'

Lieutenant Lehman shook his head and smothered a knowing laugh. The locals just didn't get it. The US Army was segregated. He'd thought that as an empire these people would follow the same strict policy.

'I'm sorry. You can work it so that our guys come one night and the coloureds another night, if you like, but we don't have them socialise together.'

Bettina felt a hot, deep anger rising up inside her as she caught the disrespect in his voice towards the black soldiers and hated it. 'Well, that's not the way we do things in England, young man.'

The lieutenant laughed casually. 'Whites and blacks do not fraternise in this man's army. The whites can attend your little event one night, the blacks the next. If you really want that. If your local girls are that desperate.'

The insinuation hit Mary immediately. He was saying that white girls who 'fraternised' with black men were little more than sluts.

353

'I thought you joined the war against that kind of thing,' she said, her voice sounding distinctly shaky.

The lieutenant eyed her with a look bordering on contempt. 'Would you go out with one of them, miss?'

'The question doesn't arise. I'm married. My husband's a pilot.'

'Bet he's not black.'

'No, he's not. But there are black people in the RAF, lieutenant. There are a lot of people from all over the empire come to fight this war. Not just America.'

She was about to stalk away from him, when she suddenly realised Bettina had gone on ahead of her and that she was alone with him. Now Bettina was out of the way, he wasn't rushing to shove her out of the door.

'Am I right in thinking that you're Jewish, Lieutenant Lehman?'

He looked uncomfortable. 'Well, yes I am . . . but . . .'

'My nephew's mother was Jewish. She told us something of how your people were treated in Austria. She told us the Germans view Jews as subhuman. You would be talked about in the same way as you talk about these people you call, *coloured,* Lieutenant. Just you remember that!'

Mary stalked out of the office bristling with a disgust that was almost bordering on hatred. Lieutenant Lehman's attitude had made her feel sick. She had to get out of here. She looked up and down the long corridor outside the offices separated from each other by little more than sheets of plywood. Bettina was nowhere in sight.

Then she heard a door open some way along the corridor.

On recognising whose door it was, Ira Lehman muttered something under his breath. The damned woman had gained entry into the colonel's office. His butt would be on the line for this.

Mary stopped in her tracks as Ira surged ahead. A bald-headed man in uniform appeared with Bettina at his side.

'Lehman. Get these ladies some tea.'

Ira knew by the look on the colonel's face that his ship was sunk. He'd probably get posted to a combat unit after this, out of the comfortable office he'd always planned to stay in for the duration.

'Yes, sir. Of course, sir.'

His face was like thunder as he stormed off. Behind him Mary was invited to join the colonel and Bettina in his office.

'Now,' he asked them politely. 'What can I do for you?'

The colonel had also been emphatic that there was to be no fraternisation between black and white soldiers; the US government was determined that they were to be segregated, and segregated they would be.

'You wouldn't want conflict in your peaceful little village now. Not good for Anglo–American relations.'

Although Mary and Bettina found it hard to stomach the US army's attitude, they had to concede that the colonel was obliged to obey US law. He also knew his men.

Ultimately they agreed they would hold two parties, though pointed out that catering for the event could present a problem.

'We have limited supplies,' she pointed out.

'We can deal with that,' said the colonel. He went on to offer his support by way of surplus supplies. 'I'll requisition some supplies from the quartermaster's stores. Anything we can spare, you can have,' he pronounced.

The first party, for white soldiers only, was to be held in mid-April, the one for Negro soldiers, a week later.

A big welcome banner had been made and stretched across the far end of the village hall. Union Jacks and the American Stars and Stripes hung below that. The food was laid out at one end on a long trestle table along with tea, coffee, and quite a lot of locally brewed cider.

Mary had offered to look after Charlie for the evening. Bettina had protested.

'No,' said Mary, shaking her head. 'You organised it. You deserve to have the fun, and anyway, I've got some knitting to do.' She held up the needles and the tiny white matinee jacket that was slowly taking shape. 'I've also got a radio broadcast to make next Tuesday. The *Kitchen Front* is doing extremely well and I'm doing a session on the best ways to bake Spam in a pie.'

'Ah, Spam!' exclaimed Bettina. 'Who'd have thought we'd have grown to like it! Everyone thought it would never catch on until they realised there was a thick crust of fat at the top of the tin. What a boon that is. I've even managed to scrape a bit of fat from the tin of corned beef I managed to get hold of this week.' Sounding exasperated by it all, Bettina sighed, laid her head back and closed her eyes. 'Oh, for a return to those days of a roasted rib of good English beef on a Sunday.' She licked her lips. 'Do you know I dream of roast beef most nights.'

'Did Mrs Darwin-Kemp make a generous donation for the dance?' Mary asked her. Mrs Darwin-Kemp had once had servants, but now had to cope with just somebody part-time coming in. She was also the first person in the village who had come into the shop demanding her loaf of bread be sliced.

Bettina sucked in her lips at mention of her close acquaintance; she didn't always see eye to eye with her. 'Not at first, but I managed to persuade her to find us a bit more.'

Mary stopped knitting. It was getting to the stage when she couldn't remember when she wasn't knitting baby clothes.

There was a querulous look on Bettina's face and a firm set to her chin.

'You didn't strong arm her, did you?'

Bettina chuckled into her hand before resting it on her cheek. She could still see the scene in Mrs Darwin-Kemp's kitchen. Eleanor had been quite adamant that she was giving all she could, declaring that working-class people were used to surviving on a lot less than people of some standing in the community.

'I mean, you can't expect us to manage without butter and a decent piece of beef, now can you? Henry's job means that I sometimes have important people to entertain. I can't give them tripe and onions.'

'She asked if you could bake a cake for her if she found the ingredients. It's for a family gathering. I said I would ask you, though I did stress that you might be too busy what with your radio broadcasts and the fact that you were expecting your first child.'

Bettina was the most forthright and honest person Mary had ever met, but all the same, she couldn't help getting the impression that other things might have gone on or been said at Mrs Darwin-Kemp's house.

'I don't mind doing it. Ruby's gone up there with her bread order this morning plus a plum pudding she ordered.' Her eyes met those of her husband's aunt. 'She supplied the ingredients for that too.'

Bettina clamped her mouth shut. Should she air her suspicions or keep them to herself?

The knitting needles ceased their incessant clicking. They were both silent, each engrossed in their own thoughts. It was Mary who broke the silence. She sighed. 'I wish Mike was here.'

Bettina nodded. 'It's hard for a young wife when her husband goes to war.'

'I suppose it's hard at any time. Those poor widows who . . .' She paused, suddenly aware of what she'd said. 'I'm sorry.'

Mary went back to her knitting. 'You don't need to apologise.'

'I think I do. It just came out. Do you still miss your husband?'

The sudden question seemed to send a jolt through Bettina's body. She sat bolt upright. 'Well,' she said, sounding as though the breath had been knocked out of her – which indeed it had. 'Now there's a question.'

'Do you mind me asking about him?'

The older woman shook her head smiling slightly sadly. 'It's nice to remember.'

'What was he like?'

'He liked his food, his drink and he liked women. Not in a philandering kind of way as such. He was fascinated by women, strong women. He didn't much care for women who didn't have an intelligent thought in their head.'

'Mike told me he fought in the war.'

Bettina clasped her hands rotating one thumb around the other as she considered her thoughts. 'Yes. He fought in the last war. And he came back. So many didn't . . .'

Her voice seemed to melt away like ice in springtime.

'It must have been hard for you – when he was away.'

Bettina gave a little laugh, a short laugh somewhere between a sigh and a chuckle. 'It was hard. It was hard too when he came back, not that his despair seemed that obvious at first. I'd just catch him looking at something quite ordinary, and then suddenly seeing tears roll down his cheeks. Half the time he wasn't seeing what was in front of him. He was back there. The memories of what he saw were still disturbing him.'

'But you helped him recover.'

'Of course. But then, I was one of the lucky ones. I had a husband. A lot of women of my generation never had a husband

and were never likely to. Three-quarters of a million of our young men died in that terrible war, leaving behind too many women and not enough men. Too many women who would never have a child of their own to cuddle and love.'

Mary was silent, seemingly concentrating on her knitting. One purl, one plain . . .

'I want Mike to live,' she said suddenly.

Bettina looked at her. She was such a pretty girl, such an innocent she thought in some departments. 'Of course you do.'

Mary stabbed her needle into the knitting. 'I want him to come home in one piece. I couldn't bear if he came home crippled or changed by his experiences.'

'Then let's hope he won't be,' murmured Bettina.

CHAPTER TWENTY-NINE

The old van they used to deliver bread had been stored in the rear shed once they had the use of the van supplied by the Ministry of Food.

Even so, they rarely used the ministry van for bakery business so Ruby had taken the bicycle, the old one her brother Charlie used to ride, the loaves of bread and the plum pudding filling out the wicker basket at the front.

Mrs Darwin-Kemp's house with its high gables and chunky chimneys loomed up out of the mist, the smell of springtime flowers and fresh buds on the trees leaving a crisply tangy smell in her nostrils. Ignoring the notice to pull the iron bell pull hanging above the gate, Ruby pushed open the back gate, squeezing between the box hedges and along the gravel path.

Old Tom, a geriatric gardener who lived in one of the almshouses at the bottom of Willsbridge Hill, was using his hoe between pristine rows of vegetables on the other side of a green lawn. Unlike most people, Mrs Darwin-Kemp had kept her lawn preferring to hold tea parties for her friends rather than grow cabbages. The vegetables were pushed to the sidelines.

It was a typical April day that brought a promise of things to come. Ruby couldn't help thinking about bluebells and house martins arriving to build their nests under the eaves. The trees and elegant shrubbery whispered in the wind, and apart from Tom there didn't seem to be anyone else around.

Never mind. She would do as she'd done before and leave the order on the kitchen table. With that in mind she made her way to the kitchen door and after parking the bicycle pushed it open and went inside.

The kitchen was very large, an old range at one end, the fire bed rumbling with heat. There was also a gas stove, quite a large one, in fact. There might be a war on, but Mrs Darwin-Kemp still entertained as often as she could and didn't seem to scrimp that much on fuel.

There was gossip in the village that she was holding a dinner party for American officers from the base. No doubt her husband had issued the invitation through one of his colleagues in London.

After setting out the loaves and the plum pudding on the table, Ruby looked through the single glass pane in the door dividing the kitchen from the rest of the house. She needed to tell somebody that she'd delivered the ordered goods as promised.

'Hello?' She rapped at the door. Nobody came.

The hall on the other side seemed totally deserted. Believing that was indeed the case, she opened the door and poked her head out. The door led out on to an inner hallway which in turn led to a larger one where visitors were received and food was taken from the kitchen and into Mrs Darwin-Kemp's dining room. Ruby called out, her voice echoing over the empty walls and ornately plastered ceiling.

The wood block flooring was a picture of gleaming cleanliness, polished to within an inch of its life. The shine was achieved by the generous application of a beeswax polish, the smell of which permeated the air. Thick rugs were placed along the shiny wooden flooring. Halfway along the hall stood a long case clock, its monotonous tick the only sound.

The house was very grand and much too large for two people. At one time it had been full of servants, though not so many now.

'Ruby.'

Her name was hissed by Gertie, the girl who had replaced Mrs Darwin-Kemp's regular parlour maid. Gertie did everything and anything around the house. She was Mrs Darwin-Kemp's Jill of All Trades. There was no such thing as a parlour maid nowadays unless you were royalty. Women, men too, earned better money working for the war effort.

'She's having tea in the drawing room with some of the Ladies' Guild. They're planning their next plan of campaign,' she whispered, her fingers over her mouth stifling a giggle. Gertie pulled off the pale-coloured gloves she was wearing. 'I tell you, Ruby, her ladyship is getting to be a right old slave driver. I've waited on them with their tea and cakes – thanks for those, by the way. I don't know what we would have done if you hadn't made them.'

'Mary made them. They looked good.'

Gertie jerked her head. 'Well, they seem to be enjoying them. Hope all these officers she's invited for this dinner party on the nineteenth appreciate them too.'

Ruby grinned. 'I did hear about it.'

'I think she wants you and Mary to cater for it,' she hissed, still keeping her voice low so that Mrs Darwin-Kemp and her guests heard nothing. 'She's invited all the high-ranking officers from the base and keeps hinting that a famous general is coming too. She's desperate to bag herself a general.'

'You make him sound like a pheasant brought down by a shooting party,' Ruby whispered back.

Gertie grinned broadly. Her crooked front teeth did nothing for her looks, but her sense of humour made up for it.

'Them officers and that general – if she gets hold of that important a personage – won't know what's hit them – not once Mrs Darwin-Kemp's got 'em in her sights!'

Both Ruby and her friend smothered a laugh, one hand clasped tightly across their mouths. Not that the laugh could be kept in any more than the giggles that exploded behind their hands.

Ruby finally controlled herself. 'I've left the bread on the kitchen table. I trust she'll let us know about the catering.'

Gertie bobbed her head. 'Everything gets left on that kitchen table. If you could see the meat and the cheese and—' Suddenly Gertie bit her bottom lip, her focus shifting nervously sidelong. 'Forget I said that.'

The moment she said it, Ruby knew she would most certainly not forget it. Something was going on here and Gertie was doing her best to hold on to her job – not there were likely to be any takers in this day and age. Bettina had told Mary she suspected Mrs Darwin-Kemp, for all her social connections, was buying food on the black market. Mary had dutifully shared the information with her sister.

'I'll let myself out then. I take it the money's in the usual place?'

It was Mrs Darwin-Kemp's habit to leave payment for goods in the teapot and to trust that if nobody was around, a person's honesty would prevail and nothing other than what was due would be taken. All the same, Ruby preferred to let somebody know she had been and was also taking what she was owed.

Ruby went back into the kitchen. Seeing as no cooking

was going on at present, there was no light on. Even so the kitchen was bright enough; in fact, it had a warm atmosphere, a bit like the bakery after a batch of loaves had been baked. There was no smell of cooking, no smell of anything much except for the earthy aroma of a basket of vegetables left on the draining board.

She put the bread in the white enamel bread bin. The plum pudding was destined for the larder.

On opening the door she found herself faced with a large truckle of Cheddar cheese and the biggest leg of lamb she had ever seen. Both were stamped US Army.

She bit her lip. Buying food on the black market was an offence. It was obvious the meat and cheese had come from the base, but via a third party. That was how the black market worked: food was stolen and handed out of the back door of an establishment – such as an army base – by somebody on the inside.

Mrs Darwin-Kemp could get in a lot of trouble buying black-market goods.

She was still in there, her body hidden behind the door when she heard somebody come in from outside. Presuming it was old Tom come in for his afternoon cup of tea, she called out a cheery hello.

'I've brought teacakes. Would you like one with your cup of tea? I made one or two extra, so don't worry about her counting them and finding one missing.'

'I sure would, honey, but perhaps another time, another place.'

She popped out from behind the door to find herself looking into a pair of blue eyes and a tanned face. His expression was one of deadly seriousness. His uniform was US Army, though differed from most that she'd seen. His shoulders were broad, his chin square and he was looking down his nose at her as though considering whether he should clap her in irons.

'I'm here on official business.'

He certainly seemed as though he meant business, standing there, legs slightly apart, hands clasped behind his back.

'Is that so?'

She stood facing him, arms folded. He hadn't introduced himself and she considered his manner overly officious, a shame really. If he wasn't so rude he'd be quite attractive.

'Yes, ma'am. I have to warn you here and now that depending on the answers you give me, we may have to involve the local police.'

Ruby raised her eyebrows. This was quite amusing. She was pretty sure he was assuming she was the lady of the house and seeing as he had failed to introduce himself properly, she wouldn't enlighten him.

'Now what can I have done to deserve that?'

Her tart response did nothing to puncture his air of superiority or lessen the ramrod stiffness of his stance, as though his spine was made of iron. 'I think you know the answer to that, ma'am. Supplies have been going missing from our supply depot, such as . . .' He dipped two fingers into his breast pocket. They emerged with a notebook and pencil. 'One large cheese, one leg of lamb . . .'

She seized her chance to teach Mrs Darwin-Kemp a lesson. 'I think you'll find them in the larder behind you.'

What to him must have sounded like a confession obviously surprised him. He looked taken aback at first but recovered swiftly, and in one sweeping gesture he had opened the larder door and surveyed the contents.

Ruby came to stand beside him. Side by side they both regarded the cheese and the leg of lamb, the latter wrapped in muslin.

'Are those the items you have on your list?' She couldn't help the amusement in her voice.

'I'll have to confiscate these items, ma'am.' He sounded very decided. 'I'm sorry, but they're the property of the US Army.'

'As I understand it, they were destined to be *eaten* by members of the US Army.'

A flicker of puzzlement came to his eyes and in that instant he seemed to see her for the first time, though almost guiltily, drinking her in then closing down again.

'I'm not sure I get your meaning, ma'am.'

'Well Mr whoever you are, I'll leave you to sort it all out. I'm off home. Goodbye.'

She was almost at the door when he headed her off.

'You don't live here? This isn't your home?' His expression flickered between surprise and disbelief.

'No.'

'But you never said . . .'

'You never asked. And you never introduced yourself.'

He made a groaning sound and rolled his head like somebody does when their neck was aching.

Ruby tilted her head to one side. 'I'm getting the impression that you haven't done this kind of thing before. Just arrived have you?'

'Two weeks ago. Declan O'Malley. Lieutenant. Military police. But I *have* done this before. I used to be a cop in New York. I need to know your name so I can check it out.'

'Ruby Sweet. *Kitchen Front* advisor. Ministry of Food.'

He took hold of his notepad and pencil. 'Address?'

Ruby was getting fed up. She needed to get home and although this young man was very handsome, there was another imprisoned in a Japanese prisoner of war camp that held her attention more. She had a half-finished letter to him awaiting her back at home. She kept writing the letters though so far had not received a reply.

She gave the officer her address and he wrote it down. She was just about to go when he stopped her again. 'What did you mean about those supplies being eaten by members of the US Army?'

Ruby couldn't help looking smug. 'Mrs Darwin-Kemp who lives here, is holding a dinner party for your senior officers. I hear there might even be a general in attendance.' She shrugged. 'I don't know who of course. Things like that are top secret.'

A look of doubt and uncertainty how to proceed flickered in his eyes.

She was feeling pretty uncertain herself.

'Have you arrested anyone with regard to these missing supplies?' she asked him.

He nodded. 'We have indeed, ma'am. One of yours I'm afraid. A local man not long out of prison named Gareth Stead.'

Ruby hummed to herself all the way home. Mrs Darwin-Kemp would be allowed to keep her supplies because it was destined for officers, but would be issued with a warning. Gareth Stead, one-time landlord of the Apple Tree public house, had been caught red-handed with a number of other items and would receive a prison sentence. She didn't know how many of his other black-market customers he'd fingered, probably only Mrs Darwin-Kemp, a presiding magistrate who'd sent him down once before. On this occasion she might not find it quite so easy – her on the bench, the defendant who had supplied her standing in the dock. How would she get out of that? Ruby smiled. She'd probably excuse herself as being sick and another magistrate would take her place.

Still, there was a plus side to her run in with the American military police – the Snowdrops, as she'd heard them called. She'd asked Declan O'Malley whether he was coming to the village dance. These dances were happening on a regular basis now and both the American soldiers and the local girls were loving it.

'Is that a personal invitation?'

She shook her head. 'I can't do that. You have to sign the list your colonel says he's put on the notice board.'

'Yeah. Sure. I think I saw it.' Something flickered in his eyes.

'I'll see you there then.'

'I'll think about it.'

'No you won't. I can tell by the look in your eyes. You've already signed it.'

Her guess turned out to be right. There he was, standing beside one of the trucks that had brought the GIs to the dance, counting them as they alighted and got into line. It was raining so there was no hanging about.

He counted his charges again before dismissing them. Once that happened, the young men who had come to fight a war took the steps up to the village hall two at a time, their voices full of bravado and laughter.

Ruby stayed at the bottom of the steps, smiling in the sure knowledge that Lieutenant O'Malley was about to look her way.

'Ma'am,' he said, touching the peak of his cap.

'Ruby,' she said. 'I'm the girl you're going to have the first dance with.'

His face was deadpan. 'Who said I was?'

'I did.'

'I didn't.'

'Are you refusing me? Come along, Lieutenant. You're here on a goodwill mission. Your job is to further friendly relations across the Atlantic. We're allies, remember?'

Was this man made of stone? He gave no sign that he was attracted to her.

'You're not doing a very good job of it,' she finally said to him. 'Now come along.' She caught hold of his hand. 'Follow me. I promise I won't eat you.'

She sensed him holding back; saw the look on his face. Something stabbed at her heart. That look reminded her of John Smith.

'I didn't know I had to dance.'

He couldn't dance! That was all it was. He couldn't dance!

She shook her head. 'So you've come here to fight, and you can't dance. We'll have to do something about that.'

'Fighting isn't dancing.' He sounded defensive.

Ruby was adamant. 'You soldiers know nothing. A quick step can get you out of heaps of trouble – fast!'

With that she grabbed hold of him and dragged him out on to the dance floor. She placed his arms around her waist. For a moment he was rooted to the spot, his eyes unblinking, staring into hers. Then she trod on his toes.

'Hey!'

'Imagine the enemy is shooting at your feet. Now lift them. One at a time, right? One, two, three . . .'

'That's great,' he said, looking down at his feet as though unsure they didn't belong to him. 'I might be needing some quick-stepping when I come face to face with the Japs.'

The Japs. The music seemed to become muted at mention of the Far Eastern enemy. John Smith was a prisoner of the Japs. Suddenly she felt guilty dancing with this handsome man while John was far away.

'I'm sorry,' she said when he asked her for another dance. 'I promised I would be home early tonight.'

She didn't admit that the promise had been given to herself. She had a letter to write and even though it might not get through to John, at least she would know she had made the effort. John deserved that.

CHAPTER THIRTY

The piece of paper on which was printed the recipe for the National Loaf fluttered to the floor and Stan Sweet made no attempt to pick it up. The recipe was to be strictly adhered to and made from a lesser refined flour than a white loaf with potato flour added. He'd already spouted the details to his daughters and niece. He continued repeating the rest of what he'd read. 'And the weight's to be reduced from sixteen to fourteen ounces. Fourteen bloody ounces! And we're not allowed to sell it wrapped and neither can we slice it for customers like that Darwin-Kemp woman.'

'Then she'll have to learn how to use a breadknife, won't she,' declared Ruby who was already mixing the first batch of ingredients for twenty of these new national loaves. 'And we'll all have to do without white bread.'

If anyone had told her at the beginning of the war that she'd get used to deprivation and carry out government directives without too much protest, she would never have believed them. They'd fared better than most simply because they'd planned things very carefully, plus gaining extra rations so they could carry out their job.

'Three to five minutes should do it,' she murmured, keeping her head down and concentrating on what she was doing.

From the start of the war her father had carried on running

the bakery, putting up with whatever directives he was given, but being told he had to adhere to prescribed ingredients and weight for his own bread had tipped him over the edge. It was his bakery, handed down from grandfather to his father and now to him. He wasn't best pleased.

Once she was sure the dough was ready, she placed it in a lightly oiled container where it would rest for fifteen minutes. After that her father would knock it back, that is, knead it this way and that over the table with his strong hands. Then it would rest for another forty-five minutes. She breathed in its aroma, noting it didn't smell any different from an ordinary loaf.

Ruby reminded him that the less grain came in from across the Atlantic the more room there was for weapons – a tacit reminder that her brother, his son, had been killed while serving on a merchant ship bringing much-needed supplies to these shores. He seemed to calm down at that, though couldn't stop himself from one last grumble. 'They're not going to like the colour,' he grumbled. 'Or the texture. It's going to be dry. I guarantee it is.'

It was six o'clock in the morning and after eating breakfast consisting of toast – courtesy of stale slices from yesterday and a scraping of margarine, they went back into the kitchen, divided up the dough into round shapes weighing fourteen ounces, not sixteen as they had been.

The dough was rested during which time they tidied up and got the next batch ready for baking. The first batch was now ready for the second shaping before being placed in oiled baking tins where they would prove again for forty-five to sixty minutes in a warm oven, before baking. They'd be done, cooling on the side by the time the shop was ready to open at nine.

Loaves for the oven were piling up all over the place,

but joy of joys, the first batch was shoved into the oven. Not long now and they would be pulled out and left to cool on a wire rack before being transferred to the shelves in the shop.

'I think I'd better serve in the shop today,' said Ruby as she and her father made their way into the kitchen. 'There are bound to be grumbles. And I have a thicker skin than our Frances.'

Ruby made tea. Stan Sweet reached for his pipe. His face was pink – as was hers – and he was sweating profusely.

'Do you think you can bake pies and make cakes with that flour?'

'Mary and I are going to try. There's not going to be much else available, although . . .'

She pretended to concentrate on making sure that the tea going into the pot was a level teaspoonful. One per person as prescribed. No more one for the pot said the powers that be!

Stan Sweet was not fooled. 'That American Frances met. She said he's with the catering corps. I've got quite used to seeing him pop into the shop with a few errant supplies, the little rascal.'

'I don't think he is a rascal.' Sighing, Ruby put down the pot. 'Is it really so wrong if he gives us a bag of white flour? A very small bag?' she added.

'Does Declan know?'

'Of course not and I won't tell him.'

'Are things serious between you and Declan?'

Ruby shrugged. 'I don't know. He's good-looking and nice, but that hardly makes things serious between us.'

Stan sifted through his thoughts and opinions while considering whether he should indulge in another cup of tea. He was frowning at the latest directive, muttering under his breath that the men from the ministry didn't have to deal with his customers. It was all very well for them to make rules, but he was the one at the sharp end having to carry them out.

His gut instinct was that the British housewife wasn't going to like the national loaf despite the claims about it having added calcium and goodness knows what else. He'd even heard somebody on the wireless hinting that it had aphrodisiac affects! And as for the leaflets they were being sent! First Doctor Carrot, the grinning carrot-shaped character dreamed up by the Ministry of Food, saying that eating more carrots was an aid to better eyesight, and now this person on the wireless claiming it helped a person's love life. Where would it all end?

'Apparently we can have some white flour for making cakes, pies and biscuits. Nobody stated where that flour had to come from, and at least it's not black market – well – not really, but if that young man . . .'

Ruby bent over, kissed her dad's head and pressed his cup and saucer on him. 'You're a doll, Dad.'

'Doll? I suppose you got that word from the Yanks too. That Declan fella.' He took a sip of tea then reached for his paper. 'Hmm!' He gave it a good shake before continuing. 'Someone says here that the Americans are overpaid, over-sexed and over here!'

Ruby laughed. 'Never mind, Dad. As long as they help win the war. Then when it's all ended, we can go back to baking white bread.'

So far Declan had been far from oversexed, at least with her. She liked him and although he avoided taking her to dances, he did take her out for a drink or to the cinema – especially if there was a cowboy film showing.

'That's what I want to be when this is all over,' he said to her. 'I want to live somewhere like Texas, not New York. It's too crowded. I want the wide open spaces and learn to ride a horse.'

'You could learn to ride a horse here. I could teach you. Gertie Fowler's dad has got a few horses he keeps at the back of the farm in Court Road.'

They'd made a date and Ruby confirmed it would be all right with George Fowler. She hadn't ridden a horse since she was about twelve years old, but hey, it was just like riding a bicycle; once you'd done it you never forgot how to do it.

At that moment, Frances came in with Charlie trailing on behind her. He was still wearing his pyjamas, the top of which he'd pulled up to his chest in order to better investigate his belly button. He went straight to his grandfather, standing in front of him jabbing his finger into his plump little belly.

'Belly button,' he said proudly as though he were the only one in the world to possess such a thing.

Stan Sweet tried to remember the time before the little boy had come into their lives, a grey time when the world seemed to have lost its colour because the war had taken his son. Little had he known that his son had left a piece of him behind and perhaps he'd never known of his existence if London hadn't been bombed. Now there was something to thank the enemy for. It was a terrible thought, one he swiftly despatched.

Inevitably, it was just him and the baby left to their own devices. Ruby went out to serve in the shop as planned. It was rumoured that Mrs Powell had taken a consignment of tinned peaches, pudding rice and Colman's mustard, so Mary had gone to join the queue that formed for such luxuries. In the city people queued for meat, butter and cream. In the country it was tinned goods.

Frances had gone to meet young Ed Bergman, a likeable enough lad but still a bit too old for a girl who had only just left school.

'He's eighteen, Uncle Stan,' Frances had proclaimed. 'Only four years older than me.'

'Eighteen.' Stan Sweet shook his head dolefully. The lad was broad-shouldered and ready to take on the world, yet only eighteen. It didn't seem right. But never mind. There was no question of her getting serious with the young man. Twenty-one years of age was a long way off. Until then she would need a parent or guardian's permission to marry.

Stan might have dozed off if it hadn't been for Charlie's continuous chattering. He was playing on the rug with Bunz, building him an armchair with some wooden bricks Stan had brought down from the attic. Being a baker was tiring work. He'd been up since before dawn and his eyes felt itchy and sore. His eyelids began to feel heavy.

His cat nap was interrupted by the shrill ringing of the telephone.

He called for Mary before remembering that she had gone out. He thought about calling for Ruby to answer the phone, but it sounded as though it was busy in the shop.

'Bloody telephone,' he grunted, struggling up from his chair.

'Phone!' chirped Charlie.

Blast, thought Stan. I must remember not to swear in front of that boy. He learned too fast.

The hallway where the telephone sat on a side table felt chilly after the living room. It was still ringing, its jangling bell resonating and making the place seem even colder.

Stan picked up the handset. It was either Mike or that

Sinclair bloke who arranged the talks and demonstrations for the Ministry of Food. He chose to believe it was his son-in-law.

'Mike,' he said. 'Is that you?'

'To whom am I speaking?'

He didn't recognise the voice on the other end of the phone, told the man who he was.

'You're Pilot Officer Dangerfield's father-in-law?'

He nodded into the mouthpiece even though he knew whoever was on the other end couldn't see him. 'Yes,' he finally said.

There was a pause. Stan felt his heart skip a beat. Something was seriously wrong.

'Is his wife there?'

'No. She's gone out. Can I help you?'

That pause again – they called it a pregnant pause because something was about to be said that was quite momentous. It could be good or it could be bad. But he had a bad feeling about it. 'My name is Carr. I'm the station commander at Scampton. It's bad news I'm afraid.'

Stan felt a lump in his throat. He thought of his daughter expecting her first child. It was unthinkable that she could be a widow before she was a mother . . .

'Is he dead?'

'No. No. Not dead, but he is badly injured. There was a lot of flak en route to their target. They were hit but managed to limp home. Despite their best attempts, the plane caught fire on landing. Michael is in hospital in Lincoln. Please give your daughter my deepest sympathy. If she needs to contact me, please do. I'll give you my number. I'm also sending a travel warrant by telegram. I'm sure she'll want to be near him.'

Stan committed the telephone number to memory. He didn't

know how he did it. His memory wasn't usually that good, but on this occasion the number stuck in his mind.

'Again, my sincere sympathies, sir. It's a great shame, but it's not all gloom and doom. They can do wonders nowadays.'

After putting the handset back on the hook, Stan wandered back into the living room and slumped in his chair, his head in his hands. First his son dead, then John Smith being taken prisoner, and now this. When would it ever end?

Charlie peered up into his face from beneath his hands. On seeing the look on his grandfather's face, his cheeky smile disappeared and for a moment he looked as if he were about to cry.

Stan forced himself to smile. 'No crying, Charlie. You're a big boy now. And so am I. Granddad's a big boy too.'

Inside his heart was breaking, but he couldn't bear for the boy to share his sadness. And anyway, what was it the station commander had said? That they could do wonders nowadays. He hoped it was true.

In the meantime he had to dig deep to find the courage to tell Mary what had happened. He wondered if anyone had rung Bettina or Mike's parents. He presumed his parents in Canada would receive a telegram.

He picked up Charlie and walked out into the shop, intending to tell Ruby first before he went to find Mary. He was surprised to find Bettina in the shop, deep in conversation with his youngest daughter. Bettina was all smiles when she saw him with his grandson in his arms. Her smile lasted until Stan told her about the telephone call.

'Does Mary know yet?' Ruby asked. 'What's happened exactly?' She looked from Bettina to her father, noting the worried looks on their faces.

Her father shook his head. 'No. I don't know the full details.

Only that his plane was hit. They got back safe, but it caught fire on landing. He's suffered burns.' He looked away. 'I don't know how badly.'

Bettina nodded and for the first time, he noticed how pale she was, how much her hands were shaking. He covered one of them with his own.

'Let's go have a sit down, Bettina. Ruby, can you make some tea and then if our Mary's not back by then, we'll go find her.'

Feeling as though she'd won a great battle rather than having spent two hours standing in a queue for tinned items, Mary swung her shopping basket and whistled something cheerful.

Just as she'd approached the top of Court Road, she noticed the steam from a locomotive coughing up over the road bridge. A train had arrived and was now pulling out of the station. Emerging from the mist, her figure solid against the spiralling steam, she saw Ada Perkins, Mrs Powell's mother.

'Hello!' she said warmly. 'It's nice to see you again. Is it a special occasion?'

'There was a need,' said Ada. 'I felt I was needed so I came.'

There was something intriguing about the way Ada said it. Nobody else could make it sound as mysterious as she did.

'And I'm sure whatever it is, you're the right person to deal with it,' said Mary. She lifted her basket. 'Tinned peaches. Luxuries we just can't do without.'

'You need them,' said Ada. 'Give your father my regards and tell him thank you for writing to me.'

So that was the reason she had arrived in the village! Her father had written to her.

'Yes. I will.'

Ada stopped abruptly. Her hat tipped forward when she frowned. 'Are you all right?'

'Yes. Of course I am,' trilled Mary, not liking Ada's expression, not wanting its air of dark foreboding to ruin her day. She was feeling on top of the world. She was married to a wonderful man and also expecting his baby. She couldn't help being all right!

Ada's dark frown was immediately forgotten and her mood persisted all the way home.

'I've just seen Ada Perkins,' she said as she breezed her way into the kitchen. 'She sends you her regards, Dad, and says to tell you thank you for letting her know – whatever it was you let her know,' she said with a laugh, not really taking in the atmosphere, not until her gaze alighted on Mike's aunt.

'Hello, Bettina. What are . . .?'

She'd been about to dig into her basket and take everything out to put away. On seeing the way everyone was staring at her – Ruby, her father and Bettina – her hands flopped on to the handle of the basket. A cold chill crept over her.

'It's Mike, isn't it?' She looked from Bettina to her father and sister. There was fear in her voice. Her hands began to shake.

'He's alive, Mary,' said her father, up from his chair and his arm around her.

He went on to tell her about the plane catching fire on landing. He reached out and laid his hands on both her aching shoulders.

'The station commander said it's understandable that you'd want to be with him, so he's sending you a travel warrant. He didn't say anything about finding you somewhere to stay, but he's left his number. No doubt he can arrange somewhere.'

Mary nodded. There was the cottage of course, the one she

had declined so many times. For some strange reason she couldn't mention it. Fate was dragging her to it.

Her sister Ruby bit her lip as she brushed her hair back from her face. 'I'll help you pack. You will be going up there, won't you?'

'Of course I will.' Mary's voice was uncommonly sharp. 'It's where I should be.' Her voice was as shaky as her hands. 'I should have been there. Then perhaps . . .'

'You wouldn't have been able to prevent it, my darling girl,' said Bettina giving Mary's arm a reassuring squeeze.

'I know. But I would have been there.'

The telephone rang for a second time that night, close to eleven o'clock. The caller asked for Mrs Mary Dangerfield.

Mary's face was pale and her hands were still shaking when she took the telephone from Ruby's hands. It was Guy, Mike's friend, calling to express his sympathies and offer help.

'If there's anything I can do, you only have to say. I have taken the initiative and put a few things in the cottage – a fire, some food, etc.'

She thanked him.

'What time are you arriving?'

She tried to clear her head, to rake the details from her mind. She knew the time the train pulled into the station simply because it would be the one Michael usually caught. She couldn't seem to concentrate.

'Look. Never mind. Give me a ring when you know. I'll be waiting at the station. The cottage is ready for you to stay in. I'll take care of you. Mike's a great mate. I'll have Felix with me. Hope you won't mind that.'

She said that she wouldn't. He sounded uncommonly cheerful and although she didn't know the extent of Mike's injuries, Guy's tone conveyed that Mike would recover. When she asked him outright, he confirmed it.

'Of course he will. I've told him that he isn't getting out of flying with me that way.' His laugh was light but kindly.

'You've seen him?'

'Of course I've seen him. He's chipper. Looking forward to seeing you too, getting out of the hospital and being with you in Woodbridge Cottage. You'll love the house. Honest you will.'

As promised Guy was waiting for her at the station, his big black dog beside him wagging its tail.

He was kind and talked all the way to the hospital, which was just as well because Mary couldn't find her voice. Her thoughts were with Mike.

'He's in a specialist unit,' he said to her, their footsteps echoing along the hospital corridor, the dog having been left in the car. 'This is the best place in the country for treating burns. Quite a lot of our chaps end up here . . .'

Mary visibly paled.

Realising he'd said the wrong thing Guy did his best to reassure her. 'Look. I didn't mean it that way. He'll be fine. What I meant was that this is the best place in the country for treating burns.'

His reassurances only went halfway to calming her down. Nurses, doctors and patients, the doors to hospital wards were passed without her really noticing.

'Hey! Gibbo!'

Mary knew instantly somebody Guy knew was hailing him by his nickname.

'Cartwright! How the devil are you?' He shook the man's hand.

Feeling as though her legs had turned to water, Mary stood there and stared. The man standing in front of her was wearing an RAF uniform. His cap was tucked beneath his arm and he was a head taller than she was. His voice had a slight lisp, but that wasn't what struck her the most. One side of the man's face was rutted and dented as though somebody had attacked the surface with a wood chisel. The skin of one eyelid was stretched from eyebrow to cheekbone giving his face a lopsided look.

Mary didn't need anyone to tell her that his face was the result of burns and the attempt of a surgeon to put him back together again.

'May I introduce you to Mrs Dangerfield,' said Guy.

'Mike's wife? Lovely to see you. I hear you're expecting a happy addition to the family. Mike told me. He was over the moon. That's why I think he'll fly through this in record time.'

Mary couldn't stop staring. The words sounded hollow. She felt Guy's hand cupping her elbow, guiding her away from the man and along the corridor. The smell of everything to do with hospitals assaulted her senses. It was bad enough any other time, but more so when afflicted with the nausea caused by pregnancy.

The burns unit was at the very end of the corridor, a pair of double doors leading into a ward of six beds, all occupied, all the patients with varying degrees of burns.

Mike was closest to the window. He was laid down flat, some kind of framework holding the bedding away from his body from his waist downwards.

'Be brave,' Guy whispered to her.

The dreadful cold feeling that had descended on her when introduced to the pilot with the burned face was hard to ignore, but Guy was right.

'Mike!'

She couldn't help sounding relieved and would have thrown herself over him if it hadn't been for the wire cage inserted beneath the bedclothes.

'Can I kiss you?'

'I'd be disappointed if you didn't.'

His voice was throaty but not groggy. As for his face . . . Mary stroked his cheek. 'Your face. It's still the same.'

'Yes.'

'The burns?'

'Nothing that will kill me – or stop me from flying,' he added with a sideways glance at his senior officer.

'I know when I'm not wanted,' said Guy. 'Mary, I'll leave you to it. Never did like being a gooseberry!'

Mike's eyes met hers. 'Kiss me, Mary.'

She felt his arms go round her as she kissed him. His hands were bandaged. She found herself stroking the raised part of his bedding, that area with the framework beneath.

She couldn't bring herself to ask how badly he'd been injured, but he saw her looking.

'My stomach, mostly, and my hands,' he said. 'My legs are fine. And as for everything else, I think it all still works, but you can never tell.'

He smiled. She fancied it was a cheeky smile and instantly knew to what he was referring. In the past she might have blushed, but not now.

'I haven't come this far for nothing. You'll get well again. I'll make you strong – just as soon as you're out of here and we're living in Guy's cottage.'

The days following Mary's departure seemed emptier than Ruby had ever known. But then, she thought to herself, it was only natural. They were twins and had hardly been apart from each other since the day they were born.

They learned that Mike had sustained burns to his upper torso and his hands. It would be some time before he flew again, but he would fly, of that they were assured. They were also assured that he'd be out of hospital and back with Mary before the baby was due in September. She also informed them that the cottage was lovely and the people at Scampton had been extremely helpful, especially Guy, Mike's squadron leader and owner of the dog who had first brought them together.

Although she missed her sister, there was no time to feel sorry for herself, no time to ponder on what might have been or even to spend too much time in the company of Declan O'Malley. There was a bakery to run, a shop to serve in, her work with the Ministry of Food, and most of all there was Charlie, the little boy who had come into their lives without warning, the reason they had to plough on regardless.

The only fly in the ointment was Gertrude Powell. Her mother Ada, Miriam's grandmother, had arrived on the train on the same day as Mary had learned of Mike's injuries, appearing out of the smoke like a ghost.

It was the talk of the village when she marched into the shop, demanded to see her granddaughter and told her to pack. 'You're coming to live with me,' she'd declared.

The customers waiting to be served had lingered to hear the rest of what was going on.

Mrs Powell ordered her mother out of the shop and her daughter to get down into the coal cellar until she'd finished serving.

Buoyed up by her grandmother's presence, Miriam had refused.

Witnesses said that she looked nervous about going back into the dingy living quarters and had dashed out of the door her grandmother was holding open declaring she had nothing of value to bring with her.

Gertrude Powell had exploded, running out after the pair

of them, her black stockings wrinkled around her ankles, her
shoes worn down on one side, giving her a bandy look.

'Ungrateful child! Come back here! Come back this
minute!'

Her attention was suddenly taken with a figure on the
other side of the alleyway dividing her shop from Stratham
House. Bettina Hicks was dressed in lilac from head to toe,
the same colour reflected in her pale hair. She was smiling
and there was a glint of satisfaction in her eyes.

'You!' shouted Gertrude, pointing an accusing finger at the
woman she hated most in the village. 'You! It's all your fault.
Just you wait, Bettina Hicks. I know your secrets and one day
I'll tell the whole world about you and your husband and that
nephew of yours. I'll tell everyone!'

Bettina's smile widened. She shook her head. 'Two can
play at that game, Gertrude. And don't you forget it!'

Ruby slid the bolts on the bread shop door and pulled down
the blackout curtain that had replaced the brown blind. She
winced at the result. The old blind had merely softened the
light in the shop; the blackout curtains darkened it.

For a moment she stood with her back to the door. Two
loaves of bread remained on the shelves behind the counter
plus a few simple scones. It was so quiet she could almost
hear herself breathe. She was alone with the smell and the
warm air drifting through from the bake house. Mary was
with her husband in Lincolnshire, Frances was out with
Charlie in his pram and her father had gone to fork Mrs
Hicks's garden.

Her gaze settled on the two remaining loaves. It hadn't
escaped her notice that food was becoming scarcer, especially
in the cities. This led her to thinking how much longer she
could go on giving demonstrations. It wasn't so much that

the ministry wouldn't provide, it was more a case of the women she was instructing having to spend hours queuing for the most mundane things.

Worrying never helped anyone, she said to herself. 'A walk,' she said and went to fetch her coat.

The early morning rain had cleared. Slate roofs glistened and drainpipes gurgled into water butts. Everyone seemed to have a water butt nowadays the reason being that if the water mains did get bombed, there would always be water to boil in a kettle or water the garden. Growing vegetables had become one of the most important activities in their lives.

Her walk took her to the bridge that went over the railway line. When she got to the middle she stopped, her arms resting on the rough stonework.

Her thoughts returned to that afternoon with Johnnie. She had felt so alive and knew Johnnie had too. In the days following their lovemaking she'd worried about being pregnant. Her fears had not been realised, but she knew beyond doubt that even if she had been, she wouldn't have cared. In that beautiful moment they had felt so alive, so determined to *make* themselves feel alive. That's what it had all been about.

A train approached from the direction of the Midlands line, the smoke from its stack billowing into the December afternoon. She straightened at the prospect of somebody she knew being on that train. It was such a forlorn hope, yet she felt that just like the lovemaking, it had to be believed in. Johnnie might be on that train.

She walked slowly to where the smoke from the train rolled over the bridge obliterating the place where it joined the road. Her heart was racing in line with her heightened anticipation.

The smoke cleared and it was as though everything had become clear. She didn't regret that moment with Johnnie. If that was all they would ever have, then so be it.

Clasping her hands together she looked down at the railway track, the train gone, the rails polished to a leaden brightness.

The year was drawing to a close. Soon the old year would be behind them. So much had happened including the fall of Singapore and Johnnie had been captured. Her Polish pilot had turned out to be married. Of the good things, finding out about baby Charlie was the best thing of all, and of course Mary getting married.

There were bound to be more difficult times ahead, but deep down she truly believed they had turned the corner. Michael was going to be fine and Mary was having a baby. Surely the world would get better. And that, she decided, is the hope we all have to cling on to.

Read on for some recipes
used by the Sweet sisters . . .

BUTTERFLY CAKES WITH CHOCOLATE

2 oz of fat
2 oz of sugar
1 level teaspoon of cocoa powder
1 fresh egg or one tablespoon of dried egg
    reconstituted
4 oz of self-raising flour
1 level teaspoon of baking powder
Pinch of salt
2 tablespoons of milk

Cream fat and sugar, beat in egg, add cocoa. Sift together flour, salt and baking powder. Keep adding a little of the milk until it is soft and creamy. Grease and flour cake tins, put a spoonful of mixture into each one. Bake for twenty minutes in a moderate oven. When cooled slice the top off each cake, add mock cream then slice the tops in half and place in the mock cream so they resemble butterfly wings.

MARY'S WEDDING FOOD

The cake

3 oz sugar
4 oz margarine
1 level tablespoon of honey
8 oz plain flour
2 teaspoons of baking powder
Pinch of salt
1 teaspoon of mixed spice
1 teaspoon of ground cinnamon
4 fresh eggs (from the local farm) or equivalent in
    dried egg
1 lb of mixed dried fruit (most of which Mary and
    Ruby had dried themselves – soft fruits, plums,
    dried apples)
1 teaspoon of lemon substitute or essence
Milk to mix

Cream sugar with the margarine then add the honey and the eggs. In a separate bowl, mix flour, baking powder, salt and spices together. Add the flour mixture to the creamed mixture finally adding the rest of the ingredients. Line a 7 inch tin with greased paper – margarine wrappers will do – and bake in a moderate oven for two hours.

Mock Marzipan Paste

4 tablespoons mashed potato
1 tablespoon of egg white
1 tablespoon of sugar
A few drops of almond essence

Mix all ingredients well together to a fairly stiff consistency. Spread top of cake with a little honey, blackberry jelly or jam. Press mock marzipan mixture on to cake and press into shape. Pinch edges and score with fork. Put back into the oven to brown. While still hot, sprinkle with grated chocolate if you have it or ice the cake if you happen to find any icing sugar in the shops.

Mary was given what must have been the very last packet of icing sugar left in the village shop so could decorate this (very small) cake with icing. Otherwise she would have had to resort to mixing dried milk (termed household milk at the time), water and sugar, perhaps with a little artificial colouring included. Luckily they had a lot of bread pudding to fill everyone up with! Nothing was wasted in the wartime kitchen.

PILCHARD PASTIES

12 oz self-raising flour or plain with baking powder
    (Remember the Sweets were bakers so had access
    to flour, though used it frugally)
Pinch of salt
3 oz cooking fat or bacon fat (or any other fat they
    were lucky enough to have saved from other meals)
Water
Tin of pilchards – 16 oz if possible
Chopped onions
Salt and pepper

Sift flour, salt, rub in cooking fat. Bind with water. Open tin of pilchards. Drain off excess fluid. Keep to one side. It can be used for other things, e.g. mixing with herbs and onion and spreading it on bread, or for the basis of a soup.

Mash pilchards with chopped onions, season to taste.
Using a teacup rim, make roundels, fill each one with the fish mixture, brush edges with milk and fold in half moon shapes. Small pasties but ideal for a wedding buffet.

CARROT COOKIES

2 tablespoons of margarine
4 tablespoons of sugar
Vanilla essence
8 tablespoons of grated raw carrot
12 tablespoons of self-raising flour

Cream fat and sugar together, beat in flavouring and carrot. Fold in flour. Drop spoonfuls into a greased tart tray. Sprinkle the tops with sugar and bake in oven for about eighteen to twenty minutes.

BACON ROLL

12 oz self-raising flour or plain flour with 3 teaspoons
   of baking powder
Pinch of salt
3 oz cooking fat or bacon fat
Water
4 oz fat bacon rashers
2 cooked leeks cut into rings or finely chopped
   whichever you prefer. Mary left them in rings
8 oz diced cooked potatoes
2 tablespoons of chopped chives

Sift the flour and salt, rub in the fat. Bind with water. Grill and
chop the bacon rashers, cool then mix with the leeks, potatoes
and chives. Roll out the pastry into an oblong shape. Place the
mixture down the middle. Starting at one end, roll over and
over until you have something that resembles a Swiss roll.

THE Official Recipe
Issued by the Ministry of Food, April 1942

   Wholemeal flour
   Potato Flour
   Salt Sea Fine
   Tap Water
   Vitamin C
   Yeast active dry

The Ministry of Food insisted on the above mentioned ingredients. It was up to the baker to use the best method as he
saw fit.